Praise for Black Earth ·

I read this in one sitting!
The synopsis tells you the basics of this story. What it doesn't tell you is that the humanity between the characters and the relationships will bring you to tears.

As the title says, I read this book in one sitting and was never bored. That's unusual for me. Even the best books will quite often have parts that don't 'flow' as well as others. This causes boredom, not so with Black Earth.

The interaction between Carrick and Erik quickly formed into a beautiful friendship that spanned the 75 million miles between Earth and Black Earth. These two main characters will keep you fully involved in this lesson in alternate history.

The story answers a lot of questions that have plagued archeologists and historians for hundreds of years. It's fun to see how everything comes together. Einstein, Hitler, and Werner Von Braun we once close associates on Black Earth, as was Julius Caesar and others. The revelations you'll discover in Black Earth will leave you floored!

The ending brought tears to my eyes and made my heart swell as it describes a love story for the ages. Better than Romeo and Juliet by far. Sometimes you'll read a good book only to have the ending be disappointing or end in a cliff hanger to be continued in the next book of an expensive series. Not here! Black Earth is so satisfying from start to finish that you'll believe you have read a modern classic.

This book is fun, exciting, and charming. You could do worse, but I doubt you could find better!

-PM Steve

Highly Recommend!
Black Earth is a well-crafted tale where the author masterfully weaves history through this science fiction love story. The enchanting character, Erik, stole the heart of this reader. Erik was the wise, gentle, witty grandfather type of character who shared his stories and wisdom with his young comrade. His painstaking yet beautiful love story ultimately changed history.

-Elaine Robinson

Not a science fiction story!
As a child, I enjoyed science fiction and have always been fascinated by astronomy and our universe, but Star Wars and other stories were just not believable to me, and I sort of outgrew it. After ordering and reading this Kindle sample, I was hooked! I purchased the Kindle eBook version, but now I must have the paperback. This was a very heartwarming story that pulled me back to earth after traveling a small portion of the cosmos. The best part was that all of it is totally believable!!! There was just enough science to make it interesting but, more than that, more heart than I ever expected from this book. We all wonder, but it's so comforting to know that we can take bits and pieces of life and imagine our own afterlife. This story definitely gave me ideas, thoughts, questions, and, most importantly, hope. The author is a friend of the family that has certainly impressed me with his first novel. Thank you, Michael. What a treat!!

-Mark Rievley

Animal Farm Revisited?
Wow! As I read this book and the lessons it teaches, I was reminded of reading Animal Farm in high school. The comparisons stop there, though. I find Michel Cook's writing much more entertaining and well woven. By the time I was halfway through the prologue, I was thinking what a good movie this could be. Now, I'm hoping it will happen. It's an epic story. Best book I've read in years! I HIGHLY recommend you read this amazing book!

-Mary B.

A Book Everyone Should Read!
A creative take on the question humans have had since the beginning of time. Is there life out there? Are we alone in the universe? Where did we, the human race, truly come from? This sci-fi novel is not just filled with adventure, laughter, and true love. It is also a story that delivers a powerful message that humanity desperately needs to hear.

-Amazon Customer

Very Exciting, I couldn't Put It Down!
I would highly recommend Black Earth: How We Got Here to any fan of the science fiction genre. The writing style reminded me of Ray Bradbury with the modern flair of Ernest Cline. I'm planning on reading it again in the next few days to see if there was anything I missed!

-Eric M.

Excellent Read!

I could not put this book down! This was a very intriguing story. I loved all the characters and especially the relationship between Carrick and Erik. The book was beautifully written, and it definitely kept my interest from start to finish. It was well thought out and will keep you wanting to turn that next page! I am hoping there will be a sequel!

-Maribeth P.

Newly Discovered Planet Reveals Mankind's Origins on Earth.

A gripping journey across our solar system to a newly discovered planet, revealing a rich history of a doomed civilization and the destiny of the planet's former inhabitants. A great read and well crafted, well-researched sci-fi novel that brings us along on one man's mission of both scientific and personal discovery. A heart-warming story that doesn't disappoint!

-Vern P.

Michael Cook is one damn good story-teller!

Black Earth will grab you at the get-go...but lots of books do that. What's different about this one is that it will reward you with a hundred little (and not so little) "wow" along the way. It's not a roller coaster of emotion...it's "damn the torpedoes, full speed ahead" kinda stuff. I didn't want to put it down and got to a point in the book where I couldn't. Science Fiction? Maybe...but not so technical that you need to be Albert Einstein to understand it. Sorta like a hammering drama that just happens to take place on another planet! I don't think I've cheered or cried reading a book ever but came close as the pages turned to the final chapter. It's lots of fun, and I cannot imagine anyone not enjoying it. Cannot wait to read another story... It doesn't have to be in outer space. Michael was just a great story-teller.

-William Marr

Hooked!

From the first few pages, I was hooked! I could not put it down, and with each turn of the page, the story became more real!

His descriptive writing style had the characters jump off the page, and I could visualize each of them along with the places he took me. He has a unique way of telling a story in which instantly transported me into the world of Black Earth! It was captivating from beginning to end!

I hope that he has a follow-up in the works since I would love to see what happens to Black Earth!!

-Rhonda Koches Haydak

Acknowledgments:

Thank you for letting me share this wonderful story with you. The story of Black Earth – How We Got Here came to me in a dream, but making that dream come true took many individuals that are all very important to me.

I'd like to thank my wife and children: Kristin, Aubrey Carin, Lola Kristine, Maggie Mae, and Carrick Michael, for helping me to breathe life into the characters that you're about to meet. I can't forget Aunt Holly; thanks for being Black Earth's biggest fan. All of these wonderful friends and family members were all so supportive in my journey, and without them, this book doesn't get written.

I would also like to thank my friends on the other side of the pond who lent their out-of-this-world expertise to tell this story. Professor Christopher Riley and Jacqui Farnham chiseled away the rough edges and helped me refine this heart-warming story; for that, I am eternally grateful. And finally, to Martin Impey, a visual poet who provided encouragement from the beginning.

A shout out to my best friend and business partner, Piyush Bhula; thanks for always being there at every turn. To my friend Doug Lambert, a poetic genius from the Windy City. To Jeremy Ledbetter for always being there and for his wonderful cover design work.

Fine Print:

This book is a work of fiction and is drawn completely from my imagination. The actual historical figures characterized in this book are intended to be portrayed in a positive light. Any references to past historical events are for entertainment purposes only and not meant to be taken literally. Any actual organizations or federal entities portrayed in this book serve only to enhance the story and are not meant to defame, devalue, or besmirch those institutions in any way.

www.BlackEarthNovel.com

"I'm what they call the poet
Inside you, I have a place
I'm the one who brings expression
To an empty face"

Michael Cook is a published poet, author, and accomplished business professional, and entrepreneur. Michael is also the owner of the #7 Escape Room experience in the World, Odyssey Escape Game, located in Alpharetta, GA, and Schaumburg, IL.

A resident of Suwanee, GA., Michael is a father of four children, a husband, a brother, and a friend.

This book is dedicated to Kristin.
My one true love!

Black Earth
How We Got Here©

What truths lie in the black void
between the stars?

A novel by Michael Cook
© 2020

Prologue – Zenith

Location: Northwest Sector of The Triad, Sub-Level 7, Barrack 5 –
Early morning hours, year unknown.

Erik awoke alone for the twenty-seven-thousand, three hundred
and seventy-seventh day. Looking in the mirror, he again realized
that he had no future, only a past.

He splashed some water on his face, there'd be no shower today,
and then wiped it away with a cloth that was in desperate need of
being laundered. He looked more resigned today than he had on
others. His sunken eyes, long since blue, were framed by wrinkles
that he wore like scars. Scars so deep, it was as if each year alone in
The Triad was a razor that put them there.

After getting dressed, Erik began his daily routine. Walking through
the dark halls, he exited the barracks, then headed to The Culina for
his morning ritual of protein ingestion. The Culina was about a ten-
minute walk from Barrack 5. It was a vast maze of kitchen areas and
seating sections that, in its heyday, served more than twelve-
thousand people daily. Each person would receive one meal per day
in one of three shifts: morning, mid-day, or night. This regimented
process went on for far too many decades to count. Today,
however, it was breakfast for one.

All of the pantries in The Culina were empty and had been for many
years. Erik's only source of food these days was a flavored powder
that, when mixed with water, would produce a thick, pasty batter.
With patience, it could be consumed as a drink; without it, a spoon
would be required. The powdered drink provided a human being
with enough protein and vitamins for an entire day. The proper
daily allowance of the nutritious substance could sustain human life
indefinitely. The granulate was kept in large canisters affixed to The
Great Wall in The Culina's largest room. Each canister was two feet
in diameter and ten feet tall and looked more like bars on a prison
cell. Symbolic, as The Triad had been Erik's prison for the last
seventy-five years. Seventy-five years since they left, seventy-five
years...since she left.

The nozzle that dispensed the powder was located at chest level for a person of average height. There were no fewer than one hundred of these canisters lining The Great Wall. Erik's favorite flavor, Red Fruit, had been gone for several years now. But out of desire, stubbornness, and some days desperation, he kept going back to the canister, hoping some powder would magically fall into the bottom of his dirty cup. Today, he would settle for Brown Maize.

After begrudgingly finishing his only meal of the day, Erik made his way to the elevator bank located in The Grand Hall. This was a circular atrium, fifteen stories tall, with elevators wrapping around it on every level: Grand Central Terminal, if you will. It was the gateway to every area of the Northwest Sector, including the monorails that led to the Southwest and Southeast Sectors of The Triad.

If you were to stand on the top level of the atrium and look over the railing, the view would take your breath away. These days, however, it was a dark abyss, a black void that Erik no longer stared into as he did in the years following her departure. It no longer teemed with life, and neither did he.

Most of the elevators no longer functioned, as electricity had been routed to serve only the necessary areas of The Triad. Waiting in front of the elevator doors for several minutes, lost in thought, Erik realized that he'd forgotten to push the Door Open button.

Once in the elevator, he took the short and solitary ride to Surface-Level 3 of The Triad. After exiting, Erik turned right and walked down a corridor that was more than one hundred feet long. The corridor walls were studded with wall-mounted light fixtures that looked like diamonds when illuminated. These days, however, they were dark and no longer shined. The only lights that illuminated his pathway now were the emergency track lights running along the floor, at the base of each wall. The loss of power indicated to Erik that his candle of life was burning down. Each time a section of The Triad lost power; it could never be restored. This was due to The Triad's Energy Conservation System, or ECS.

At the end of the corridor, Erik entered The Triad's History Library, an incredibly large and cavernous facility, roughly ten-thousand square feet in size. Though absent of books, the History Library was filled with hundreds of blinking computers and monitors, seven hundred and ninety-eight to be exact. Erik knew this number well, as he had counted them on many occasions. The computers sat alone, humming with historical data that, unless shared with others, was useless information. Not to Erik, though. The knowledge found here was the only reason he rose in the morning. It stood as the only cerebral outlet for this withering old man.

Erik liked The History Library, not only because it offered an escape to an otherwise imprisoned man; but because it was also the coolest place within The Triad. Though the sub-levels were kept at 82°F, the surface-levels were set at 92°F. Heat is the number one computer killer, and because of this fact, The Triad's computer systems ensured that The History Library remained at 75°F and no higher.

Here, in The History Library, Erik was most comfortable and relaxed, making it easier for him to delve into his planet's history. This was the part of the day when he learned of another time, a time that was not his. This period in time had, nevertheless, become his past, present, and future. The knowledge gathered in The History Library helped Erik to make sense of why he was here: his origins, his purpose, but most of all, his sacrifice.

Today, he would continue watching where he'd left off the day before. Erik was reading about and viewing a period in time that was four-thousand years before this one. It was a time that had ultimately forecast the end of a once-proud civilization and determined the final plan for what would become of his kind: humankind.

After his daily historical intake, eight-hours of reading and viewing chaos and destruction, war, and its aftermath, Erik made his way to The Triad's outer observatory deck on Surface-Level 5, the top level of The Triad. This was the warmest place in The Triad, a balmy 98°F, due to the massive, heat-shielded, triple-paned glass facade. Though it was warm, it was the only place in The Triad that gave him true peace. It was the closest he could be to what he had always wanted to be: a man with a future.

As far as the eye could see, which wasn't very far, was a vast tapestry of darkness, both of landscape and of sky. Erik would sit, just staring out of the massive observatory glass canopy for hours. He imagined what this place looked like when it was still alive and filled with color. A place where the future was once promised, and the past could be fondly remembered without tear.

Nostalgia and heat caused Erik to nod off. He now dreamt of the time before the others had gone Home. He dreamt of what became of them; and what might've become of him if only he'd gone Home with them. Most of his dreams these days, however, were not of the recent past; but rather the distant. His daily history lessons had crept into his present and became what he remembered most. A time so long ago, the mind could be tricked into believing that it never actually existed.

For more than seventy years, Erik had been studying the past twenty-thousand years of his planet's history, but mainly the last six-thousand. He believed that if he had been alive during the critical times of monumental human failure, the catastrophic loss of common sense, and the epidemic of irrationality, then maybe, just maybe, he could have done something to prevent the unraveling of his civilization's existence. Erik concluded that mankind's greatest flaw was its inability to learn from its past mistakes.

Flashing lights and sirens.

Erik was suddenly rocked into consciousness. He wondered for a moment if this was part of his dream. But no. This was the day he had hoped for but never actually thought would come. A day that, when it came, might not even matter. But on this day, matter it would.

Chapter 1 – Haleakala - House of the Sun

Location: Maui, Hawaii, USA. Haleakala Space Observatory, atop Maui Mountain – September 19, 2019.

Young budding astronomers Colye Justman, 29, and Phillip Blakely, 28, both Ph.D.'s and recent graduates of Stanford University, were preparing for their shifts. They would start at 8 pm and finish at 6 am, Aleutian Time Zone.

The two sat at their desks, just ten feet apart, in an open-air room with little privacy. Checking emails and texts on their smartphones, neither paid much attention to their job duties. Instead, the two discussed who had a better chance of securing a date with the 'new girl,' Dr. Kristin Pruett. Pruett was a Harvard graduate who'd recently joined the Haleakala team.

The two had finally settled in when, at 12:07 am local time, Colye Justman observed an anomaly in the night sky. While studying the sky from the Charge Coupled Device of the new Pan-STARRS 3 telescope, he saw something that would change everything we know about our origins. Something that would forever alter our history, not only here on Earth but in the Universe as well.

The Pan-STARRS 3, a 60-inch in diameter telescope, has the ability to image a swatch of sky roughly forty times the area of a full moon, surpassing the capabilities of any similar-sized telescope on Earth or in space. The PS3 was primarily designed to search the skies for asteroids, but on this night, it did something much more.

On a night in which Jupiter and Saturn were prevalent in the night sky, the bored and distracted Colye Justman looked beyond what he was assigned to do; search for distant asteroid fields. Instead, he veered deep into the galaxy, taking in the majesty of the night sky and the 1.7 billion stars in the Milky Way alone. As he studied an area East by Southeast, along the Ecliptic Plane, he saw something that, in his experience, simply could not be there: a black hole. Not the scientific version, but of an actual black dot obstructing his view of the stars that lay behind it.

After several minutes of disbelief and the rubbing of his eyes, he called out to Phillip Blakely. "Blakely! Get over here! Fast!"

Blakely dismissed him until Colye shouted, "Get your ass over here! NOW!"

Blakely reluctantly let his feet fall from his desk to the floor, slowly made his way over to the Pan-STARRS 3 CCD screen, and then looked at the feed.

Justman asked him to look closely. "Do you see anything out of the ordinary?"

Sarcastically, Blakely responded, "No! I see stars. And a lot of them. A billion and a half, give or take."

"Look again! Right here!" He pointed to an area in the field of view in the bottom left-hand corner of the CCD Feed screen.

"LOOK! Do you see it?!" he yelled.

"Dude, if you're talking about the speck of dirt on the feed, yeah, I see it."

"That's not a speck of dirt, you idiot!"

"Colye, you're crazy," Blakely replied dismissively. "It's just lava ash on the sensor, that's all. There's no heat signature being detected. Man, the new girl's got you seeing things! Clean the sensor. If it's still there after that, we'll talk."

Justman pushed Blakely out of the way, telling him to, "Fuck off!" He was sure about what he was seeing: a black sphere.
Confused, he muttered to himself, "What's causing the occultation of the stars?"

Through the night, Justman studied the anomaly and noticed the black mass occulting other stars as it moved slightly against their backdrop. When considering the Earth's position, Justman was able to calculate how far away it was. To his horror, he realized that the black dot was much closer than he would have expected.

While it was impossible to determine the black sphere's exact size, Justman estimated it was roughly the same as the Earth, or perhaps a bit smaller. He based his calculations on the occultation time of the stars that it passed in front of.

"This isn't possible!" he shouted out loud while removing his glasses and rubbing his eyes over and over again.

He kept calculating what he saw and exhaled in disbelief. His data suggested that the black dot was roughly the same distance from the Sun as Earth. That meant that it would fall into the Inhabitable Zone.

By the time he'd finished his observations, it was after 2 am, and Colye found himself debating whether or not to call his boss, Dr. Nick Castle. Blakely talked him out of it, stating that, "If you call him at this hour, he'll fire your ass!"

Colye agreed and continued his examination of the anomaly in the sky for the remainder of his shift. His best guess was that the black sphere had an approximate diameter of 7,600 miles, compared to Earth's 7,917. So, larger than Mars, at 4,212 miles across, and much bigger than the Moon, with its diameter of 2,158 miles.

More importantly, Justman's crude calculations suggested that the discovery was only about seventy-five million miles from Earth compared to Mars' current distance of one hundred and sixty-five million. Nagging questions persisted, though.

Why had no one noticed it before? he wondered.
It appeared not to reflect any sunlight, so Justman surmised that the object must be absorbing all of the solar radiation that contacted it.

So why isn't it radiating the heat back out into space? Why isn't it hot? Why isn't it visible in the infrared? The questions kept coming.

Per protocol, Justman entered all information that he'd collected into his journal and assigned the black mass the official name ILK-87b.

The end of his shift arrived, but Justman didn't go home. Instead, he waited until 8 am when his boss, Dr. Nick Castle, was scheduled to arrive. Pacing the floor impatiently, Justman watched as the clock ticked slowly up to 10 am, but still no sign of Dr. Castle.

Breaking protocol, Colye decided to share his findings with the new girl, Kristin Pruett.

Exhausted, he cautiously approached the office of Dr. Pruett. Tapping gently on her office door, Justman asked, "May I have a word with you?"

She obliged him and invited him into her tiny office, a nine-foot by nine-foot room with no windows and no pictures hanging on the walls. Maneuvering around two file boxes stacked on the floor, Justman pulled out a chair opposite Pruett and took a seat in the cramped quarters.

"Sorry about the mess," she said, embarrassed by the anticipation that he was about to ask her out to dinner.

Sitting uncomfortably in his chair, Justman opened his journal. Tentatively, he shared the findings that he'd gathered the night before. Pruett listened intently and, when he'd finished, looked at him with an amused smile.

"You know, you didn't have to go through all this trouble just to ask me out on a date."

Confused, Justman muttered, "What? Huh? I'm not asking you out on a date."

Suddenly he was very unsure of himself. "No-no! I need you to take a look at my findings from last night. I think I found something up there that's not supposed to be there!"

After reading through Justman's notes, Dr. Pruett agreed with Blakely's conclusion that his findings simply weren't possible and that they must be some kind of mistake or misinterpretation.

"A case of sleep deprivation, perhaps?" Pruett raised an eye-brow.

"Do I look tired to you?" snapped Justman, as his bloodshot eyes sagged and watered.

"Yes, you do!" confessed Pruett. "Colye, there's no heat signature there. No heat, no planet."

"Never mind then!" In frustration, Justman turned toward the door.

Just then, he saw Dr. Castle entering the building.

"Dr. Castle! Sir, may I have a moment of your time?" asked Justman.

"What? What are you still doing here?" asked the rushed and perturbed Castle, who was running late.

"That's what I wanted to tell you..." responded Justman before being sharply cut off by his boss.

An abrupt Castle said, "Make it quick; I have a call with Dr. Archibald Grassley in fifteen-minutes."

Grassley, a world-renowned astrophysicist, and Director of the Harden Institute in New York City would be calling to discuss the upcoming presser about the new Pan-STARRS 3 telescope.

After hearing what Colye Justman had to report, Castle broke one of the golden rules of science by saying, "That's impossible!" He then added, "Why are you wasting my time?"

"But sir....!" pleaded Justman.

The meeting ended abruptly, and Justman went home feeling dismayed, discouraged, and completely defeated.

At the end of his call with Grassley, Castle joked that one of his guys spotted a black sphere in our Solar System last night that was roughly the same size as Earth.

Instead of saying goodbye and hanging up, the always curious Grassley interjected, "Now-now, wait a minute, what did you just say?"

Castle explained further and was stunned when Grassley asked him to email over the entirety of Justman's findings. "At once!" he urged.

Later that night, Castle's phone rang while he was in the shower. His wife Carolyn barged into the bathroom and yelled, "Honey, Dr. Grassley's on the phone. He says it's urgent!"

Castle yelled back, "Tell him to hold on!"

In a towel and dripping wet, Castle took the call. His wife looked on and saw his jaw drop as he listened to what Grassley was saying. When the call ended, Castle instructed his wife, "Get Colye Justman from Haleakala on the phone; I've got to pack a bag!"

Moments later, Castle grabbed the phone from his wife and said to Justman, "Meet me at the airport in one hour. We're going to New York!"

Chapter 2 – Black Earth

Location: Washington D.C. NCN National Cable News Network Studios, The Situation Center with Bear Winston – September 30, 2019.

"This just in!" announced Bear Winston, anchor of NCN's nightly news show. "An astonishing discovery is being reported by the International Astronomy Union in Munich, Germany. A large object, roughly the size of Earth, has been detected some seventy-five million miles from our planet."

"First spotted by the Haleakala Space Observatory in Maui, Hawaii, on September 20, 2019, the discovery was made using the facility's new Pan-STARRS 3 telescope, the most powerful telescope of its kind, either on Earth or in space. The discovery is causing concern and speculation throughout the scientific community."

"To shed more light on this developing story, I'm joined by the world-renowned astrophysicist, Dr. Archibald Grassley, Director of the Harden Astronomy Institute in New York City."

Winston swiveled in his chair to face his guest. "Dr. Grassley, can you give our audience your expert opinion on this fascinating new discovery, which has the scientific world struggling for words?"

"Well, Bear, as you know, I personally never struggle for my words," joked Grassley. "I want to start by saying that without the curiosity of Dr. Colye Justman of the Haleakala Space Observatory, the discovery of what is now being called ILK-87b may have gone undiscovered for another century or two."

"I was in Munich just two weeks ago for the IAU conference, which was actually rather boring, and this discovery came out just two days later. My guess is they'll be inviting us back in the near term to discuss this rather exciting development."

"But how...?" Winston began, almost stuttering in his attempt to form the question. "How in the world, forgive the pun; how in the Universe, could we have missed what appears to be another planet in our solar system after all of these centuries?"

Grassley perked up in his chair and responded, "Well, Bear, the first thing we have to remember is that space is called space for a reason; there's a lot of it. And since William Hershel discovered Uranus in 1781, Neptune by Urbain LeVerrier in 1846, and Pluto, discovered by Clyde Tombaugh in 1930; astronomers have basically been looking beyond our own Solar System and have apparently, shall I say, missed the planet for the stars," he chuckled heartily while looking very pleased with his sense of humor.

"The other challenge is that nearly all celestial bodies in the Universe either radiate light or reflect it, our nearest example being the Moon. But this new, rather large body…," chuckled the heavy-set Grassley, "actually absorbs it, meaning it's black."

"What do you mean, black?" challenged Winston as he leaned across the table towards Grassley.

Grassley calmly responded, "The surface of ILK-87b appears to be covered with some type of carbon substance; nanotubes perhaps."

"Nanotubes?" asked Winston, looking perplexed.

"Yes," said Grassley, wearing his teacher's hat. "Nanotubes are like tiny carbon trees that absorb all the light they contact. If that's what's on the surface of this newly discovered planet, then it would be nearly invisible to us here on Earth. You see, Bear, if something in the night sky is completely black and is also seventy-five million miles away, it would be visually undetectable, no matter how powerful the telescope."

"I've heard of the term Vanta Black and that it's the darkest material on Earth; is this similar?" questioned Winston.

Grassley leaned forward as if to underscore his credentials and said, "Yes, but even blacker than Vanta Black."

"The way I see it," added Grassley, "this new discovery is similar to the August 2011 discovery of TrES-2b, a Jupiter-sized planet about 750 light-years away. That planet was first observed by NASA's Kepler spacecraft a little more than two years after its launch. TrES-2b only reflects one-percent of the sunlight that reaches it, so it was difficult to spot, even for a computer-controlled telescope. That makes the observational discovery of Dr. Colye Justman, in conjunction with the Pan-STARRS 3, all the more remarkable."

"This is all very interesting...," said Winston, looking a little lost.

"I do believe that this young man just found himself a place in our history books," proclaimed Grassley.

"This is the most excited I've been about any discovery in the cosmos in my lifetime, and I'll tell you why. ILK-87b is calculated to be about seventy-five million miles from Earth. Mars is currently more than one hundred and sixty-five million miles away, meaning humans can go there and investigate. Sorry everyone, but Mars will simply have to wait!" exclaimed Grassley, with an excited smile.

"One more thing Bear. This discovery will likely be the most important discovery, not just of our time, but of all time."

"Should we be worried about extraterrestrial life on our new neighbor?" joked Winston nervously.

"I'm so glad you asked that question," smiled Grassley.

"Why is that?" asked Bear, with a reciprocating smile.

"Bear, from our calculations, ILK-87b falls into what we in the astronomy community like to call the Goldilocks Zone.

"Goldilocks Zone?" Winston looked puzzled.

"Yes. Meaning it's not too hot; not too cold," smiled Grassley, always happy to preach about the cosmos. "The Inhabitable Zone, otherwise known as the Goldilocks Zone, is an area around a star where the temperature is just right for liquid water to exist."

"Ahh, Goldilocks! I get it," said Winston. "So again, what are the chances...?" asked Winston, for the second time before Grassley interrupted.

"The answer is no; it would be implausible that life currently exists on ILK-87b due to its surface properties and its atmosphere's absorption of light. Surface temperatures would be far too high to sustain life as we know it." Grassley paused, largely for effect, before continuing. "But wouldn't it be astoundingly great if it did?" he concluded with his trademark grin.

"And..." again Grassley paused, cognizant of the millions of viewers tuning in for the live broadcast, "life would've almost surely existed at some point in its planetary history. That's why I'm so excited about this discovery." Grassley settled back in his chair and revealed a look of satisfaction on his face.

Moments after the interview concluded, during the commercial break, Grassley pulled Winston to the side. "Listen, Bear," he whispered, "I didn't want to alarm your viewers, but there's a little-known fact about this discovery that has the scientific world confounded," Grassley looked around nervously to see if anyone else might be listening.

"What's that?" asked Winston.

"As I mentioned to you moments ago, ILK-87b is completely black and doesn't reflect any light. What this indicates to me, and many others, is that the surface is likely many hundreds of degrees Fahrenheit."

"Yes, you alluded to that during the interview," Winston again looked perplexed.

Grassley paused before leaning in. "Bear, are you familiar with infrared technology?"

"Of course I am," Winston looked offended.

"Bear, there is no heat signature radiating from this black mass." Grassley was beginning to sound nervous. "That's causing many of us in the scientific community a great deal of consternation," he confessed.

"What exactly are you saying?"

"Off the record, I'm saying that if that planet is hot, and it's not radiating an infrared heat signature," he paused and looked both ways before whispering, "then something's causing it not to."

Winston's look of confusion turned to fear as he muttered, "Are you suggesting...?"

"Technology!" said Grassley, finishing Winston's thought.

They shook hands, and Grassley promised to keep Winston apprised. As he left, Grassley put his index finger to his lips as if to say, "Shhhh."

Without speaking, Winston nodded his head in agreement. Grassley winked at him and departed The Situation Center studio. Those out of earshot witnessed a pale-looking Winston standing alone and looking a bit unnerved.

Location: Munich, Germany – October 7, 2019.

The IAU had finished its annual conference in Munich on September 18, just two days before ILK-87b was discovered. Now, it invited back experts from around the world, this time to discuss the implications the discovery would have on all future space exploration plans.

While the worlds of science and space exploration were abuzz, the world at large remained slightly skeptical and quiet. News coverage of the recent events began to wane. The average person wasn't sure what to make of the discovery, unaware of exactly what it meant for life on Earth.

Mild protests formed in the streets of Munich outside IAU Headquarters. The Flat Earth contingent turned up, as did some Moon landing deniers, but the crowds were small and peaceful, and news outlets paid them little attention.

Location: Los Angeles, California – October 25, 2019.

In Britain, the BBC had been airing old interviews and documentaries featuring Riley King, Professor of Planetary Science at the U.K.'s Lyons University, discussing the Moon landing and debunking conspiracy theories. While in Los Angeles, Professor King was actually appearing live as a panelist on cable television's Right Time with Will Sparks. King was part of a panel that featured astronomers Cynthia Nye and Dr. Colye Justman. The special guest that night was Dr. Archibald Grassley.

The show was focused on what the host of the show, Will Sparks, dubbed Black Earth. This would be the first time ILK-87b would be called by that name, and it would stick. Sparks was skeptical that a black planet had actually been discovered, and the panel discussed his views. They joked about the possibility that life might actually exist on the newly discovered planet.

When Grassley was invited out, he sat to the left of Sparks. Immediately Sparks launched in, chiding Grassley on his suit vest and necktie, which were both adorned with images of planets and stars. Laughing, Grassley defended his fashion sense as nerdy cool.

Sparks began the interview by challenging Grassley on how he could have possibly missed a tenth planet in our solar system.

"Now, Will," began Grassley, "I have to correct you on that one. With Pluto officially being demoted to a dwarf planet in 2006, ILK-87b is the new ninth planet in our solar system, not the tenth!"

Undeterred, Sparks quipped back, "Who even cares if anyone lives on what people want to believe is a Black Earth?"

For a moment, Grassley seemed almost lost for words before finally blurting out, "Will, did you just call ILK-87b Black Earth?"

"Yeah, and what if I did?" Sparks didn't seem to care about the fuss Grassley was making.

"It's got a hell of a ring to it!" said the charismatic, African-American icon. "Sounds like someplace I'd like to visit one day," he chuckled as the audience erupted in laughter.

"Well, if you'd told me that it was you who'd discovered Black Earth, I definitely would've thought it was a hoax, knowing you. You're always looking for the camera!" Sparks clapped his hand on Grassley's shoulder and added, "I wouldn't put anything past you!"

Although Grassley went on to recite familiar lines from the Winston interview, he went on to say, in a more serious tone, "As we sit here today, there is significant research underway that will likely result in an unmanned expedition in the coming years."

While Grassley was always on the front lines, preaching the gospel of astrophysics, the rest of the scientific community wondered how it would focus its collective energy on ILK-87b. Observatories around the world began pointing their most powerful telescopes towards the black sphere. Astrophysicists, astronomers, and scientists were on their heels, desperately trying to explain how this black mass could have gone unnoticed for centuries.

Most experts in the scientific community were careful to avoid the heat signature issue. It was a question that was begging to be answered. And while the majority celebrated the discovery, some privately dreaded trying to make sense of it all.

By late November 2019, NASA held emergency meetings to discuss delaying or even postponing their Mars-related expeditions, waiting until more information could be gathered. The meetings' results were hardly reported by the press as curiosity about the new discovery continued to wane.

People around the world began to realize the new discovery had not changed their day to day lives, and when the media realized that had happened, the news cycle soon reverted back to the two main stories they had been following before the announcement of the discovery: the Presidential Democratic debates ready to begin, and the fact that the current President was under a cloud of impending impeachment, something that had consumed the media industry for over a year.

Chapter 3 – Space Race

Location: Washington, D.C. NASA Headquarters – January 3, 2020.

At NASA Headquarters in Washington D.C., officials mulled over the notion of canceling their planned Mars 2020 Rover Mission, scheduled for August, and focused instead on ILK-87b. The change would effectively put the United States back in the lead of the modern-day space race, regaining its prominence over new-comer China. The Chinese space agency had been late to space exploration, having sent its first astronaut into orbit only as recently as 2003. But it had since jumped to the forefront. On January 3, 2019, China had landed its unmanned Chang'e 4 Lunar Rover on the far side of the Moon. No other spacecraft had previously ventured there, aside from a few botched NASA crash landings.

While NASA was congratulatory in public, behind the scenes, there'd been concern that the United States was losing its place as the world leader in space travel, innovation, and technology. Those fears, however, were washed away with the discovery of ILK-87b and the anticipated diversion of the 2020 Mars mission. The U.S. was again poised to regain the lead in the space race.

On the first anniversary of the historic landing of Chang'e 4, the news coming out of China was not about its space program, however. The World Health Organization was reporting cases of pneumonia on an unprecedented scale, first detected in the city of Wuhan, in the country's Hubei province. In the following six-month period, the disturbing news would distract the world from the new planetary discovery.

Meanwhile, NASA's announcement to send an unmanned probe to the black planet, which caught its rival countries off guard, went largely unreported by the Press. Instead, the world's population was beginning to focus on the unfolding epidemic in China that was rapidly spreading to other countries around the globe.

Location: New York City. United Nations Headquarters – January 13, 2020.

The U.N. General Assembly was called to action by the E.U., Russia, China, and India, who all agreed that the first exploratory mission to ILK-87b should be an international effort, resting on the shoulders of many nations. They sought a U.N. resolution that would block the United States from going it alone.

On January 20, 2020, the U.N. Security Council, by a vote of 11-4, agreed that the U.S. should proceed with its planned expedition. However, in a subsequent ballot, the Council unanimously voted that any future manned expeditions to ILK-87b must include an international coalition.

By early February, NASA was working overtime to reconfigure plans and retrofit equipment in an effort to make the unmanned journey to ILK-87b on schedule. During interviews, retired NASA employees likened what was happening at NASA to the 1960s fervor that led to the moon landing in 1969.

One of the biggest concerns that NASA had was the fact that ILK-87b's surface appeared to be so black that an orbiting satellite, at any altitude, would likely not be able to photograph the surface and its terrain. This didn't deter them, though. If needed, NASA would dust off old technology used by the Magellan spacecraft in the early 1990s to map the surface of Venus. They would repurpose it to image ILK-87b's surface by using a technique called synthetic aperture radar. The mission had one clear purpose: get to ILK-87b fast and find out as much as possible.

The Mars 2020 rover mission, with its goal of landing a new rover on the red planet, was officially scrapped. NASA instead shifted its focus entirely to an ILK-87b exploration program.

The ditched Mars mission had goals of addressing high-priority scientific questions. It would have investigated not just the potential for life on the red planet today but also whether Mars might have been inhabitable in the ancient past. The new mission to ILK-87b would attempt the same objectives but would address those questions from a low Black Earth orbit instead of landing a rover.

NASA had a tough call to make about how best to orbit the black planet. For weeks, the experts scratched their heads over three alternatives. The first was a polar orbit, with an inclination of 90°, orbiting North to South. This would allow the orbiting spacecraft to see virtually every part of the planet, as it rotated below, and it had support from a large section of the NASA team. The second was a Sun-synchronous orbit, which would allow the probe to pass over one part of the planet at an altitude of around 800km. For this to work, the orbiting spacecraft would have to shift its orbit daily, but, on the plus side, it would mean they could count on continuous sunlight for taking pictures. The final option was a geosynchronous orbit, where the probe would orbit ILK-87b at the same rate it rotated, meaning it could observe nearly a full hemisphere of the planet below.

Different experts lobbied hard for their favorite option. Finally, NASA leadership decided that a polar orbit would give them the best chance to scan low-altitude, hi-resolution images. It would switch to a geosynchronous orbit after thirty days, so the orbiting camera could then focus on particular areas of interest.

In the several years leading up to the discovery of ILK-87b, NASA had been developing a hi-resolution camera that could map even the darkest planetary surface. The camera would combine infrared, radar, and night-vision capabilities. The project had been set for completion in early 2021. However, with the discovery of ILK-87b, that date was brought forward to coincide with the upcoming mission, causing no end to the sleepless nights for the technicians involved. The new camera was officially named Infinity Horizon.

Another issue concerning NASA was its ability to communicate with any future manned missions to ILK-87b.

Until now, communication between Earth and rovers on the surface of Mars had been transmitted via satellites. Due to the great distance between the two planets, there were long delays. Comms could take anywhere from three to twenty-two-minutes to arrive since the signals only traveled at the speed of light: almost 671 million miles per hour. NASA officials decided that if they ever did send astronauts to ILK-87b, that kind of delay would be unacceptable. So, NASA decided it would create a new satellite system named Interlink.

The plan was ambitious: Interlink technology would consist of a series of mini-satellites called CommSpheres. The mini-satellites would act as communication beacons and would be positioned at intervals of 500,000 miles along the designated route from Earth to ILK-87b. The CommSphere satellites would be able to shift their positions based on the two planets' planetary alignment. However, preliminary findings suggested that ILK-87b was trailing Earth by a steady seventy-five million miles. It appeared to be in the same elliptical orbit of the sun as Earth.

Before being deployed, each satellite would be slightly larger than the size of a basketball. When they were released, each tiny CommSphere satellite would unfold and extend its mini antennas, looking more like the traditional satellites orbiting Earth.

Once fully operational, the satellites would use SC or Superluminal Communication. This technology, which had only just recently been implemented with the Interlink system, had been in the development and testing stages for more than five years.

SC technology was controversial. In the past, it had been considered only hypothetical. That was until December 2019, when a groundbreaking study revealed that it worked. The research had shown that tachyonic particles, which move faster than the speed of light, could be used to send comms. This suddenly made FTL, or Faster Than Light communication, possible, disproving the Lorentz-Invariant theory, which suggested that FTL was impossible.

If all went as planned, the SC technology would allow communications to travel at 10x the speed of light, making comms with a planet seventy-five million miles away instantaneous. That would mean NASA's Mission Control could communicate directly with any spacecraft en route and with the astronauts during any future manned missions or even with the black planet's surface.

Superluminal Communication was so novel that it had never been used before. Under normal circumstances, years of testing would take place before deploying new technology for space travel communications. But, if a crewed mission were to go to Black Earth soon, there would be no time for that. The prototype CommSphere satellites would be put to the test for real, with astronaut lives potentially at stake. Due to tachyonic particles' volatile nature, the CommSphere satellite's life span was expected to be no longer than five years.

To get them into space, the mini-satellites would piggy-back on the unmanned mission to ILK-87b. The Infinity One spacecraft would carry a payload of one hundred and fifty of the CommSphere satellites and release them along the path to ILK-87b.

NASA engineers and scientists raced to complete the Interlink system for the scheduled launch of Infinity One on August 16, 2020.

The Interlink System would be mission-critical, as the goal of such a communication system would not only enhance the speed of communication but would also help to mitigate the SAD phenomenon or Separation Anxiety Disorder. This type of disorder would likely take hold of an Astronaut's mind as he or she drifted farther and farther away from Earth. While common mainly in toddlers, children can experience SAD through adolescence. However, while uncommon in adults, NASA psychologists worried that the vast distances the astronauts would travel might cause problems when the larger-than-life planet Earth completely disappeared from their view.

During the long periods in which astronauts occupied the International Space Station, they only looked out of a window to see Mother Earth rotating below. The fact that Earth remained visible at all times made it far easier to be away from home for long-duration missions.

Astronauts heading further out into the Solar System, however, would have to cope with the stresses of living in deep space while at the same time being millions of miles away from their friends and their families. This isolation could prove depressing, posing psychological challenges ranging from hallucinations to full-blown panic attacks that would risk astronaut and craft. All of this was in stark contrast to the 1960s cultural portrayal of astronauts having the 'Right Stuff.' NASA wanted the world to see American astronauts as superheroes and not mere mortals suffering from mental health disorders.

And it wasn't just the astronauts' minds that NASA had to worry about. Space exploration takes a toll on the body too. For decades, NASA doctors had known that space travel could have a severely adverse effect on the brain, for all intents and purposes making it age faster. The list of dangers was seemingly endless: Microgravity, high levels of ionizing radiation, and psychological isolation. These were problems for any astronauts, but traveling into deep space could multiply them one hundredfold.

That's why the Interlink system was so valuable. It would allow astronauts to communicate with their friends and family through email and radio communication. The great distance between them and Earth would seem much more bearable, which might help them cope better with the many hazards of deep space travel.

Finally, after many months of planning and retrofitting the original Mars probe, the new Infinity One spacecraft was ready. On August 1, 2020, NASA technicians began packing the Infinity Horizon camera into the craft and adding the payload that would deploy the Interlink communications corridor.

Press reports of NASA's progress provided a welcomed distraction for many around the world and a much-needed reason to celebrate. In the previous eight months, every country across the globe had been rocked by the horrific effects of the COVID-19 pandemic, which had originated in the city of Wuhan, China.

Tens of thousands had died, and many more had lost their livelihoods since the world had remained closed for business while the virus ran its course. At NASA, though, working in clean environments, such as the High Bay Clean Room, was the norm. Scientists there had pressed on throughout the outbreak towards their urgent goal of prepping for the space mission.

Location: Titusville, Florida. Cape Canaveral Air Force Station, Space Launch Complex 41 – August 16, 2020.

"We have lift-off!" exclaimed Mars Johnston.

The rocket carrying the Infinity One spacecraft successfully cleared the tower and was headed for a low Earth orbit on the way to beginning its journey to ILK-87b. Before it could escape Earth's orbit, it needed to achieve Escape Velocity, the velocity required to escape the Earth's gravitational pull. In the case of Infinity One, that meant exceeding speeds of 25,000 miles per hour before launching itself into outer space.

The seventy-five million mile journey would take four months, during which NASA scientists could take somewhat of a breather after their headlong dash towards the launch date. But they weren't going to be completely idle. As the spacecraft traveled towards Black Earth, it would deploy its payload of one hundred and fifty CommSphere satellites at five-hundred-thousand mile intervals along the route. Each time a tiny satellite was released, it unfurled itself and went into operation. Back on Earth, the satellites were tested and, one by one, found to be communicating flawlessly. This was a great relief to NASA officials.

At last, the monumental voyage was almost over. It was now December of 2020, and as Infinity One neared ILK-87b, it began its pre-programmed braking maneuver. This caused it to slow its pace so that it could be captured by the black planet's gravity and enter its orbit.

It was at this point that Infinity One detected a faint heat signature coming from the fast-approaching black mass. Though the signal was weak, the black surface was definitely emitting some sort of heat energy. However, that explained very little to the scientists on Earth, who were busy sorting through the limited data at their disposal. The mystery still remained: what was stopping infrared telescopes on Earth from reading the black planet's heat signature?

That question would remain unanswered for the foreseeable future. Since the early part of 2020, most governments had quarantined their populations in their homes due to the COVID-19 pandemic. The world's citizens were relegated to watching the news for updates on the health crisis. With the hourly onslaught of bad news, the public became wary of the doomsday prognosticators and simply tuned out.

The one-year anniversary of Black Earth's discovery was fast approaching, and news coverage began to shift away from the pandemic and onto Infinity One's journey to Black Earth; people had a reason to tune back in. Broadcasts became more hopeful and were now considered a welcomed distraction. News outlets experienced soaring ratings as audiences around the globe were glued to their TVs and smartphones, anxiously awaiting the first glimpse of Black Earth.

Conspiracy theorists, Flat-Earthers and skeptics, donned their face masks and descended upon major cities. They filled the streets, protesting the authenticity of ILK-87b, now dubbed Black Earth by both believers and non-believers alike.

The whole world needed something positive to cheer for, and Infinity One fit the bill. Astrophysicists, astronomers, and astronauts, now collectively referred to as 'The A-Team,' were being treated like rock stars. Along with any recently acquired information, their opinions and expertise were in demand by educational institutions, private corporate groups, and the public at large.

Dr. Colye Justman was now a household name and had been recently promoted to the new Director of the Mauna Kea Observatory in Hawaii. And, as Infinity One neared its destination, he was photographed by paparazzi having dinner with fellow astronomer Dr. Kristin Pruett.

Black Earth inspired people of all nations to go outside once again and take in the wonder of the Universe. Between the COVID-19 pandemic and the newly discovered ILK-87b, whether for better or worse, the world felt smaller, and its thousands of varied communities felt more like one.

Chapter 4 – Straight Lines

Location: Houston, Texas. Christopher C. Kraft Jr. Mission Control Center, Building 30 – December 23, 2020. 9:20 am CST.

The initial pictures sent back by Infinity One were processed and released to a limited number of Mission Control staff. What they revealed was shocking, and NASA officials immediately decided to mark them as classified. To explain away the delay in publishing the images, NASA concocted a plausible story. There were, NASA announced, technical issues with Infinity One's capability to transmit visual data. Additionally, the Infinity Horizon camera was experiencing technical difficulties. The announcement, however, was far from the truth.

Inside the halls of NASA, jaws were on the floor. Those involved in the processing and dissemination of the images were issued gag orders. They were forbidden to share anything they saw, even with their closest family members.

What they observed was something most people had long considered possible, given the vastness of our Universe. Still, it was something most had never thought they would live to see.

The initial images transmitted back from Infinity One were too dark and yielded little detail. However, the radar mapping transmitted back hi-resolution images. These vivid images revealed two incredible things.

Firstly, and to the surprise of all the experts, the atmosphere of ILK-87b was, for the most part, clear, with no apparent cloud cover. Secondly, and most shocking, the images revealed shapes that would be inconsistent with a celestial body absent of intelligent life, either past or present. The initial images astonished, amazed, and struck fear into all who witnessed them. Deep breaths and lumps in throat were much abound.

As NASA officials with top-level clearance sat around a table strewn with the disturbing images, many struggled to maintain their composure. Flight Director at Mission Control, Marcus 'Mars' Johnston, was filled with dread. He spoke for everyone in the room when he uttered the words, "God doesn't do straight lines," echoing a line from his favorite movie, *Prometheus.*

Once the team had taken time to digest the pictures they were seeing, they immediately started to rethink their strategy for Infinity One. Mars Johnston issued the order to maintain the spacecraft's trajectory in a polar orbit, retracting the original order to change to a geosynchronous orbit after thirty days. This order would maintain the satellite's low-altitude access to virtually every point on the black planet's surface. Their goal was to scan the surface as closely as possible to solve the mystery of why atypical surface features were seen on a planet other than Earth.

December 23, 2020. 12:20pm, CST.

James Lorenstine, NASA's Chief Administrator, and Flight Director Mars Johnston sat in a sound-proofed room waiting to be patched into a video conference call. It was a call neither had ever imagined they would make. They sat alongside each other in silence as they waited for the call to begin. Each was lost in his own thoughts.

Lorenstine regained his focus more and more with each ping of an arriving guest. One by one, the big cheeses of the National Security Agency, followed by those from the Department of Homeland Security, the White House's Office of Science & Technology, and, finally, the Joint Chiefs of Staff pinged into the call. For now, the President of the United States, POTUS himself, was not part of the conversation.

Everyone had already been informed that the call was highly classified. No one would be permitted to discuss or disseminate any of the subject matter until the Joint Chiefs of Staff had briefed the President.

Lorenstine and Johnston had agreed that they needed to ease into the call due to the shocking material that was about to be shared. Johnston began by explaining that sensors on the probe had confirmed that the surface of ILK-87b was black in its entirety. He made sure to stress that there were no signs of activity on the surface and that the probe had also detected a strong magnetic field, suggesting that the planet had a geologically active interior. Some of the assembled callers began to wonder why their busy schedules had been interrupted for a mundane science lecture.

At that point, Lorenstine took over the call, glancing disapprovingly at Johnston as he prepared himself for the difficult news he needed to disclose. Gasps and curses emanated from the participants' video feed as he began his shocking 'show and tell' of the images that had been recorded. What they illustrated, littered across the surface of ILK-87b, was infrastructure that looked as if it belonged on Earth. More than one of the participants on the call sank back into their chairs, frightened by what they saw. There were buildings, bridges, and even a sizeable launch platform with a tall tower at its center. This last structure, more than any other, had terrified the NASA technicians who first saw it. Lorenstine didn't have to point out to his audience of officials that it looked remarkably similar to a rocket launch pad.

The call erupted into chaos for several minutes. These weren't just bureaucrats and scientists; they were also men and women with families and loved ones. What they suddenly had to contemplate was almost too much for some of them.

"Ladies! Gentlemen!" Lorenstine eventually called the meeting to order. "Please. I must continue."

He brought up more slides, this time of the natural terrain. "We don't see any significant bodies of water on the surface, although we have found what appear to be remnants of river and lake beds. Across the surface, we see deep basins, which appear to be signs of ancient ocean floors."

Lorenstine closed the slide show, and his face re-appeared on his audience's screens. "These are only preliminary observations," he began his carefully rehearsed summary.

"We'll need to gather more data. However, for right now, there is nothing to suggest life currently exists on ILK-87b. We have found neither smoke, light, nor movement in the images."

What was unmistakable, though, to all those on the call was that life did exist at some point in its recent planetary history.

The call concluded shortly thereafter. Everyone was eager to process the information. They all agreed that absolute secrecy was imperative. They knew that if word got out about what had been discovered on ILK-87b, it could cause an international panic. But, of course, in their hearts, they all knew that a leak would be inevitable at some point.

It was during this call that Mars Johnston found himself, for the first time, referring to ILK-87b as Black Earth.

Location: Washington D.C. NCN National Cable News Studios, The Situation Center with Bear Winston – December 29, 2020. 9:45 am EST.

BREAKING NEWS.

Bear Winston unexpectedly appeared on television screens and mobile devices across the country.

"We interrupt our regularly scheduled programming to share what can only be described as shocking news!" Winston appeared composed but slightly shaken; a few pages of notes laid disheveled on the table in front of him.

"In just the past several minutes, we've heard of an incredible discovery on the surface of the planet we're all now calling Black Earth, and for good reason!" exclaimed Winston. "It was just a little more than two weeks ago; the Infinity One spacecraft entered the orbit of the black planet, ILK-87b. It didn't take long before images of the planet's surface were transmitted back to Earth. It's what those images are revealing that has insiders astonished."

"Confidential and trusted sources are reporting to NCN that the pictures from Infinity One's camera appear to show some type of infrastructure on the surface of the planet. It's being reported to us that scientists close to the Infinity One probe are suggesting that the structures they're seeing can only have been created by..." he broke off momentarily and stared earnestly into the camera. "Please don't be alarmed by what I am about to say: It seems they can only have been created by some type of intelligent life form. It's still early, but we'll be following this breaking news closely. We'll report back to you every step of the way." Winston shuffled his notes as he finished up. "Stay tuned. We'll be right back with our experts to break it all down."

Not since the 9/11 terrorist attacks on New York City and the Pentagon in Washington, D.C., had the world been so consumed by the news coming out of the United States. The populations of every country were glued to their TVs and smartphones, anxiously awaiting more information.

Location: Roswell, New Mexico – January 2021.

Business in the small town was booming. Hotels were sold out, and once-empty parking lots were filled with campers and motorhomes while parks were littered with tents. Storefront windows were covered with signs that said, SOLD OUT, and local museums were booked out for weeks. Trekkies, hippies, and nerds alike, lined the streets, happy to hang out with other alien enthusiasts. Roswell, New Mexico, was back in the spotlight.

Roswell was originally made famous by an alleged 1947 UFO crash. The U.S. military had always maintained that it was merely a conventional weather balloon. It wasn't until the late 1990s that the U.S. Government declassified documents about the event, which revealed that the object was actually a nuclear test surveillance balloon. However, UFO enthusiasts remained unconvinced, often citing a local ranch hand's initial reports of a flying disc. Even the mainstream media was beginning to question the declassified documents released some twenty years earlier.

Facebook exploded! The Area 51 Raid was back on again, with tens of thousands of curiosity seekers signing up! Facebook experienced the Internet Hug of Death, a temporary blackout, going off-line for the second time in less than a year. The social media giant was unable to sustain user traffic due to the world's curiosity regarding Black Earth.

Flat Earther blogs gained millions of new followers by perpetuating conspiracy theories about the discovery. Moon landing deniers declared that NASA was 'at it again', claiming that governments of every country were complicit in the outrageous fabrication. The phrase, 'It's a lie!' was seen everywhere, from billboards to hats and t-shirts. It became the battle cry for millions of skeptics.

Location: Rome, Italy. Vatican City – January 24, 2021.

Pope Francis, the 266th Pope to lead the Catholic Church, held prayer in St. Peter's Square. News helicopters circled above, transmitting pictures of the largest congregation ever to amass there. Some commentators estimated that more than 65,000 of the faithful had flocked to see and hear the Pope. Many in attendance and around the world feared the rapture.

Location: Washington, D.C. – January 25, 2021.

With great fanfare, the new American President announced plans to send a manned expedition to ILK-87b by the end of 2021. The spaceship carrying the crew of eight men and women would be called New Horizon.

November was tentatively scheduled for the launch. That timeframe would allow for the roughly four months it would take to cover the seventy-five million miles between Earth and our nearest neighbor, Black Earth.

NASA confirmed that the Mars 2020 Rover, built originally for the scrapped trip to Mars, would be used for the mission. The rover already had instruments that could test the chemical make-up of the planetary surface. Now, it was being retrofitted with advanced drills that could collect core samples, rocks, and sediments. This would give NASA valuable data about the black surface, which could then be transmitted back to Earth long before the manned crew returned home. Additionally, the samples the rover collected would be brought back for further testing by the astronauts landing there in March of 2022.

The biggest challenge facing NASA was the change of planetary destinations from Mars to Black Earth. The spacesuits created for the Mars mission had been designed to protect the astronauts from extreme cold, with temperatures on the red planet ranging from minus 80°F to minus 195°F. On the other hand, Black Earth was thought to be closer to 1200°F, so heat, rather than cold, would be the problem.

And it wasn't as if NASA could simply pick a different spacesuit off the rack. Spacesuits, known to the experts as Extra-Vehicular Mobility Units, or EMUs, were advanced technology. Before the mission to ILK-87b, EMUs had only ever been designed to protect an astronaut from temperatures ranging from a frigid minus 249°F to a stifling hot 250°F. It was back to the drawing board for NASA engineers.

As they began work, the EMU department estimated that each spacesuit for this mission would cost as much as $250 million. There would be one for each of the eight astronauts, plus two back-ups, or ten in total. That brought the bill to a whopping $2.5 billion just to outfit the crew.

The mission would also provide scientists with the ability to use technologies that addressed conditions on Black Earth. It would then try to characterize Black Earth's surface and other environmental conditions. Anything that might affect the astronauts' welfare to conduct additional scientific experiments on the black planet was considered.

Early data from the probe revealed a strong, planet-wide magnetic field. This suggested to NASA scientists that a strong magnetosphere was likely protecting the surface from solar storms and galactic radiation.

Location: Helsinki, Finland. Messukeskus Convention Center – April 27, 2021.

Scientific leaders and decision-makers from every space agency in the world converged on the Messukeskus Convention Center for a five-day meeting. The conference had two main goals. The first was to review NASA's findings from Infinity One. The second was more controversial: to narrow down a long list of astronaut candidates being considered for the upcoming mission.

On day one, attendees came to grips with the Infinity One data. They discussed details of ILK-87b's surface conditions, its temperature, and its apparent infrastructure. Tempers flared when some of the more conservative leaders denied what everyone else could plainly see; that architectural infrastructure did, in fact, exist on the planet. The word blasphemy was used over and over.

The main topic of conversation among the delegates was the mystery of Black Earth's surface temperature and color. It seemed incomprehensible that no heat signature could be detected through infrared technology, even though the data suggested surface temperatures ranged between 1100°F -1300°F.

Planetary geologists racked their brains, speculating about the composition of the black surface and its ability to absorb nearly all the light that contacted it. Many pointed out the similar properties of carbon nanotubes. They speculated that the surface might be layered with something comparable, be it natural or synthetic. A few of the eccentric scientists even suggested that something or someone might be trying to conceal the black planet from those on Earth.

On day three, some experts began to criticize NASA's radar mapping, with Indian and Chinese astronomers suggesting that China's new Aperture Spherical Telescope, called FAST, would be a better option for studying the black planet's surface. The $170 million, 500-meter-wide radio telescope, completed in 2016, had been designed to study distant pulsars, among other things. By the end of the day, however, a consensus was reached, no other Earth-bound telescope could better map the black planet. Assigning FAST to the project would make China the second biggest contributor, after the U.S., to the international effort to map Black Earth's surface.

Across the span of the five-day conference, a team of psychologists, space travel experts, and bureaucrats concentrated on a more human challenge: creating a shortlist of candidates for the crew of the historic mission. Experience protocols were set aside as the team needed to include mission specialists in various sciences and, of course, a medical doctor.

NASA would be heavily involved, but it wouldn't have the final say on the crew. The United States was providing the spacecraft, but it would be crewed by an international team. This crew would be multi-national, incorporating the best of the best personnel from around the world.

Inevitably each country was vying for its own candidates to be picked. Throughout the week, the crew composition became a giant jigsaw puzzle. Solving it was fraught with sensitive political considerations. From official discussions to late-night conversations over vodka and beer, international diplomacy was as much a part of the process as rational decision-making. However, by day five, world leaders and the science community had done their jobs. The crew list wouldn't be published for months, but a full team, with understudies for every member, had been agreed upon.

The cost for the participating countries would be high. Still, the overall price would be small for Earth's global community of nations. The international consensus was that the mystery of Black Earth needed to be solved by working together, no matter the cost. The world's population was growing restless and demanding answers. The mission to get humans to Earth's nearest neighbor had to happen fast and, if that meant abandoning long-standing protocols, then so be it.

Location: Toronto, Ontario, Canada – May 2, 2021.

A publicly undisclosed G8 Summit was convened in Toronto. It would include the Russian Federation, which was brought back into the fold considering the discovery of ILK-87b. The leaders of Canada, Germany, France, Italy, Japan, the United Kingdom, the Russian Federation, and the United States arrived in Toronto in absolute secrecy. They gathered at the world-famous Casa Loma mansion. Normally a tourist attraction, Casa Loma was closed for renovations, and the public was unaware of the meeting. To maintain confidentiality, the leaders entered the castle through the horse stables.

After making the 800-foot walk, the world leaders made their way into the gothic-style mansion through a once-secret tunnel. Casa Loma was built in the early 1900s and served as the primary residence for financier Sir Henry Pellatt. With 98 rooms, covering nearly 65,000 square feet, it was outfitted with the most elegant furnishings and art that the world had to offer.

In the early evening hours of the first day, the eight leaders assembled in Casa Loma's Great Hall, the main room for social gatherings. Enormous Canadian and British flags hung from the rafters some forty feet overhead. A giant table adorned the room, and beautiful chandeliers hung high overhead, beside a balcony that ran the length of the room, more than fifty feet.

The Great Hall's fireplace was graced by a large painting of Sir Henry Pellatt himself, nestled between its mantle and the double lofted doors of the master suite high above.

The ambiance of the magnificent hall was the perfect setting for the summit. Surrounded by the splendor of what the world once was, the world leaders would begin a dialogue about what the world might become.

One by one, they sat at the great table while aides, interpreters, and stenographers, were stationed behind them and around the room. Topic du jour was Black Earth.

Wide-ranging discussions would take place over the two-day summit. The first and, as it turned out most contentious, would be what the world leaders knew of Black Earth before its 'accidental' discovery.

German Chancellor Angela Merkel looked directly at the new U.S. President and Vladimir Putin, President of the Russian Federation. Her challenge to them was pointed. "Speaking on behalf of the other six leaders in the room, we would very much like to know what the United States and Russia knew about ILK-87b prior to its actual discovery on September 20, 2019."

President Macron of France launched in. "Russia and the U.S. have been traveling to space since the 1960s. Are we expected to believe that this is a new discovery?"

Vladimir Putin was quick to respond. Speaking in heavy Russian, his interpreter repeated his words. "First, let me say to all of you, the Russian Federation is thankful to be reunited with our fellow G8 countries. We understand our value to this group and to the world. We do not plan on being a distraction in this or any future matters. "Now, to your question, Chancellor Merkel and President Macron," Putin's words were interpreted.

"Speaking on behalf of the Russian Federation, its scientists, its astrophysicists, and our entire space agency, we knew nothing of ILK-87b prior to the Americans' so-called accidental discovery. Perhaps," he said as he deliberately turned in his seat to stare down the new American President, "your questions should be pointed at the U.S."

The new American President didn't hesitate. "Let's be clear about the discovery of ILK-87b. We first discovered it on September 20, 2019, at 12:07 am, Aleutian Time Zone. We have no reason to believe anyone from the United States of America, either past or present, knew of its existence before that day. I strongly urge all of you to focus away from conjecture and paranoia. We must wrap our heads around what this discovery could mean for the delicate psyches of the people we're here to represent and protect. Not only our countries collectively, but of all the countries of the world," he explained.

"We could be on the precipice of global hysteria, fueled by genuine fear. A world-wide frenzy could lead to the systematic breakdown of our great societies. In a few short months, New Horizon will have reached ILK-87b. Then we'll find out if what our eyes have told us is the truth. We'll likely have answers to ancient questions about how we got here and whether or not we are alone in the Universe."

Canadian Prime Minister Justin Trudeau had been nodding throughout the President's speech. Now, he cleared his throat and calmly added his own thoughts. Rising from his chair, he declared, "The world as we know it may never be the same after the year 2021. While we quibble over trade agreements, election meddling, pandemics, and climate change, we may have just come face to face with the second half of our human history.

"Whatever else we find out, our Universe just got a lot smaller and, now more than ever, we must present a united front. We must erase the silly idea of nationalism from our vernacular."

Around the table, the world leaders chorused their approval.

Two days of detailed discussions and negotiations followed. In a ground-breaking show of unity, the summit concluded by drawing up a pledge. The world leaders committed to a multi-national effort to get to Black Earth and return with answers that would "reassure the people of our great planet." The pledge ended with momentous words: "No matter the findings, we are safe, and we are united as one people, one planet, one Earth."

Chapter 5 – New Horizon

Location: Titusville, FL. Cape Canaveral Air Force Station, Space Launch Complex 41 – November 25, 2021. 12:17 pm EST. Thanksgiving Day.

While many Americans were tuned into the Macy's Thanksgiving Day parade, most of the world was tuned into the NCN – National Cable News network. The cable news giant was airing a special report on the manned mission to Black Earth. The journey would carry humans deeper into space than they had ever been before. The program was filmed live from NASA's Space Launch Complex in Titusville, Florida. It would include interviews with the New Horizon spacecraft crew members, fittingly set to launch on Black Friday, November 26, 2021.

On television and smartphone screens around the world appeared NCN Journalist Jonathan Cooper. He sat alone in an outdoor studio just one-thousand yards from the massive rocket ship.

"Thank you for joining us today live from Florida," said the charismatic Cooper. "We're here today to share with you remarkable images and stories coming out of NASA regarding the upcoming launch of the New Horizon spacecraft. We'll also be sitting down to chat with some of the brave men and women that will be making the historic trek to what the world is referring to as Black Earth."

"It seems like just yesterday that NCN broke the incredible story to the world, that our planet, planet Earth, suddenly had a new neighbor. While not actually new, Black Earth appears to have always been there; we just couldn't see it," explained Cooper. "ILK-87b was discovered seven hundred and ninety-seven days ago; now dubbed by all, Black Earth."

"This program is dedicated to one of the most remarkable and historic space missions of our time," said Cooper.

"It's now exactly T-minus twenty-four-hours to lift-off. Behind me, you can plainly see in the distance, sits the most powerful rocket since the Saturn V Rocket series."

"Not since the Apollo program took a total of twelve American astronauts to the moon, over the course of nearly four years, and returned them safely to the Earth a total of six times between 1969 and 1972, has the world so eagerly anticipated a space mission."

"The New Horizon spacecraft, built by Boeing, is designed to fly human beings farther from Earth than any man or woman had ever traveled before. The cost of this mission is a whopping $73 billion."

"Since the expedition is a multi-national endeavor, the cost is being incurred by the following nations: the United States has invested $32.1 billion; China, $15.75 billion; India, $5.25 billion; the United Kingdom, $4.5 billion; Germany, $3.7 billion; Japan, $3 billion; Italy, $1.5 billion; the Russian Federation, $1.75 billion; and Canada and France, each coming in at $2.75 billion. That's a lot of money!" exclaimed Cooper, looking astonished.

"The contributing nations have all agreed that, as part of their financial contribution, each would share in whatever scientific gains were made on ILK-87b."

"As mentioned earlier, the New Horizon craft and crew will travel further than any humans before them. For perspective, let me share with you some amazing numbers. The farthest distance ever traveled by humans was in April of 1970, when the Apollo 13 astronauts, at an altitude of 158 miles, flew around the far side of the Moon, a whopping 248,655 miles from Earth. The one-way journey to Black Earth, however, would be just shy of seventy-five million miles. That's a lot of miles!" said Cooper, raising his eyebrows and exhaling.

"The very capable crew of the New Horizon spaceship will be comprised of eight veteran astronauts who all, except for three new-comers, have worked closely with each other during their time on the International Space Station."

"We're joined now by U.S.A.'s Mike Swimmer. Captain Swimmer will be piloting the New Horizon craft and will also serve as the mission's Commander. Mike, may I call you Mike?"

"Of course," said Swimmer, in a deep voice that seemed to match his rugged exterior, in a royal blue NASA jumpsuit.

"Welcome to our live broadcast, and thank you for being here. NASA officials tell me that I only have a few minutes with you as it's just hours before launch."

"I wonder if you could tell the world a little bit about yourself?" asked Cooper.

"Sure, I'm Captain Mike Swimmer. I'm forty-three-years-old, and I'm originally from Austin, TX., but I've lived in Houston for the last twelve years with my beautiful wife, Sarah. We have three daughters together; Kennedy, who'll be sixteen tomorrow, Jessica, who's fourteen, and Clarissa, who's eleven."

"Wow! That's a lot of girl power in your house!" said an impressed-looking Cooper.

"They've definitely got me outnumbered, but I hold my own," smiled a proud Swimmer. "They're all great kids. My wife does an amazing job keeping us all grounded."

Cooper laughed, "Was that a little pun there?"

"Completely unintended," smiled Swimmer.

"Mike, I think what the world wants to know is," Cooper paused in an effort to formulate his question, "what emotions are you experiencing right now, just hours before you take off to a place that is so mysterious? I mean, are you excited, scared? What are you feeling right now?"

"I mean, it's a wide range of emotions. Excited for sure, scared no, but anxious, yes. Just incredibly proud of the team that we've assembled and to be a part of history," humbly expressed Swimmer.

"So, Mike, I understand that you're a fourteen-year veteran of NASA but have never actually been onboard the International Space Station; is that right?"

"That's correct," said Swimmer. "You see, I'm a pilot, and they generally only send scientists to the ISS."

"You'll have to forgive me," said an embarrassed Cooper. "That makes too much sense!" blushing a little.

"It says here that you piloted three shuttle missions from 2009-2011. Can you tell us a little more about that?" asked Cooper.

"Gosh, it doesn't seem that long ago," expressed Swimmer. "So, I Co-piloted the 2009 Atlantis Shuttle, served as the Pilot on the 2010 Endeavor mission, and then piloted the Discovery mission in 2011."

"You must be excited to get back in the saddle," suggested Cooper.

"How has NASA kept you busy over the last ten years or so since canceling the Shuttle program?" he asked.

"I'm actually a flight trainer for NASA and have worked with various space agencies around the world, like Roscosmos in Russia, CNSA in China, ISRO in India, and JAXA in Japan."

"Wow, lots of acronyms there!" the two men smiled.

"I understand that space travel runs in the family. Can you share a little bit of your lineage with our viewers?" asked Cooper.

"Yeah, sure. My great uncle is the late Alan Shepard."

"I just learned of that yesterday and find it fascinating!" revealed Cooper. "For those of our younger viewers that don't know the name, I was wondering if you can remind those watching from around the world just how significant your uncle was to the history of manned space flight?" requested Cooper.

"My uncle was one of the original seven Mercury astronauts, known as the Mercury Seven, and was the first American Astronaut in space in 1961. He would later go on to Command the Apollo 14 mission that landed on the moon in 1971."

"So, he walked on the moon?" clarified Cooper.

"Oh, yes!" said a proud Swimmer. "He was the fifth man to set foot on the moon and the only man to hit a golf ball while on the surface," smiled a beaming Mike Swimmer, with his adrenaline pumping, now sitting at attention in the canvas director's chair on the outdoor canopy set.

"So, that famous video of an astronaut swinging a golf club on the moon was your great uncle?"

"It was!" said Swimmer.

"Well, I see you're being pulled away. My producer is waiving at me frantically, just off-camera," offered Cooper.

"Listen, all the best to you and thank your family for me, as I know that they are also sacrificing a great deal, being without their husband and dad for more than eight months," expressed an appreciative Jonathan Cooper.

"No problem, thanks for having me!" said Swimmer. "Going to share some time with the family before they quarantine us."

The two men shared a hearty handshake, and Cooper welcomed in his next guest.

"Joining me now on the set is a man who has spent more time in space than any other astronaut in the history of any space agency, Co-Commander, Dr. Carrick Michaels. Welcome, Carrick!" said Cooper.

Michaels walked onto the set wearing his NASA jumpsuit. His strikingly good looks were a television producer's dream. Standing at an above-average 5'11", his dirty blonde hair seemed to be glowing in the Florida sunlight. While his crystal clear blue eyes sparkled as they seemed to mesh with his blue uniform. Cooper saw a little Robert Redford in the young astronaut.

The two men shook hands before sitting down, with Cooper looking overly impressed with Michaels' movie star image.

"Thanks for having me!" said an unpretentious Michaels. "Unfortunately, I only have a few minutes with you, but I'm very happy to be here," said an excited-looking Michaels.

"Well, I'll get right to it then," opened Cooper, as he looked over a few loose-leaf papers in his hand.

"Please tell us a little bit about yourself," encouraged Cooper.

"My name is Carrick Michaels, and I'll be thirty-one next month," he smiled. I'll be serving as the mission's Chemist."

"Ah, let's see, what else?" he asked himself aloud.

"I am originally from Suwanee, GA, and, oh yeah, I want to say Hi to my mom Maggie and my girlfriend Lola, they're standing right over there!" said an excited Carrick Michaels, pointing to two women standing just off-camera and giving them a little wave.

Cooper also waved at the two women standing behind him. It was clear that the two were anxious to share a Thanksgiving dinner with the most important man in each of their lives prior to the mission that would take him away from them for the following eight months.

After reciprocal waves, Cooper launched in with what he perceived as a rather exciting announcement. "I'm delighted to share with the world, right here as we speak, that you'll be the first person to step foot on Black Earth! How does one earn such an honor?" asked an excited Jonathan Cooper, fully understanding how big of a moment this was for him as a journalist. He would be the only journalist to interview Michaels pre-flight.

"Well, I'd like to say it's a long story, pun intended," he chuckled, "but I am actually the youngest member of the crew. I was approached by NASA Administrator James Lorenstine and Flight Director Marcus Johnston about the idea, and of course, I jumped at it."

"Why you, though?" asked Cooper, trying hard not to sound dismissive. "I mean, what was the criteria?"

"Yeah, so, it actually has nothing to do with how long you've been with the program; I've only been with NASA for a little under five years; it's actually about how many hours you've logged in space."

'Wait! So, you've logged more hours on the ISS than anyone else in the world? That's amazing! How many?" asked a visibly excited Cooper.

"16,464 hours! It's the longest anyone has spent in orbit!" proclaimed a smiling Michaels.

"That's amazing!" said Cooper. "I'm trying to do the quick math in my head...," he said while being cut off by Michaels.

"It's six-hundred-eighty-six days!" offered Michaels.

"Did you sign up for that, or did they make you go?" asked a smiling Cooper.

"No, I signed up for it! My first stint lasted a year, right out of training, and then two six-month missions, give or take a few weeks," he said, wearing his pride on his sleeve, along with an American flag and the NASA logo.

"Remarkable!" said Cooper. "So, half your time with NASA has been spent in space then?"

"Not quite, but my girlfriend thinks I'm a fugitive, running from someone or something," he joked, then found her eyes offset and gave her a wink and a smile.

"So, I think I read somewhere that your late father was a famous Navy pilot; is that true?" asked Cooper while hanging on Carrick's every word.

"Yes, my father was a Lieutenant in the United States Navy, his name was Mike Michaels, and yes, he made quite a name for himself during his career. He was a Top Gun Instructor for several years," responded Carrick, with a subtle look of discomfort on his face as his demeanor sagged.

Thinking that Carrick had finished speaking, Cooper launched in with another question, "Wow, that's amazing! Listen, one of our viewers tweeted in and wanted to know why close friends call you 'Rock'?" asked a rather curious Cooper. "Is that some sort of a nickname? If so, it's awesome!"

"Yeah, that's a long story and...," a slightly embarrassed Carrick began to respond before being quickly cut off by Cooper.

"My apologies Carrick! It looks like we're being cut short again," said a reluctant Cooper. "Listen, you have a big day tomorrow and a big next eight months. You get going, and I, along with the rest of the world, will look forward to seeing you descend that latter shortly after you land on Black Earth."

"Thanks for having me, Jonathan! Oh, and by the way, my girlfriend and I are news junkies and big fans of yours! It was great to meet you!" confessed Carrick Michaels.

"Well, likewise. I'm a big fan of yours too. Thanks for giving us some of your valuable time before lift-off," said a very appreciative Jonathan Cooper.

"Okay, time for a commercial break. We'll be right back to meet more of the crew members. Stick around!" announced Cooper.

Minutes later, Cooper re-appeared on T.V. screens and mobile devices around the world.

"Welcome back, everyone. Unfortunately, I'm sorry to report that during our break, we were notified by NASA officials that we won't have a chance to interview the other crew members who agreed to sit down with us. Instead, we'll be sharing images of the other team members and sharing a little bit about their stories.

"On your screen now is a picture of Russia's Alexi 'Cosmo' Popov, who was selected for his credentials in Biology. Popov will be third in command and is a native of the beautiful city of St Petersburg. At forty-two-years-old, he's the longest-serving cosmonaut in the Russian space agency, Roscosmos," continued Cooper.

"Next, we go to China's Liu 'Lisa' Yaping. Yaping won her place on the crew for her Geology training. She's thirty-four-years-old and comes from the Chinese capital of Beijing. Yaping's been working for China's space agency for six years. Apparently, she's quite the expert at shooting pool; she wanted us to know, although I'm not sure how useful that will be in space," remarked a smiling Cooper.

Next up, India's thirty-eight-year-old Piyush Bhula, one of the foremost Astrophysicists in the world. Piyush hails from Navsari, Gujarat. As he's known to his friends, P-Diddy will be running all the physics experiments on the mission. This was a big assignment for him, but one he is well prepared for since India had already selected him for the crew of their planned 2027 Mars mission."

"While the five astronauts mentioned so far have all worked together for years, with some spending many months together on the ISS, there are three other members of the crew that were brought in for their specific academic and professional skills," revealed Cooper.

"Dr. Kaley 'Kinzi' London is one of them."

Viewers on T.V. were shown an image of a beautiful, blonde-haired, blue-eyed woman, who had a smile as big as the rocket ship that could be seen in the distance, just over Cooper's left shoulder.

"She'll serve as the crew's Medical Doctor," said Cooper, "so part of her job is to keep herself and the other crew members safe and well. She's thirty-two-years-old and was born in Seattle, Washington. While she's relatively new to the NASA space program, London is following in her mother's footsteps. Kate London formerly served as a physician on two space shuttle missions back in the 1980s."

"Another newbie is a thirty-eight-year-old Australian, Oliver Taylor. Known as Ollie to his crew-mates, he'll serve as the Co-Pilot on the New Horizon spacecraft. Ollie hails from Australia's easternmost city of Brisbane. While he's only been in the Australian space program for four years, he's logged more hours of simulation training in robotic aero-braking than any other astronaut in the world," exclaimed Cooper.

"And finally, we see on your screen, Japanese astronaut Satoshi 'Sun' Kanai, who'll be rounding out the team. Kanai was born in Yokohama in 1988 and is a Meteorologist. Though he's logged only six months on the ISS, his experience as an astronaut, a Meteorologist, and an Oceanographer in the Japanese Maritime Defense Force, makes him uniquely qualified for this mission."

"Okay, we'll be going to a commercial break, but after that, we'll be meeting with Mission Control's Flight Director and NASA's Chief Administrator James Lorenstine. Stay with us!"

After completing the interviews with the NASA Executives, Cooper closed the broadcast by saying, "The International crew will be in space for more than eight months and will cover a distance of more than one hundred and fifty million miles. History will remember these brave men and women as the greatest space explorers of all-time," declared Cooper.

"If successful, five of the crew will land on ILK-87b and investigate Black Earth's surface astrobiologically, looking for signs of current or past life. Additionally, the exobiology program will include the return of soil and air samples for later scrutiny back on Earth. But above all, the Surface team's mission will be to explore with their eyes, their brains, and their human curiosity, something that still, in the twenty-first century, exceeds the capabilities of our autonomous, remote exploration robotics. As planetary geologist and designer of many Mars missions, Michael Malin once said, "When it comes to looking for signs of life, there's no substitute for boots on the ground, a hammer, and a hand lens."

"For NCN, I'm Jonathan Cooper. Signing off. Please join Bear Winston and me tomorrow morning for more coverage of this historic mission. Until then," nodded Cooper.

Chapter 6 – Lift-off

Three-hours prior to launch, the astronauts entered the ship's cockpit, accompanied by the Close Out team, who would be the last people to see them before lift-off. The Close Out team's job was to strap the crew into their couches and prep them for departure. Once they'd been positioned in their couches, each crew member would begin their launch protocols. Lying in a reclined position with control panels of switches above their heads, each would monitor switch position settings and data sensor activity of more than one-hundred controls. They were frequently interrupted and asked to speak into their helmet mics so that Mission Control could make sure that each team member's Comms were functioning properly.

Just before launch, some of the team members surveyed the crew compartment and nervously smiled at each other, while others had their eyes tightly closed with fists clenched in fear. Before closing her eyes, Kinzi London nervously glanced over at Carrick. He returned her nervous smile, then both closed their eyes.

Mike Swimmer and Ollie Taylor studied the instrument panel above their heads; Michaels couldn't help reflecting on the journey in front of them. It would take them to a place never previously seen by humans. They would travel distances never before traveled by mankind. And finally, they would see things that humankind had never seen before. The thought was sobering.

Before countdown, the team heard the reassuring voice of Mission Control's Flight Director, Mars Johnston, as he ran through the final countdown.

"4, 3, 2, 1. Ignition! ...We have lift-off!" sighed the overwrought Johnston.

Far below them, the massive thrusters burned their fuel and made the sound of rolling thunder. The rocket's power violently shook the crew compartment, and the team felt as if they were being shot skyward out of a giant cannon.

By the time the bottom of the rocket reached the top of the tower, it was already going one-hundred miles per hour. As the rocket shook, rumbled, and shuddered upward, Michaels tried to align every nerve in his body to the vibrations of the launch. Because he'd experienced lift-off on three other occasions, he searched for any sign that something might be wrong so that he could react instantaneously to any emergency. Going through his mind, though, was the fact that the massive thrusters were in control right now and that he and the others were simply along for the ride. An emergency of any kind during this phase of the mission would likely lead to a sudden and violent end.

The engines' roaring chorus was punctuated after seven-minutes by a thudding boom, as the first stage of the primary rocket was detached, and the secondary engines took over.

Looking out of his window, it seemed to Michaels that they were flying through a fireball. After that, the ride became smoother. Across the crew, compartment eyes opened, and fists unclenched, then a burst of static came over the helmet comms.

"What a ride!" said Mike Swimmer, punching fists with Ollie Taylor. The entire crew was excited to be alive! Back at Mission Control, many miles below, was a celebratory staff jumping up and down in triumph, finally able to breathe again.

At Mission Control, Mars Johnston could be heard whispering, "Good luck and Godspeed. The world is with you!"

Within twelve-minutes, the secondary rocket engines cut as the spacecraft went into Earth orbit. And just ninety-minutes, their engines re-ignited on a retrograde trajectory that would carry them away from Earth. Within five-hours, the entire Earth was visible from their windows. After seven days, they were able to block out the Earth with their thumbs. And after a month, planet Earth was in their past and Black Earth in their future. For the next eight months, these global heroes would call the New Horizon spaceship home.

December 13, 2021 – The world's population was captivated by the New Horizon spaceship's recent launch. Still, they were also growing impatient with NASA and the U.S. Government over their lack of transparency regarding the images captured of Black Earth. Nearly a year had passed since Infinity One had begun sending pictures back to Earth, and still, no photos had been released to the public. It was also clear that no pictures had been leaked to the press because no self-respecting journalist could have resisted getting the credit for breaking the explosive images to the public.

The disturbing images NASA was hiding from the public were only shared with a few national agencies. Marked as classified, they were passed onto the NSA, the CIA, the FBI, the White House Office of Science and Technology, the Department of Homeland Security, and the Department of Energy. As a courtesy, the U.S. also released highly redacted pictures to the G8 Plus 5 Group's world leaders.

In the interest of public safety, every governmental organization who had them kept the images and their descriptions under lock and key. Powerful search engine robots, operated by NASA, were constantly on the lookout for any image that had crept onto the web or the dark web. When the bots detected any of the images' digital signals, they automatically redacted them.

Orbiting at an altitude of two-hundred fifty-six miles above the surface of ILK-87b, roughly the same altitude as the International Space Station orbits the Earth; the Infinity Horizon was still sending images, with more than twenty-thousand transmitted to date. The images captured surface details at pin-sharp resolution. In fact, the Infinity Horizon camera was performing far beyond its expected capabilities. The U.S. Military kept this revelation a secret from other world powers. They requested that any images shared with other nations be blurred slightly before they were sent so as not to alert other governments to the advanced technology possessed by the United States.

Internally though, the pictures and what they revealed were causing concern and distress. In the darkest corners of NASA, over quiet conversations, staff discussed whether the world's safety might be in jeopardy. Since the first images were taken of ILK-87b, more than three dozen NASA and government employees had been treated or hospitalized for mental health-related illnesses. Another six requested early retirement, while one even committed suicide.

Entire cities seemed to have existed on ILK-87b at some point over the previous several centuries. However, those cities didn't look ancient. Instead, they appeared to be more modern than Earth's most contemporary and sophisticated metropolises. The ILK-87b cities, though, were in ruins. Something catastrophic seemed to have happened on Black Earth; something so violent that it appeared to have wiped out the entire population of every species that might once have existed on the black planet.

In addition to skylines and cityscapes, reservoirs, dams, and what appeared to be futuristic power plants also seemed to have been devastated by some type of cataclysmic event. An event that likely altered the existence of any and all life that once existed there, dooming the black planet.

Some cities appeared to have been pulverized into oblivion, as craters marred most of the landscape around nearly all of what appeared to be former population centers on Black Earth.

Some suspected meteor storms while others pointed to the fact that no such body of meteors, large enough to wipe out an entire planetary population, had ever been recorded in our history. This fact, however, was not relevant, as the meteor storm advocates argued that the tracking of meteors only began as recently as the mid-1830s, when Denison Olmsted, an American Physicist, Professor, and Astronomer, invited some of his Yale College students to join him in monitoring the Leonids, in 1833. The Leonids are prolific meteor showers associated with the comet Tempel–Tuttle; they occur roughly every thirty-three years and were first witnessed around 902 A.D., and usually occur early in the month of November. Even a large meteor body like this, though, would not have had the power to ravage Black Earth.

After orbiting Black Earth for more than a year, Infinity One had digitally mapped most of the planet and cataloged it into tiny block sectors, roughly five-hundred by five-hundred miles wide. Those sectors were ranked by relevance and importance. Those that were absent of any apparent infrastructure were marked as low priority. They included topographical features like dried-up oceans, lakebeds, and mountain ranges. These were passed on to geologists to pour over at a later date. Those sectors that indicated areas populated with infrastructure were classified as top-priority and were sent for immediate analysis.

One sector, in particular, was getting a lot of attention. Cataloged as G7.164.598.622, the area appeared to have very little crater activity. It revealed infrastructure and buildings that seemed completely intact. This sector would be the first destination targeted by the New Horizon surface exploration team.

January 3, 2022 – Thirty-nine days into the one-hundred seventeen-day journey and flying at a record speed of 26,658 miles per hour, New Horizon had traveled nearly twenty-five million miles but still had more than fifty million miles to go. It was expected to make low Black Earth orbit sometime on or around March 21, 2022.

Aboard the spaceship, the six male and two female crew had finally settled in. They learned a great deal about one another. Friendships had developed in the close quarters of the craft. Most of the crew already knew each other well, having spent many months together on the ISS. Ollie Taylor, Kinzi London, and Sun Kanai had not previously worked closely with any of the other crew members outside of mission training but meshed nicely with the team. While some disagreements had occurred, the mood was generally light-hearted. Silly jokes often filled the air, followed by laugh-out-loud moments. The astronauts often sat together, playing card games, or chatting. A small reading group had even formed as the crew shared their small stash of books.

And then there was Carrick Michaels, who'd always seemed to be staring out the window during his me-time. Carrick would stare for what seemed like hours. His crew-mates often wondered what was going through his mind. He veered deep into the darkness and saw beyond the stars and the black void of space. Most people look up to the sky at night and see the stars in all of their beauty. Carrick, on the other hand, looked up and saw the black void beyond them. What was the black abyss of space hiding? What lay ahead for he and the crew of the New Horizon? What universal questions would finally be answered after reaching Black Earth?

The rest of the crew took Carrick's forlorn silences in stride. They would prefer to socialize with him during their downtime, but no one interpreted his self-imposed isolation as a snub. They accepted him for who he was.

The camaraderie between these Best of the Best grew stronger with every passing mile. It was as though all the things that kept individuals from different corners of the world apart didn't apply in deep space. The crew was no longer distracted by the boundaries, borders, or barriers that might otherwise divide this diverse group of modern-day *Magellans*.

In the weeks leading up to the launch, people on Earth referred to this diverse crew using the term which referred to Ferdinand Magellan, the Portuguese explorer who was first to circumnavigate the Earth a little less than five-hundred years ago.

Onboard the New Horizon spacecraft, accommodations, quarters, and compartments were similar to that of the International Space Station. They included eight sleeping pods, three lavatories, a galley for food preparation and consumption. Near the back of the spacecraft was a pressurized airlock that led to a unit containing the two surface rovers. These were aptly named Black Horizon Rover 1 and Black Horizon Rover 2. Each rover could carry up to three astronauts at a time and had a battery life of one-hundred-hours. They were the pinnacle of space exploration technology and cost a whopping $1.1 billion each.

Regardless of the price tag, NASA had decided to take two rovers along to provide redundancy in case one failed or became damaged. The two rovers would also give the surface landing party more flexibility. After touching down on the black surface, the astronauts would have only fifty-hours to conduct all of their experiments before heading back to the spacecraft for their return trip home. The Black Horizon landing rovers, however, would not be joining them. They would have to remain on the surface.

For the New Horizon landing module to escape the estimated gravitational pull of ILK-87b, it would need a huge amount of thrust. To achieve this, it would have to be 1,600 pounds lighter on take-off than it had been when it landed. So, there would be no room for the rovers. Failure to depart the surface on the first attempt would render its occupants new residents of Black Earth.

If this tragedy were to unfold, the five astronauts designated for surface exploration would likely only have three days to live. The Lander was designed to provide minimal life support for an additional seventy-two-hours beyond the mission's designated timeline. There would be absolutely nothing the remaining three crew members, orbiting overhead, could do to save the doomed ground exploration crew.

Location: Houston, Texas. Christopher C. Kraft, Jr. Mission Control Center, Building 30 – January 15, 2022.

In the private offices of NASA's hierarchy, senior leaders were worried. New images from Infinity One had revealed something inexplicable and acutely disturbing. A light had been detected, emanating from a structure in the much-studied sector of G7.164.598.622. This revelation caught all of those involved off guard, with some excited and curious while others were quietly fear-stricken.

The sector that had sparked the most interest by those involved had an area within it that had a sui generis-shaped structure that was as enormous as it was unique. A three-sided megaplex, with anchoring buildings in each corner, each with five sides.

When Mars Johnston sat down alone in his office to view the images, the buildings immediately made him think of the Pentagon in Washington, D.C.
Mars was very familiar with the Pentagon; as he'd spent about half his time working at NASA's headquarters in D.C.. Ever since the Space Shuttle program shut down in 2011, he'd been required to travel back and forth from Houston to Washington monthly, and had been to the Pentagon several times over the years.

Intrigued by what the images showed, he decided to research some details of the Pentagon, which served as the United States Department of Defense headquarters.

Its sheer vastness struck a chill in Mars as he compared the photos from Black Earth to actual photos of the Pentagon. After opening his laptop, Mars Googled some technical details about the Pentagon. Searching the internet, he quickly learned that it was the largest office building in the world, with more than 26,000 military and civilian employees working there daily. It covered an area of 28.7 acres and was located in Arlington, Virginia. It had a floorplan of 6.5 million square feet, spread over five surface-levels and two sub-floors. American architect George Bergstrom had designed the building. Construction had started on September 11, 1941, and finished on January 15, 1943.

Mars scrolled slowly through web images of the architectural plans. He could see that the complex was made up of five concentric rings of buildings that got smaller from the outer ring to the innermost. A five-acre center plaza was covered with grass and trees and labeled as Ground Zero. Ironic, thought Mars since that was the name given to the area around New York's twin towers, that had been devastated by terror attacks on September 11, 2001. The twin towers hadn't been the only target, though.

Exactly sixty years after its construction began, the Pentagon had been hit too. American Airlines Flight 77 had been hijacked and flown into the building's western side, killing one hundred and eighty-nine people. One hundred twenty-five people had lost their lives on the ground, along with fifty-nine victims and the five hijackers on board the airliner.
Mars toggled back and forth between the images from ILK-87b and the plans for the Pentagon. They were unnervingly similar. The three-sided goliath in sector G7.164.598.622 was anchored with three buildings that were shaped exactly like the Pentagon. Using high school geometry, Mars calculated that the triangular structure's interior area was approximately 4.5 square miles.
Mars knew it would be important for the surface Landers to have some idea of what they were dealing with regarding the size of the megaplex during their surface exploration. He quickly pulled a legal pad from the top drawer of his desk and began jotting down notes on the building's size and shape.

He also noted that the ILK-87b structure appeared to have no lifeforms associated with it. The mammoth structure appeared to be completely dark and uninhabited. The only exception was the recently detected light.

Mars was not the only NASA employee who was deeply curious about the structure. Unlike the rest of the planet's metropolises, this massive building seemed untouched by either time or global devastation. The small stitch of light emanating from the top of the Northwest Sector might very well have been nothing more than a reflection of the sun's light. The mystery, however, remained. Investigating it would become the top priority of the New Horizon crew.

Chapter 7 – Iron Will

Location: Deep Space. The New Horizon Spaceship – January 22, 2022.

Through the dark expanse of space, the New Horizon crew crept towards Black Earth. The craft and its occupants had been in space now for fifty-eight days and had traveled more than thirty-seven million miles. They were nearing the half-way point to ILK-87b, and for some of the crew, this was a beacon of hope. However, other crew members were getting fidgety and beginning to act like little kids in the back seat of a car driven by Mom and Dad during childhood. 'Are we there yet?' While those words hadn't actually been uttered, the look on the crew's faces said it all. The scientists displayed apathy almost hourly, as they were getting itchy and simply wanted to get to work on the historic experiments that would take place after landing on the surface of ILK-87b. The crew also hoped to answer the question of how architectural infrastructure could possibly be on Black Earth.

As the crew's medical doctor, it was Kinzi London's job to monitor and maintain the other astronaut's health, and that included their psychological wellbeing.

On any long-duration space mission, highly organized schedules help to keep morale high. On the New Horizon, days were divided into three blocks of eight-hours. The crew was expected to sleep for eight hours and work for another eight. Kinzi would ensure that her crew-mates completed a minimum of four hours of exercise per day. This left the team with four-hours of what they referred to as 'Me' time. Most read or played games while others chatted about life or their families back home, while some just internalized what awaited them on the black planet.

There was no diurnal change in space, but to give them a sense of normality, the astronauts' days were laid out as they would have been on Earth. Day and Night were organized on Houston time. When it was night-time in Texas, they slept. When it was daytime, they exercised, ate, worked, and played.

The 9 to 5 of each workday was highly structured so that the missions' scientists would remain focused on their research. Though essential, the experiments could also be tedious and mundane and would not be as exciting on the journey out as they would be when they got to Black Earth. On the other hand, the lab housing biologist Alexi Popov's work was a particular draw for the others. He experimented with growing plants in zero gravity, and the plant life on his lab table made him a popular man.

The New Horizon pilots, Mike Swimmer and Ollie Taylor, remained occupied monitoring the integrity of the spacecraft. They continuously audited fuel usage and instrument readouts. When they weren't conducting routine maintenance, they worked through doomsday emergency scenarios. If the incident onboard Apollo 13 had taught NASA anything, it was that you needed to be prepared in case the 'what-if' actually happened.

Kinzi London's daily routine was perhaps the most mundane, even though it was highly significant. She performed regular tests on every member of the crew, including herself. Each day, the information from her blood tests, breathing examinations, heart rate monitoring, and a host of other evaluations was transmitted back to NASA's Mission Control.

The crew's diet typically consisted of three meals a day: breakfast, lunch, and dinner. Space nutrition was extremely advanced because the ISS had been operating for well over twenty years, sending back millions of data points about astronauts' health. The food provided was perfectly balanced to supply them with sufficient vitamins and minerals. The men onboard were allocated roughly 3300 calories a day, while the women only required about 2000.

The New Horizon pantries were stocked with more than two hundred different food and beverage options. The crew would consume fruits, nuts, peanut butter, chicken, beef, seafood, candy, brownies, and many other foods. Drinks for the crew included coffee, tea, orange juice, fruit punch, and lemonade. As long as they stuck to their daily calorie intakes and made healthy choices, they could eat and drink whatever they wanted.

In addition to diet, Kinzi also kept a close eye on the astronauts' physical exercise regimens. There were no exceptions to the daily training sessions. Mission Control allowed no shirking. For the more physically active crew members, four-hours in the gym was a breeze. For others, it was more of an effort. It was Kinzi who coaxed and cajoled them through. Rigorous exercise would help ensure that the surface crew would be physically able to transition from four months of zero gravity to the gravity of a planet nearly the size of Earth.

A team of doctors on the ground in Houston monitored the crew's vitals closely. They then sent back daily updates so that Kinzi could tweak each astronaut's nutritional intake and exercise regimen. The goal was to ensure that the team stayed at peak fitness.

The crew also expressed their apprehension about what might be discovered on a planet that was clearly inhabited by intelligent life form at some point in the last five hundred years. To date, NASA had only provided the team with limited data, which only added to the team's consternation. At one point, Kinzi overheard Alexi Popov whispering to himself, "Only thirty-eight million miles to go, only fifty-nine more days...only!"

When Kinzi communicated her concerns to Mission Control, Mars and his team began to formulate a plan to ease the anxieties onboard. NASA had continued to analyze surface images from ILK-87b, but it seemed sensible to release information to the New Horizon crew on a 'need to know' basis only. And many NASA officials believed that, until they were closely approaching Black Earth, the astronauts didn't need to know details unrelated to their journey prior to entering the orbit of the black menace.

It was Mars Johnston who turned this policy on its head. In a high-level meeting, he finally lost his temper. He rose from his seat, banging his fists on the table. "Morale is waning onboard!" as his forehead looked like an atlas of popping veins.

Mars simmered, "They're up there wondering what's waiting for them on Black Earth. All the while knowing that we have that information, and we're keeping it from them. We need to give them something. The unknown is a powerful drug. We can either let that drug fuel psychological unrest. Or we can harness it. These are highly trained and mentally strong explorers. Give them what they need."

The meeting ended with Mars getting his way. It was decided that Mission Control would release carefully chosen photographs to the crew and provide them with a list of activities for the surface exploration team. Several hundred images were sent to the crew, none of them too alarming. Pictures of the triangular mega-plex in sector G7.164.598.622 were redacted so that the exact shape was not revealed.

Onboard the spacecraft, the astronauts gathered around their dining table in the galley to go through the pictures sent up from Mission Control. Some wedged their legs under the low slung table; some placed their feet in foot straps mounted to the floor; others simply floated free. They viewed the downloaded media on their tablets. Up until this point, they'd known that infrastructure had been spotted on the surface of ILK-87b but couldn't appreciate the scale of it.

It was more than half an hour before the crew started to talk about what they were looking at. And when they did, their reactions were divided. Some, like Mike Swimmer, felt all the more excited. "We're part of something big here, people," he told the others.

"That's easy for you to say," Cosmo Popov countered in his heavily accented Russian. "You're not going down there."

When flipping through the crew's job functions when on the surface, Kinzi noticed that she and Carrick would be investigating a strange structure in sector G7.164.598.622. The first thing she noticed was a set of notes from Mars Johnston. The look of curiosity melted from her face. Mars' notes suggested that a light had been detected in the Northwest section of the mammoth building. It was probably nothing Mars had written, but he wanted the surface crew to be aware.

Kinzi glanced at her fellow crew members, now hotly debating the notes and images.

Kinzi then nudged Carrick and pointed out what she had read. He looked at her as if to say, let's chat later. She couldn't shake the feeling that alien life might still exist on the black planet.

Later, before the team's sleep schedule, Kinzi observed Carrick staring out the window again. With a hand full of radar images, she floated over to him and asked, "What exactly are we looking at here?"

Carrick looked uncertain and responded by saying, "Not sure, but we're going to find out soon enough."

Kinzi took a minute before nervously asking, "Why do you think they assigned you and me to investigate the mega-structure?"

With a straight face, Michaels responded, "Isn't it obvious? We're clearly the two best looking Astronauts on board this ship!" trying to bring some levity to a stressful situation.

Both laughed off their nervousness and settled into a more serious tone when Kinzi asked again, "No, really; why us?"

Carrick pondered for a moment and said, "Kinzi, it's what we were meant to do. Every past experience we've ever had in our lives has led us to this exact moment in time. This is our destiny," he proclaimed.

Kinzi looked at him for a moment and then said, "Wow! You're so full of shit! Does that line actually work with the ladies back on Earth?" she flirted. Carrick just grinned.

With the mood lightened a bit, Kinzi floated away, and Carrick went back to staring out the window. He was again searching for the answers as to what secrets were hiding in the black void behind the stars. Would Black Earth help to satisfy his curiosity?

NASA's decision to release the photos worked like a charm. Anxiety and fear produced adrenaline, and the much-needed shot in the arm delivered a renewed sense of pride. A new energy was felt, and the team's sense of purpose was restored. Mission accomplished, sort of.

Location: Houston, TX. Mission Control – February 3, 2022.

With the New Horizon crew in better spirits, NASA received some more good news in early February. It came in the form of infrared scans of Black Earth's atmosphere, which were quickly transmitted up to the spacecraft.

Convening a meeting, mission astrophysicist Piyush Bhula took the crew through the findings. The scans showed that Black Earth's surface temperature was far lower than most physicists on Earth had predicted. The general consensus had been that the surface temperature on ILK-87b was somewhere between 1,000°F and 1,290°F. With their advanced cooling technologies, the Extra Mobility Units could withstand up to 1,327°F max and only for one-hundred-twenty minute periods. As it turned out, the new infrared scans showed surface temperatures between 800°F and 840°F in direct sunlight and 580°F at night. To give the crew some context, Piyush explained that the Moon has a surface temperature of 260°F when facing the Sun and minus 280°F with no direct sunlight. The upside was that the team conducting ground experiments would be able to stay in the hostile environment for several hours longer than previously thought before needing to seek refuge in the landing module.

The news also suggested that Black Earth likely hadn't been black for very long. At its current temperature, Piyush estimated that the planet had probably been absorbing the Sun's energy, rather than reflecting it, for just a few thousand years. Any longer than that, the surface would be much hotter, perhaps up to 1,600°F.

With temperature data pouring in, the mystery of why infrared heat signatures could not be detected from Earth remained unsolved. Piyush held numerous discussions with physicists on Earth to discuss this, but all the experts were baffled for the moment.

Chapter 8 – Orbit Insertion

Location: Deep Space. Onboard the New Horizon spacecraft – March 15, 2022.

Butterflies were in full effect in the bellies of each and every one of the New Horizon crew. After one hundred and ten days in space and having traveled more than seventy million miles, the crew had awoken early to prepare the ship's precious cargo's readiness, the two Black Horizon Landing Rovers.

With just under five-million miles and a mere seven days to go, the New Horizon was a beehive of activity. Spacesuits were checked, double and triple checked; approach calculations were studied; New Horizon's fitness was monitored, and the flight path and deceleration plan for orbit insertion were reviewed.

Every evening, Mike Swimmer and Ollie Taylor sat in the galley going over their procedure for getting into orbit around Black Earth. To do this, they needed to drastically reduce their speed as they approached the planet.

A technique called Orbit Insertion – Deceleration would be used when capturing into orbit around the black planet. The shedding of excess velocity would be achieved via a rocket firing known as an orbit insertion burn. During the maneuver, the pilots will fire the spacecraft's engine in their direction of travel in an effort to slow its velocity relative to the target, enabling New Horizon to enter into Black Earth's orbit.

As a contingency, another technique that could be used against Black Earth's less than tangible atmosphere is called Aerocapture. Aerocapture would use the friction of the atmospheric drag in an effort to slow down the spacecraft enough to get it into orbit. This would be very risky, however, as it had never been tested for an orbit insertion. However, this maneuver would only be used if the orbit insertion burn failed to slow the spacecraft enough to enter into the black planet's orbit.

Generally, orbit insertion deceleration is performed with the main engine. The spacecraft gets into a highly elliptical capture orbit. The apocenter can only be lowered with further decelerations, even using the atmospheric drag in a controlled way; this is called aero-braking. Aero-braking lowers the apocenter and circularizes the orbit while minimizing the use of onboard fuel. To date, only a handful of NASA and ESA unmanned missions had performed robotic aero-braking. The New Horizon pilots onboard, however, had spent hundreds of hours simulating this type of maneuver. Mike Swimmer and Ollie Taylor were more qualified than any other spaceship pilots in the world, which is why they were selected for the critical mission to Black Earth.

The astronauts went through every part of their preparations carefully. Each of the Surface Landers carefully checked through the equipment they were taking, repeatedly packing and repacking everything to get it just right. Still, each of the final seven days felt like a week to the team. By now, the Surface Landers had spent hundreds of hours studying images of ILK-87b's terrain. They had identified interesting target sites for their science experiments, but Kinzi and Carrick had their sights firmly set on sector G7.164.598.622 and the mega-plex located there.

Carrick stepped up his vigils at the spacecraft windows, looking for signs of the black planet, but he couldn't discern its form.

The upbeat tension onboard was mirrored on Earth. News coverage across the world's media outlets reported the craft's progress. Everyone was nervous and impatient as they awaited the moment of truth: contact with Black Earth. The anticipation level was high, and with a lot of luck, backed by years of training, these eight men and women might make an incredible discovery. Earthlings might finally have an answer to the age-old question: "Is there life out there?"

March 21, 2022, a mere nine hundred and fifteen days since Dr. Colye Justman first discovered ILK-87b, the New Horizon began the process of deceleration as it rapidly approached Black Earth. After many months of preparation and rigorous training, the crew understood the duties they'd been tasked with and were up to the challenge.

In the previous thirty days, the crew spent many hours studying images of ILK-87b's rough terrain. They had their sights firmly set on sector G7.164.598.622 and the three-sided mega-plex located at what was now the epicenter of NASA's focus. But first would come the hard part, entering low orbit after rapid deceleration.

Mike Swimmer's heart-rate monitor recorded a calm fifty-four beats per minute at his seat in the cockpit as he began his orbit insertion maneuvers. "Houston, we are now shutting off auto-pilot and are ready to manually guide New Horizon into orbit around ILK-87b. I'm happy to say that we now have a radiant heat signature on our screens."

Back in Houston, of the many questions needing to be answered, the question of why no heat signature could be detected from Earth loomed large at Mission Control and the scientific world writ large.

"That's good news, Mike!" responded Mars Johnston, speaking into his headset.

Around him were no less than sixty technicians, statisticians, engineers, and communications experts, all sitting in front of glowing computer screens and control panels. Mars himself was pacing the floor paying close attention to the three one hundred and fifty-inch television screens on the front wall of the three-thousand square foot room.

"Houston, we are now shutting off auto-pilot and will manually guide New Horizon into orbit around ILK-87b," confidently announced pilot Mike Swimmer.

"Copy that, Mike! We can see the shutdown on our end," said Mars while squeezing a miniature Earth stress ball. Just moments before, he was using it to play catch with himself and bouncing it off of the walls; now, he was clawing at it like a bear would its prey.

At Commander Mike Swimmer's side, his co-pilot Ollie Taylor checked his instruments and prepared himself for the maneuvers that would take them into orbit around the unseen planet.

Nerves were on edge for all on board, but particularly for the two pilots as they only had one chance to get the orbit insertion right. Both men smiled and chorused, "Here we go!"

Commander Swimmer relayed more information to Earth. "We are approaching ILK-87b at a speed of 9,671 feet per second, and we are approximately 44,000 miles from its surface.

Talking through each process, one step at a time, Swimmer fired the spaceship's thrusters in their direction of travel. The spacecraft began to slow soon after. Swimmer counted down the speed in real-time, but it was quickly evident that this maneuver was not enough. They would need to perform the aero-braking process.

Mike Swimmer knew it was time to let Ollie Taylor do his job. "I'm now handing control of the craft over to Ollie," he told Houston. Ollie furrowed his brow in determination, "Let's get this thing done!"

Every second of Ollie Taylor's training had been leading to this moment. His hands slightly shaking on the controls, he fired multiple boosters to make minute changes to the craft's trajectory so that they could collide with the atmosphere at the right angle. The minutes felt like hours to him as he guided the New Horizon into orbit. His hand faltered, and he almost misfired a rocket when Swimmer suddenly gasped.

"Ollie, check this out!" exclaimed Swimmer.

Ollie looked beyond Swimmer to where he was pointing out of the cockpit's porthole. An immense black mass was obstructing the view of the stars that lay beyond it.

"Jesus! That's impressive!" said Ollie.

"Kinda creepy if you ask me," said Swimmer, returning to his tasks.

Within minutes he reported to Mission Control that New Horizon had successfully entered Black Earth's orbit. Their headsets were filled with the sounds of celebrations back in Houston.

March 22, 2022. Just sixteen-hours after entering into Black Earth's orbit, the surface crew were awakened by Sun Kanai. The mission's meteorologist would be helping the Surface Landers prepare for their departure.

Before donning their EMUs, each surface crew member would breathe pure oxygen for three-hours to acclimate their body to the artificial environment of their spacesuit. Each member of the team would then assist another, with two getting dressed concurrently.

Around the world, everyone knew the names of these heroes of space exploration. The person commanding the Surface Lander was the mission's chemist, Carrick Michaels. Medical doctor Kinzi London would accompany him; geologist Lisa Yaping; physicist Piyush Bhula; and biologist Alexi Popov.

Together they began the process of suiting up. The EMUs were incredibly complex pieces of protective gear, and it took more than seven-hours to outfit the entire surface crew. Each member of the team assisted one another, with two getting dressed concurrently. Sun helped Carrick into his suit. After each was outfitted in their $250 million duds, they squeezed through the airlock that linked the New Horizon craft to the Black Horizon Landing Module. They went in by twos, guiding each other through the airlock and into the cramped inner crew compartment.

For those making the journey to the surface of the black menace, the Black Horizon landing module would be a tight fit. The craft's exterior was thirty feet long by seventeen feet wide, while the crew cabin was only eighteen feet long by sixteen feet wide.

The crew compartment accommodations would be less than ideal as it was jammed with five couches that would support the crew during acceleration and deceleration. The couches would also position the crew at their duty stations and support the spacecraft's translation and rotation hand controls, lights, and other equipment. The landing module also included one lavatory, a small food galley, and storage units for rock samples and other collected matter from the surface. At the head of each couch was an EMU storage compartment for use when the crew was able to disrobe for purposes of sleep and lavatory use.

The Black Horizon surface Lander was packed with four days worth of rations, medical equipment, experimental devices, and storage units, as well as the two Black Horizon Rovers.

First in was medical doctor Kinzi London, followed by physicist Piyush Bhula. Sixty-minutes later, Cozmo Popov and Lisa Yaping nestled into the landing module. After Sun Kanai was done outfitting Carrick Michaels, he assisted him in loading into the module, and the pressurization process would soon begin. Kanai exited the Lander and then sealed the airlock chamber door; it was now only a matter of sixty-minutes or so before separation of the landing module would occur.

When the Lander was fully prepped, Sun Kanai informed Mission Control back on Earth. "Houston, we are ready for auto-command separation of the New Horizon landing module; you have control," he reported.

With that transmission received, Mars Johnston replied, "Roger that New Horizon, we have control!"

"5, 4, 3, 2, 1!" then a nervous pause came from Johnston.
"We have separation of the Black Horizon Landing Module from the mothercraft New Horizon," came word from Mission Control's Flight Director.

And just like that, in an instant, the landing module began to float freely away from New Horizon. The mood surrounding the tightly fit astronauts was tense. The team wore nervous smiles due to the anxiety and the overwhelming feeling of what those onboard called cosmic vulnerability.

"There's no turning back now," declared Bhula.

Michaels motioned to him a nervous thumbs-ups and an uneasy smile.

Kinzi London's eyes were closed while the others were purposely not making eye contact with one another.

Back in Houston, Johnston said to the team in the Lander, "The world is watching; let's make this look easy."

Location: Two hundred miles above the surface of ILK-87b – March 22, 2022. 3:00 pm, CST.

It was now sixty-minutes before touchdown when Mission Control gave the New Horizon landing module the 'go' to initiate its de-orbit burn. The craft would fire its engines in the opposite direction of the surface, which would allow it to penetrate Black Earth's atmosphere. Some of the crew were full of fear as the black abyss below looked to swallow them up. Most of the crew had their fists clenched and eyes closed, but Carrick Michaels was busy studying the landing radar in an attempt to find a smooth spot to set down the surface Lander.

"Holy Shit!" shouted Carrick Michaels out loud, as something in the bottom right-hand corner of the radar screen captured his attention.

It was the massive and foreboding triangular structure that appeared on his radar. The mega-plex loomed large across the otherwise baron surface just miles from their designated landing spot. That would be the first time Carrick would actually see the entire structure, and it was far bigger than he could have imagined. His focus now shifted to a soft landing, as his crew-mates were all a little more nervous after his, 'Holy Shit!' utterance.

After a descent of one hour and thirteen-minutes, the Black Horizon Lander safely touched down at exactly 10:54 am CST Houston local time. With its landing, history was made. Not since December 14, 1972, when Gene Cernan and Jack Schmitt landed on the moon, had any human being landed on a planetary surface other than planet Earth.

Back at Mission Control, there were sixty sighs of relief while billions of people witnessed the historical event around the world. Most were not even alive when Apollo 11 touched down on the Moon in July of 1969. The huddled masses around the world watched in disbelief and amazement at what they saw. Not one of them would ever forget where they were when five of their fellow Earthlings touched down on a planet seventy-five million miles away. Champagne corks flew in celebrations around the globe.

While on Black Earth, the exploratory surface crew could once again breathe. Kinzi London finally opened her eyes and allowed tears of relief to make their escape. While orbiting above, pilot's Mike Swimmer and Ollie Taylor, along with meteorologist Sun Kanai, shared a few fist-bumps and cheers. Their celebration included a toast, with each taking a swig of recycled urine.

The surface crew, though, had no time for celebrations. They had work to do. Carrick reviewed each astronaut's planned surface activities with them. This took four-hours, after which the crew ate a small meal. Then, working to his schedule, Carrick ordered them all to take a ninety-minute nap before they disembarked.

Up next, the making of history.

Chapter 9 – Erik

Location: Surface of Black Earth – March 22, 2022.

Preliminary readings outside the New Horizon landing module indicated high levels of carbon dioxide and nitrogen but nearly imperceptible oxygen levels, with the surface temperatures recorded at 816°F. With the crew scheduled to be on the actual surface for three to four hours on day one, they would have plenty of sunlight to get their work done.

Because the surface was non-reflective and the atmosphere void of oxygen, the Sun, high above, looked more like a very bright star in the night sky. At the very least, the Lander and its equipment, along with the white spacesuits, would offer some point of reference and assist the explorers with their bearings.

For the astronauts on board, who'd previously experienced spacewalks outside of the International Space Station, such lighting conditions would seem somewhat familiar. In the darkness of outer space, the sun appears brighter because there's no atmosphere to absorb or reflect its light energy. Because of ILK-87b's thin atmosphere and because the surface was blacker than black, the team would experience similar lighting conditions to that of a planet without an atmosphere.

The amount of light reflecting off of the EMUs, surface Lander, and the tools brought with them would be at best vibrant, at worst, blinding. The surface explorers would have to employ their helmet visors when working outside of the landing module. However, they would accomplish very little at night as the planet's blackness would absorb any artificial light source they brought with them. Therefore, all activities would suspend at sundown.

Inside the landing module, the team was preparing to egress the craft. Carrick Michaels was chosen to be the first to step foot on the surface of Black Earth, as he had logged more time in space than any of the others on the surface team. Michaels would join the ranks of Neil Armstrong, as the only other person to be first to set foot on another celestial surface, with Armstrong first doing it on the moon, on July 20, 1969.

Carrick, feeling quite nervous and apprehensive, looked at the team and saw that they were all staring back at him with nervous smiles. Envy wouldn't be the right word to describe how the other surface explorers felt towards Michaels. However, what was undeniable is that each secretly wished they could be the first to step onto the strange and mysterious black planet.

Bhula gave the 'thumbs-up' to Carrick while Kinzi said, "Go get 'em, Cowboy!"

Yaping followed with words of encouragement in her native tongue while Popov said, "Go make some history, kid!"

Carrick's smile back to them could hardly mask his feelings, though. He wasn't afraid of what lay outside of the Lander. Instead, he was melancholy at the notion that his father, United States Navy Lieutenant Mike Michaels, was not alive to see his only son advance the human cause on such a universal stage.

A second later, Carrick turned and stepped into the airlock chamber, which would separate him from the support of his comrades, and there, he stood alone. The tug of Black Earth's gravity was greater than he thought it would be, or might it have been the weight of the world back on Earth, with billions watching from around his world and listening to this monumental feat.

Crackling, in his ear, was the voice of Marcus 'Mars' Johnston. Johnston said, "Carrick, audio goes live to the world in twenty seconds."

"Don't trip going down that ladder, son," he joked, hoping to take the edge off of the nerves that must've been paralyzing Carrick.

"One more thing," said Johnston, "say nothing about any infrastructure that you might see." With that, Mars counted down, "4, 3, 2, 1..." He paused then said, "You're live, son."

Though his crew-mates would join him in just a matter of minutes, that moment belonged to him. He hit the hatch release button with his right hand and then cranked the handle securing the outer hatch door. Pushing the door open, he stared into the blackness, a darkness that neither he nor any man had ever stared into before. Carrick was unable to see the ground beneath the Lander, as the surface provided no reflective value. It was a sight that NASA was unable to simulate back on Earth. It was as if the Lander were floating above a massive black hole, and only the stars overhead could provide any context to the black planet's horizon.

As Carrick surveyed the night sky, he witnessed seeing more stars than he had ever seen before. ILK-87b was known to have no moons. That, in conjunction with the non-reflective surface, made the light from distant stars seem brighter and more vivid.

While unable to see the actual surface, Carrick's depth perception would be useless. Though the Lander's outer lights lit his path down the five-step ladder, he had to rely on the Heads-Up Display, or HUD, on the inside of his helmet shield to visualize any surface features. Carrick saw a rather flat surface with very few large objects, such as rocks or other debris.

After another moment of reflection, Carrick did an about-face and stepped back down onto the top step of the ladder while firmly gripping the exterior handrails. The world was now able to see him and were holding their collective breath.

Steadying himself, he took one step, then another, and then slowly descended the ladder into history. Standing on step three of the ladder, Carrick couldn't help but remember meeting Neil Armstrong while attending a U.S. Navy Memorial Service at Purdue University when he was only ten-years-old. Carrick attended the event with his mother, Maggie. The event was a tribute to the Navy's 'Best of the Best' who had fallen in service to their country. Armstrong was one of the speakers on that day and actually mentioned Carrick's father by name.

After the event was over, Neil Armstrong presented Carrick's mother with the U.S. Navy flag, folded into a triangle; he then thanked her for her sacrifice. Armstrong then extended his hand to shake Carrick's. Armstrong's hand swallowed that of little Carrick's, and the emotion that overcame the fatherless young boy was profound. It was at that moment, and because of Armstrong's words, that Carrick would become an astronaut one day.

Armstrong kneeled down, grasping Carrick's shoulders, and whispered in his ear. "Son, your father, touched the sky as one of the bravest pilots who ever lived, perhaps you, his son, will grow up and one day touch the stars and not just the moon as I did."

Armstrong then stood, rustled Carrick's hair, and then continued down the line shaking the hands of others who had also lost loved ones. His words would echo in Carrick's heart and mind from that moment on.

Carrick now stood on step four of the ladder and the world, once again, held its collective breath. Reaching for the satchel strapped to his waist, Carrick made sure the flag he brought from Earth was indeed there. The flag he carried was the very U.S. Navy flag that Neil Armstrong had presented to his mother that day back in the summer of 2001. Each of the astronauts would plant a flag recognizing each of the contributing countries. But Carrick would plant this one. On Black Earth, he would leave behind a tribute to his father, his mother, the legend of Neil Armstrong, and the memory of a small child that grew up without a father.

Now, on step five, Carrick recited to himself the words he would utter when touching down on the black surface and hoped he didn't mess up.

On March 22, 2022, at exactly 5:00 pm CST., Michaels' boots hit the ground, and he uttered the words that were to become part of every history book in the world, words that would transcend language itself.

"With two feet planted on Earth's nearest neighbor, Humankind takes another step towards the universal truths of our origins. I am proud today, not as an American, but rather as an Earthling, for all that we have accomplished together; through boundless dedication, sheer determination, and iron will," pronounced Carrick Michaels.

The world now had a hero, a seemingly invincible and fearless explorer who would go on to inspire millions of kids to dream big for many decades to come. What the world couldn't see or hear, though, through the grainy images televised far and wide, was that their hero had tears running down his face as he descended that ladder into immortality.

"And we're clear!" the words of Mars Johnston crackled in Carrick's helmet. Those words indicated to Carrick that the live feed was off.

Now standing alone on Black Earth, Carrick exhaled and took a moment for himself. At that moment, he released a flood of hard work, hard luck, and heartbreak. The world could not hear the young man cry, but his crew-mates in the Lander, orbiting overhead, and those back in Houston could.

In his mind, Carrick's life flashed before him. For the first time since lift-off, he realized that everything that ever had happened to him in his life led him to this moment in time. All the good, all the bad, the loss of his father, the black hole in his heart, everything had led him here.

Those who witnessed his flood of emotion had a moment to themselves. Thousands of individuals involved in the project to get humans to Black Earth all had their own stories of sacrifice, determination, and heartbreak. In that instant, they too let it go. While no one had the courage to look at anyone around them, they knew. They knew that Carrick's moment of human triumph was theirs too. Mars Johnston just stared at the big screen at Mission Control, tears running down his face, and for a moment, just a moment, he looked at Carrick and saw his son.

Over the course of the next hour, the remaining surface explorers exited the Black Horizon landing module. The first order of business would be to release the Black Horizon Rovers from their housing units. The process went relatively quickly after they released the twelve handle clamps holding each rover in place. From there, the team used the Lander's hydraulic arms to lower the rovers down onto the surface.

By the time all scientific experiment equipment was unloaded and staged on the black surface and the Black Horizon Rovers were readied for their relatively short journey, sunlight began to wane. It was now 8:36 pm back in Houston, but days on ILK-87b were shorter than on Earth as the planet's rotation moved faster than Earth's. A single rotation of Black Earth took just under twenty-hours versus Earth's twenty-four-hour rotation cycle. After just three-hours and thirty-six-minutes on the black surface, the exhausted crew called it a day as the sun disappeared beneath the western sky of Black Earth.

It appeared that sunrise and sunset were off between Houston and ILK-87b. The time difference was roughly five to six-hours and would continue to be off-set for their remaining time on the surface.

Once the crew was back onboard the pressurized landing module, the team removed the top half of their spacesuits and stowed them in the compartment at the top of their crew couch.

Sitting down on his couch, Carrick opened up comms with Mars Johnston back in Houston and began to review the schedule for the next day.

"Well done, son," said a stoic Johnston.

"Thanks, Mars. That was tougher than I thought it would be," said a humble Carrick.

"You made us all proud. I won't forget what I saw today," said Mars, echoing what the world felt.

"Okay, okay! You're gonna make me cry again."

"Suck it up, kid! We've got some work to do before shut-eye," laughed Mars.

Over the next hour, the two scheduled the crew's task orders to fit into the fifty-hours or so that the team could remain on the surface. Now that the astronauts had experienced surface conditions for the first time, they had more of an idea of what was achievable. Mars asked Carrick how the crew was dealing with near-Earth gravity after four months in space. Mission Control was acutely aware that they couldn't pile too much activity on any one of the Surface Landers. Their muscles had to adjust to the weight they were suddenly bearing, and Mars and his team didn't want to drive anyone to the point of exhaustion or even collapse.

While Carrick worked on the schedule, the rest of the crew relaxed and recapped their time on the surface.

As Cosmo Popov stored away a sample of the black surface composite, he asked the others to look at his hand.

"That's amazing!" said Yaping, "It looks like the tips of your fingers are missing!" she said as they all sat in astonishment.

"Look at your boots!" said Popov to the others.

Everyone looked down and saw what appeared to be missing feet, as portions of their boots were covered with the strange black substance and were basically invisible. Whatever the substance was, it created the mind-blowing optical illusion that their boots were simply not there.

Yaping sprinkled some of the mysterious black powder into the center of her palm, then looked down to see what appeared to be a bottomless hole. The crew members were all amazed, and after the wonderment subsided, they took in their eerie surroundings, and each were reminded that they were very far from home.

After finishing his call with Mars, Carrick ended the fun by saying, "Do you guys realize you may be holding radioactive poison in your hands? Are you crazy! Put that stuff away!" he ordered.

Yaping's fingers were covered with the black dust, and with an alcohol wipe, she removed the substance from her middle finger on her left hand, held it up, then asked Carrick jokingly, "What finger am I holding up?"

"Ha-ha!" responded Carrick, with a look of acknowledgment that he was probably overreacting.

The entire crew laughed out loud, and Carrick's mood was lightened. His mood resembled his exhaustion from the day's events, and the harmless banter helped to shed the weight of the burden and responsibility that they all carried.

After cleaning up and storing collected samples, the crew enjoyed a dinner that consisted of vacuum-packed roast beef, mashed potatoes & gravy, macaroni & cheese, and fruit.

For a short while after dinner, the crew discussed their objectives for the next day. Though exhausted from experiencing gravity for the first time in four months, the team would spend another forty-plus-hours on the surface before rejoining New Horizon, orbiting overhead.

Three of the scientists, geologist Lisa Yaping, physicist Piyush Bhula, and astrobiologist Cosmo Popov, would be working together at a location that was close to the Lander. The site had been chosen as an interesting feature that appeared to be some sort of dried-up riverbed.

Once there, Yaping would collect solid and gaseous matter, plus any liquid she could find. These samples would be studied to see if earthquakes, volcanic eruptions, tsunamis, or landslides, might have played a part in the current condition of ILK-87b's black surface. Meanwhile, Piyush Bhula would conduct ground experiments to see how energy and matter interacted with each other on Black Earth. Finally, Cosmo Popov would search for any signs of organic material on the surface. Popov was trained to search for promising samples that might show signs of life. Specific structures in rocks can give away clues that organic matter might once have lived within them. Popov would collect any samples that looked promising and store them for later testing on the way back home and, eventually, on Earth.

Chemist Carrick Michaels, and Medical Doctor, Kinzi London, had been tasked with a different responsibility, though; they were to investigate the three-sided megaplex and would be manning the Black Horizon Rover 1 to do so. The journey would take several hours the following day because each side of the triangular structure had been calculated at roughly three miles. The two would focus first on the Northwest Sector of the massive complex, the location where the mysterious light was spotted.

It was now time for the team to rest, and Carrick called for lights-out on the Lander. As the crew exchanged 'goodnights,' three of them could see that Bhula and Popov had already fallen asleep, with Popov snoring loudly.

It was now lights-out, and the crew was somewhat comfortable after completely shedding their pressurized suits. All were asleep with the exception of Kinzi London. With one arm folded behind her head, she looked out the window and saw nothing but darkness. While this helped the others sleep, it made Kinzi apprehensive about her journey the next day to the triangular mega-plex. A minute or so later, Carrick woke up, and through foggy eyes, looked over at London and saw that hers were wide open.

"Can't sleep, huh?"

"Nah, a little nervous about tomorrow, that's all," said Kinzi.

"Me too," responded Carrick.

"You're nervous? The way you handled yourself today was impressive. Now I know why they call you Rock."

"Nerves of steel!" she added.

"You're kidding? I was shaking like a leaf going down that ladder," he confessed.

"Besides, Rock comes from my name."

"Your name?" inquisitively asked Kinzi, turning on her couch to face him.

"Yeah, Carrick is Irish; the name is Gaelic, meaning Rock."
"Mystery solved!" said Kinzi, nodding her head with the revelation.

"We were all wondering, but no one had the nerve to ask you," she added.

She paused for a moment and said, "That makes sense," while wearing a smile.

"How so?"

"Well, you're not all that big, so Rock didn't really come to mind when we first met, and I looked you up and down," she said with a wicked grin.

"No comment," said Carrick.

Both were quiet for a minute or two before Carrick confessed, "I saw it on the radar today during our approach in."

"Saw what?" asked a confused Kinzi.

"IT!" said Carrick, eyes wide-opened.

"Ohhh!" realizing what Carrick was saying, "Was it as big as it looked in the pictures?" she asked.

"Bigger!" he said, raising both eyebrows.

"I can't sleep just thinking about it. How'd it get there?" she questioned aloud.

Carrick closed his eyes and whispered, "We're gonna find out tomorrow," and then went back to sleep.

Two-hours later, Kinzi awoke in a cold sweat and surveyed the compartment, forgetting for a moment where she was. It then dawned on her that she was on Black Earth, and her dream, from a moment ago, would unfortunately not change that fact.

Location: Black Earth – March 23, 2022.11:00am, CST, Houston local time.

After a hearty breakfast and hours of gearing up, the crew disembarked from the Black Horizon landing module just after sunrise. The sun blinded them upon egress of the Lander, causing all to lower their visors when facing it.

While the other scientists set off to begin their soil, rock, and air sample collections, Carrick Michaels and Kinzi London mounted Rover 1, then began their brief journey to the mega-plex, roughly two miles away. The two would rely on ground radar to lead the way as they were in total darkness, even though the sun was high in the sky. Once there, they'd begin the process of perimeter inspection in hopes of acquiring visual confirmation of where the light emanating from the Northwest Sector of the dark structure was spotted.

The journey there was an arduous one due to the many large rocks and craters they encountered along their path. Kinzi was behind the wheel and had to rely on her helmet's Heads-Up Display as well as the radar mapping screen on the rover.

"I think I've got a handle on this radar visual on the HUD," she reported to Carrick.

"Well, I hope so; we're only moving three miles an hour!" joked Carrick, laughing at his friend, who was feeling pretty proud of herself.

As Kinzi drove, Carrick had time to take in the darkness. "Where are we?" he wondered to himself. "What am I doing here?" he thought while shaking his head.

The terrain was also covered with hills, valleys, and what appeared to be dry riverbeds. While the sun was rising quickly, the surface was jet black, rendering no reflective value, so everything was dark even though it was the middle of the day. Both astronauts wished their white spacesuits were not so bright. Their helmet visors helped to relieve the stress on their eyes, though.

Out of nowhere, London's eyes began to focus in on a distant silhouette, and she shouted, "Oh my God! Can you see that?!"

Kinzi immediately stopped the rover, and the two raised their visors and squinted to see what appeared to be the mega-plex they were searching for.

Carrick followed with, "Jesus Christ! It's massive! Kill your HUD, Kinzi!

"Can you see it?" he asked.

"Yes!" shouted Kinzi in response. Both sat in awe.

Only the top of the structure could be seen as the millions of stars behind it helped frame the black structure.

Clicking back on their HUD, the two were staring down a monstrous structure on their radar. This was the first visual of anything that resembled something that appeared to be manmade. Apprehension filled the air as the two got closer and realized just how big the mega-plex was.

Michaels broke the silence. "Okay, what the fuck is this?!"

The crew orbiting above quickly chimed in with, "Everything okay down there?" asked Mike Swimmer, orbiting some two hundred-fifty miles above the surface.

"Yes," said London. "It's just....," she paused, "what we're seeing down here isn't possible," as the two and their vehicle were dwarfed by the mammoth structure, even though they were still several hundred yards away.

"New Horizon, are you guys seeing this?" asked Carrick.

"No, we're just seeing a black screen, no visuals yet," stated Swimmer from high above.

"Why? What are you picking up?" asked Ollie Taylor.

"Whatever it is, it's big!" exclaimed Carrick. "Keep an eye on your radar."

At that moment, the rover drove over an embankment and stalled into a ditch, leaning downward at a 45° angle. The two were leaning heavily against the dashboard of the rover. Carrick, busting chops, said, "I thought you had a handle on this thing."

"Ha-ha asshole!" quipped Kinzi as she restarted the battery-powered rover. "Here, you drive it!"

Minutes later, the rover drove over an embankment and settled on what appeared to be a road.

"What the Hell! Now we're driving on an actual road?" Carrick couldn't believe what they were seeing.

The two glanced over at each other at the same time and, without words, conveyed their absolute surprise, shock, and terror at what they were witnessing.

"This can't be real!" exclaimed Carrick.

Kinzi was speechless at that moment and swallowed hard as she stared at the black monster that looked more like something built on Earth rather than anything possible on another planet.

The structure before them appeared to look exactly like the Pentagon in Washington, D.C. It looked to be about seventy-five feet tall with deep window basins but didn't reveal actual glass. Kinzi surveyed the structure as Carrick drove the rover.

Carrick stopped the rover again, and the two just stared. Kinzi kept flicking her HUD on and off really fast; she tried to compare the radar with the silhouette.

It was at that moment that she shouted the words, "I see it! I see it!"

"See what?"

"The light!" she shouted.

"Look up! Look up!" shouted Kinzi, pointing to the top of the behemoth.

Carrick killed the HUD in his helmet and focused his attention skyward, and then saw it too.

"I'll be damned!" he said, as they both witnessed a light emanating from a window atop the structure.

After driving another hundred yards or so, Carrick stopped the rover, and the two just stared in awe.

Carrick asked, "Kinzi, have you ever been to Washington?"
"I'm from Seattle, you dumbass!" she replied with a look of confusion.

"No, D.C., Washington, D.C.?" asked Michaels.

"Well, of course!" responded London.

"Does this, whatever it is, look familiar to you?" he asked.

"Oh my God, I'm going to be sick," she said, as a look of horror ravaged her face?

"The Pentagon?!" she said. "I was just there last July."

"Where the hell are we? What the fuck is happening?" Carrick whispered to Kinzi.

Just then, their gloved hands met and clenched out of fear.
"New Horizon," paused Michaels, "are you getting these visuals?" he asked.

There was stunned silence from the orbiting craft when after a moment, the radio crackled, "We can't believe what you're seeing down there!" responded Swimmer, as he called Sun Kanai over to the cockpit monitors for a look.

For just an instant, all involved imagined that this might be some kind of human experiment, almost like something from the Twilight Zone, the television show from the 1960s.

"Knee-knee-knee-knee, knee-knee-knee-knee," chimed Michaels, followed by a nervous chuckle.

"You guys proceed with caution!" said Ollie Taylor, co-piloting from above.

As they got closer to what appeared to be the front of the mega-plex, the road they were driving on widened from roughly four lanes to eight, even though no visible lines could be seen on the road surface.

The surface, like everything else on Black Earth, was covered with a fine black carbon powder. It was as if they laid breadcrumbs out on the road. It would've been hard to get lost when returning to the module as the rover's tire tracks were prevalent, and with the absence of any significant wind gusts, the tracks would've remained visible indefinitely.

Back at the Lander, the other three scientists continued their experiments and were completely unaware of what Michaels and London had found. While their radio frequency was tuned into that of Michaels and London, the two had switched their frequency to that of New Horizon's, orbiting above.

Location: Houston, TX. Mission Control.

The team back on Earth experienced radio blackout as the moon passed between Earth and ILK-87b. They were unable to receive any of the transmissions between any of the astronauts on the surface, nor from New Horizon, orbiting Black Earth overhead. It would be another seventeen-minutes before communication was restored. The following seventeen-minutes changed everything human beings had ever believed regarding the origins of mankind.

Location: Black Earth. Northwest Sector of The Triad – March 23, 2022. 1:56pm, CST.

The outer door of the Northwest Sector's main entrance opened to find two stunned astronauts standing frozen in fear. The two astronauts were drenched with light as it poured out of the interior of the structure. The astronauts were caught off guard as they were unaware that they were standing near an entrance of any kind.

Just as Kinzi's hand managed to find Carrick's again, the radio crackled in their comms, and Mike Swimmer and Ollie Taylor shouted at nearly the same time, "Get out of there, right now!"

For whatever reason, all fear suddenly evaporated in the hearts of Carrick 'Rock' Michaels and Kaley 'Kinzi' London. It was as if both knew that everything human beings thought about the universe was about to change in the most unimaginable way.

Both looked at each other and, without words, took five steps forward into the chamber, between the inner and outer doors, stopped, and didn't look back to witness the outer door close. With warnings not to proceed, the crackling in their comms died at that moment, and all radio contact was lost. Both shed tears, but didn't weep, closed their eyes, and with gloved hands still clenched, awaited their destiny.

After what seemed like forever, the chamber completed a temperature regulation process, and within several minutes the inner door began to open. Standing at attention before them was a withered old man with chest out.

The man raised his hand to his forehead and saluted the astronauts before saying, "What took you so long?"

Chapter 10 – The Triad

With the Moon no longer interrupting contact between Mission Control and the New Horizon spacecraft, garbled messages from Black Earth's orbit began to bleed through the headset of Mars Johnston and others listening in from Houston. What they heard was the sound of panic and commotion coming from the three astronauts onboard New Horizon.

An alarmed Mars tried to make sense of what was happening. "New Horizon, this is Mission Control, we can hear you, but we can't make out what you're saying; repeat!"

"They went in! They went in! They entered the mega-plex!" yelled Mike Swimmer.

"We ordered them not to, but they went in anyway!" Ollie Taylor's voice came through.

"We've lost all contact with Michaels and London! Please advise on how to proceed!" requested Swimmer.

Johnston took a second to process what he was hearing. "What do you mean they went in?"

Taylor came back on the comms. "They went into what appeared to be an airlock, then we lost all contact with them!" he yelled.

Swimmer chimed in. "We advised them not to enter, and they just went in without saying a word; they ignored our commands!"

Johnston looked around the Control center, absent of words, and realized what he had just heard. The large mega-plex was an actual building, and it had an airlock. The gravity of that fact delivered a gutshot to everyone in attendance. With that, everyone listening knew that intelligent life form did, in fact, exist in the universe. Hostile or friendly? Past, or present? Those were the questions now faced, and those questions would not be answered for another several hours.

Back on the surface, the other three scientists, conducting tests near the landing module, were unable to reach their fellow surface explorers. Out of concern, they changed their radio frequency to New Horizon's, orbiting above.

"Surface crew to New Horizon, do you receive us?" Bhula came through on the comms.

Swimmer shouted the order, "Return to the landing module at once and await further instruction!"

"But what about the others?" asked Bhula.

"Get in the module NOW!" demanded Commander Swimmer. With the three remaining astronauts safely back in the Lander, Swimmer explained to them what'd happened.

Four-hours on the surface were as long as the astronauts could remain outside the module without risking dehydration and other heat-related effects. This fact did not escape the remaining astronauts in the module, and they began to grow even more concerned with the whereabouts and condition of both Michaels and London.

Location: Black Earth. The Triad – March 23, 2022. 4:30 pm, CST. Houston local time.

Carrick and Kinzi had now been outside the landing module for five-hours and thirty-minutes, and their air supply would've been running low.

Their spacesuits contained two oxygen tanks that could provide breathable air for anywhere between 6.5 to 8 hours and included a carbon-dioxide removal system. The amount of usable air to breathe would vary depending on how much physical or mental exertion was used by the two astronauts, or rather, how much oxygen was burned due to their heart rate. Either way, Kinzi, and Carrick were fast approaching a critical period in time, and no one knew of their current situation.

While it was believed the two wouldn't have used very much physical exertion due to the Black Horizon Rover's use. However, it was believed that their heart rates would've elevated due to what they had witnessed while on rover patrol, thus burning more oxygen. Additionally, fear of the unknown when entering the structure would have burned additional energy.

Nevertheless, the team on the surface, those orbiting Black Earth, and those back in Houston were all quite concerned with the two astronauts' fate, who seemed to go willingly into the mega-plex.

March 23, 2022. 8:00pm, CST.

As nightfall approached, Mars Johnston ordered the remaining Surface Landers to stay put in the landing module until first light. No matter what scenarios the two astronauts were presented with, both Carrick Michaels' and Kinzi London's oxygen supply would have run out by now, and only a miracle would result in the two still being alive.

The following morning, at 11:30 am CST, the process of search and recovery would begin.

Location: The Triad – March 23, 2022. 8:00pm, CST, [Minus six-hours].

Kinzi and Carrick appeared to be standing face to face with a man, an old man, with his hand extended as if wanting to shake.

"My name is Erik."

Michaels looked at London first, then reciprocated by extending his hand to shake Erik's while Kinzi nervously looked on.

"Welcome to The Triad," said Erik.

"The Triad?" asked Kinzi.

"Yes," said Erik, "this is where I live."

"Who are you, and what is this place?" asked an apprehensive Michaels, desperately trying to look fearless and in command of the situation.

Erik chuckled and said, "That's a four-thousand-year-old story!" Pointing to their hefty EMUs, Erik said, "You might want to take off your helmets and turn off your air supply. Oxygen's a precious commodity around here."

He coughed and continued with a scratchy voice. "You'll have to excuse me; it's been a long time since I've talked this much. Please forgive the sound of my voice. Trust me, the air quality in here is fine."

Both astronauts checked their oxygen monitors. These illustrated two things: the amount of oxygen remaining in their tanks and the oxygen levels outside of their spacesuits. The levels on the exterior of their suits indicated a mixture of gases; they included: oxygen, nitrogen, argon, carbon dioxide, and minute traces of methane. In other words, air in which they could breathe.

After a few moments of consternation, Michaels, followed by London, removed their helmets. Each took a nervous breath and looked at the other with relief.

Erik turned and said, "Follow me; I'll give you a brief tour of the place."

Carrick, echoed by London, said, "Wait a minute, we're not going anywhere with you!"

"What is this place? Who are you? And how did you get here?" demanded Carrick.

Erik smiled and said, "I was born here and have lived here my entire life. My guess is that the two of you are from Home and have come here to see if any life form still exists? Well, here I am, and there you are; what's next?"

"Home?" asked London with a puzzled look.

Carrick cut in sharply, with a disingenuous look. "We are from the planet Earth, but you already know that. You look and sound American. What country are you actually from?" he asked.

Erik spread his hands out in a conciliatory gesture. "I'm afraid I don't know what American is. Is that where you're from? I would've guessed that you were from Home. So, planet Earth? American? Which is it?"

Puzzled, alarmed, and very frightened, Carrick stared Erik down. "My name is Dr. Carrick Michaels, and this is Dr. Kaley London. We are from the planet Earth and have traveled seventy-five million miles to get here. We are to investigate any signs of intelligent life forms on this planet."

"Seventy-five million did you say?" asked Erik.

"That's correct," replied Carrick.

Erik acknowledged Carrick with a nod. "Well, it's very nice to meet the both of you," expressed a chipper, Erik, who was visibly thrilled to have visitors.

"Call me Kinzi," said London, with a nervous smile.

"Kinzi it is then!" smiled Erik.

"I don't know if I'm intelligent, but I'm definitely still alive; last time I looked in the mirror anyway," he joked. "Not for long, though, I guess."

The conversation seemed to go in circles for another minute before a frustrated Carrick barked, "Are we your prisoners?"

"Prisoners? I'm guessing that word means captives?" Erik looked puzzled and wondered to himself why Carrick would think that.

"No, I am not holding you captive. You came to my door, and here we are. If you come with me, we can sit down and talk for just a moment," he offered.

The two agreed to follow Erik, but they made it clear that they couldn't stay for long.

"Of course," conceded Erik, as they began to move deeper into the building. "I'm sure your shipmates are beginning to wonder where you've wandered off to."

The three walked down a long corridor with walls that appeared to be made of stainless steel. Studded along the hallway were dormant light fixtures that, Carrick suggested, "Look like diamonds."

"They are diamonds," responded Erik. "All of them. Your eyes are keen young man. In this darkness, they don't shine like they used to."

Carrick responded by saying, "The look of a diamond is unmistakable; even in the dark, they still sparkle."

"But those can't be diamonds," he added, "they're too large, and there's too many of them."

Erik curiously asked, "Why does that surprise you? Every lighted wall fixture and window-pane in The Triad is made of diamond," he said while looking confused.

Kinzi suggested to Erik, "Diamonds are a rare commodity on Earth." To which Erik responded, "They're as common as salt on Zenith." Carrick had a look of shock on his face and sarcastically said, "My girlfriend would love it here!"

Kinzi pushed Carrick, and both laughed out loud for a moment before their facial expressions turned serious again.

London turned back to Erik and asked, "Zenith? What's Zenith?" Erik responded, "That's the name of the planet you landed on a few hours ago."

"How do you know how long we've been here?" quizzed Carrick, looking towards Kinzi, both with the knowledge that they'd landed the day before.

"It would have been hard to miss that fireball drop out of the sky!" he joked. "Actually, The Triad detected your arrival. I was sleeping as you approached the main entrance," he joked, "you woke me up. I really don't know when you actually arrived."

There was an uncomfortable moment of silence.

"So, when did you arrive?" asked a curious Erik.

"About one day ago. Do you measure time in days on Zenith?" asked a sarcastic Carrick, trying to trip up the stranger.

"Of course, I'm pleased that you do too," said Erik.

Carrick, looking perplexed, didn't know what to say next.

Kinzi noticed that Carrick was tongue-tied and chimed in. "So, how many other places like this are there on Zenith?" Kinzi asked.

Erik responded, "This is it. This is all that remains."

"How many others are there in The Triad?" asked Carrick.

"It's just me, and it has been for a very long time," said Erik.

Kinzi looked skeptical; she kept turning and looking over her shoulder as if to suggest she thought there were others nearby. Internally, she was very skeptical of everything Erik had to say, particularly his claim that he was indigenous to Black Earth and why he kept referring to Earth as Home.

Carrick, on the other hand, was more curious than he was suspicious.

Over the next few hours, Erik showed them official offices, observatories, meeting rooms, lavatories, and the barracks. Erik explained to Kinzi and Carrick how he came to be alone in The Triad. He explained that seventy-five years ago, the last shuttle left Zenith and made its final journey to Home." I have to assume that Earth and Home are the same."

"Why's that?" Carrick wondered aloud.

"The distance," answered Erik. "There is only one planet in the Solar Complex that could be within that proximity of Zenith.

Carrick and Kinzi looked at each other, confused by Erik's reference to the Solar System.

"I remotely escorted the remaining 27,914 Zenithians, minus one; me, to their new home on what you call your planet Earth, or what we've always referred to as Home," explained Erik.

He continued, "After thousands of years of robbing Zenith of its natural resources, the planet eventually went dry, and water became the most sought after of all natural resources. Temperature and tensions quickly rose, and war ensued. It was a war that resulted in the total annihilation of Zenith."

"The remaining residents of our planet were forced inside, away from the depleted atmosphere and toxic heat. This place, The Triad, became our last haven of hope and our only refuge; it was our final residence before being shuttled to Home."

"For six-thousand years, Zenith has been transporting its population to your planet. You are both descendants of Zenith; your ancestors are Zenithian," proclaimed Erik.

Michaels looked at London and then back to Erik, smiled, and dismissively said, "Bullshit!"

Erik didn't know what the term 'Bullshit' meant but surmised that Carrick didn't believe him.

He shrugged his shoulders. "I can prove it."

"Please do," challenged Carrick.

Erik asked both of them, "Does the building in which you stand look at all familiar?"

Both Kinzi and Carrick looked at each other and confessed that it did.

"Yeah, so what? What does that mean?" challenged Carrick.
"The man who designed this building, Canfield Ripley, died some four thousand years ago, but his plans were on a shuttle that left for your planet ninety years ago. The goal was to build a portion of The Triad as a tribute to Zenith and its contributions to your planet, the planet that we call Home. This pentagon-shaped structure was to be built in the capital city of the strongest, most advanced nation on your planet. If you have such a building on your planet Earth, then it would've certainly been built less than ninety years ago," said Erik.

Both Carrick and Kinzi looked at each other nervously and had no words. They just stood there in silence for a moment and tried to make sense of what the old man was saying.

"From the look in your eyes, Kinzi, I'd say that structure did indeed get built and that it was less than ninety years ago."

Michaels did a quick search on the Honeywell armband computer, incorporated into his spacesuit. The signal was weak, but after several seconds Carrick turned to Kinzi and said, "Construction on the Pentagon was started in 1941."

Kinzi did the quick math in her head, stared into Carrick's eyes, and said, "That was eighty-one years ago!"

At that moment, Kinzi dismissively turned to Erik and said, "Yeah, well, you're from Earth, so you would've known that. You'll have to do better than that!" she added.

Erik sighed, "Kinzi, if I'm from your planet, who brought me here and when?" he asked.

Kinzi thought about it for a moment and stuttered, "Gi, Give me a second..."

Erik said, "The last shuttle for Home left seventy-five years ago; it made its last migrant drop at Latitude N33.373442°, Longitude -104.529393°."

Carrick did the quick math in his head and said, "1947" under his breath. He then asked Erik to repeat the coordinates; he entered them again as Kinzi looked on.

"Oh my God!" exclaimed Carrick, "1947!"
He then showed Kinzi, who leaned in and squinted to read the results on his armband. Kinzi turned ghost white, started to say "Rah......!", and then fainted.

Kinzi regained consciousness a few moments later; with Carrick and Erik hanging over her, she shouted, "Get him away from me!" She then reached for her helmet and screamed, "Get me the hell out of here! Now!" now screaming.

Carrick helped her on with her helmet, and they all walked to the same airlock from which they'd entered.

Erik seemed resigned to their departure and, prior to activation, asked, "Put on your helmet, son; I need to activate the door. To which Carrick responded, "I'm not leaving!"

Kinzi screamed at Carrick, demanding that he put his helmet on while hitting him in the chest.

"I'm not leaving this place. I'm not going," repeating himself.

Michaels then looked at Erik, seeking affirmation, at which point Erik acknowledged him with a nod and a look that revealed his revelry and surprise.

Carrick calmly said, "Kinzi, listen, if he's telling the truth, then we're descendants of this planet. If he's lying, then he's clearly from Earth; either way, I'm in good hands. Go get the others and bring them here tomorrow," he instructed.

The instant London was out the door, she screamed into her comms, "Can anyone hear me!?"

Her voice crackled across the poisonous atmosphere of ILK-87b, startling both her crew-mates in the Lander and those orbiting overhead.

In an instant, the team members responded, "Yes, we can hear you! Where are you?" both Swimmer, overhead, and Bhula back at the module chorused together.

Through her tears, she cried, "I'm on my way back!"

Swimmer, fearing the worst, yelled, "Where's Michaels?"

Kinzi let out a raw moan and, through her tears, said, "He's still in there, and we need to get him out!"

At this point, the team in Houston, orbiting overhead, and those in the Black Horizon Lander, were on high alert and realized that Kinzi was still alive, but how? It was now 10:47 pm CST, nearly twelve-hours after exiting the Black Horizon landing module, and at most, she would've only had eight-hours of air supply.

The silence in the Lander was deafening; Bhula had his head in his hands and thought, "She should be dead."

Their faces went from despair to joy, back to despair again when they considered the fate of Carrick Michaels, who was unaccounted for by everyone except for Kinzi.

Kinzi made it back to the Black Horizon Lander long after the sun disappeared beneath an ocean of black. Once safely back on the landing module, she was welcomed with open arms and tears of joy and relief.

Everyone inquired as to the fate of Carrick Michaels and how it was that she didn't run out of oxygen. Kinzi went on to tell them that the Pentagon-shaped building had breathable air and that she and Carrick entered. She purposely made no mention of a man named Erik.

She explained to the surface crew, Houston, and her three crew-mates orbiting overhead that their air quality indicators suggested the megaplex's interior atmosphere was similar to that of Earth's. With the external conditions outside the module having high amounts of carbon dioxide and temperatures over 800°F, that fact was very hard for everyone to comprehend. Those in communication did a quick introspective and rationalized that if there was oxygen inside the structure, there must've been intelligent lifeforms.

Location: Black Earth. Black Horizon Landing Module – March 24, 2022. 11:30 am, CST. Forty-eight-plus hours on the surface of Black Earth.

With direction from Mission Control, the crew disembarked from the Landing Module. Today they were supposed to be wrapping up their sample collections and on-site experiments. Instead, they would set out to find Michaels.

The four astronauts, London, Bhula, Yaping, and Popov, mounted the two rovers and followed the tire tracks back to the entrance of The Triad. Upon approach, the astronauts were in disbelief as The Triad towered over them. London, though, was solely focused on getting her friend back.

Roughly forty-minutes after setting out on the two Black Horizon rovers, the group stood in front of The Triad's main entrance, which appeared to be twenty feet high. After about fifteen minutes, the massive airlock door opened, making the sound of escaping air.

Everyone stepped into the airlock without hesitation, except for Popov, who said apprehensively, "I'm not going in there!"
The trio shouted, "Get in here!"

Popov, however, had made up his mind. He rationalized to the others that someone had to stay outside in case the group never emerged from the structure.

"Listen, until we know that Carrick's alive, I'm in charge," he said. "So, I'll be staying put," he added.

To his relief, the group concurred. They continued on without him, even though protocol required two of them to remain together as the Black Horizon Lander required two astronauts to engage the vessel upon lift-off.

Once the exterior door closed, Popov quickly regretted not following them in. Now alone, on the black planet, he felt quite fearful of his surroundings, considering the recent events.

The three astronauts waited for the heat regulation process to be completed when the inner airlock door finally opened. There, they saw Carrick Michaels, and joy and relief flooded their faces. Kinzi lunged at him to hug him and then, with two fists, began punching his chest.

"Alright, alright! Calm down!" said Carrick, grabbing Kinzi by the shoulders and gently pushing her off of him.

The team was shocked to see that he wasn't wearing his EMU. After the inner airlock door closed, Michaels stepped to the side to reveal a little old man standing behind him; it was Erik. Bhula and Yaping both gasped and took two steps backward.

"What the hell?!" exclaimed Yaping. Bhula still couldn't catch his breath and turned to Kinzi for an explanation.

Drenched in guilt and feeling apologetic, London looked at the other two and said, "I couldn't tell you everything back at the Lander in fear you wouldn't come here to help me retrieve Carrick."

"Well, you should've!" said Yaping, now regretting her decision not to stay with Popov.

There was stunned silence when with a smile, Carrick said, "Come on, let me show you around a bit."

Erik said nothing; he just smiled and, with arm extended and palm up, pointed down the dark hall and let Carrick lead the way.

For the next two-hours, Erik and Carrick showed the team around, desperately trying to convince them that Erik's origin was Black Earth. Carrick tried to make the case that the planet Earth was populated by human beings from Zenith, or better known as Zenithians.

While the team was in awe of the massive and sophisticated facilities, Michaels was the only one that actually believed Erik's tale. The rest remained unconvinced. Eventually, Yaping insisted it was time to go.

As the team began putting their helmets on, Bhula looked over at Carrick and said, "Where's your suit?"

He continued, "It's going to take a quick minute to get you suited up; come on! We need to get going!"

The look on Carrick's face said it all, and at that moment, Kinzi shouted at Carrick and said, "Get your fucking suit on NOW!" Carrick squinted his eyes slightly, tilted his head to the left, and said, "I'm not going with you."

Kinzi teared up while the other two astronauts demanded he go with them.

Carrick was insistent. "Yeah, I'm not leaving here. I'm in charge, and I'm staying," he said.

"What about your Lola?" asked Yaping.

"What about your mom?" asked Bhula. "You would do that to her?"

While Bhula tried frantically to raise New Horizon on his comms, Carrick said, "Listen, tell everyone I love them, and I'll come back soon, but I am not leaving this place, not right now," instructed Michaels. "Cosmo is in charge now."

Everyone knew that future expeditions were eminent with the discovery of what appeared to be human life form on ILK-78b, and should Michaels not return with them, they would surely see him again. At least that's what they hoped.

Kinzi wasn't sure, though, and was devastated that Carrick was staying behind. She somehow felt responsible, but more importantly, she felt more connected to Carrick after their experience of entering The Triad together the day before.

As the astronauts exited The Triad, Popov could see that there were only three.

"Where the hell have you guys been?" said a pissed-off Popov. "You were in there for hours!"

Popov walked closer to the airlock and tentatively looked in, "Where in the hell is Carrick?!" looking even more perturbed.

"What was that kid thinking?!" he tried to reason.

To his visible displeasure, the astronauts tried to explain what had happened. Popov, who had been in constant contact with Houston and the team orbiting above, radioed again, and told everyone that "Michaels failed to emerge from the mega-plex."

"Mars screamed, "What the hell do you mean, 'failed to emerge'?"

The trio orbiting overhead could be heard shouting expletives.

On the way back to the Lander, Popov notified New Horizon and Houston of the events that had transpired and Michaels' refusal to come with them.

Mars Johnston was through the roof. "I don't care what he wanted; you should've knocked him over the head and dragged his ass back to the module!" he shouted.

"What in the hell were you guys thinking?" he finished. Johnston was a former Marine, and the notion of leaving behind one of their own was unconscionable.

It was too late. What had been scheduled as a fifty-hour expedition to Black Earth had already turned into more than fifty-four. Life support resources were running low on the lander. The crew had to return to New Horizon without further delay.

Before lift-off, the crew had to push Carrick to the back of their minds in an effort to conduct pre-launch activities. After all checks and re-checks were completed, the astronauts donned their helmets and gloves, carefully strapped themselves onto their couches, and prepared for lift-off.

Across the vast expanse, instructions went back and forth between Earth, the New Horizon spacecraft, and the surface module.

Popov radioed: "Black Horizon Lander to Houston. We're good to go."

Houston to New Horizon: "Mike, everything good on your end?" Swimmer to Mission Control: "Roger that. We're ready to receive Black Horizon."

Houston to the Black Horizon Lander. "Alexi, you're good to go. Initiate countdown."

"Roger that, Houston."

At 5:01 pm CST, on March 24, 2022, the landing module's crew compartment separated and jettisoned skyward to re-enter Black Earth's orbit. As they lifted-off, Kinzi had one last glimpse of the black abyss outside the cabin window. Then she turned to look at Carrick's empty harness and began to cry.

Just over fifty-four-hours after touchdown, and exactly forty-eight-hours and one-minute after Michaels uttered his now-famous words, they were gone.

Behind them, a dark, desolate planet, that for now and for the foreseeable future, had two residents, where just days before, there was only one.

Chapter 11 – Fallout

Location: Deep Space. New Horizon Spacecraft – March 30, 2022.
Six days after lift-off from Black Earth.

The journey back to Earth was somber. Everyone felt like they
could've done more to persuade Carrick to come back with them.
Over the four-month trip, Kinzi London found herself staring out the
same window that Carrick did. Like him, Kinzi was now consumed,
not by the beautiful stars, but rather the empty black vacuum that
lies beyond them.

"It's okay, kid," said Cosmo Popov as he floated up from behind. "It's
not your fault. Carrick is strong-willed; he clearly had his reasons for
staying."

As Kinzi turned to look at Cosmo, he noticed that she had tears in
her eyes. She said nothing to him and instead turned back toward
the black void.

"Listen, I should've gone in," said Cosmo. "Maybe I could have said
or done something to make him come back with us."

His words fell on deaf ears. Kinzi was inconsolable. Cosmo chose to
leave her alone at that moment as he empathized with her feelings
of regret and the feeling that they all could've done more to
encourage Carrick to return with them.

In hindsight, however, Kinzi somehow knew that Carrick was never
going to leave with them. She saw something in his eyes when they
came face to face with Erik. Jogging her memory a little more, she
recalled that it was Carrick that found her hand before the two
walked into the airlock. It was him, not her, that leaned into that first
step towards The Triad.

Kinzi rationalized that some sense of history must've taken over his imagination and that he was somehow connected to Black Earth. What happened the night he spent in The Triad, she wondered? Did Erik brainwash him? Did he learn or see something that made him feel obligated to stay? Or was being the first 'boots on the ground' so intoxicating that he needed more. Whatever it was, Kinzi was determined to see her friend again.

Location: Kazakhstan, Central Asia – July 19, 2022.

The bumpy ride of reentry into Earth's atmosphere and colliding with the ground, at a survivable 15 miles per hour, was over. Now came the hard part. Facing the world, and recounting what they had seen up there, was going to be difficult. "Not so fast!" would come the edict from NASA.

The returning crew was quarantined for fifteen days while all their vital signs were checked and triple-checked. During that time, they were debriefed by a constant stream of agencies. NASA, NSA officials, and government representatives from the other participating countries met with the astronauts more than a dozen times. It was made abundantly clear which public statements would be acceptable and what they would not be allowed to say.

Dr. Kinzi London would be the most outspoken of the seven New Horizon astronauts.

"So, a cover-up?" said London, firmly. "That's what you're asking of us?" She paused for a moment. "Insane! I won't do it!" she said.

"First of all, a cover-up is not what we're asking of you." Michael Rogers, Head of the National Security Agency, was stern. "Second of all, we're not asking you anything at all. We're telling you. This is a matter of national security and will be treated with discretion."

"Gimme a break!" shouted London. "It was one guy up there, not a Space Force."

"Yes, but we don't know who he is or what country holds his allegiance. Until we do, all of you will say only what's agreed upon," finished an unflinching Rogers.

Location: Washington, D.C. NCN Studios – July 21, 2022

Breaking News – "This just in!" pronounced Bear Winston. "A rather uncomfortable story is unfolding regarding the astronauts who just recently returned from ILK-87b."

"We've been hearing from several family members and friends of Dr. Carrick Michaels, one of the six scientists and two navigators aboard the New Horizon spacecraft. The crew recently returned from what many are now calling Black Earth. However, our sources are telling us that they don't know where Michaels is."

"NASA has confirmed that all eight astronauts who traveled to the newly discovered planet returned safely. But we now believe that might not be the case."

"Stay tuned; we'll be providing more details as they come in."

As questions regarding the whereabouts of Dr. Carrick Michaels persisted, pressure mounted in the halls of NASA. The number of people who knew about the situation was growing. More than two-hundred and fifty personnel now knew that Michaels hadn't returned home. In addition to his seven crew-mates, there was the staff at Mission Control, hundreds of government officials from the U.S. and other participating countries, along with the recovery team in Kazakhstan. Now that the news had been leaked to the press, there was no way the lie could be contained.

The White House had been flooded with calls from its Ambassadors of more than sixty countries. Representatives of foreign leaders, and the G8 leaders themselves, bombarded U.S. Government officials with questions regarding the whereabouts of Dr. Carrick Michaels.

In the White House's Oval Office, the phone rang. Germany was on the line.

"Mr. President," the new German Chancellor began, "in Toronto, in May of last year, you spoke to my predecessor about the value of transparency. Today I speak on behalf of the other G8 leaders when I tell you that we expect full disclosure in this and all future matters. Hiding the truth from the world will simply not stand."
"Forgive me, Chancellor," said the President. "In good time, I will be in touch with you to address all of your concerns. Now please, let me move on to finding out more facts from my security officials."

Eventually, the U.S. did get back to the German Chancellor and the other world leaders regarding the fate of Dr. Carrick Michaels. In consultation with the G8 Plus 5 Group, a consensus was reached. It was decided that the world must know the truth regarding the whereabouts of Dr. Carrick Michaels and what had unfolded on Black Earth.

Location: New York City. United Nations Headquarters – July 31, 2022. 12:00 pm EST.

A special session of the U.N. Assembly had been called, with one hundred and ninety-three member states in attendance. The body would be addressed by the President of the United States of America, otherwise known as POTUS.

Standing behind the President was a group of individuals, all with their own connection to Dr. Carrick Michaels and to Black Earth. Maggie Michaels, his mother, stood tall beside Carrick's long-time girlfriend, Lola Cook. James Lorenstine from NASA accompanied Marcus Johnston. Off to the side was a small group of scientists. Dr. Riley King, Professor of Planetary Science, stood with Dr. Archibald Grassley, world-renowned Astrophysicist, and Dr. Colye Justman, Director of the Mauna Kea Observatory in Hawaii and the man who discovered ILK-87b.

"Ladies and Gentlemen in attendance," the President began. "I first want to say that I am talking to you today only after consulting these very special and well-informed people that you see behind me." POTUS gestured to the group of people standing behind him. "Even as I acknowledge the courage, wisdom, and expertise of these global patriots, I speak with you with much trepidation and with butterflies in my stomach. What I am about to share with you are words that will be uttered for the first time, and possibly the only time, in our human history."

"Throughout the ages, we have reached out to the stars in the hopes that they might tell us of our origins. We've gazed from afar, and through modern technology, we've studied up close. Today, I bring you some, not all, but some of the answers to the age-old questions that we as humans have always asked. Questions that have been posed for as long as there have been people on Earth."

"As you all know, on September 20, 2019, Dr. Colye Justman, standing behind me and to my left, discovered the planet many are now calling Black Earth. Then, on December 12, 2020, infrastructure was observed on Black Earth using our Infinity One unmanned probe. This discovery was first leaked to the press on December 29, 2020."

"Subsequently, the U.S., in cooperation with the seven other G8 world leaders, put together an international team of the world's finest scientists and space aviators. From there, we embarked on a mission that would answer the most ancient yet most contemporary question of all-time: are we alone in the Universe?"

"On March 22, 2022, we landed a crew of exceptional astronauts safely on the surface of ILK-87b. That's a day we'll all remember for the rest of our lives."

"On that day, we heard the profound words spoken by our beloved, Dr. Carrick Michaels. If I may, I'd like to recite his words to all of you here today."

Despite having a working teleprompter, POTUS produced a page of embossed paper from his inside jacket pocket. Glancing up at his audience for a second, he began. "Dr. Michael's said, 'With two feet planted on Earth's nearest neighbor, humankind takes another step towards the universal truths of our origins. I am proud today, not as an American, but rather as an Earthling, and for what we have accomplished together; through boundless dedication, sheer determination, and iron will.'"

POTUS then refolded the paper and returned it to his pocket.

"Along with that monumental achievement, there was a discovery made. One that allows me to say to you here today," he paused for several seconds before continuing, "we are, in fact, NOT alone in the Universe."
The room was filled with audible gasps and chatter. POTUS continued regardless, courageously speaking over the clamor.

"I stand here today, as a fellow Earthling, and tell you that we have not just discovered life form on ILK-87b. Rather we have discovered our own life form. We have found a fellow human being on what I will now and forever refer to as Black Earth."

Many on the assembly floor threw up their arms in disgust. Some ran their hands over their faces, overwrought by disbelief. More than a dozen representatives tore off their headphones and stormed off the assembly floor, and at least two people fainted. The hall was in an uproar for several minutes before the President spoke again.

"Please! My fellow citizens of planet Earth. The United States of America promises that we will be transparent with you. We will work closely with you and with scientists from around the world. We will never give up in our quest to learn more of our shared universe and to subsequently share those findings with you."

"I want to finish by sharing with you a rather amazing display of courage. Over the past few weeks, people have speculated that one of our astronauts did not make the return trip home from Black Earth. They are correct. I am proud to tell you that our very own Dr. Carrick Michaels made the selfless decision, on his own, to remain on Black Earth."

"Dr. Michaels, whose mother is with me today," POTUS gestured back and to his right, "is a chemist from Suwanee, Georgia. He earned his Ph.D. at Cornell University, and he is the greatest of all American heroes. His crew-mates brought home a message from him to his family. He believed that he had been led to Black Earth for a reason. He decided he would return to Earth only after he learned more of the planet and our origins. Dr. Michaels is currently on Black Earth. I can assure you that he is safe, and he is shielded from its inhospitable atmosphere."

POTUS turned to look over his right shoulder and then back to those in attendance. "I want to make something very clear to the family of Dr. Michaels and the world at large. Dr. Michaels will be safely returning home no later than the summer of 2023."

"As I speak with you here today, we are planning another journey to our nearest neighbor, Black Earth. The journey there and back will once again involve an international coalition, comprised of some of the same brave men and women that have already traveled to the black planet."

"At the beginning of the first day, at the beginning of the first month, at the beginning of the new year, a spacecraft fittingly named New Beginning will travel to Black Earth. Its astronauts will learn more about the planet and will bring home our universal hero, Dr. Carrick Michaels."

The President finished his speech by saying, "May God bless all the people, of all the nations, of our world and of our Universe."

POTUS thanked those in attendance and exited the stage, flanked by two Secret Service agents, followed by his other special guests.

The President of the United States did not say in his speech that NASA had no idea what condition Michaels was in or even if he was alive. In fact, NASA officials were incensed by his speech. It was foolhardy to have guaranteed the safe return of Carrick Michaels by the summer of 2023. The new leader was making the first big gamble of his young presidency.

Location: Planet Earth – Month of August 2022.

Around the world, some celebrated while others rioted in the streets. People who were proud to say they were atheists joined those who were afraid to, dancing in the streets. "*I told you so!*" they cheered to anyone who would listen.

Cable Television's Right Time with Will Sparks was picked up for another five seasons, and Sparks was given a sizable pay raise. Sparks had always been one of the most charismatic and outspoken atheists. Now, everyone wanted to be a guest on his show.

The Flat Earther population dwindled, and conspiracy theory websites and blogs reluctantly reported an 80% drop in clicks. Meanwhile, the religious right screamed blasphemy from the rooftops. Sales of both telescopes and bibles went through the roof. While at the same time, church attendance around the globe dropped considerably.

The world's population, by and large, received the news with open arms and mind. There was almost a sense of relief as much of the world's population always somehow knew that humankind couldn't be alone in the vastness of our universe.

Back at NASA, few details were disseminated to the press regarding the discovery of what could only be assumed was human life found on the black planet. An international body was assembled to take over all public relations and decide what information would be shared with the world.

What was transpiring was no longer a United States-led news story but rather a human one. Few details would avoid censorship from that point on.

When arranging its mission to ILK-87b, NASA had great forethought when preparing for the New Horizon journey to Black Earth. The agency followed through on a previously unannounced launch of a small spy satellite into orbit around Black Earth.

The Walker Trace satellite would monitor transmissions coming from Black Earth's surface and then transmit those signals back to Earth in near real-time. It would accomplish this by using the Interlink Communication Corridor. The U.S. Military was resolute in its unwillingness to share its advanced technologies with the rest of the world. Even the G8 Plus 5 would remain in the dark regarding the Walker Trace satellite's true capabilities. The codename of this secret operation was Operation Laser Focus.

Since Carrick Michaels was left behind, the Walker Trace satellite had been monitoring Black Earth for any signs of life. It was picking up faint radio transmissions but nothing that provided NASA with any useful information.

Location: Hartford, Connecticut, USA – August 7, 2022.

The Ivy League Science Council, or the ILSC, had been tasked with studying samples brought back from Black Earth, and what they learned was riveting.

Geologists from the ILSC, along with three scientists from the mission to ILK-87b, Lisa Yaping, Alexi Popov, and Piyush Bhula, all came to the same determination. The scientists agreed that changes to soil and rock samples, which normally would've taken centuries, likely occurred in only decades on Black Earth. Soil samples that were brought back also revealed high levels of carbon in the form of particles called Carbonites.

The scientific findings were revealed in a press conference, aired live on the NCN news network, and included many world-renown scientific experts. The conference was widely reported on by dozens of news agencies from around the world.

During the conference, it was disclosed that the blacker than black particles held no reflective value and that early testing revealed that they absorbed 100% of the light they came in contact with. The samples also revealed high levels of oceanic basalt from oceanic crust, suggesting that the oceans on Black Earth dried up, and then the pelagic and marine sediments found at the bottom of the ocean, along with calcium carbonate found in Calcareous ooze, relocated far and wide.

Geologists concluded that the volcanic eruptions that spewed the basalt were not only powerful but also incredibly violent. Geologists also theorized that the eruptions were numerous and widespread. The samples collected were from an area far from any perceived dried-up oceans; and at much higher land elevations.
The team speculated from the ILSC that the oceanic soil relocation occurred during explosive eruptions from volcanoes that were once beneath great oceans. These eruptions seemed to have launched ash and soil particles thousands of feet into the air, which then traveled vast distances before being deposited in other geographic areas.

The high percentage of oceanic basalt found in the soil samples also suggested to scientists that the basalt must have traveled hundreds, perhaps thousands of miles, and been airborne for long periods of time.

Finally, the scientists concluded that tornadoes and enduring monsoons might have plagued Black Earth. Oceanic crust deposits carried by these storms must have dumped the basalt onto the surface over many centuries, resulting in its current black desert conditions.

However, they concluded that more samples from the various regions of Black Earth would need to be collected and tested to support their conclusions.

Chapter 12 – God

Location: Black Earth. Top level of The Triad, Observatory Deck, Surface-Level 5, Northwest Sector of The Triad – March 24, 2022. Exactly 5:01 pm CST.

Erik and Carrick stared out of the triple-paned, diamond-glass observatory window and watched as the Black Horizon Crew Compartment jettisoned skyward.

"Well, there they go. You sure you made the right decision?" Carrick spoke with a lump in his throat. "Not sure. Guess it doesn't matter now, though."

Erik wondered aloud, "You hungry?"

Carrick laughed. "Starved, actually. Hope whatever you're serving is better than space food."

"C'mon, Pal." Erik chuckled as he began to walk away. "You're in for a real treat!"

Making their way to The Culina, Erik told Carrick he had a lot to share with him. "I hope you're a good listener," he grinned.
The two walked side by side for a few minutes when Erik finally confessed, "Listen, you stink. After a shower, I'll get you some extra clothes that I used to wear a long time ago; they'll probably fit you; I've lost some weight over the years."

"I stink?" Carrick laughed. "You smell awful!"

"Well, it has been a couple of weeks since my last shower, and I wasn't exactly expecting company. You'll have to excuse me." Erik then picked at his shirt and gave it a cautious sniff. "It's all about water conservation around here," he added.

"Please tell me you're not gonna shower with me?" Carrick joked.

"God! It would be terrible if I were trapped in this place with an old pervert." He threw back his head and laughed out loud at the thought.

Erik didn't get the joke. "What does pervert mean?"

"Don't worry about it," he laughed aloud.

Minutes later, at The Culina, the two sat down to eat.

"Holy shit! This is awful!" gagged Carrick as he forced down a bitter concoction called 'Lemon Leaf.'

Through pursed lips, "That's it, that's all you've got?" desperately trying to rid his tongue of the bitter taste.

"We're out of my favorite, so I thought I'd offer you one that we had plenty of," explained Erik. "Considering you're gonna be here for a while, I don't want you ingesting what's left of the Brown Maize."

"I would've loved to have offered you some Red Fruit. Ahhh, it was the best." Erik gazed over at the empty canister with a look of benign resignation.

As the two made their way back to the barracks, Carrick admired the steel-gray corridor, "What's with the stainless steel walls?"

"Those aren't steel walls; they're platinum."

"Platinum? Man, this place just keeps getting better! Diamond glass and platinum walls? I don't even wanna know what the floors are made of." Carrick shook his head in amazement.

"Platinum is great!" lauded Erik. "It's a noble metal; it's non-toxic, non-reactive, and has a high melting point. Plus, it's incredibly easy to manipulate."

Carrick tried to keep a straight face. "Good grief, you're not always going to give me the long, drawn-out answer to everything I ask, are you?"

Back at the barracks, having enjoyed separate showers, the two sat in adjacent bunks and talked.

"How many bunks are in here, anyway?" Carrick was curious.

Erik knew the answer without even having to think. "There are barracks located on each of The Triad's ten sub-levels. Every sub-level has a total of thirty barracks. Each of those once housed four hundred people."

"There're four hundred beds in here?!" challenged Carrick. "Where?"

Now standing, he looked deep into the dark and cavernous space of Barrack 5. He quickly did the math. The bunks were arranged in stacks of four high, and he could see that they were aligned in rows of four, across the width of the room. It was impossible to see more than ten rows deep down the length of the barrack since the light was so low.

"Damn! How far back does this place go?"

"It's twenty-five bunks deep, but I haven't been back there in decades," said Erik. "There's nothing back there for me."

"Ouch! Talk about no privacy when this place was full, huh?"

"I didn't realize how much my privacy meant to me until you showed up," teased Erik.

"Hey, I can grab another bunk back there if you'd like?" offered Carrick, pointing to the black void in the back of Barrack 5.

"I rather like your company. I actually miss the sound of people talking before they'd fall asleep. The sound of silence feels more like death. You actually feel alive when surrounded by other living things," confessed Erik.

After a moment of silence, Carrick remembered something from the tour Erik had given him earlier. "Why do you still sleep in here at all?"

They'd explored other sections of The Triad after the other astronauts had gone, and Erik had shown Carrick several well-appointed, private quarters on Sub-Level 3. They looked much more comfortable than the spartan barracks.

Erik sighed. "What little family and friends I once had, all lived in Barracks 5 and 6. This is the only place that I still feel close to their memory."

"God, that's sad. I hope my friends come back for me at some point. I don't want to end up sleeping outside, next to what's left of the landing module."

They both laughed.

Erik's next question took Carrick by surprise. "That's the second time you referenced the word 'God.' What does that mean?"

Carrick was confused. "I don't understand the question."

"What does the word 'God' mean?" clarified Erik.

"You know, the man upstairs." Carrick pointed skyward.

Erik looked up and patiently reminded Carrick that there were no other people there. Not on the level above them, or anywhere else in The Triad or on Zenith.

It suddenly dawned on Carrick that Erik not only didn't believe in God but that he didn't even have a concept of what the term meant.

"Wow!" said Carrick. "Now that's a long story."

"I'm not going anywhere," smiled Erik.

Realizing that it would be a long night, Carrick started a conversation that would be an uncomfortable one for some people back on Earth.

Carrick began, "Even though I'm an atheist, I think I can explain the concept of God, the Devil, and religion.

"What's an atheist?" Erik interrupted.

Carrick laughed, "This is definitely going to be a long night! Be patient with me. You're going to have lots of questions."
Erik nodded in affirmation.

"Since the beginning, on Earth anyway...," said Carrick, "...people have believed in a greater good. Most people believed that they weren't alone in the Universe. They believed that something greater than themselves was at work, pulling the strings of their actions, their decisions, and their fate."

"In the early days of life on Earth, people weren't exactly sure what or who was guiding them; they just knew there was something. They looked to the skies above for answers and believed that their God or Gods lived in a place called Heaven," his eyes strayed upward."

"People believed that if they lived a good life and believed in God, that they would be rewarded with eternal life after death. They believed there would be a place waiting for them in Heaven," explained Carrick.

Erik nodded, completely engrossed in Carrick's story. "So, where is this place called Heaven?"

Carrick pointed upward again. "In the sky."

"If you had lived in the ancient society of a country called Greece a few thousand years ago, you would surely have believed in Gods. The Greeks had a God for everything. A love god, a rain god, a fire god. Basically, there was a God for everything that could not be explained.

"Did you say Greece?" asked Erik while shaking his head. "We had a section of The Triad called Greece. Those who lived there were called *The Greek Society.*"

"No, kidding?" said Carrick, looking surprised.

He continued, not wanting to get distracted. "Today on Earth, beliefs are more fractured. Some believe in a god, and those people are considered religious. Some don't, and those are called atheists. And then there are people who aren't sure either way, and we call them agnostics.

"Me personally," said Carrick, "I do not believe that there is a God in Heaven, or for that matter, anywhere.

Carrick was beginning to enjoy giving Erik a history lesson. "Some of those religious people also think there's a kind of fiery alter-God. An entity that encompasses all evil. In the country of America, where I live, the main religion is known as Christianity, and people read the stories of the Christian God in a book called the Bible. One part of the book, the New Testament, describes this evil entity as Satan or the Devil. The Bible says that the Devil started off as a good angel. In fact, he was portrayed as the Prince of Angels until he led a revolt against God. His punishment was to be forever banished from Heaven, along with his mutinous flock of angels."

Carrick glanced up at Erik. "Are you following me so far?"

Erik, without words, nodded; his face cradled in his hands as he listened intently.

Carrick continued, "Scripture, which is just another word for the Bible, says that Satan carried out his struggle against God by seducing humans into committing something called sin. Sin is defined as a transgression against the law of God."

Erik, who'd been absorbing every word, finally chimed in. "I'm following you, but this all seems a bit farfetched and a little hard to comprehend. Are you telling me that humans on Earth actually believe that someone, or something, is floating around in the Universe, making decisions for them? It's interesting," he clarified. "it's just really difficult to believe. There were no such beliefs on Zenith."

Carrick threw up his hands. "I agree! I personally believe that Gods were created to satisfy the curiosities and fears of humans. For example, when lightning flashed across the sky in the early days of history, humans on Earth thought it meant their Gods were angry. When it rained, it was a sign that their Gods must be pleased because it meant their crops would grow. But that was just because they didn't understand what caused precipitation!"

"I think most people fear what they don't understand. And they want to believe they're not alone in the Universe. It comforts people who are dying to believe they're going to a better place, be it Heaven or Nirvana."

Carrick was beginning to wonder if he was overwhelming Erik with too many details. But Erik still seemed to be digesting it all.

"Although I am an atheist," continued Carrick. "I do believe that all religions have a place in society. It's okay with me for people to have faith in anyone or anything. I think a person should be able to worship another person, a spirit, or an ideology. Whatever they want, in fact! And I accept that faith is the cornerstone of all religions. It's the belief in something we can't see, hear, touch, or feel." Carrick stared straight up towards the bottom of the bunk above. "I just don't personally believe in any of it. I'm kind of shocked that so many people still do."

Erik didn't speak. He just listened intently as Carrick talked.

"My guess is that about half the population on Earth don't believe in God at all. Or, at the very least, they aren't sure if God actually exists. Since the early days on Earth, most humans have basically been forced to believe in God. Each section of the planet Earth, each collection of people, were obligated to believe in that sect's God, or there would be a heavy price to pay."

"What kind of price?" Erik wondered aloud.

"In the early days, you could be killed for criticizing the local God or simply for doubting its existence. Nowadays, you probably wouldn't get hurt. Maybe just ridiculed. Even today, though, in some cultures, denying the existence of God can have brutal consequences. It just depends where on planet Earth you live."

Carrick was just getting warmed up. "There's been an overt brainwashing of religion. It's happening right now and is terribly unfair to young people."

Erik looked confused. "Please explain," he encouraged.

"The notion of God has been drilled into our psyche since before we could walk or talk, reason or question. Believe it or not, we were brainwashed."

"I'm not familiar with that term," said Erik while looking confused.

"It means to manipulate a person's way of thinking or use of logic. It causes confusion and is done repetitively until a person no longer questions the very things that should be questioned," explained Carrick.

"That's awful!" said Erik.

It was difficult for Carrick to answer that question without thinking about all the times his father's death had been reasoned away as 'God's will' or something that was 'meant to be.' He couldn't escape the fact that he was angry. He'd been cheated out of a childhood that should've included the one thing he'd didn't have: a father.

But who was he supposed to be angry with? A God he didn't believe in? Friends and family who'd argued away his father's death as fate? Or maybe he was angry with his father? Could he possibly have caused the accident that killed him? Or was he angry with the Navy? These were the questions Carrick asked when he looked out beyond the stars. But, in reality, he knew those questions would never be answered. In the end, he was just sad that he and his father had never known each other.

Gathering his thoughts, Carrick remembered that he was telling a story, and Erik was waiting for him to carry on. He sat up and swung his legs around over the side of the bed so that he was facing Erik. "Here are some examples of brainwashing," he continued.

"When someone would sneeze, people would say, 'May God bless you!'"

Erik put his hand out as if to slow Carrick down. "Wait, I don't understand."

Carrick replied, "Years ago, it was believed that when you sneezed, a part of your soul left your body. So, you were a little closer to death. People wanted to comfort you, so they said, 'God bless you.'"

"Here's another, 'Mommy, why did my father have to die? In my case, my mom said, 'That's the way God intended it to be.' I wasn't expected to question that notion. That always bothered me and was what first caused me to question God and religion."

"Even the currency in America is marked by religion. The phrase, 'In God we trust,' appears on both coins and paper currency. Here's another example; in my country, school-aged children are required to pledge allegiance to our flag, and 'one nation, under God'." Carrick grimaced at the thought. He'd become so passionate about this subject that he'd almost forgotten Erik was there.

The old man's voice jolted him back to his bunk in the barrack. "So, explain to me again why it is that people look upward for answers?"

"You got me. I have no idea why." Carrick shook his head. "Science has dispelled a lot of the old mythologies. Once we determined why water fell from the sky, we simply called it precipitation. Science replaced ignorance as humans began to evolve on the intellectual level. In ancient times, anything that couldn't be explained was attributed to a god. Once we found explanations, it became science."

Erik went to speak, but this time Carrick held up his hand. He had one last thing to add.

"Life ends, and death comes to every living thing. That's not a truth that we like very much, so we feel compelled to put a positive spin on the negative reality. I call it the 'opposite rule,' meaning there are two sides to everything. Where you have light, goodness, God, you must, in theory, have darkness, evil, Satan. Where there's hot, there's cold. Where there's up, there's down. Yes, no; in, out. I could go on for days."

"Please don't!" smiled Erik, waiving off Carrick.

Carrick hardly heard Erik's request and was on a mission to educate him.

"On Earth, we can't ignore the fact that there's evil among humans. Every day we hear about violent acts like murder, rape, assault, and many more. I think humankind couldn't account for the origins of this evil, so they had to blame someone else other than their God. Enter the Devil. If you believe in the Devil, then you certainly believe in God. If you believe in Heaven, then you certainly believe in Hell, the opposite of Heaven."

"It's even in our language. If you think about the words good and God, you will see subliminal messaging there. Same with the words evil and Devil. The message implies that God is inherently good, and on the opposite side, that the Devil is evil. Or how about the word dog?"

Erik looked confused again.

"Did you even have dogs or pet animals on Zenith before it all came crashing down?" Carrick asked.

"Pets? Yes," Erik replied. "I have no idea what a dog is. But if you're referring to domesticated, furry animals, then the answer is yes. Zenithians had many species of animals that they kept as companions. Our words for them were 'Docgas,' but never dog."

Carrick nodded slowly. "Well, on Earth, we have a specific type of pet called a dog. I can only theorize as to how they got their name. But the word itself is important. Dog is God spelled backward. And when you look deeper, you see the subliminal message. On Earth, people refer to a dog as 'Man's Best Friend.' Carrick came to an exultant end.

"Fascinating!" Erik hadn't taken his eyes off Carrick through his whole speech. After a moment of silence, Erik asked Carrick if he was done.

Carrick grinned. "I can go on if you'd like?"

Erik interjected quickly, "No-No, I think I got your point."

Carrick laughed, a little embarrassed at having talked for so long.

In the darkness of Barrack 5, Erik lay on his back and stared upward at the bottom of the bunk overhead. "I think I understand why they looked up to the sky, believing someone else was there."

"I'm listening. By all means, please; solve the mystery!" begged Carrick.

"My guess is that it could be two things," stated Erik.

"Go on!" encouraged Carrick.

"From the time Zenithians were old enough to learn, we were taught about a future life on Home. We spent our lives preparing for the day when we would travel to Earth. Each and every one of us looked up and dreamt of the day when we would go Home. In a sense, our Home was your Heaven."

"So, you're saying that after Zenithians got to Earth, they still looked towards the sky because they had done so their entire lives?"

Erik shrugged. "It seems plausible that they would remember where they came from, doesn't it? And they'd surely remember all the loved ones they had lost or left behind."

"What's the other reason you think people on Earth look to the heavens?"

"Carrick, we shuttled Zenithians to Earth for roughly six-thousand years."

"So what?"

"Each time a shuttle left Zenith, it set out on a course that helped determine what regions of Home to populate."

"Okay, and....?"

"Before ending at its destination, the shuttle was programmed to fly over its previous destinations, in some cases, hundreds of years later."

"Why?" Carrick asked.

"We needed to know if the previous migrant drops of Zenithians had thrived. If they hadn't, we learned and re-calculated. We re-evaluated and mapped more suitable geographic locations. Places with more sustainable climates. And we also sent unmanned shuttles to map the Earth and record the progress of past migrant drops."

"While that's all very intriguing, I don't see what you're getting at," challenged a rather confused-looking Carrick.

"Don't you understand?" asked Erik.

"I'm completely lost."

Erik tutted, impatient for the first time. "Most times, we went back to previous locations, and Zenithians had expired, with no trace that they were ever there. But, other times, thousands of times, we had survived and flourished, forming communities and regional civilizations."

"Still not getting it!" exclaimed a dumbfounded Carrick.

"Maybe people on the ground, some of whom were generations older than those who'd migrated to Earth... Maybe they saw the shuttles!" offered an enthusiastic Erik.

"They might've looked up and seen something greater than themselves, something they couldn't explain or understand. Don't you get it?"

Carrick's jaw dropped, and he leaped up, nearly banging his head on the bunk above. "UFOs!" he exploded.

"U-F-what?" Erik was stunned by Carrick's reaction.

Carrick, with a look of revelation on his face, shouted again. "UFOs! Unidentified Flying Objects! I get it NOW!"

Carrick sank back down into his bunk, thinking out loud. "Of course, that's it! It makes perfect sense. They couldn't explain what they saw, so it had to be a God."

Both men were exhausted. The two laid in silence for several minutes. Carrick with a big smile on his face while Erik's was creased with baffled wonderment. He was still trying to process the notion of people inventing an imaginary figure in the sky to praise and worship instead of just asking the question, why. It seemed strange to him that they hadn't just demanded answers until the unexplained was finally explained.

After lights-out, Carrick lay awake for some time. He was sure his companion had drifted off to sleep when Erik's voice floated sarcastically out of the darkness. "You're not always going to give me the long, drawn-out answer to every question I ask, are you? I simply asked what the word God meant."

Carrick laughed. It wasn't long after that both men were asleep.

Chapter 13 – The Human Races

Location: The Triad, Barrack 5 – March 25, 2022. The next morning.

Today Carrick and Erik woke up a little early. This day would mark the beginning of Carrick's indoctrination into Zenith's past. Using separate basins, the two splashed a little water on their faces before planning out their day.

"You ready?" asked Erik.

"That sounds a bit ominous. Ready for what?"

Erik smiled and said, "Today, my friend, you're getting the first of what will be many history lessons to come. But first, breakfast."

"Great, 'Lemon Leaf' again? Ugh!" said Carrick, with a look of disgust.

After arriving at The Culina, Carrick decided to get a little nosy. He asked Erik if he could take a look around.

"Sure." Erik swept his arm back to indicate that Carrick could go where he pleased.

As Carrick wandered away, Erik moved to the long-empty Red Fruit canister and tapped it out of habit, as he had for many years. Erik's days often felt like weeks, his weeks felt like months, and sometimes, his months felt like years. As he stood in front of the canister, he thought about how different life had become since Carrick's recent arrival. With this budding young friendship, Erik was creating fresh memories for the first time in more than seven decades. Memories that he knew would make him smile when he reflected on them. He liked Carrick so far and, if he'd ever had a son, he'd have wanted him to be like Carrick.

As usual, he looked into the bottom of his cup, no Red Fruit there. Erik sighed and moved to the Brown Maize canister. He dreaded the day his second favorite flavor would run out too.

Carrick, meanwhile, was walking around the kitchen area, opening doors and cabinets. Eventually, he stumbled across a switch panel. Inside were buttons marked with the different flavors of all the powdered drink mixes.

"Ahhh, the motherload!" he mumbled under his breath.

He checked up and down the panel until he spotted a button, and there it was, a button labeled Red Fruit. When he pushed it, the satisfying click likely meant he'd finally get to taste the sweet, powdered nectar that Erik had been talking about.

"That was easy," he said aloud, extremely pleased with himself. He wondered how Erik could've missed it over the many decades he'd been here alone. It was marked with the words Manual Powder Refill Control. He shook his head and smiled, then headed back into The Culina's great hall to find out what was so special about Red Fruit.

Moments earlier, as Erik poured water into his cup, drenching the Brown Maize powder, he'd heard a poofing sound. He shrugged it off. He figured it was Carrick moving items around in the next room. A few moments later, Carrick strolled in, acting like he owned the place and wearing a sly grin on his face. Erik said nothing. He admired the young man's air of confidence, although he wasn't sure why Carrick looked so pleased with himself.

Carrick walked right past and, without a word, held his cup beneath the nozzle of Erik's old favorite, Red Fruit.

Erik began to say, "I told you, there is no...," when suddenly, a hefty portion of red powder fell into Carrick's cup. Erik wore a look of amazement as Carrick made his way to the water dispenser, acting as if nothing had happened.

Astounded, Erik watched as Carrick filled his cup with water and began to stir. Carrick licked the metal stirring utensil and nonchalantly commented, "Mm-mm, this is quite tasty."

Erik didn't speak. He dumped his cup into a nearby basin and almost ran to the Red Fruit canister. He leaned in and bent down under the nozzle, tilting his head upward to inspect the dispenser more closely. Straightening up, he shook his head and smiled. He took a portion of the red powder, drenched it with water, and stirred it slowly as he joined Carrick at a nearby table.

After they'd both savored the sweet-tasting red substance, Erik got up, rubbing his belly, and wiping his mouth.

"Okay wise guy," he said, "you gonna tell me what just happened?"

"Nope." Carrick looked smug. "I'll tell you tomorrow. After a full day, we'll be able to consider it one of many history lessons."

"Touché."

"Okay, I have to ask," Carrick pondered aloud, "if there's a Culina on every level, why not just find some more 'Red Fruit' there."

"You think for a second that I haven't inspected every powder canister, on every level of the Northwest Sector of The Triad?" asked a rhetorical Erik.

"Yes, your curiosity seems to have ended at the now full canister right over there." Carrick was drenched with sarcasm.

"You're on a roll today!" said a slightly perturbed Erik. "Every level has different flavors. Trust me, I checked; there's no 'Red Fruit' in any of the other nine Culinas in the Northwest Sector."

"But what about the other sectors?" winked Carrick.

"Ugh! You're killing me!" Let's just get to the library!"

The two exited The Culina and began to walk.

Halfway down the hall, Erik realized how much he was enjoying having Carrick around. Even though his jokes were bad and his stories long.

Erik then put his arm around Carrick's shoulder in a fatherly gesture. Carrick looked at the hand on his right shoulder and then looked back to his left. "This doesn't mean we're going to share a shower later, does it?" They both laughed out loud. Neither said anything more about it, but each of them had experienced an unexplainable connection.

Exiting the elevator on Surface-Level 3, they turned right, and Erik led the way down the long hall. As they headed for The History Library, the lights on the walls once again caught Carrick's eye. "Are those fixtures really diamond?" he asked.

"They are," answered Erik. "But I still don't understand why you find them to be so special; they're just glass."

"Just glass?" Carrick looked baffled.

Erik opened the door to The History Library, and they entered. Carrick looked around and exclaimed, "Holy Shit!"

Erik recoiled, "I thought for sure you were going to say, "Oh My God!"

"Where are all the books?"

"No books, my friend," responded Erik.

"There haven't been books on Zenith for many centuries; I've only seen images of them. I would love to read one someday, though. Let me know if you have any recommendations," smiled Erik.

Carrick asked, "How many......?," and before he could finish the question, Erik said, "Seven hundred and ninety-eight."

"Wow! That's a lot of computers!"

"Why no books?" wondered Carrick aloud.

"Apparently, they're bad for the air quality in The Triad," he offered. "Hmm, that's interesting," thought Carrick.

Carrick walked around for several minutes, admiring the computer stations. Each included a high-resolution, liquid-glass monitor about forty inches tall; a tablet for data commands and every one of them seemed to show a different part of Zenith's history.

At the end of two long rows of computer stations, Carrick saw something that amazed him. A 4D, holographic image island. It was about ten feet in diameter and a foot high, like a circular stage. On top of it, to Carrick's astonishment, life-sized figures seemed to be moving around.

Erik came up behind him, hands clasped behind his back. "Go ahead, step up onto the island and into the past."
Nervously, Carrick glanced back at him. "Can I?"

Erik acknowledged him with a nod of approval, and Carrick cautiously stepped up onto the platform. He was immediately immersed in another place and time in Zenith's history.

He looked down at his feet and actually felt as if he was standing on a futuristic city street. Two-wheeled cars whizzed by, and people passed him on moving sidewalks. There were no traffic signals that Carrick could see, which caused him some confusion. Beside him on the street, a vehicle was idling. Carrick bent down to peer into the window. Inside the car, he saw a heads-up-display that illustrated to the driver whether they should stop or go. The driver looked at Carrick, smiled, and then zoomed away. Carrick was surprised; surely, the driver couldn't actually see him.

Carrick saw people, human beings, going about their day in a modern city. Although he knew he was in a hologram, Carrick felt as if he was really there, wherever there was. He actually felt a breeze on his face and blowing through his hair.

As Carrick surveyed the landscape, he saw a young woman standing across the street. He watched her and, after a moment, the woman turned and looked his way. Just for a second, Carrick pretended it was Lola. He stared into her eyes and realized that she was staring back at him. Frozen in fear, he felt unable to look away. Then, to Carrick's astonishment, the young woman gave him a wink and a smile. Completely freaked out, Carrick quickly jumped back down off of the platform, shaking his head in disbelief.

"What just happened?" he asked, breathing heavily.

"You just stepped back in time, my friend. The period that you were in was five-thousand years ago on Zenith."

"Five-thousand years ago?" Carrick was stunned. "But it was so futuristic!"

"That was a thousand years after the first shuttle carried Zenithians to Earth and more than a thousand years before The Great War," said Erik.

"The Great War?" asked Carrick, looking curious.

"We'll talk about the war in due time," promised Erik.

"But the people, they looked so happy. They didn't appear to be on the verge of extinction," said Carrick.

Erik nodded in resignation. "In the beginning, people simply ignored the changing climate. Each year it got a little warmer, and people just grew accustomed to it. They spent more and more time indoors and adapted to the rising temperatures. The human species is good at adapting to their surroundings."

Carrick nodded in agreement.

"Most people denied what they were seeing and feeling. Some shouted their concerns in the streets, but they were largely ignored. The people in power only did what they had to, to stay in office. They went along with what the masses wanted to hear."

Erik walked to the edge of the platform and looked in at the scene playing out there. "The scientists knew what was happening, though. They understood that inaction would result in an irreversible chain of events that would doom our planet.

"My territory, Austriaca, was out in front of the climate crisis. We began building underground shelters and digging deep for water reserves. The Triad sits on the largest water reserve on the planet, that made Austriaca the future target for many low-lying territories."

"Your territory?"

"Yes, my territory. The Triad sits on land that was formerly known as a country called Austriaca. My ancestors lived there.

"Austriaca, you say?"

Yes. Today, The Triad is all that's left of a once-proud nation and planet," answered Erik.

"On Earth, we have a country called Austria," revealed Carrick.

Erik smiled. "Well, now you know where the name likely came from. It makes me happy that Zenithians paid homage to our once proud civilization."

Erik went back to his story; sadness once more painted his face. "Many island populations, near the center ring of Zenith, had to flee because of rising sea-levels. Other countries ran out of fresh water when lake beds and rivers went dry. This mass migration into neighboring territories caused conflicts throughout the mid-latitudes of our planet. In Zenith's entire history, prior to the drought and rising temperatures, there had never been global, national, or even regional conflicts."

"At first, local skirmishes were ignored in regions where the land elevation was high, and water was abundant. These nations just pretended that the problem didn't concern them. Leaders shielded the public from the truth by controlling the information reported by communication entities."

Carrick was listening to a familiar story but didn't want to interrupt.

"It was at this time that regional governments secretly began building and amassing armaments. Satellites were launched into orbit that had atomic energy weapons capabilities. Some even had massive lasers that could take out power supplies over large landmasses and population centers. Within just a thousand years," Erik said, "territories formed into countries, and those countries created and maintained borders. It was those very borders that spelled the beginning of the end for Zenith."

"Why?" asked Carrick, "Why were borders the beginning of the end?"

"Once you have borders, you're essentially telling people to stay out. This then leads to racial segregation because if you're native to a geographic region, you want people who aren't to stay away. With less interaction from different races, you begin to feel more comfortable with your own kind. And before you know it, you have nationalism. The divides grow greater, and the seeds of hatred are sown."

Carrick found the narrative hard to believe. "But Zenith would have been so advanced," he countered. "With no borders for thousands of years, the populations would have basically mixed, and the gene pools would have merged nearly into one."

"Our planet was a utopia," Erik agreed. "Everyone lived harmoniously for eons. And then it changed, in practically the blink of Zenith's eye."

Carrick perked up. "What changed?"

"Are you familiar with tribalism?" he asked.

Carrick sat down on a seat nearby. "Sure," he answered. "Tribalism is loyalty to your own kind. Although we also use the term on Earth to describe people with shared interests. Kind of like birds of a feather..," he trailed off.

"Birds of a what?" asked Erik.

"Nothing. Please continue," Carrick gestured for Erik to go on.

"New words began to enter our language. Like homophily. Heard of it?"

Carrick shook his head. No.

"It's the human tendency to form friendship networks with people of similar occupations, interests, and habits," explained Erik. "Some tribes would be located in geographically proximate areas, like cities or regions. However, as technology advanced, platforms like telecommunication networks enabled groups of people to form using digital tools, like social networking. My guess is that you've witnessed this on Earth to a lesser degree?" suggested Erik.

Carrick nodded soberly.

"Tribalism also implies the possession of a strong cultural or ethnic identity that separates one member of a group from the members of another group. Based on strong relations of proximity and kinship, members of a tribe tend to possess a strong feeling of identity that usually creates a negative opinion of other tribes. Intense feelings of common identity usually lead people to feel tribally connected," explained Erik.

"As Zenith advanced, so did the ability to communicate to the masses; it was called The Social Convey."

"Social media," Carrick whispered to himself.

Erik stated that the ability to communicate with anyone, anywhere, instantly caused people to become more and more curious about people, cultures, and places.

"The age of The Social Convey led to the rapid change of how people viewed themselves and others, and this ultimately led to a reversal in the development of the human psyche."

"People's minds began to de-evolve as critical messaging was replaced with unimportant mass communication. This form of information was designed to numb the mind and cause it to fall into a state of compliance. People no longer valued their own thoughts and instead placed higher importance on what others thought. The masses were shepherded by powerful, corrupt intellectuals who were motivated by self-interest rather than the good of humankind. Ordinary people began to feel small and insignificant, and this insecurity caused people to withdraw. They began judging others, classifying everyone else in terms of social standing, wealth, health, lineage, and race."

Carrick couldn't believe the parallels between Zenith and Earth. He sat in silence as Erik went on.

"Zenith's population centers were wildly diverse for centuries. But when global warming started, along with the degradation of our natural resources, there was a great change. For the first time in our recorded history, Zenithians began to see the differences in each other as opposed to the commonalities that had made our global society great. This, coupled with several decades of The Social Convey, led to the first signs of racial intolerance and, ultimately, segregation."

"When did all of this happen?" asked Carrick.

"The tribal instincts of humans first began to show around nine-thousand years ago," replied Erik. "Over the span of just one century, Zenithians began gravitating back to the regions of their ancestral roots and origins. Around one-thousand years before The Triad was built, and around a thousand years after the first shuttles left for Home, a new ideology took over the fragile democracies that once ruled our world."

"It was the birth of a very dangerous political movement called *The Segregationist Party*. Their ideology was based solely on intolerances of the most obvious physical differences between humans: skin color, hair, and eye color, as well as ancestral and geographic origins."

Erik's anger was evident in his clenched fists as he recounted this period in his planet's history.

"The Segregationist Party began to control mass communication networks and took over The Social Convey, which had already softened the minds of the masses. This was the entry vehicle needed for the pervasion of the human psyche. The Segregationist Parties hi-jacked critical thinking through a barrage of false narratives and destructive propaganda. This went on for decades until the damage was irreversible. Zenithians began to retreat to their corners of the world and would not come out again until the last of The Triad's population was forced to integrate."

"So, you're saying that Zenithians instinctively reverted to their ancestral corners?" asked Carrick.

"It didn't happen overnight, but that's exactly what they did!" answered Erik.

Carrick looked profoundly concerned. It was a tale that felt horrifyingly familiar. Erik, though, had more to say.

"From that point on, barriers grew taller and deeper, both physically and psychologically. Within three or four generations, there was no turning back. It was the beginning of the end."

"In fact, the populations of Zenith began to revolt against the pilgrimage to Earth. Unless they could be divided into separate geographical locations on the new planet, they would simply refuse to go. The three central race classifications were Caucasoid, Negroid, and Mongoloid. Because of the tribal friction, they began their segregation on Zenith a thousand years after the first pilgrimage to Home. Sorry, I mean Earth, as you call it." Erik gave Carrick a faint smile.

"Couldn't they just say they didn't want to go Home?" Carrick wanted to know.

"That was not an option our leaders gave us. You have to remember that we were fighting to save the human race from extinction. Concessions were made, however, and a referendum was held on the plan to segregate the races. The majority voted to segregate." "So, the separation of races began on Zenith. Back then, the GSA, or *The Global Survival Authority*, was in control of The Triad. It had initially been conceived as *The Succession*, but the plans changed after the vote to segregate. Instead, The Triad was built with three sectors of equal size, one for each race. Three-mile-long conduits connected each of the sectors so the races could stay far apart."

"The Succession?" queried Carrick.

"In due time."

Erik continued. "The Triad was completed a little more than four thousand years ago. Then the three sections of The Triad were evenly populated with 120,000 people from each of the three races, 360,000 people in total. Those left outside The Triad would eventually perish over the next one hundred years, at the hands of Zenith's harsh atmosphere and world war."

"The three sections were simply known as the Northwest, Southwest, and Southeast Sectors. We're currently standing in the northwest corner of the Northwest Sector. All three sectors were finally vacated when the last shuttle left for your planet seventy-five years ago."

Carrick shook his head in astonishment, thinking back to the moment he and Kinzi realized that the last shuttle had arrived on Earth in 1947.

"That's when the remaining population of Zenith was relocated to Earth. The remaining population, with the exception of one, me." Erik's face went dormant.

After a moment to himself, he went on. "The Triad segregation would be replicated on Earth, with the three main geographic migration locations resembling the sectors of The Triad."

Struck by curiosity, Carrick asked, "Can you display a map of the Earth on that thing?" He pointed at the holographic island.

Erik entered a few keystrokes on a flat, translucent touchpad, and then a transparent, rotating hologram of the Earth instantly rose from the platform.

"Cool!" pronounced Carrick. He jumped up and asked Erik how to stop it from rotating.

"Just touch it," said Erik.

Carrick nervously extended his right arm and, with a single finger, cause the rotating Earth to stop. When it did, he exuded a release of uneasy tension.

Carrick asked Erik to point to the three geographic locations that the shuttle transported the three Zenithian races to. His face now wreaked of curiosity. Given what Erik had said about The Triad segregation, the places Erik indicated came as no surprise to Carrick.

The first migrant drop he pointed to was on the African continent.

"Let me guess," Carrick said. "The Negroid population was relocated there?"

"That's correct."

Next, Erik rotated the holographic image of the Earth slightly to reveal Southeast Asia.

"Mongoloid?" asked Carrick.

Erik nodded in the affirmative.

Spinning the hologram a final time, Erik indicated Northwestern Europe.

"Caucasoid?" Carrick spoke almost to himself. This visual triangular image would stick with him.

The most obvious question of all suddenly struck Carrick. "Why were you left behind?"

Erik sighed. "In due time, I will answer that question. In due time young man."

Chapter 14 – The Liaison Network

Location: Black Earth. Northwest Sector of The Triad, Barrack 5, Sub-Level 7 – April 15, 2022. Early morning hours.

Carrick had been on Zenith for twenty-two days, and he was feeling a little closed in. Erik could see that he wasn't himself, so, at breakfast, he asked him if he was ready for another history lesson.

"I'm bored! Carrick moaned. "I want a tour of The Triad."

"I'll make you a deal," Erik bargained. "If you sit through another day of history lessons, I will take you on a tour tomorrow. I must warn you, though, it will take several days to show you all the things you need to see."

Carrick immediately looked more upbeat. "That's a deal! I'm going to hold you to it!"

Sitting in The History Library, the two embarked on a history lesson that would explain to Carrick the impact climate change had on Zenith. He would learn what ultimately forced the population to flee the planet for good. But first, Carrick had a question.

"Erik, I've been meaning to ask you something that has confounded scientists back on Earth since we first discovered Zenith."

"By all means. Let's get your question answered, young man."

"On Earth, we've been searching the Universe for as long as we've been curious about life, our origins, alien lifeforms, you name it. Along the way, we developed technology to help us see deeper into the Cosmos. The vast majority of our telescopes are on Earth, but we also have hundreds of highly technical telescopes orbiting the planet. And there are many more exploring the Universe on unmanned spacecraft."

"Okay, so what's your question?"

"Infrared heat signatures?" inquired Carrick. "Does that mean anything to you?"

"Ahh, yes! I was wondering when you were going to get around to asking me about that," said Erik, with a smile.

"How'd you do it? How in the hell did you hide the heat signature of a planet the size of Zenith for thousands of years?"

"Pretty cool, huh?" Erik replied.

"Well, you gonna tell me?"

"Infrablue," Erik boasted.

"Infra...what?" asked Carrick, shaking his head with curiosity.

"In simple terms, Infrablue technology masks the heat being radiated from the surface of Zenith."

"That's amazing, but how did you actually implement the technology?"

"Let me show you how it all works," offered Erik.

On the image island, Erik pulled up a hologram of Zenith. It was big, easily eight feet by eight feet in Carrick's estimation. A little larger than the holographic image of Earth Erik had shown Carrick a few weeks earlier.

"So, what are we looking at here?" asked Carrick.

"You see all the white dots on and around the planet?"

Carrick looked closer to see where Erik was pointing. "Those are satellites!"

"That's a lot of satellites!" commented Carrick. "I can't believe we didn't hit one on the way in."

"That would never happen. They are all equipped with anti-collision technology."

"Nice!"

"Now, watch this!" Erik hit a button on the floating keypad, and the results took Carrick's breath away. Before his eyes, a thin blue line connected every satellite with every other satellite within its line-of-sight. It looked like a giant blue spider's web wrapped around Zenith.

"My God, that's incredible! A company on Earth is developing something similar right now," said Carrick. "It's called Starlink; it'll be used for telecommunications. It's still in the early stages, though. It'll be years before it's actually functional."

"This system is called The Spectral Web, and it's about two-hundred-years-old."

Mesmerized by the blue web, Carrick asked, "So how exactly does it work?"

"All of the blue lines that you see emit a cold signature, which counters the heat signature coming from Zenith. The blue lasers essentially cloak the surface heat and make Zenith invisible to Earth."

"But why would it need to be invisible to Earth? We wouldn't have been a threat to Zenith; not now, not then."

"Carrick, I think you're being a bit naïve," countered Erik. "We were smart enough to understand that at some point, some of the migrants who went Home might want to find out where Zenith was, and not for any honorable reasons. What if corrupt Zenithian factions on Earth wanted to expose Zenith and its Liaisons to the rest of the world? What if they decided to return to Zenith to pillage our resources, secrets, and data?"

"What's a Liaison?" asked a puzzled-looking Carrick.

"A Liaison is a person on Earth that helps migrating Zenithians assimilate upon their arrival."

"Gotcha." Carrick attempted to process Erik's words.

"But why? Why would Zenithians want to expose Liaisons or any of Zenith's secrets?" he asked Erik, not completely understanding.

"There is information here in The History Library that could greatly benefit Earth, but also do it great harm," said Erik. "Not all Zenithians were good people, Carrick. We suspected that if they were corrupt on Zenith, then they would be even more corrupt on Earth. Zenith's technology could be a precious commodity on Earth. A migrant could acquire great wealth by selling it. And don't forget about the shuttle manifests. They contain passenger names, and the details of location drops. Information like that could help a former Zenithian find another migrant. They might seek retribution against someone who opposed them politically or rivaled them in social standing or wealth, both here on Zenith or Home."

"Retribution? That just doesn't make any sense to me," said Carrick.

"This all seems a little far-fetched. To suggest that these manifests were some kind of NOC lists seems a bit crazy."

"What's a NOC list?" asked Erik, looking curious.

"It's a list of agents or spies: N.O.C. meaning Non-Official Cover. I'm going to need you to tell me what all of this means. What's going on here?" asked a now concerned Carrick.

"Okay, here we go!" said Erik. "Carrick, I can't imagine they still exist, but it's likely..."

Erik was cut off by Carrick's demand. "Get to the point!"

"Bear with me, son," Erik raised his hands, motioning surrender. "We have, or at least we had, a secret organization on Earth that was filled with Zenithian patriots. They helped migrants to assimilate on Earth. We called them Liaisons."

"When a migration shuttle date was announced, there were celebrations on Zenith because thousands were going Home. On Earth, however, I have to imagine that it was a busy and confusing time. Liaisons would've been preparing to receive the incoming migrants. Tens of thousands of migrants would be dropped off at thousands of locations around your globe. Each migrant needed a home to live in, not to mention a backstory on Earth that didn't previously exist. That wouldn't have been an easy feat. It would have meant the fabrication of birth certificates, medical and educational records, detailed family, and professional histories."

"Sponsor families had to be organized in order to host the migrants until they were assimilated into society. These sponsors were first or second-generation Zenithians or sympathizers of the migration cause."

"That's unbelievable! How was it even possible to coordinate something so complex?"

"We had an entire department in The Triad dedicated to the effort. More than one-thousand Raconteurs worked on the Liaison Program. Remember, except for the last five shuttles, migrations happened anywhere between fifty and one hundred and fifty years apart."

"Hang on! A Racon....what?" Carrick shook his head side to side as the whole concept was extremely confusing.

"So sorry, Carrick. Please forgive me. Raconteurs were story-tellers. Every migrant needed a story, and our Raconteurs had thousands of stories cataloged, and they worked full-time daily to create more."

"Geez!" said Carrick, as his head figuratively spun.

"Now, as I was saying. The Liaison Network worked to ensure everyone had at least two sets of backstories and that those could be woven into the stories of past migrants. It was all very complicated. Layers of data and information were incorporated into each story."

"So, past migrants knew who was coming to Earth and when?" asked Carrick.

"No, not until a few days before the shuttle was due to drop off its human cargo. Only the secret Liaison Network on Home knew, and then the preparations began."

"Wow!" Carrick was definitely no longer bored. He couldn't quite believe what he was hearing, yet it sounded faintly familiar.

"For centuries, people on Earth have speculated that societies of powerful individuals secretly control the world. I always thought those were just conspiracy theories." Carrick pondered the notion that those paranoid myths might actually be real. He was having a hard time wrapping his head around the thought that this might be true.

He wondered aloud, "How would you even pull something like that off? How could a secret like that stay secret? Thousands, if not millions, would have known."

"As I mentioned," Erik replied. "The Liaisons were global patriots. The screening process to become one didn't take months; it took years. The Liaisons had to be entirely trustworthy, as they held all of Zenith's secrets on Home. It was their responsibility to help people adapt to life on Home. And...," he paused momentarily, "the Liaisons were entrusted with the task of making sure our recent migrants would ascend social, economic, and political ladders."

"You're telling me that first-generation Zenithians held high political offices on Earth?" Carrick never thought he had the capacity to be shocked by anything new, but this stunned him. He was now on his feet, walking erratically back and forth, almost not believing any of what he was hearing.

"Yes. The goal was that our people would hold leadership positions in corporate, social, and political settings," Erik leaned in, feeling he needed to justify himself. "We had to make sure contemporary migrants held some power. That was the only way to make sure future Zenithian migrants could secretly make it Home without incident. And you have to understand; forged documents were necessary to ensure professional and educational backgrounds could be validated. To do this, we needed important figures in governmental and educational institutions in every country and region on your planet."

"Who? Who were these people? What you're suggesting is that these secret societies do, in fact, exist. That sounds preposterous!"

"Preposterous?" Erik asked. "Look around you, Carrick! The entire planet of Zenith was unnoticed by Earth for eons. Yet, you don't believe it's possible Zenithians went unnoticed for just a few centuries? Again, I think you're being naïve."

Erik's softened his tone. "Listen, Son, I don't know who these people were; that sort of information was way above my clearance level. The officials on the shuttle were the only ones in contact with the Liaisons on Home. I was merely given longitude and latitude; I was never in contact with them and was never privy to who they were. Even if I had been, I wouldn't tell you," Erik tried to raise a smile out of an unsmiling Carrick. "You could be one of the bad guys," he winked.

"You're a funny man!" Carrick unwillingly cracked a smile.

"Carrick, listen, I was just the remote shuttle pilot. Only Zenithian government officials knew all of the details. And anyway, the communication network between Zenith and the Liaisons was dismantled decades ago. After the last shuttle was announced and the relevant information was transmitted to Earth, it wasn't needed anymore. My guess is they're either all dead by now or too old to make a difference."

"The original Zenithians might be dead," Carrick agreed, "but the secret societies could still exist, even though Liaisons are no longer needed. The good and the bad elements of Zenithian society could still be coordinating their efforts."

"Anything is possible! Look at the two of us, just sitting here talking to each other! Five years ago, you wouldn't have thought you'd be here with me right now," smiled Erik.

"You're right. Five years ago, I was only halfway through the astronaut training program, not even sure I'd succeed," Carrick said, more humbly. "No way I thought I'd be on a black planet, seventy-five million miles from home."

Erik, on the other hand, had always thought it was possible. He'd always dreamed that a day just like this one would happen. Lost in thought, the old man watched the holographic image of Zenith rotating on the platform. Carrick gave his questions a rest for a while. He got up and took a closer look at the satellite web around the planet. Eventually, he broke the silence.

"How did Earth communicate with Zenith, Erik? I mean, communication technology wasn't very advanced on Earth until long after the last shuttle came."

Erik was stirred from his trance. "For many years, we used the transmitters from downed shuttles that never made it back to Zenith; there were several over the millennia. Short wave radio transmissions were used later, from around one hundred and thirty-five years ago.

"Listen, I'm not an expert, but wouldn't radio waves get bounced back down to Earth by the particles in the atmosphere?" said Carrick, casting some doubt.

"You are smart, Carrick!" an impressed-looking Erik conceded. "Yes, but if the receiver, both on Zenith and the Migration Shuttle, was sensitive enough, which they were, the signals could be detected."

Carrick just shook his head. He continued to be shocked by Zenith's advanced communication abilities.

"In fact, The son of one of our Liaison's, Heinrich Hertz, who was actually born on Zenith and migrated Home when he was just a small child. He was the first person on Earth to discover the science of electromagnetic radio waves. That was already an ancient technology on Zenith, but it was new to Earth. So, radio could then be used to send signals to Zenith after years of no communication between the two planets. That was due in part to the downed shuttles eventually going dark. After that, another former Zenithian, Guglielmo Marconi, continued the efforts to communicate with Zenith by inventing long-distance radio transmissions."

"After that, we got busy with the rapid succession of migrant shuttle missions. The last five happened in just sixty-one years. The fear was that with advanced technology budding on Earth, we might be discovered by scientists who knew nothing of Zenith." Erik paused to contemplate the slowly spinning globe before them.

"It was at this time that the remaining scientists, engineers, doctors, and government officials from Zenith migrated to Earth."

Carrick was still confused. "So, if the Liaisons could be trusted, why was Zenith so paranoid about their secret getting out?"

"As I told you, we were acutely aware that not all of our people had the best intentions. They might someday want to advance their own cause on Earth by exploiting Zenith and all of its riches. We simply couldn't risk it, and precautions were taken."

"Do you really believe former Zenithians would have exposed the secret?"

"Carrick, we sent all of our people; only I was left behind. For thousands of years, Zenithians, with both good and bad intentions, were sent Home. We knew that great societies would emerge, and integrating the best that Zenith had to offer while appealing to some, might threaten others in the hierarchy of those societies. Once we became aware that Earth was advancing to the point where Zenith could possibly be discovered, we had to become undiscoverable."

Carrick shook his head in awe at the great secret that had been kept for thousands of years. It was hard to contemplate. "Why wouldn't the corrupt few just reveal that Zenith existed? Reveal all of the information and technology wealth that Zenith had to offer?" he wondered aloud.

"Those are questions that I cannot answer," responded Erik. "It would have been assumed that not all those migrating from Zenith would be welcomed by the masses, particularly those in power on Home. We were careful to limit the information regarding dates and locations of future migration shuttle missions; only those on the manifest that could truly be trusted were privy."

"Why share that information at all?" Carrick wondered aloud. "Someone had to be aware that a shuttle would arrive at a certain geographic location on a designated date. That was the only way the migrants could be met and welcomed by the Liaisons on Home."

"I have so many questions," Carrick smiled. "But for now, just tell me one more thing about the Liaisons. If this information was secret and above your clearance level, how do you know about migrants like Hertz and Marconi."

"With the flurry of shuttles going Home in the final years, Remote Shuttle Pilots heard things they probably shouldn't have."

He then smiled and added, "You don't spend seventy-five years alone in The Triad, with its immense library at your fingertips, without uncovering a juicy fact or two about the people who migrated long ago," he said, with only mild hubris.

Carrick grinned and tapped his nose conspiratorially. "Well, I promise not to tell anyone back on Earth that you opened the doors to The History Library to me." He stood and looked around at all the monitors stretching across the library. He knew that the story Erik was sharing with him was an enormous gift. He turned back to Erik and asked, "Why are you telling me all of Zenith's secrets, anyway?"

Erik exhaled heavily. "I will be dead soon, and The Triad will go dark soon after that. If I don't share this information with you now, then it dies with me. I simply don't want that to happen. I trust you, son."

"I trust you too!" said Carrick.

Chapter 15 – Black Rain

Location: Black Earth. Northwest Sector of The Triad, The History Library – April 15, 2022. Late afternoon.

As the two men continued to sit and talk, Carrick told Erik that Zenith and Earth's story seemed almost too fantastic to believe.

At that, Erik laughed. "You recently traveled seventy-five million miles and walked through the front door of The Triad. And just before I faded into oblivion. Now that, I find hard to believe!"

Carrick laughed. "I have so many more questions I'd like to ask, but what else did you want to show me before my tour tomorrow?" Erik turned back to his floating keyboard. "Let me show you something that will explain why we're both sitting here today. I think you'll better understand how all of this came to be." He tapped a few buttons, and another image of Zenith appeared, this time without the satellite web.

The hologram was impressive. "It's beautiful!" Carrick exclaimed, walking around the platform to get a better look. "It almost looks like Earth; only the continents are different shapes and sizes. It even has polar ice caps!"

"This is Zenith, seven-thousand years ago," Erik said. "This is just before we began to understand the effects that pillaging a planet for many millennia would have."

Erik swiped upward into thin air, and a holographic slider appeared. Swiping left to right slightly on the slider, he moved forward through Zenith's history. "Now, this is Zenith, six-thousand five hundred years ago. Do you see any difference?"
Carrick's eyes widened. "Please tell me those are rain clouds?" he asked, knowing that they couldn't be.

In parts per million, Erik explained that the carbon dioxide levels went from 350 to 2320 in a mere five-hundred-year period. Carrick knew that such high carbon dioxide levels would be extremely harmful to humans and most other lifeforms.

"That's when health issues began to be noticed," Erik stated.
"No, kidding!" agreed Carrick.

"It started with headaches and insomnia, and then people started becoming lethargic and nauseous. It was at this time that space travel and exploration became more accelerated and advanced. Before this point in our history, we had only launched satellites into orbit, and most of them were unmanned. Zenith has no moons to explore, so we had to search farther afield. Within proximity, Earth was the only planet we knew of that was suitable for life. We got lucky! Earth and Zenith are on the same ecliptic plane revolving around the Sun, and Zenith trails Earth by only seventy-six million miles."

"We knew living there would be hard on Zenithians initially due to the pollinated atmosphere versus The Triad's pristine air quality. It was estimated that life expectancy would be cut roughly in half. But, regardless of that, we had to start considering migrating there."

"Wait a second!" Carrick interrupted. "Did you say seventy-six million miles?"

"Yes, as of six-thousand years ago, Zenith trailed Earth by seventy-six million miles."

"Wow! Our trip here was only seventy-five million miles. That means..."

"Yes, I do recall you telling me that shortly after your arrival. Are you certain of the distance?" Erik recognized the discrepancy.

"That's a silly question! Yes, I'm sure!" said a mildly offended Carrick. "Why?"

"Uh-Oh!" Erik let out a mild gasp.

Carrick's face went white. "Holy shit! We're on a collision course!"

"If the calculations are correct, it would appear so. But do the math, Carrick. Impact wouldn't occur for another 450,000 years," assuaged Erik. "I think we'll be okay," adding a smile.

"Yeah, but still...," said Carrick, unable to finish his thought.

"Okay, Carrick, let's not get distracted," Erik called Carrick's attention back to the globe in front of them.

"On Zenith, before the population was forced indoors, the average life expectancy was one hundred and five years. On Earth, it would be about fifty. As it turned out, the first Zenithian migrants died out within twenty years. At that point, we had to re-calculate and send manned shuttles to Earth for air and soil quality testing. It would be another three hundred-fifty years before the second migration shuttle went back. This time, the migrant population was still detected in the areas where they were dropped off for as many as one hundred years after arriving on your planet. There was a problem, though; it didn't appear that they were flourishing. Almost no infrastructure or population growth could be detected."

"I'm confused, Carrick challenged. "With all the advances on Zenith, why didn't you just bring the necessary tools, equipment, and technology with you. You left those people there to die. Explain that one to me!" he demanded.

"Okay," said Erik. "This won't be easy to rationalize, but there was a very good reason. We knew our population needed to relocate to survive. So, we educated the migrants about the living conditions on Earth and taught them to accept life on Earth without any of the comforts of Zenith. We ensured that the relocated population would never refer to Zenith again. We needed to make sure they understood that what they were leaving behind was a dead planet and that they should never consider coming back."

"Why?" demanded Carrick.

Erik sighed. "The first migrants were selected from parts of our population that were less educated, less sophisticated, and therefore less able to find their way back to Zenith."

"Guinea Pigs?" whispered Carrick.

"We knew that if we sent our best and our brightest, within several hundred years, they would have the ability to come back," Erik protested. "Zenith was heading straight into a world war that would devastate the planet. It was about to become even less inhabitable! We needed our people to look forward, not back."

"I do admit, though, it was almost brainwashing, what we did. Kind of like Earthlings forcing religious beliefs on their masses," he smiled slyly at Carrick. "But it was necessary so that they would never want to return to Zenith or ever have the ability to do so. We needed the human race to start from scratch; live off the land, so to speak. "The indoctrination started at birth; all that people ever heard was that they were going Home. The educational curriculum was focused only on Earth and how to survive there, after their migration."

"So, the migrants knew about Earth's history?"

"No, they were only educated about things like the atmospheric conditions and how to survive."

Carrick found that rather mystifying.

Erik continued, "It was clear though, that once a Shuttle took them Home, there was no looking back. The only communication back would be through the Liaison Network."

"Oh, I see. It wasn't even possible for those migrating Home to know the history of Earth?" Carrick asked rhetorically, his curiosity satisfied. Erik nodded. "That's why entire family structures would travel Home together. There was no looking back, no communication in either direction, except for when a migration shuttle was announced to the Liaisons."

"As they grew up, Home, or Earth for you, became their Heaven, so to speak. They looked up at the sky and imagined being there. They actually wanted to go. The difference is that your planet Earth was a real place and not an imaginary one, like God or Heaven. Zenithians could actually schedule time in the Astronomical Research Observatory. There, through powerful telescopes, they could actually see Earth.

"That's amazing!" Carrick was incredibly excited about this revelation. "I want to see Earth! I bet it looks amazing from this distance!" He sat, looking like a kid at Christmas."

"Over here, son!" Erik tried to regain Carrick's attention by snapping his fingers in his face.

Carrick snapped out of it and was all ears.

"Home would be a place where they could live in peace and breathe in clean air, without ever having to face war or climate change again."

Carrick looked grim. "You do realize that that was a death sentence for your people?"

"You mean 'our' people," Erik said, "we're all humans!" He slid the timescale another five hundred years forward and pointed at the globe. "Now that's a death sentence."

"Watch this," said Erik. He touched a button on the holographic slider, and a surface temperature layer was revealed on the hologram.

What Carrick was looking at now was a poisonous atmosphere, with clouds that were nearly black. The readings indicated surface temperatures had gone from an average of 72°F to 92°F. Around the mid-latitudes, they topped out at 120°F Zenith's surface went from looking similar to Earth's to something far less recognizable.

Erik pointed to the top and bottom of the translucent globe. "The polar ice caps were completely gone by this time, for hundreds of years, black, microscopic pollution particles accumulated on the densely packed ice. The caps began to absorb the Sun's heat rather than reflect it, which caused a rapid melt-off. Rising sea-levels then swallowed up the mid-latitude island chains. They simply vanished beneath the oceans. Continents shrank, and coastal populations were forced inland. This created over-population in the areas that were nearest to freshwater lakes and rivers." Passion took over Erik's voice as he highlighted the doomed areas on the holographic globe. "The people we were shuttling to Earth would live far longer, even with no tools, no technology, none of the comforts of Zenith."

There was an urgency to Erik's commentary now. He played out more readings on the globe, showing the CO2 levels reaching 5000 parts per million. He explained that as CO2 concentrations rose, the other gases in the atmosphere were altered. Breathing became increasingly difficult. Plant and insect life began to die off rapidly. Over the next several hundred years, vegetation became scarce. Thousands of species went extinct as atmospheric oxygen levels plummeted.

"It was at this point that the GSA, or Global Survival Authority, was created. It was comprised of one representative from each country," explained Erik. "The GSA secretly prepared for more regular and rapid transfers of people to Home. On Zenith, plans were laid to build more indoor housing facilities. These complexes would be placed near freshwater sources where possible."

Erik moved the slider a little farther to the right, and, to Carrick's horror, nuclear holocaust played out across the globe. The atmosphere was now filled with radiation, carbonites, volcanic ash, even higher levels of CO2, and moisture from the evaporating oceans. Black rain began to fall and coat the planet.

"The surface became darker and darker and subsequently absorbed more of the Sun's heat. Rising oceans and expanding surface layers caused tectonic plates to shift, and volcanic fury was unleashed on Zenith. In turn, the volcanos released ash and toxic vapor into the air, enough to shorten our days to just a few hours of sunlight. The air became even more toxic, and surviving outdoors was now impossible without some sort of breathing apparatus. A death sentence, huh?" asked Erik, turning to see Carrick's stunned face.

"By this time, human beings on Earth were starting to thrive. Our imaging from returning shuttles illustrated to us that many civilizations were proliferating, with likely none thinking or even knowing about life on Zenith. This period in our history became known as the Vacation Era."

Carrick raised his brows in an 'ah-ha' moment.

"Zenithians never spoke again of what they left behind and would never desire to go back. They would assimilate with existing Earth populations, and by this time, the intelligence levels of relocating populations were greater. One would assume at this time that Earth was beginning to evolve more." surmised Erik.

"Let's test your theory, Erik," challenged Carrick. "Where would a shuttle have dropped off migrants during the period you're referring to? Give me longitude and latitude. And a timeframe."

Erik turned to his keypad and brought up a hologram of Earth. He entered some information and, almost immediately, a beacon appeared on the image. Its coordinates were longitude 31.270695° and latitude 29.533438°.

As Carrick looked closer, his eyes widened, and he shouted, "I'll be damned! Ancient EGYPT!" The year was roughly 3000 BC or about 5100 Earth years ago.

Later that night, the two laid in their separate bunks. Carrick was exhausted from the day's revelations. Before closing his eyes, he wanted to ask one more thing.

"Erik, earlier today, we discussed some of the secrets that Zenith possesses. I have just one more question for you."

"What is it, son?"

"Have you ever heard of the term cancer? It is a disease caused by the uncontrolled growth of abnormal cells in the human body."

"Nope! Never heard of the term or of the condition," answered Erik, before closing his eyes and turning to go to sleep.

Carrick thought to himself, "I bet the cure for many diseases, and even cancer, is buried in The History Library."

Chapter 16 – Carrick

Location: Black Earth. The Triad. Sub-Level 7, Barrack 5 – April 16, 2022. Early morning hours.

Carrick woke up a little early in anticipation of his big day; Erik would be giving him a tour of The Triad. Not wanting to wake his new friend, he just laid in his bunk thinking about his girlfriend, Lola Cook. It was less than a year since he and Lola had been out ring shopping. Everyone, especially Lola, was anxiously waiting for Carrick to pop the big question. Carrick seemed to be having cold feet, though.

The two first met while they were studying at Cornell University. They'd now been dating for more than six years and were both in their early thirties. Both families thought it was time for Carrick to ask her to marry him, and they were beginning to grow impatient. Lola, in particular, couldn't understand why he hadn't proposed yet. She never questioned his love for her and never thought for a moment that he was the cheating type. So, what was the hold-up?

Not even Carrick knew the answer to that question, and now he was seventy-five million miles away from making that decision. Maybe, he speculated, that was the real reason he stayed behind on Black Earth.

Being a scientist and an astronaut kept Carrick busy and away from home a lot. Even when he spent a year on the International Space Station, followed almost immediately by two additional six-month stints, his absence had been manageable for Lola. After all, it was in the name of science and service to the international community. But Carrick knew that his decision to remain on Black Earth was incredibly self-serving. He was still sorting through what motivated him to stay behind.

Lola managed her own expectations since life was hectic for her too. She was wrapping up Med school, and, after that, she'd be moving onto a twelve-month internship at NYP – Weill Cornell Medical Center in New York City. Blaming their busy schedules for his lack of commitment was just an excuse for Carrick. He simply wasn't ready to take the plunge. Something in his life was missing, and he had to find it. The problem for Carrick was that he didn't know what it was.

Lying in his bunk, it dawned on Carrick that Lola was nearly finished with school and that he wouldn't be there for her graduation in the fall. Fast on the heels of this thought, it occurred to him that Lola had no idea if he was okay or even if he was alive. Her sadness must be unbearable, he thought. In a moment of panic, Carrick suddenly realized his decision to stay behind on a planet seventy-five million miles from home might be the proverbial straw that broke the back of their relationship.

Both of them would be turning thirty-two in December, and unless NASA got back to Black Earth by August, he would also miss her birthday. Yep, he's sure of it! She'd never wait for him. Not this time, not after this stunt.

As Carrick thought more about what he had done, he began to realize that staying behind, without any forethought, was both a foolish and selfish act. He doubted many people would be able to forgive him. He could almost picture his mother Maggie, at home on Earth, worried sick about her only son.

Maggie Michaels became a single mother before Carrick was even born. His father, Michael Erickson Michaels, a Lieutenant in the U.S. Navy, had been killed in 1990 while conducting a Naval training exercise near Guam. Michaels was out on an aerial maneuver, which would consist of a 'touch and go' from an aircraft carrier when his plane experienced technical difficulties. The F-8 Crusader he was flying experienced full engine failure over the Western Pacific Ocean, about two-hundred and fifty miles south by southwest of Guam, south of the Mariana Island chain. A calm and collected Michaels had radioed in that he had to eject. He was still in radio contact when he reported that his canopy failed to open. That was the last time anyone would ever hear of him.

Michaels had ditched near the Mariana Trench, the deepest part of any ocean on Earth, at a depth of around 36,100 feet. Neither his plane nor his body were ever recovered. Salvaging, or even searching for the wreckage, would've been incredibly difficult due to the depth of that part of the ocean.

The accident happened on June 11, 1990, when Mike Michaels was only forty-two-years-old, and Carrick's mom, Maggie, was just thirty-two. They'd been married for just two years, and Maggie was three months pregnant with Carrick. She delivered her only child, Carrick, on December 12th. Maybe not having a father, or at least a father figure, was what Carrick had been missing for his entire life.

Carrick never knew his father, and his mother chose never to remarry. She never wanted her son to be confused about who his dad was. His father would always be Lieutenant Mike "The Hammer" Michaels, United States Navy Pilot; not some stand-in replacement dad. In his childhood home, his mom had placed framed pictures of his father all over the walls as a constant reminder of the father who couldn't be there in person.

As a child, each time Halloween came around, Carrick's mom would dress him up as a fighter pilot. Eventually, Carrick had grown tired of it. He would've rather dressed up like a football player or an astronaut instead. When he turned 16, his mom gave him one of his father's flight suits as a birthday present. More like a birthday past, thought Carrick. He'd tried it on only once, alone in his room. Looking at himself in the mirror, wearing his father's uniform, made him cry. He quickly took off the flight suit, put it back in the box, and never took it out again. He knew he was never going to fill his father's shoes or uniform, for that matter. He didn't plan on being his father's replacement, not in his mother's eyes, nor anyone else's.

Carrick knew from the age of ten that he wouldn't follow in his father's footsteps by going into the Navy, even though that would fulfill his mother's dream. With the Naval Academy calling, it would have been an easy, predictable choice. The Hammer had been a legend within the Naval ranks, and Carrick's future would have been assured if he'd followed his father's path. But that wasn't going to happen, and he damned sure wasn't going to be a pilot either. He'd be a scientist instead, and maybe even an astronaut one day.

Carrick snapped out of his funk. Now sitting up in his bunk, he looked across the barrack and saw Erik sleeping soundly. He felt great empathy for the tired, old man. Erik had been alone on this dead planet for more than seventy-five years. The last significant memories he had were of watching his family and friends get on the final shuttle to Earth. How heartbreaking that must've been.

Feeling a little less sorry for himself, Carrick was beginning to see that he might have a purpose on Black Earth. Maybe he was here to fill the hole in Erik's heart. His mere presence would give the old man some companionship before he perished into the nothingness of this black island in space. It also occurred to Carrick that he would be leaving Black Earth inside of a year. What would become of Erik then? Surely there'd be other missions to the black planet, and Erik would have more company, but Carrick was growing fond of the old man and would miss him after he'd gone home.

About sixty-minutes later, after returning from The Culina, Carrick kicked the bunk that Erik was sleeping on and woke him up.

"Mind your foot, young man," Erik said sleepily. "Unless you want to lose it."

Carrick was enthusiastic. "Big day today! I finally get my tour of The Triad, after more than three weeks in this Godforsaken place."

"You know, for a non-believer, you sure do reference God a lot." He rubbed his eyes and got up from his bed.

"Figure of speech. Sorry," said Carrick, handing Erik a cup.

"What's this?"

"Well, it was supposed to be breakfast, lunch, and dinner in bed, but you had to go ahead and get up," said Carrick sarcastically.
Erik looked into the cup and looked back up at Carrick. With a stern face, he barked, "You can never bring food down here, EVER! Do you understand?"

Carrick swallowed hard, took a half step backward, then stuttered, "Ah, ah, I'm sorry! I, I didn't know...," He felt like a little deer in daddy's headlights.

Erik's angry expression dissolved, and then he laughed out loud. "Just messing with you, kid! Take it easy." He then raised his cup, took a swig, and said, "Red Fruit, Mm-mm, my favorite. Thanks, pal!"

Carrick tried to laugh it off, but his feelings were hurt. He muttered, "That wasn't funny, old man!" His emotions were still out of sorts from earlier in the morning when he thought of Lola.

"You want to hug it out and then grab a shower?" joked Erik.

Carrick rolled his eyes and said, "No, thanks!" He turned to walk away and began to snicker. Soon, both men were laughing uncontrollably. Once the laughter had died down, Carrick saw that the tears rolling down Erik's face weren't just from hilarity. He was genuinely crying.

"Everything okay, old man?"

"Yes." Wiping the tears away from his cheeks. "It's just...", he paused, "I haven't laughed like that in more than seventy-five years."

Carrick thought he was kidding again and busted his chops by saying, "You're going to need to pull up your big boy pants and get it together; we've got a big day scheduled today!"

"Roger that!" said Erik with gusto.

Chapter 17 – The Tour

Location: Black Earth. The Triad. Surface-Level 5, The Astronomical Research Observatory – April 16, 2022. Later that morning.

"I'm in heaven!" Carrick pronounced. He couldn't believe his eyes as he stared into the viewfinder of the most powerful and advanced telescope that he had ever seen. "I can't believe it! No observatory on Earth could ever lockdown a view like this of a planet so far away. I think I can see our Moon too!"

The visual captured by the mega-telescope revealed the blue marble of Carrick's distant world. An image every person on Earth has seen a million times. A tiny white dot could also be detected orbiting the blue marble. It took Carrick's breath away.

"I'm sorry I didn't tell you about it sooner. I feel terrible." Erik stood beside him, looking over his shoulder.

"Don't worry. Now that I know about it, though, I'm gonna want to come up here from time to time. I hope that's okay?" Carrick mentally crossed his fingers in hope.

"Of course!" said Erik, smiling in affirmation.

"I'll be honest, though. This will make my time away from Home much easier to bear."

"Was that little Home comment intended?" asked Erik, thinking that Carrick was on his game.

"Yeah, you know. I thought I'd throw you a little nod, as thanks for showing me this place."

Erik was impressed with Carrick and smiled. While Carrick stood busy staring at the Earth through the massive telescope's viewfinder, Erik flipped a switch, and each of, what totaled, thirty monitors lit up the room. Even Erik was impressed; it had been years since he'd been back to the observatory.

"You know, you can just look at it from these monitors, right?" Erik pointed across the room from where Carrick was standing. The expansive room was decked out with liquid-glass monitors of all sizes. The one Erik was pointing to was an incredibly high-resolution monitor that stood opposite of the telescope's viewfinder. The monitor was two-hundred inches across and seventy-five inches tall and captured an image of Earth that filled the screen. The other monitors captured Earth from varying distances. However, Carrick acted like a little kid when looking at the moon from Earth through his first-ever telescope.

"No, really, come over here, Carrick," encouraged Erik, motioning to the enormous monitor with his hand for the second time.

"No, this is more fun." Carrick's eye remained glued to the viewfinder.

"Carrick, come over here for a minute. I want to show you what this thing can do," insisted Erik for the third time, again motioning.

"Fine!" said the ten-year-old version of Carrick.

Carrick turned away from the view-finder to see what Erik had been asking him to look at.

"Holy shit! What's all this!" said the adult version of Carrick. Unable to control his emotions, after turning to see the room adorned with his home. Planet Earth illuminated the room in shades of blue, green, and white. For a brief moment, Carrick was transported home.

"Watch this!" Erik turned a dial, and the telescope zoomed in on a part of India.

"Wait! What!" exclaimed an excited Carrick, standing there in awe.

"You can get that close-up?!"

"Yes, sir!" nodded Erik with a smile. He knew that this would please his young friend.

"We have to come back here in twelve-hours; I want to show you where I live!" Carrick acted like a little boy the night before Christmas morning.

"I've looked through a lot of telescopes, but this is amazing. I'm seeing something no other human from Earth has ever seen from anywhere near this distance. The farthest used to be from our moon."

"Well, not exactly," Erik reminded him that, "Tens of thousands of Zenithians who migrated to Earth saw what you're seeing right now."

"You know what I mean!" clarified Carrick. "Any living human being, anyway."

At that moment, Erik's face was invaded by emptiness. He went white and became silent for a while; Carrick too absorbed to notice. After a few minutes of dead calm, Carrick pulled himself away from the massive monitor, thinking that Erik had left. Erik hadn't gone anywhere, though. Carrick observed the old man standing quietly in a shadow, just several feet away, staring into nothing.

"Erik, you okay?" Placing his empathetic hand on a withering shoulder, Carrick felt a creeping sense of guilt. He wasn't sure why, though.

The old man took a few deep breaths, and gradually the color began to seep back into his face. He motioned for Carrick to follow him. "C'mon, I want to show you something cool."

Location: Sub-Level 7.

After a thirty-minute walk, with almost no words, Erik opened the door to a room on Sub-Level 7. A plaque on the door read Survival Storage Unit. Erik led the way inside. The lights hadn't worked in decades, but Erik instinctively reached for the light switch anyway. When nothing happened, he switched on his headlamp and instructed Carrick to do the same. Carrick, looking a bit apprehensive, did likewise and followed close behind. The room was long and narrow, and the headlamps barely illuminated the back of it.

In the room were an assortment of items: uniforms, helmets, safety suits, equipment, and oxygen tanks.

"What is this place?" asked Carrick.

"This is where you go…," Erik paused for a moment before finishing, "when you've outlived The Triad."

"What the hell does that mean?"

"This is my life support system when everything just stops. The Triad is only meant to live for so long. For years it's been systematically shutting itself down in preparation for the end of its usefulness. The only reason it's alive now is because of me. It's designed to die shortly after I do. I'm almost one hundred and fifteen-years-old, after all. I know; I look good for my age," he bragged.

"Here on Zenith, once the population was forced indoors, we breathed clean air and ate only what our bodies actually needed. As a result, average life expectancy jumped from about ninety to around one hundred and twenty-five years, during a period of just one hundred years. Amazing what the human body can accomplish if you don't abuse it," Erik smiled crookedly.

"Wow, and wow! A life expectancy of one hundred and twenty-five years?" Carrick raised his eyebrows. "And you're one hundred and fourteen-years-old? Man, I'm sorry I called you old earlier. That's crazy! On Earth, we're lucky if we live to be eighty."

"The Triad is set to shut itself down in fifteen years or so. If I'm still alive then, it will shut me down too."

"Or so?" challenged Carrick.

"It could shut down sooner; it may go a little longer. There's no way to tell."

"Well, that's pretty scary," said Carrick.

Erik shrugged his shoulders, "I'm ready to go when it's ready to go."

At that moment, Carrick was reminded that Erik had lived a long time alone in this prison. He reasoned that he wasn't too motivated to live on forever.

Erik chimed in, "Just how bad are things on Earth? Please don't tell me that humankind is setting another planet on fire?"

Carrick's face didn't deny it; Erik's showed frustration. "Can't we ever learn from our own damned past mistakes? It's as if history doesn't count for anything. Humans just keep going down the same paths. Enough already! That's the reason I've been rotting alone on this planet with no one to talk to and no human interaction for all of these years!" sighed Erik, with a look of defeat on his face.

"Yeah, it's getting pretty bad. If we don't fix things in the next twenty-five to thirty years," he paused, "we may be headed for the same fate as Zenith."

"Temperatures soaring? Polar caps melting? Sea-levels rising? People starting to get nervous?" asked Erik.

Carrick acknowledged with a "Yes, yes, yes, and yes." His fingers checking imaginary boxes.

As Erik pondered the image of a doomed Earth, Carrick wandered around the room. He picked up one or two items and looked them over with interest. Finally, he turned back to Erik.

"What if you do outlive The Triad?"

Erik shrugged his shoulders. "Then, I come here."

"To do what?"

"To buy a little time before dying with it."

"But no matter how many tanks of oxygen there are, they wouldn't last you more than a few weeks, maybe a month," thought Carrick.

Erik picked up a small metal case and rotated it in his hands. "It's not running out of oxygen that I fear most; it's the heat. When this place loses power, the temperature will get up to 300°F in a matter of a few days. At that point. I'll have a few choices, and none of them are good. I can suffocate or die of heat exhaustion." He flipped the metal case up, and it landed neatly in his hand. "Or I can end it with this."

Erik opened the case and motioned to Carrick to look inside. Nestled in a close-fitting housing, Carrick saw a metal syringe with what appeared to be a CO_2 cartridge attached to it.

Carrick said, "That looks like the kiss of death."

Erik smiled half-heartedly. "Pure death in a syringe. We call it The Black Widow. "

Carrick shuddered. "You guys have those on Zenith, too?"

"Have what?" Erik didn't understand.

"Never mind!" Carrick asked, "Do you know what heat does to the human body?"

"Yes, I do, actually. But my guess is that, with you being a chemist, you're going to give me the long drawn out answer anyway, aren't you?" asked Erik.

"Yep!" said Carrick unapologetically. "Heat can kill you directly by inducing heatstroke and indirectly by causing damage to many of your vital organs like your brain and kidneys."

"The problems begin when your body has trouble keeping its core temperature close to 98.6°F," explained Carrick. "Basically, your nervous system tries to cool down your body every time its core rises a degree or two. It attempts to divert blood away from your organs and toward your skin. Blood carries a lot of heat with it, so your best chance of cooling it off is to get it to a place where it can cool down. From there, your sweat glands begin to release water, which has a cooling effect as perspiration evaporates from your skin. The problem is that if the air surrounding the skin is humid, your sweat has nowhere to go, and it just sits on your skin. This exacerbates the problem by trapping the heat in your body, raising your core temperature even more.

"Let me guess, then I die?" Erik asked sarcastically.

Carrick waved his joke aside. "Once your core gets above 104°F, you're in big trouble. Elevated temperatures lead to increased pressure in your skull and decreased blood flow to your brain."

"Okay, okay, I get it!" protested Erik.

"I'm just saying," said Carrick.

"I'll take the needle!"

"That's what I was trying to tell you!" explained Carrick.

"Oh, and by the way, I'm a scientist too!" Erik gently reminded him. "What was your field of study?"

"Do you mean, what is my field of study?" smiled Erik. "Present tense please! I'm a Biologist."

"Wow! No wonder you seem to know me so well. Get it?" joked Carrick.

"Ha-ha! Yes, I get it," smirked Erik, unimpressed by Carrick's little biology joke.

The two men examined the items in the room as if to take inventory. Although The Triad was due to shut down in fifteen years, the ECS, Energy Conservation System, had been slowly shutting down non-essential systems for several years in an effort to conserve energy. Erik had no control over this process. He couldn't be sure he would actually outlive The Triad or if the shutdown might suddenly accelerate. Both knew that if things went south in a hurry, they'd need to act fast.

Erik handed Carrick what looked like a flimsy set of silver overalls. "Put these on, young man," he commanded.

"This looks like a cooling suit, but I've never seen such a thin one before." Carrick pinched each shoulder, holding it up to his body to check for size.

Erik reminded Carrick that humans on Zenith were inventing highly technical items for millennia before any invention ever happened on Earth.

"Whoopie!" Carrick retorted sarcastically. "Well, we've got some pretty cool stuff on Earth too."

"Touché," said Erik smiling. "You're from there after all," he winked.

Erik selected several more items for each to wear, creating a small pile on the table in front of them.

"Where the hell are you taking me?" asked Carrick. "Should I be scared?"

"The places we're visiting today no longer have life-sustaining resources. I'm taking you beneath the ten sub-levels of The Triad."

Carrick's eyes flew open. "There are sub-sub-levels? Good grief!"

"Hey, you asked for a tour! Now you're getting it!" Erik tossed him a pair of gloves, and they began to suit up.

Soon both were decked out in heat-resistant-cooling suits, boots, gloves, and helmets; and were equipped with roughly five-hours of oxygen.

The two made their way to The Grand Hall. Standing on Sub-Level 7, Erik hit the 'Down' button on the elevator panel for the first time in many decades. They exited the elevator on Sub-Level 10 and made their way down several hallways before reaching a door marked with an unequivocal warning: *Do Not Enter.*

Carrick hesitated, "You sure you want to go in there?"

Erik paused. "When I was a kid, we used to sneak down here all the time. Didn't need a heat suit then, though."

"Listen, it's gonna get a little noisy in there, so stay close and don't assume I can hear you unless you're looking right at me."

Erik showed Carrick how to switch on his oxygen and close the shield on his helmet. Only then did he open the door.

Erik led the way down several flights of stairs. At the very bottom, they walked down another long hallway and came to a door marked Black Diamond Reactor. Carrick was nervous, but he tried not to show it. He gave Erik a nervous thumbs-up sign and a weak smile, and they went inside.

The two entered the Control Center portion of the reactor, and their headlamps revealed an enormous, glowing diamond. It was roughly twelve feet by twelve feet across, roughly the size of an SUV on Earth.

Carrick thought to himself that for a building as modern as The Triad, the Control Center almost felt cave-like. Though there were very modern and advanced switch panels and control boards, with dozens of monitors, the ceiling looked like chiseled granite.

The giant diamond appeared to be levitating, half above ground level and half below. A pink glow radiated from its core. The light was bright enough to illuminate the control panels arranged around the circular platform on which the two men stood. They both stared at it in wonder.

Carrick yelled into his comms. "It's amazing!"

"Looking at that never gets old," Erik shouted proudly. "Turn off your headlamp for a moment."

Carrick couldn't believe his eyes; the glow was amazing. "Is that what I think it is?" he asked.

"A diamond? What gave it away?" yelled Erik.

"It's beautiful! What does it do?" uttered Carrick.

"It provides power to the Northwest Sector of The Triad. It's what's keeping us alive. In fifteen years or less, it won't be glowing anymore; I'm afraid to say."

"But how? Where does it get its energy from? How does it work? You said diamonds were nothing special! You said that they were as common as salt on Zenith. That's what you said!" protested Carrick. Unable to fully hear Carrick, Erik motioned for them to leave the room. The humming and vibration was a little too loud for conversation.

Once back in the hallway, Erik asked Carrick to repeat his last question.

"I was asking where it got its energy from? And how does it work? You said diamonds were nothing special!"

"Okay, so I downplayed their value, sort of." Erik conceded. "Not all diamonds are created equal. This one came from a place known as the Gibraltar River Valley. When it interacts with a nuclear fusion switch, it becomes supercharged and can provide energy for roughly one hundred years. After that, like everything else around here, it dies."

"So, this one's been in place for eighty-five years then?"

"I see you're good at math too," wisecracked Erik.

Carrick ignored him. "So, each sector of The Triad has one of these diamonds?"
"Yes, but the other two are dead," said Erik.

"As the populations dwindled in each of the three sectors, the Energy Conservation System took over and channeled the remaining power to the Northwest Sector. The other two Diamond Reactors expired soon after we integrated those populations into the Northwest Sector. For many, it was the first time they'd ever seen a human being with skin color different from their own."

"How did it go?" asked Carrick.

"Not good; people were afraid of each other. Nobody trusted anyone. The older population didn't want the younger population to interact with those outside of their own race. However, the younger generation was much more receptive to learning about the strangers from the other sectors of The Triad. It was crazy!"

"Some fringe groups were opposed to letting people of color into the once, Caucasian Only Northwest Sector, and protests broke out. It went on for many months. There was lots of violence, and two people were actually killed during that time."

"Geez," grimaced Carrick.

"Like I said, it was crazy! Things got so bad that the agitators were moved up in the migration queue and placed on the next shuttle to Earth. After that, civility was restored. You could only imagine what it was like," said Erik.

"I wouldn't have to imagine that at all!" Carrick continued to be amazed by the parallels of human history on Zenith and on Earth.

They left the Diamond Reactor behind and began a long walk to a section that controlled plumbing in The Triad.

As they walked, Erik told Carrick that the diamond he'd just seen was similar to those that powered the migration shuttles.

With a straight face, Erik reminded Carrick, "Don't forget, there's more than one downed shuttle on Earth."

Carrick stopped in mid-step and recalled an earlier conversation the two had had, "Wait, that's right! You mentioned that yesterday! How in the hell did you hide something that big? Nations would go to war to get a hold of one."

"Don't worry; no one will ever find them. Not unless the oceans dry up!"

"Why were shuttles ditched on Earth? Why not bring them back here?" asked Carrick.

"The plan was always to bring them back, but as you can imagine, over many millennia and several hundred missions, things didn't always go as planned. Some of the early shuttles either crash-landed or had computer or propulsion malfunctions preventing them from returning to Zenith."

"With regards to the final shuttle, everyone on board knew we were bringing it back to Zenith. We told them that it would return so that they would never be tempted to search for it. We made it so they would never desire to come back here. If they knew the shuttle that took them away from Zenith was right under their noses, they would always believe it was possible to find it and return to this dying planet. It would've offered the migrants false hope."

"But you said they were indoctrinated and wanted to go to Earth. I'm confused," said Carrick.

"Well, as you can imagine, with tens of thousands of migrants on board, surely some would be apprehensive and want to either not go Home or would want to return to Zenith after getting there," rationalized Erik.

"That makes sense," said Carrick with a look of acknowledgment in his raised eyebrows.

They walked on in silence. "Wait, though," Carrick stopped again. "You didn't answer the question. Why didn't you return the final shuttle to Zenith?"

Erik was becoming frustrated. "For the same reason, we told the migrants it was returning to Zenith. It had to be a one-way trip. If I knew that the shuttle was here on Zenith, I would always long to go Home with the others. To see my mother, my brother, and to see her again,....," he broke off, clenching his fists.

"I would've worked every hour of every day, trying anything and everything to retrofit the shuttle so that I could pilot it Home. It would have all been in vain as it simply would have been impossible. I couldn't do that to myself. That was a part of my sacrifice. So, I buried that shuttle in the deepest part of Earth's ocean, where no one will ever find it. Ever!" he cried.

Carrick had gone pale but didn't push back because he could see that Erik was fighting deep emotions.

After a ten-minute walk, during which Erik seemed to calm down, they entered a section of The Triad called the Hydro-Oxy Exchange. Erik referred to it simply as 'The Hydro.'

"On Earth, water is also called H2O, as it's two parts hydrogen, one part oxygen," said Carrick.

"Hello! I'm a Biologist," said Erik, rolling his eyes.

They continued walking through the complex when Erik offered, "When the surface water resources on Zenith evaporated, the populations of each country had to go searching for subterranean water reserves. As it turned out, Austriaca was lying on top of hundreds of reserves, which made my ancestral nation a target for mass migration. As the climate became more hostile to human life, so did the leaders of foreign powers. The Great War broke out as countries became desperate to ensure the survival of their own people."

The two stood and chatted in front of three massive water pipes that ran vertically up out of the ground and upward through the ceiling; they appeared to be about ten feet in diameter, in Carrick's estimation.

"The biggest water reserve of all...," Erik paused and smiled, "lies right beneath our feet. Well, it's actually more than five miles below the surface, and it's encased in granite. See these pipes right here?" said Erik as he slapped his hand on one of the three massive pipes. "They are coming up from that water reserve."

"I was wondering what these were. What are those three over there?" Carrick pointed to three similar-sized pipes on the opposite side of the massive, dark, and dank facility.

"That's the water coming back down out of The Triad," offered Erik.

"Not much coming down these days, huh? The two of us don't create too much waste," chuckled Carrick.

"More than waste!" Erik bounced back, "It takes a lot of water to keep The Triad cool."

"How much water flows through these pipes?" Carrick tapped the pipes the two stood next to.

"Let's put it this way; there's enough water down there to last for another five millennia. So, let's just say, The Triad will run out of electricity and oxygen long before it runs out of water."

Carrick's eyes widened. "You son of a gun!" he exclaimed.

Erik shrank back. "I don't know what that means, but you look pretty serious right now."

"You told me that it was 'all about water conservation around here,' those were your words! You smelly old man, you lied to me?"

"Ah-hem!" Erik cleared his throat defensively. "Again, I don't know what you mean by 'Son of a gun,' but I was kidding about the water conservation. I was just being lazy. I didn't want to take a shower every day. I never had to before you got here. Old habits die hard, I guess."

Carrick smiled. "I'm just messing with you!"

The two men laughed, leaving The Hydro behind them.

Back in the climate-controlled portion of The Triad, the two dropped off their life-support gear. Erik took Carrick to see the classrooms where children were prepared for their future lives. Interactive screens on the walls showed lessons about survival on Zenith, the origins of The Triad, and how to survive on Home. There were also specialized classrooms, where the most advanced children took extra lessons. The curriculum lists were long, including physics, biology, chemistry, astronomy, medicine, neurology, meteorology, nuclear fusion, and nuclear propulsion.

From there, they visited offices where government officials worked. And they toured the communications hub and space observatories scattered throughout the upper levels of The Triad. By this point, they'd been on the go for roughly eight-hours, and both were completely exhausted.

Back at Barrack 5, each showered. The shower area was massive; it contained hundreds of shower stalls that were only slightly bigger than a phone booth. Adjacent to the showers were sinks and modernistic lockers of some sort; that's where the two kept their clothing. In between the shower and locker areas were the laundry facilities; inside, there appeared to be hundreds of what looked like dry-cleaners as opposed to traditional washers/dryers. Some still contained clothing that once belonged to Zenithians who had long since migrated Home. Carrick found this to be eerie. It was as if they were grave sites to a generation long since gone, on Zenith, and on Earth.

The two were now back in Barrack 5, getting ready to go to sleep when Carrick decided he had to have his curiosity satisfied. "Erik, you mentioned two things today that really piqued my interest, and I'd like to know more."

"Fire away," replied Erik.

"Earlier, you mentioned your mother and your brother leaving on the shuttle. But you also mentioned 'her,' and then you trailed off. Who is 'her'?"

"First of all, it would be who *was* her, not who *is* her. You said it yourself; people on Earth are lucky if they live to be eighty." Erik stopped and took a deep breath. "Her name was Lilly. She was the only woman that I ever loved, and I think she loved me too."

He paused awkwardly, and Carrick tried to fill the silence. "I always loved that name," he said. "When I was little..."

Erik cut him off. "Who's telling the story here?" he asked. "This is difficult enough as it is. Let me finish." Again he needed to take a breath, but this time Carrick kept quiet, waiting for Erik to go on.

"We were best friends and had known each other since we were toddlers. We were born just one day apart, in the same month of the same year, so we went to class together for many years. She eventually became a medical doctor while I became a biologist. We worked closely together, and the connection between the two of us was undeniable," Erik smiled to himself.

Cautiously Carrick inquired, "Did you ever tell her how you felt?"

"No, I didn't, and before you ask why not, I'll tell you. I was afraid."

"Afraid of what?"

"Are you going to let me finish, or what?" asked Erik. "I was afraid she wouldn't love me back. I was afraid that she would tell me that her heart belonged to someone else or that she didn't see me in that light. I was just afraid, afraid of it all. As a scientist, I calculated the odds. The chances of her saying something other than 'I Love you' were far greater, so I just couldn't bring myself to do it."

"That's ridiculous!" Carrick couldn't stop himself from raising his voice. "You should've told her! At least then you would've known. You both would've known! All these years later, wondering whether or not she loved you, that must've been torture!"

"Still is," sighed Erik. "You don't get it, do you? The thought of knowing that the only woman I ever loved didn't love me back was simply not an option. How could I have gone on for all of these years? I would've gladly spent my days out here alone in The Triad, believing that she loved me, rather than a life on Home knowing that she didn't. The truth of her not loving me would've been much harder to take than the torture I've endured alone here for all of these decades! At least this way, I can believe in my heart that she did, in fact, love me."

Carrick was unsettled. "So just like that, you let her go Home without you?"

"She was the biggest part of my sacrifice! She was my sacrifice!" Almost shouting, Erik cried, "How could I have selfishly asked her to stay if I didn't actually know that she loved me. If I had been sure, I would've absolutely asked her not to board that shuttle."

"That's my point," said a visibly frustrated Carrick, "you should've asked her if she did. You could've been together this whole time!"

Erik's anger seemed to have run itself out, and sadness had taken over. "But if she'd said no. Then what would I have held onto for all of these years? She made my sacrifice worth it."

Carrick shook his head in disagreement. "I still don't understand, but that's just fine! Maybe it'll hit me someday when I'm flying alone through space or out for a casual drive on a rover, zooming across some random black planet! Whatever!"

As Carrick carried on getting ready for bed, he was pissed. Erik, though now seemed more at peace with himself.

Right before lights out, Erik asked, "What was the other question you had for me?"

Carrick couldn't believe that he'd lost his train of thought. "Today, you were talking about ditching the shuttle in the deepest part of Earth's ocean. I need to know exactly where that was? I know you can't answer that question now, but tomorrow, when we get back to The History Library, I'm going to need you to show me."

Erik had a blank stare on his face.

"First thing in the morning, okay?" said Carrick, a look of determination on his face.

Carrick removed his shirt, fluffed his pillow, and laid down with his back to Erik.

Erik, however, wasn't done. "You think I don't know the exact location where I terminated my only hope of being close to Lilly again? I'm a little insulted."

Carrick turned in his bunk to face his friend. "I didn't mean anything by it. I just..."

Erik cut him off. "Latitude 11.3733° N, Longitude 142.5917° E." He knew it by heart.

"That's the western Pacific Ocean, near Guam!" said a stunned Carrick.
"I don't know what you call that body of water. All I know is that I mapped the entirety of Earth many times, and that was the deepest part I could find."

Carrick sat up slowly. His voice had reduced to a whisper. "That's where my father is buried!"

"What do you mean buried?"

Carrick rubbed both hands down his face and said, "I never told you this, but my father died thirty-one years, three hundred and nine days ago. He was a pilot for one of our military branches, and his plane went down in a terrible accident." He could feel his eyes becoming watery.

"You were just a baby then. How much do you remember of him?"

"I wasn't even born yet. That's an extraordinary coincidence, those two events happening within miles of each other, some forty-three years apart. It seems as unimaginable as it is unexplainable."

Carrick closed his eyes, knowing he was going to lose plenty of sleep, trying to reconcile what he'd just learned.

Chapter 18 – Walker Trace

Location: Planet Earth. Washington D.C., NASA Headquarters – August 29, 2022. 9:00 am, EST.

In a large conference room at Two Independence Square, a group of grim-faced officials gathered to discuss a strategy for communicating with Black Earth.

NASA's Chief Administrator, James Lorenstine, and Mission Control's Mars Johnston were hosting the meeting, and they had some illustrious company. Jennifer Stanton, Director of the Department of Homeland Security, had just arrived. She was hanging her jacket over a chair across the table from the Secretary of State, Mike Truman. Around the oversized conference table, several administrative assistants were pulling out notepads and folders, and a stenographer was readying himself to take an official record of the meeting. A junior NASA official was handing out information packets to each of the attendees.

As notes rustled and coffee was poured, Chief Administrator Lorenstine stood and walked to the front of the fifth-floor room, where glass windows overlooked the busy D.C. street below.

He watched the cars and people racing about their normal lives until the noise died down behind him. Then he turned to call the meeting to order. "Ladies and gentlemen, thank you for coming. As you know, we're here to discuss a strategy for communicating with Black Earth and ultimately retrieving our astronaut and American hero, Dr. Carrick Michaels, from Black Earth."

"How exactly do you plan on doing that?" demanded Secretary Truman.

"As I said, we're here to discuss that," Lorenstine replied, ignoring Truman's belligerent tone. "At this time, I'd like to introduce all of you to NASA's Marcus Johnston. Marcus heads up Mission Control and will oversee the program that we're calling Operation Safe Return. Marcus will be reviewing our plan at length, and he'll take questions at the end of his presentation. However, you can feel free to jump in anytime if you're unclear about the information being communicated. Marcus," Lorenstine gestured to his colleague, "please proceed."

"Thank you, Jim." Johnston collected his papers together. "Firstly, I want to thank you for coming in today. I understand that some of you got an early start and just landed at Reagan a couple of hours ago. I'll try my best to keep it brief. Secondly, please call me Mars," He looked around the table with an exaggerated smile, attempting to seem as likable as possible. The attempt fell flat, and the room remained silent as stoic faces looked on.

"Okay," Mars continued, "Now before I get into the nuts and bolts of it all, I do have one point to make. Only a handful of people in Washington, Houston, or anywhere else around the world are privy to what you're about to see and hear today. The information that I'm going to share with you today is highly confidential and top secret." There were nods of acquiescence around the table.

"If I can now direct your attention to the monitor to my left." Mars fumbled with the LCD remote control and dropped it on the table before regaining control. "I'm going to show you some highly classified images, taken from a communications satellite that we currently have orbiting ILK-87b, better known as Black Earth. What you may not know is that this satellite is not our Infinity One satellite, which has been orbiting Black Earth since August of 2020. This is a different craft, known as the Walker Trace satellite, named after its designer, Ben Walker Trace. We launched it from the New Horizon spacecraft, but with rather less publicity attached, if you see what I mean." Again, Mars tried a winning smile. Stony faces stared back, so Mars pressed on.

"While Infinity One's mission is to map the surface of Black Earth, Walker Trace is designed to pick up sounds. More precisely, it is designed to scan designated areas for anything resembling radio or human voice transmissions."

How does it work? Using sound waves?" Director Stanton inquired.

"Hearing a conversation from space using sound waves is not possible," Mars explained politely. "Sound waves travel through the air, and in space... well, there is no air, of course... and where there is no air, there can be no sound waves."

Stanton quickly apologized. "I meant to say radio waves," she clarified unconvincingly.

"We won't be using radio waves either," Johnston replied. "We'll be using lasers."

He clicked a video graphic onto the monitor, showing how the laser system worked. "The Walker Trace listening network is highly sophisticated. It can detect subterranean sounds such as volcanic activity, small earthquakes, and even tremors resulting from tectonic plates' slightest shifting. And, more specifically for our purposes today, it can, in theory, hear a conversation on the planetary surface, from its orbit, 300 miles above."

Secretary of State Truman sat forward in his seat. "This sounds interesting. Tell us more, please."

"If you'll look at the graphic here, you can see the Walker Trace satellite is equipped with twenty-six lasers. These can be pointed to a specific target on Black Earth. With the precision that only a laser can provide, we can mark a designated point that is smaller than the size of a quarter. This will allow us to target windows, for example. If we can touch the laser to the glass, we can hear everything that's happening in that particular room or any adjoining rooms that share a wall, floor, or ceiling with the targeted room. We can then transmit those sounds back to Earth in near real-time. To do that, we use three smaller geostationary communications satellites that span the entire planet, each positioned in orbit at 120° apart. Communications then come back to Earth via the Interlink Communication Corridor.

Please take a look at the insert in your packets; it's titled Interlink Communications." Around the table, the attendees flipped through the documents in their packets and pulled out the relevant insert.

"In lay terms, if we contact someone or something, we can communicate with the person or thing in near real-time," explained Johnston.

"Thing?" asked Director Stanton, with a pale look of concern on her face.

Mars smiled while Administrator Lorenstine took over. "We're keeping all possibilities on the table for now," he said.

Lorenstine gestured to Johnston, who continued his presentation. "The Walker Trace satellite has been orbiting Black Earth since March 23rd after it was secretly launched from our New Horizon spacecraft. At first, its mission was to monitor for any seismic activity. However, since Dr. Michaels made the unexpected decision to remain on Black Earth for an indeterminant period, our goals have shifted."

"Currently, the satellite is targeting this structure."

Johnston displayed an aerial shot of a triangular campus on the monitor, consisting of three pentagon-shaped buildings and a conduit-type housing that connected the three corners.

"To date, the Walker Trace has not picked up anything that resembles manmade audio or actual voices. What we don't know is the chemical make-up of the structure. Some dense metals could hinder our efforts as they might lessen the performance of the lasers. For now, we're focusing on what appear to be glass portions on the top levels of the Northwest Sector of the structure, seen here and here." Mars pointed them out on the monitor.

"What's so important about that particular location," asked Jennifer Stanton.

"This is where a light was previously detected," Mars answered. "And it's near where our two astronauts, Dr. Kaley London, and Dr. Carrick Michaels, first entered the structure," he concluded.

Secretary Truman had been studying the monitor closely, with great concern, as Mars talked. "Those buildings look very much like our own Pentagon! Are we sure that's not our handy work up there?" he asked.

Lorenstine responded with confidence, "If there were only two people in the Universe that knew the answer to that question, it would be God and me. And I can assure you, that is not the handy work of the U.S.A."

"With all due respect," Secretary Truman snapped, his words drenched with disrespect, "you don't head up the United States Government. You are not the keeper of its many secrets." He sat back, observing the much younger man with obvious disdain.

"No, I don't, and no, I'm not," Lorenstine calmly pushed back. "But I do head up the only agency on this planet that could get the men and materials to Black Earth to construct that building. It surely isn't the Russians; they couldn't even get a man out of Earth's orbit, and the Chinese have only just made it to the moon. As for India, they may have recently gotten a craft to orbit Mars, but they are new to the scene, and what we're looking at there would have taken years to build. It's either us or it's aliens, of that you can be certain," he finished, with great passion.

This time, no one challenged him.

Chapter 19 – The Sacrifice

Location: Black Earth. The Triad Shuttle Launch Pad – August 29, 2022.

Erik and Carrick drove onto a massive launchpad, one from which more than seven-hundred-thousand Zenithians began their migration to Earth. For Erik, this was a solemn place. It was just below the launchpad that he last saw his Lilly, right before she boarded the final shuttle mission to Home.

The launchpad was positioned directly in the middle of The Triad, in an area shaped like a triangle, measuring three miles by three miles by three miles. Outfitted in Zenithian space suits, the two drove toward the very center, Carrick marveling at the sheer size of the area.

"This is huge!" he said. "I never envisioned the shuttle being this big."

"The shuttle had a max capacity of 30,000 people," Erik told him. "It was designed to drop off its human cargo and return to Zenith in a matter of only four months."

Carrick marveled. "Much faster than us then. New Horizon took four months just to get to Black Earth, one-way."

Erik nodded modestly. "Each shuttle was designed to make twelve round trips, and then it would be retired. Its parts would then be used in the production of the next shuttle."

"Why only twelve trips?"

"In the entire six-thousand years that we shuttled Zenithians to Earth, we only lost one shuttle due to an accident on lift-off. It was on the thirteenth journey to Home. Shuttle 13 broke up sixty seconds after lift-off from Zenith. Millions of Zenithians were in attendance, and billions more watched from their tablets. As you can imagine, it was a horrifying spectacle. From that day on, our leaders decided never again to allow a shuttle to complete more than twelve missions. The actual number thirteen became synonymous with pain, disaster, fear, and dread. No one migrating to Earth would have ever confidently boarded a shuttle attempting its thirteenth mission."

"How many died in the disaster?"

"Only thirteen-thousand people died, but they were some of our absolute finest," Erik stressed. "That particular mission was targeted to modernize Home. Shuttle 13 was filled with doctors, scientists, engineers, architects, craftsmen, scholars, you name it. Thousands of our best people went down with that shuttle."

"From that point on, it was decided that no person with an advanced education would board another shuttle Home until the last five shuttles left Zenith."

"Okay, so let me get this straight," said Carrick. "Shuttle 13, carrying 13,000 Zenithians, broke up while attempting to escape Zenith's atmosphere? Killing everyone on board? Is that what you're telling me?"

"That's correct."

"Well, that explains it then!" said Carrick.

"Explains what?"

"On Earth, the number thirteen is also synonymous with bad luck and bad things in general. People dread the number," explained Carrick.

Erik chuckled. "It sounds like Zenithians took some superstitions with them when they left for Home."

After reaching the center of the launchpad, the two walked around for a few minutes. Standing there in the 800°F plus temperatures, Carrick began to feel uncomfortable despite his temperature-controlled spacesuit. "It's getting a little warm out here. How old did you say these suits were?" he asked.

Erik smiled. "These suits are likely the most advanced space gear in the entire Universe."

"You know, you've gotten good at not actually answering my questions," quipped Carrick. "How old are the damn suits?"

"Thirteen-years-old!" responded Erik with a straight face.

Carrick grimaced and began to feel slightly panicked.

"Just kidding!" joked Erik, still straight-faced. "They're actually eighty-five-years-old!"

"Well, that makes me feel a little better. But eighty-five is pretty damn old." Carrick was only somewhat relieved.

"Carrick, what's eight plus five?" asked Erik, trying to rattle Carrick a little more.

After doing the quick math in his head, followed by another look of impending doom, Carrick shouted, "Son of a bitch!

"Jesus Christ! Get me back inside!" said Carrick. "Next time, I'll wear my EMU," he added.

"You had me freaked out with the number 13, and now you have me shitting in my pants! Old and unlucky! You're gonna give me a heart attack!"

A minute later, the two mounted the Shuttle Rover.

"So, Jesus Christ, what does it mean?" asked Erik as he activated the rover's battery supply.

Carrick, still annoyed, shook his head as if to say, "Forget it!"

Erik drove them back to the Northwest Sector's interior main entrance.

Recovering himself, Carrick couldn't help but be impressed by the vehicle. "This rover's badass," he admired. "It's much better than ours. How old is it?"

"It's six-hundred and fifty-years-old," Erik stated matter-of-factly. Carrick gasped in astonishment.

Erik laughed openly now. "Just kidding, it's only a hundred and thirty," he laughed. Carrick couldn't stop himself from joining in.

Location: Northwest Sector's Command Center, Inner Observatory deck facing the Shuttle Launchpad, Surface-Level 5, Top level of The Triad. An hour later.

"Okay, so why did we have to go outside to the actual launchpad? Couldn't you have just shown me some aerial footage?" asked Carrick.

"I could've, but I really wanted to ride the Shuttle Rover again. And I wanted you to experience the pad up close before you saw this view." Erik pointed south through the triple-paned, diamond-glass window. "Tell me what you see."

"Not much!" said Carrick.

"Look again. Beyond the actual launchpad. If you look a little further, you should be able to make out the inner portions of the Southwest and Southeast Sectors of The Triad."

"Jesus, you're right; I can see both corners. The launchpad is massive! How is it possible that I'm able to see anything out there with all of that black carbon substance covering everything?" Carrick looked astonished.

"The inner and outer observatories of all sectors, along with the launchpad, needed to remain clean of the black particles," Erik explained. "So we have an electromagnetic shield that repels the ferromagnetic elements in the carbon soot. The reaction keeps those surfaces clear of the black material. It won't be long before it all goes black, though. The ECS will cut power to the shield soon, I'd imagine."

Carrick, however, was still fixated on the scale of the area. "How big was the shuttle?" he asked.

Erik didn't need to check. "The shuttle was 250 feet tall, with a diameter of 680 feet and a circumference of 2136 feet. It had an interior space of 125 million cubic feet, with five different levels. Each had a total floor area of 1,345,000 square feet."

"My God, that was the mother of all ships! How did you guys even get that thing off the ground?"

"Do you remember how big the Black Diamond Reactor was? A power source that can keep an entire sector of The Triad running for a hundred years; that's what powered the shuttle," said Erik, proudly.

"Yeah, but what about the propulsion system?"

Erik said, "First, tell me about Jesus Christ? You keep mentioning the phrase whenever you're angry, impressed, or scared."

"Another long story, I'm afraid, I'll tell you before bed," said Carrick.

"Great, you're going to make me wait, and now I have to suffer through another one of your long bedtime stories! I can't wait!" said Erik sarcastically.

Carrick sat engrossed for the next hour as Erik talked him through the shuttle's complex propulsion system. No conversation about the shuttle could fail to bring Erik's thoughts to the last ever migration journey. It was on Carrick's mind too.

Once Erik had talked himself out, Carrick gently asked, "You've mentioned that you made a sacrifice, my friend. Will you tell me more about it?"

Erik sighed; not sure he was ready to tell the story. But here they both were, and he had no one else to tell. If not now, then when?

"Let me start with the shuttle and why someone was required to stay behind. The shuttle was pilot-less. Every step of its journey was directed by a Remote Shuttle Pilot or Controller, sitting in a Command Center like this one. Each sector of The Triad has its own Command Center. From there, the Controller directed the entire mission."

"Why no pilots?" wondered Carrick aloud.

"The fear was that if pilots were flying the shuttle, there would always be the possibility of human error. After Shuttle13 exploded thousands of years ago and rained down debris and bodies to Zenith, we had to remove the human variable. However, the biggest reason was that human pilots possessed human emotion and would have the ability to turn the shuttle around and return it to Zenith. There was also the chance that pilots would possibly succumb to an angry mob, being forced to return to Zenith against their will."

"Yeah, but a remote pilot could also turn it around if they wanted to, right?" countered Carrick.

"Of course. But the psychological state of a pilot, millions of miles from Zenith, would have been far more fragile. An onboard pilot might be wrestling with many different emotions, as well as the monumental responsibility of handling the craft."

"We simply left nothing to chance. It was I who volunteered to be the last Controller for the final shuttle mission. I was uniquely qualified as I had been the Controller on the previous mission that'd occurred fifteen years prior. I was just twenty-five-years-old back then. By the time of the last mission, I was nearly forty. Plus, I was the only Controller who wasn't married with children. It was meant to be, that's all. I was the right man for the job," concluded Erik.

Carrick thought about those Zenithians who had left and what Erik must have meant to them. "You were their hero!" he exclaimed. "I can't believe there aren't statues and monuments all over planet Earth in your honor."
"I bet they're calling you a hero right now, as we speak," said Erik.

Carrick shrugged his shoulders. "Nah, most times, someone has to die to be considered a hero."

This prompted Erik to wonder aloud, "Hmmm, maybe they are calling me a hero after all."

"Oh. I'm sorry, Erik, I was just saying," Carrick apologized. It was slowly dawning on him that Erik was likely going to die alone on this empty planet. A planet void of all that Erik once knew and the person he still loved, Lilly.

"Carrick," Erik broke into his thoughts, "you have to understand that all Zenithians made a great sacrifice in going Home. Everyone who went to Earth left behind advanced technology, medicine, the safety of The Triad, and everything they had known for their entire lives. Sometimes that included friends, family, and loved ones. They understood that they made their individual sacrifice so that the human race could live on."

Carrick took a moment to digest that. He considered how hard it would be today on Earth for the self-consumed population to forfeit their luxuries for a simpler life. It also occurred to him that not all people on Earth had it so good, with millions dying each year from starvation, disease, and lack of fresh water.

Both men silently reflected what the word sacrifice really meant, but Erik was the one who understood it personally.

It was Carrick who broke the silence. "Tell me more about Lilly. She was a Doctor, huh?"

Erik nodded.

"My Lola is about to graduate med school later this year," said Carrick, struck by the similarities.
Erik stared out the window into the past, smiling at his memories of Lilly.

"You know, she's really easy to describe. If a blind person were to ask me what Lilly looked like, I would tell them to imagine the feeling of a cool breeze hitting their face. If a deaf person asked me to describe the sound of her voice, I would explain to them that it sounded like the way flowers smelled. I know that that sounds like a strange way of describing someone, but that's the best way that I could sum up her beauty. You know what I mean?"

Carrick took a moment before answering. "Yes, I think I do," he said, with a warm smile on his face as he too looked off into the distance.

"So, you two never...," Carrick cleared his throat noisily. "You never sealed the deal?"

"You mean, did we ever have gender relations?"

"Well, yes, although that's not how I would describe it. Well... Did you?"

Erik laughed and said, "You described it as 'sealing the deal,' is that how people on Earth refer to it?"

Carrick laughed too and said, "Touché."

"Yeah, we did it," Erik answered casually, with a half-smile and blushing a little.

"Wait. What? Why didn't you tell me that before?" Carrick gave Erik a gentle shove.

"I don't kiss and tell."

Carrick responded with a quizzical look and said, "They had that saying on Zenith too?"

"Still do," said Erik as he smiled again.

"Details please?" demanded Carrick.

"Like I said, I don't kiss and...."

Carrick quickly cut him off. "Now you listen to me! I'm stuck on this Godforsaken planet with a crusty old man, without the love of my life, Lola. You're going to give me details, and you're going to do it now!"

"Okay, okay!" Erik threw his hands up in the air, motioning surrender. "Lilly was about five foot, seven inches tall, and she had blonde hair and blue eyes. She spoke softly, but she had an air of confidence. She was smart too and quick to pick up on things. It was a challenge for her not to finish a person's sentence because she knew exactly what they were trying to communicate. She was everything a man could want," He paused, and Carrick didn't interrupt.

"I never understood it!" confessed Erik.

"Understood what?"

"I never understood why she never married or was never with a man before me. Both men and women desired her on Zenith, yet she never committed to anyone. I always thought it was due to her work as a doctor; she stayed incredibly busy. She was the only medical doctor in the Northwest Sector," Erik added proudly. "Maybe she liked girls?"

"No, no! Not at all! That wasn't it!" said Erik, frustrated.

"I know exactly what it was," said Carrick smugly.

"Okay, Einstein, what was it?" Erik was slightly annoyed.

"It was you! She wanted you! And you were too God damned afraid to tell her you loved her!" he shouted.

"You think?" pondered Erik aloud, rubbing his chin.

"Wait a second! You just called me Einstein," said Carrick, clearly stunned.

"Yeah, so what?"

"Albert Einstein? questioned Carrick

"It's a figure of speech," replied Erik. "What's the problem?"

"Albert Einstein? I knew it!" Carrick shot up from his chair in disbelief, knocking it backward and almost stumbling. "You're from Earth! Goddammit! You've been playing me the whole time!"

Startled by Carrick's reaction, Erik hurried to help him. "What are you talking about? Albert Einstein was Zenithian. He went to Home on a shuttle around one hundred and thirty years ago. A pretty kooky guy by all accounts. He was young when he left, only in his twenties, but starting to sprout gray hair, so the stories go. It was always messed up too."

"Bullshit! He would've been a child one hundred and thirty years ago, not a grown man with gray hair!"

"No, the guy I'm thinking of was a Controller. I heard he did one mission and then demanded to go Home on the next shuttle. I only know about him because he was kind of a laughingstock. I wasn't even born back then, but I read that he thought he was smarter than everyone else. He was convinced that if he went to Home, he would transform the place. As I understand it, he was a smart guy, but some people thought he was too smart for his own good. He became the butt end of many jokes, which persisted for many years, long after he'd gone Home. Apparently, he had dyslexia and had difficulty reading the shuttle manuals," Erik mused. "He was given a hard time about that. No wonder he wanted to go to Earth so badly. People always wondered if he'd accomplished anything on Home. I guess he must have if you know who he is."

Carrick righted his chair and sat back down slowly.

"So, did he actually go on to become an important person on Earth?" asked Erik.

"That can't be!" said Carrick. "The years...," he paused, doing the math. "The age. It doesn't add up!"

"Carrick, listen, you forget that we live a lot longer on Zenith. Look at me, I'm one-hundred and fifteen-years-old, and I still feel great. I look good too!" Erik said with a smile, trying to derail Carrick from his shock. "It's possible it's the same guy. We were taught from the time we were little to assimilate ourselves on Earth. To blend in with the local population. He would've never told those around him his real age. And his backstory would have covered up his origins. Listen, I'll pull up a picture of him tomorrow when we return to The History Library. We have a catalog containing images and biographies of every Controller there ever was; he'll definitely be there! Yep, that'll settle it," said Erik reassuringly.

"But Einstein was a scientist, and you told me that Zenith didn't send its best and its brightest. That's what you said!" Carrick was still having trouble believing his friend.

"Actually, I told you we saved our best and brightest for the last five shuttles to Home. He was on the fourth to the last shuttle Home. As I understand it, he was studying to be a physicist, but he wasn't done with school yet. Again, these are just stories that I've heard. Even his instructors thought he was eccentric."

"Carrick, keep this in mind; I told you that we wouldn't send our best and brightest until the last several shuttles. The fact is people grow old. In Einstein's case, several in his family were getting quite old; If we no longer needed him here, we would have given him and his family the chance to see what many called 'The New World,' particularly since we were so close to the last migration of Zenithians. I'm not lying to you, Carrick, not now, not then, nor would I ever," he assured his young friend.

"Anyway," he smiled, once again attempting to divert Carrick, "I thought we were talking about Lilly?"

"We are. I'm sorry! I didn't mean to insinuate that you were a liar," apologized Carrick. "Tell me all about her. Tell me everything!"

"It happened the night before she left for Home," Erik reminisced.

"What did?" asked Carrick curiously.

"We sealed the deal," Erik grinned, a little embarrassed. "We were in her barrack, Barrack 6. Everyone else was celebrating because they were going Home to make a difference. They, and their families, were actually going to breathe in the fresh air. Remember, they had never been outside of The Triad. Now they would walk on grass, smell the flowers, and feel raindrops on their faces. Until now, they had only seen images of Zenith before the climate changed and The Great War decimated our planet. They had also seen images of Earth taken by returning shuttles. They knew Earth was beginning to turn the technology corner, and they couldn't wait to contribute. An Evolution Revolution is what they kept saying was coming to Home. Apparently, it did. The fact that you're here with me today must mean they made quite a contribution. I wonder what contribution Lilly made to her new home. I guess I'll never know," he trailed off wistfully until Carrick prompted him to carry on.

"Well," Erik continued, "we stood talking in Barrack 6. There was so much to say, but words were hard to come by. She asked why I had come to see her. I told her I just wanted to say goodbye and to tell her that I wished her well. I said that I hoped she contributed to her new Home. That's when it happened."

"That's when what happened?" asked Carrick for the second time.

Erik's voice went soft. "She said the words."

"What did she say, Goddammit? Just tell me already!" demanded Carrick.

Erik snapped back, "You know, for an atheist; you sure do reference God's name a lot!"

Erik paused, "Patience, young man, patience," he then continued telling his story.

Erik fondly remembered. "She said, 'Well, you came here to say goodbye to me, so say it.'"

"At that moment, I didn't say anything; I just held her in my arms and kissed her for the first time. I had never kissed a woman up until that moment in time; it was more than I could ever have imagined. I became a different person at that moment. It felt like she did too. Someone, anyone, could've walked in, but they didn't. It was as if our special moment, one in which we both had waited a lifetime for, was supposed to be uninterrupted," said Erik. He'd never discussed that moment with anyone else before, and recounting it for the first time gave him a feeling of conciliation. It was as if he was properly processing the experience for the first time.

"So, then what happened? What did you guys say to each other afterward?" Carrick leaned forward, eager to hear Erik's response.

"That's just it. There were no words. We just got dressed, and I left."

Carrick was dumbfounded. "That's when the words 'I love you' were supposed to be spoken, you dummy!"

"I know! But we were both left speechless. The next day, I saw her when I was transporting everyone to the Shuttle Staging Area beneath the launchpad. I helped her with her bag and hugged her. While I held her, I whispered goodbye into her ear. She smiled and winked, then said, 'Last night's goodbye was better. Let's not call it goodbye; let's just call it Until we someday meet again'."

Erik was smiling, but Carrick could see tears welling in his eyes.

"It was awkward. I just hugged her again, and then she boarded the shuttle. And that was it."

Erik finally looked at Carrick directly and saw that he, too, had tears in his eyes. They exchanged no more words until they got back to Barrack 5 later that evening.

Later, back at the barracks, lying in bed, Erik said, "You told me you were going to tell me about this Jesus guy."

Carrick nodded. "Okay, here we go! Basically, people believe that Jesus was the Son of God. Our history tells us that he was born over two-thousand years ago to a virgin mother. He was eventually tortured and killed for his beliefs and teachings by being hung on a wooden cross until he died. That type of death is called crucifixion."

"I'm confused," said Erik, "what do you mean a virgin mother? I'm not following."

"Wait! You'll have many more questions, believe me. Let me get through this, and hopefully, some of them will be answered. Before his execution, he was known as Jesus of Nazareth. After his death, he became known as Jesus Christ, the Son of God, the Savior of all men. Christ wasn't an actual word or name, though. It was derived from the Greek word Christos, which translates as Messiah, meaning leader, or a savior, for a cause, or a group of people."

Erik nodded to show he was keeping up. Carrick pressed on with his story.

"Early into Jesus' adulthood, he became a traveling preacher and a supposed healer. By his early thirties, he was a public figure. During that brief time, a little more than a year, Jesus attracted a lot of attention for his beliefs and his teachings. Somewhere between the years 29AD and 33AD, I'll explain the time period later, he went to a city called Jerusalem to observe Passover, a festival in the Jewish religion. His arrival was celebrated with great psychological significance. The Roman authorities, who ruled Jerusalem, took notice."

"While he was there, he was arrested, tried, and then executed on the orders of the Roman governor, Pontius Pilate. History would later recount that a few high-ranking Jewish officials, who owed their power to the Romans, conspired to have Jesus put to death. It's said that they were jealous of Jesus and viewed him as a threat to the religious status quo. Others said that an unruly mob singled Jesus out to be crucified."

"What does the term Romans mean?"

"The Romans were a large and powerful empire that dominated great land masses and ruled harshly over their people and their conquered territories," replied Carrick.

Erik nodded, his chin in his hands as he followed Carrick's account.

"So," continued Carrick, "it is written that Jesus had twelve followers or disciples while he was alive. After his death, they became convinced that he had been resurrected three days later. The disciples claimed that Jesus had appeared to them. In turn, they converted others to believe in him. This eventually led to the foundation of a new religion, called Christianity." Carrick exhaled completely, realizing how crazy the account of Jesus' life must sound to someone who'd never heard it before.

Erik echoed his thought. "That's quite a tale!"

"Yeah, but what many Christians don't want to admit is that the story of Jesus is peculiarly similar to that of an ancient Egyptian named Horus."

Erik opened his mouth to ask Carrick who Horus was when Carrick threw up his hands and said, "Don't ask! It'd be another long story!"

"Okay, okay!" agreed Erik. "Well, that was another fantastical story! When you first mentioned Jesus Christ earlier, I got confused for a moment and had to rack my brain. I was reminded of a Zenithian who had a similar name and the same initials."

"Who's that?" asked Carrick.

"Some big shot and his family, from a long time ago, his name was Julius Caesar."

Carrick was floored. He shook his head in disbelief until Erik chimed in. "Well, I'm guessing by your expression that we'll be busy in The History Library tomorrow!"

"Albert Einstein and Julius Caesar?! This place just keeps getting better!"

Before the lights went out, Carrick turned back to Erik and asked, "Did you have a birthday go by and not tell me about it?"
"How'd you know?" inquired Erik.

"A few months ago, you told me you were almost one hundred and fifteen. Today you said that you're one-hundred and fifteen, present tense. I didn't have to be Einstein to work that one out."

"Well done," conceded Erik. "I don't celebrate birthdays anymore, though. They're sad reminders for me." His voice struck a melancholy tone. "Besides, you gave me a birthday gift this year just by being here."

"When was it?" asked Carrick.

"About seventy-eight history lessons ago," smiled Erik.

"Clue me in next year; if I'm still here, I'll hook you up with a cup of Red Fruit." That made them both chuckle.

After a few minutes of silence, Carrick said, "Erik listen, I recognize your sacrifice. If no one from the last shuttle is still alive on Earth, I want you to know that someone from Earth recognizes what you gave up for all Zenithians and all Earthlings. I'll never forget it for as long as I live.

Oh, and one last question...," said Carrick. "If you ever saw Lilly again, what would you say to her?"

Erik simply responded, "I love you."

Chapter 20 – Back on Earth

Location: Washington, D.C. NASA Headquarters – August 29, 2022. 2:15 pm EST.

Continuing their discussion earlier in the day, NASA officials talked through the logistics of a communication strategy from Earth to Black Earth. As they worked away, sleeves rolled up, Chief Administrator James Lorenstine and Mars Johnston burst back into the room.

"Team, Mars, and I have some great news to share with you!" Lorenstine exclaimed. "As you know, Mars was due to return to Houston this afternoon. I've asked him to cancel his flight. And for an excellent reason. Take it away, Mars!" said Lorenstine.

Mars had a big smile plastered on his face. "I'm very pleased to tell you that about an hour ago, we received some incredible information. Just after our earlier briefing with the Secretary of State and Director of Homeland Security, Jim and I got the call. It's the news we've all been waiting and hoping for since March 24th. We now have evidence that Dr. Michaels is very much alive. Carrick's alive, everyone!" Johnston was clearly ecstatic. The room, which had been quiet until then, erupted with cheers, high-fives, and tears of joy.

Mars waved for the jubilant officials to calm down. It was almost impossible to call the room to order. He had to raise his voice to make himself heard. "Our Walker Trace satellite, never before tested due to time constraints, appears to be working marvelously! We've gotten word that voices were recorded coming from the interior glass canopy section of the triangular campus' Northwest Sector. That's the location we've been so curious about. We've confirmed that one of those voices is that of Dr. Michaels. From the dialogue transcript, which is very limited, not only have we discovered that he's alive, but that he's healthy and safe!"

More cheers erupted across the room.

"I can't go into much more detail than I already have, but I just wanted to make sure you were all aware. Our next steps will be focused on bringing our native son back home to his family."

Sixty-minutes earlier, Lorenstine had placed a phone call he knew would bring considerable relief.

"Mrs. Michaels, this is James Lorenstine from NASA. I have great news to share with you."

There was an audible gasp from Carrick's mother, Maggie Michaels, at the other end of the line.

"Carrick is okay!" Lorenstine said. "I have been waiting to make this call since March 24th."

"Oh, thank God!' cried Maggie.

"I can officially confirm to you that, as of one hour ago, we received a transmission from Black Earth. It indicated to us that your son is very much alive and well. I cannot share further details, but voice authentication records confirm that it was indeed Carrick, and he was speaking in a very relaxed tone."

"When is he coming home?" interjected Maggie.

"I cannot answer that definitively at this time," said Lorenstine.

"But we do know that Carrick is doing just fine. Maggie, he's alive, and we're going to bring him home!"

Lorenstine assured Maggie that a manned mission would soon commence and that a lift-off date would be announced in the coming weeks. He asked her to hang up the phone and confidentially call her family and friends to share the news.

While James Lorenstine was on the phone with Maggie Michaels, Mars slipped out into a corridor to make a phone call of his own.

"Lola, it's Mars Johnston from NASA. Listen, I'm calling you from my cell phone as this is an unofficial call. In fact, it could cost me my job. I'm not permitted to call you as you're not officially a member of Carrick's family."

"Mars, What is it?! Is he okay?!" Lola's words sounded labored.
"It's good news, Lola! He's alive!" said Johnston, with muffled enthusiasm. "Listen to me. I can't share many details with you, as the information confirming he's alive is classified. What I will share with you, completely off the record, is that on the transcript we recorded, Carrick was heard saying your name. He even referred to you as the love of his life."

"Don't lie to me, Mars!" Lola sobbed.

"Lola, I would never make something like that up," Mars looked up and down the hallway, conscious of the fact that he should end the call soon. "I want you to keep an eye on the news this evening. It will all be confirmed publicly later tonight. Oh, and one more thing... In the coming days, the launch date will be set for later this year. Keep your hopes up, Lola."

"Wait! Mars, you said he was heard talking. Talking to who? Is there another astronaut up there with him?" asked a confused Lola.

"Look, I've said too much already. Unfortunately, I cannot answer that question right now. Thanks for understanding. I'll talk to you soon."

"Thank you, Mars," said Lola, more at peace with herself.

"All the best, Lola!"

And with that, Mars ended the call.

"Who was that?" asked James Lorenstine as he walked up behind Johnston.

"Oh, that was my ex-wife, Karen. We just received some great news. Our son, Brandon, just got accepted to Yale on a baseball scholarship." Johnston hated lying to his boss.

"You must be very excited!"

Mars replied nervously, "We are! Yes, sir! So excited! Yep!"

Lorenstine didn't seem to notice. "Oh, and by the way, we're meeting with Jim Clapper, the new Director of the CIA, at 5:00 pm today. It'll be in Langley, at the Bush Center. Let's drive over in my car so that we can discuss the next steps. We need to have our act together."

"CIA? Wasn't he the Director of National Intelligence? I thought he retired," said Mars.

"He did, but the new administration brought him back last week," said Lorenstine as he walked away.

Location: Langley, Virginia. The George Bush Center for Intelligence, CIA Headquarters – August 22, 2022. 5:15 pm EST.

"Okay, folks, please have a seat." Jim Clapper motioned everyone to take a seat in the chairs around the table.

"As you may know, we received some good news today regarding our boy, Carrick Michaels. If you haven't already heard, he's alive, and from the sound of things, doing just fine. Now, while NASA's going to handle getting him back to Earth, we need to discuss a matter of a more delicate nature. The audio recording contains dialogue between Dr. Michaels and another man, whose identity is unknown at this point. We intend to get to the bottom of who this unidentified man is and from which country he hails. The audio we have was made possible by our new spy satellite orbiting Black Earth..."

"Ah-hem, it's not actually a spy satellite," Mars Johnston interjected. "Rather, it's a high-powered, laser-focused hybrid, and it bears little resemblance to anything we currently have orbiting Earth. It's called Walker Trace."

Clapper looked stunned at being interrupted. "I'm sorry, who are you?" he asked.

"Director Clapper, you'll have to excuse Dr. Johnston," Lorenstine rushed to his defense. "Marcus Johnston is the head of Mission Control, and he's been heading up the surveillance program monitoring Black Earth."

"Ahhh, very good. Now, as I was saying..." Lorenstine kicked Mars under the table as if to suggest that he stay quiet until he was called upon.

Clapper went on to say, "On the recordings, we hear two men talking. Through voice recognition analysis, we have confirmed that one of them is, in fact, Dr. Carrick Michaels. The other person is simply referred to as Erik. Two other people, Lilly, and Lola are also mentioned in the recording. It will be our job to figure out who these people are."

Mars Johnston chimed in for a second time. "For everyone's edification, I can tell you that Lola, Ummm..." Mars lurched as Lorenstine's foot once again connected with his leg, "Lola would be Lola Cook, the girlfriend of Dr. Michaels," he finished.

"Well, that's fine investigative work, Mr. Johnson. We'll make a note of that," said Clapper dismissively.

"It's actually Johnston, with a T. And, for the record, it's Doctor Johnston," Mars clarified with a lump in his throat and an uncomfortable smile as he was kicked under the table for the third time.

"Duly noted Dr. Johnston; with a T. Now if we can get on?" Clapper dragged his eyes away from Mars. "All of our foreign intelligence officers have been redirected to seek any information that might shed light on the national origins of this person, or entity, Erik."

At the end of the meeting, Clapper pulled Administrator Lorenstine and Mars Johnston to one side. The three men stood awkwardly together in silence as the room cleared.

Once everyone else had left, Clapper addressed them in an exaggeratedly polite tone. "Gentlemen, I want to thank you for your efforts with regards to Operation Laser Focus. However, at this time, you will no longer be heading up this program. My hope is that you don't feel slighted and can understand that this situation has become an issue of national security," he drawled.

"Of course, Director Clapper," said Lorenstine.

"Yes, sir," Johnston concurred, feeling uneasy.

"The two of you will be busy moving forward, with the efforts to return America's hero safely back to Earth," Clapper concluded.

As the three men were leaving the room, Clapper let Lorenstine go ahead. He then tugged on Mars Johnston's arm as if to say, wait for a second, you're not going anywhere.

"Dr. Johnston, May I have a moment?" Again the extreme politeness filled Mars with dread.

"Of course," he replied, completely on edge now.

"I want to apologize," Clapper said, "for mispronouncing your name and not recognizing your hard-earned Ph.D."

"Oh, not at all, Director Clapper."

"Your career in NASA is well documented and storied," continued Clapper.

Marcus tilted his head forward and smiled slightly in acknowledgment, caught off guard by the Director's compliment.

"But I can assure you that it will all be over in an instant the next time you pick up the phone and share classified information with a civilian."

The smile ran from Mars' face, and the knot of dread hardened in his stomach.

"Don't lose any sleep tonight over this. It's understandable why you made the call to Lola, but classified means classified! Do you understand?"

"Yes, sir!"

The two shook hands as Clapper placed his left hand on Mars's right tri-cep in a warm gesture, hoping to calm him down a bit. Clapper exited the room as Mars stood in a puddle of fear. He took a deep breath and exhaled slowly before composing himself. Lorenstine was waiting for him in the hallway. "What was that about?" he asked.

"He just wanted to thank me, I mean us, for the great work we're doing back in Houston."

Location: Washington D.C. NCN National Cable News Network Studios, The Situation Center with Bear Winston – Later that day.

NCN – Breaking News.

"This just in!" said Bear Winston. "Just moments ago, the White House announced that America's newest hero, Dr. Carrick Michaels, is alive. Officials cannot say what evidence led them to this conclusion, but they confirm that Dr. Michaels is, in their words, fit and well. They've also said that our Government's leaders, along with the rest of the G8, will be discussing when we can get back to Black Earth to safely bring Dr. Michaels home."

"Stay tuned, as we'll be turning to our experts for more commentary after a short break. We'll be right back!"

Chapter 21 – A World at War

Location: Black Earth. The Triad, Surface-Level 3, The History Library
– August 30, 2022.

Looking at a forty-inch liquid-glass monitor near the front of The
History Library, Erik asked Carrick, "Is that him?" while pointing to
the man he knew as Albert Einstein.

"I can't believe what I'm seeing!" Carrick exclaimed. "This is crazy!
Albert Einstein was from Zenith?! I just don't know what to say."

"What about him?" asked Erik, indicating a man captioned as Julius
Caesar.

"It looks like a very young version of him, but I can't say for sure,"
replied Carrick. "Pictures of Julius Caesar are all artist interpretations
because there was no photography on Earth when he was alive.
The only way to determine if your claim is valid would be to
calculate the number of years since Zenith's Julius Caesar was sent
to Earth. And then we can see if the time matches up. I minored in
history as an undergrad in college, and I did a paper on Julius
Caesar. His accomplishments were astounding. How many years
does it show since he migrated to Earth?"

"I'm guessing that the word college refers to advanced education?"
surmised Erik aloud.

"You got it!" said Carrick.

His curiosity satisfied; Erik entered some data into the transparent,
floating keypad. "It shows here that the shuttle Caesar traveled on
left Zenith 2,120 years ago."

"Hmmm." Carrick rubbed his chin. "History books on Earth say he
was born around 100BC, so the years do line up. Does it say how
old he was when he left Zenith?"

"It's right here. He was twenty-two, and that he left with his mother,
Aurelia, and his father, Gaius Julius Caesar, along with his..."

Carrick cut Erik off. "With his two sisters, I know. I'll be damned! That's him!" Carrick sat and stared at the screen in stunned silence, almost unable to comprehend these revelations.

After a moment, he collected himself. "Does it have any other details about him prior to leaving Zenith?"

"There's a lot of information here. I remember reading about his family some thirty years ago when I studied that particular shuttle manifest and the people who were on it," said Erik.

"If you've studied every shuttle manifest, there's no telling how many of Earth's most celebrated historical figures you've read about." Carrick shook his head in wonder. "The more we talk, the more I believe everything that you say."

"Well, if you didn't believe me, the truth would be right here in this library. Okay," Erik went back to the keypad, "it says here that one of his ancestors was a Regional Governor in Austriaca. His father, Gaius, was a Hansman in The Triad's 27th Precinct. It also says that their family was very prominent in The Triad's political circles."

Carrick was intrigued. "What's a Hansman?"

"Basically, it was a Chief of State, someone who controlled everything that happened on that particular level of The Triad. Gaius was Chief of State for the entire Surface-Level 3, responsible for everything from educational and governmental reform to post appointments. It says that Julius studied at the Citadel, which was a military academy in The Triad, and that he was a fiduciary scholar. I don't know what that means, though."

"It means to manage assets that aren't your own," explained Carrick. "He must have been studying for life on Earth. That's definitely him!" "What did he do on Earth that made you do a 'paper' on him in college?" asked Erik.

"Geez, that's hard to sum up; he had so many great achievements. Do you have a whole day to discuss it?"

"Please make it a short story. You tend to go on and on," Erik shot Carrick a grin.

Smiling back, Carrick launched in. "Well, first of all, Julius Caesar was an incredible military tactician and governor of people. He led his country to a commanding victory over the Gallic tribes. That helped Rome to secure the River Rhine, which they considered a natural border."

Erik nodded his head, not understanding most of what Carrick was saying but letting him continue anyway.

"Caesar was a highly decorated war hero. He defeated some of the finest military minds in our world's history, including Pompey, the leader of the Roman Republic, and an Egyptian pharaoh named Ptolemy," explained Carrick.

"Without a doubt, though, his most enduring legacy was his referendum of the Roman calendar; he basically sought to add ten days to the calendar to better align it with the solar calendar. He then renamed two of the summer months. One of them he called July, short for Julius, after himself; and another he named August, short for Augustus, after his great-nephew and adoptive son."

"So, Earth has a twelve-month calendar?" asked Erik.

"Yes, it does. How many days does the Zenith calendar have, by the way?"

Erik didn't answer; he just smiled.

Carrick smiled back. "Three hundred and sixty-five?"

"You got that right," Erik nodded.

Both men laughed, and Carrick admitted that perhaps the idea of a three hundred and the sixty-five-day calendar wasn't such an original idea after all.

"Anyway, his list of accomplishments goes on and on. Those are just a few examples. His name was so revered that years after his death, the name Caesar actually became a title given to someone when they ascended to the throne.

"I just have one issue with all of this, though," mused Carrick, "there's documented history of people like Julius Caesar and Albert Einstein. All the way back to their births, the whens, and the wheres of their lives. History suggests they didn't just fall out of the sky as you claim. How do you account for that?"

"Oh, I don't know. I guess it just depends on who was writing the history books. Did it ever cross your mind that a Zenithian took pen to paper and recorded the history they wanted to endure?" asked Erik.

After a brief moment of silence, Carrick spoke up. "Ahh, I get it. They needed to weave these significant figures into Earth's history in order for all of it to make sense to future generations," he reasoned aloud.

"Thanks for the abbreviated summary!" Erik smirked. "Now, we need to move on. Today, my young friend, I need to tell you about The Great War. Come with me."

Erik led Carrick to what appeared to be a twenty-foot wide, liquid-glass monitor on the back wall of The History Library. Fiddling with a keypad, he brought images up on the screen, showing the planet as it descended into chaos.

"The Great War was the event that hastened the climate catastrophe, that eventually drove Zenithians indoors for the remainder of their time on this planet."

"If you recall, the rising coastlines near the mid-latitudes of our planet deluged hundreds of island chains around the globe. Eventually, millions succumbed to heat, famine, lack of fresh water, and disease. Millions more retreated deep into either the northern or southern hemispheres. Many were taken in as refugees by neighboring provinces, nations, and regional territories. Others perished at the borders while waiting for safe passage."
Images on the screen showed wretched people, their few belongings strapped to their backs. They appeared to be begging for help as border guards pointed futuristic weapons at them.

"That looks awful! It's like watching a bad movie!" said Carrick.

"What's a movie?" asked Erik. Carrick just shook his head.

On the screen, nation after nation felt the impact of the heat and rising waters. Regional conflicts broke out, and blood filled the streets as freshwater became increasingly difficult to find.

Erik gave Carrick a grim running commentary. "The greatest nations of Zenith, those with the most wealth and resources, didn't get involved. They simply watched from the sidelines as the survival of the most desperate played out before their eyes. Government officials failed to act, and the citizenry rebelled because of it. Local government facilities were taken over, and after just a few years, once-massive countries were fractured into splinter groups of empathetic crusaders and lawless rebels from the societal fringes."

"As the smallest nations fell, there were only three global powers left on Zenith. They controlled the satellites and aerial space fleets. A once-powerful, naval-ready nation went by the wayside because, as the oceans dried up, so too did their fleets."

"Jesus!" said Carrick. In shock over what he was seeing.

The images on the big screen revealed monorail conduits built beneath what were once vast oceans. The intricate maze of diamond-glass tunnels reminded Carrick of underground subway systems in large metropolises on Earth. Every country seemed to be connected by this high-speed, non-stop transportation network.

Erik kept up his dismal account. "The three remaining countries left standing were Austriaca, Norway, and Maricopa. These were the three most powerful countries pre-war, and the only countries left standing post-war."

"Austriaca had the highest elevations and Zenith's most abundant water reserves, along with the largest population of educational institutions. The country also boasted the most diverse population on Earth, pre-segregation."

"Norway had the highest population levels, the most sophisticated military, and the largest geographic landmass, although much of it was unpopulated due to rough terrain."

"Maricopa had the greatest agricultural wealth and, in many respects, fed our world," said Erik.

"Before the war, the three nations formed a pact called *The Alliance Accord*, governed by a leadership council called *The Allied Assembly*.

The three nations agreed to develop a succession plan that would ensure the survival of the human race. The leaders would pool the resources of their nations. They'd bring together the world's best engineers, architects, craftsmen, educators, medical experts, and scientists. Together they would build and populate a massive facility called *The Succession*.

"The Succession was to house the remaining Zenithian population once The Great War had ended. There would be four corners of The Succession." Erik pointed to a 3-D blueprint illustration that revealed all levels of each corner of what the mammoth mega-structure would look like. "It would house agricultural facilities in one corner, scientific facilities in another, space exploration in the third, and medical facilities in the last."

"That thing looks impressive!" said a wide-eyed Carrick. "I thought The Triad was big; that would have dwarfed all of this."

Erik nodded in agreement and continued. "It wasn't meant to be, however. The plan fell apart when the Segregationist Parties rose up. The referendum was held, and it was decided that the races should be separated. It was then that the plans for The Succession disintegrated. Instead, the facility would become known as The Triad."

"The Triad would have three corners instead of four, with each of the three sectors in the shape of a pentagon. The five-sided sectors would serve as a tribute to Zenith's original founding Principles of Democracy: A Representative Government; Individual Rights; Rule of Law; Right of Speech; and Right of Health," explained Erik.

Carrick grimaced, "Kind of a contradiction; no?" he argued. "How's that?" asked Erik.

Carrick was dismissive. "Well, The Triad separated people based upon their race! There's your contradiction. So much for individual rights.

"Yes, I see your point. Now that I recall, the party in the minority got to choose the design. Perhaps that was a concession made by those in the majority."

Erik continued. "The three main buildings, or sectors, as they became known, would have five surface-levels and ten sub-levels. "Canfield Ripley, The Triad's architect, designed it so that each sector was an exact replica of the other two. Each level, fifteen in total, of each sector, could house up to eight-thousand residents. So, there'd be 120,000 residents per sector. A grand total of 360,000 Zenithians would spend their remaining days enclosed in the facility until they either migrated Home or died waiting. The sectors would be known simply as the Northwest, Southwest, and Southeast Sector."

"Incredible!" said Carrick under his breath.

"Much like the original plan for The Succession, each sector would have designated surface-levels specializing in five human need categories: medicine, space exploration, agriculture, astrophysics, and genetic science."

"The Triad would be built in the highest elevations of Austriaca and sit atop the world's largest water reserve. It would take seven years to complete, and then a lottery called The Chance would begin."

"A lottery?"

"Yes, a lottery. To see who would populate The Triad."

"How did it work?" asked a curious Carrick.

"Each of the three nations was allowed to pre-select no more than 30,000 individuals who were masters in their field of study; the brightest and the best. These people, and their immediate families, were automatically granted access to The Triad. After that, everyone else went into the lottery."

"The Allied Assembly issued bar-coded numbers to each family in the three nations. Then, random numbers were drawn, and those families whose numbers came up were granted an invitation to live in The Triad. They could decline if they chose, but none did. The original lottery winners became known as The Lucky Seven."

"Why the number seven?" asked a curious Carrick.

"The records don't indicate why, but my guess is because it took seven years to build The Triad. Perhaps that's it," Erik suggested.

"The Lucky Seven, huh? That's wild!"

"Why is it wild?" asked Erik.

"On Earth, the number seven is considered a lucky number."

Erik smiled with pride and continued with his history lesson.

"The lottery process itself took many weeks, and then it was another several months before The Lucky Seven had all relocated into The Triad."

"After this place was populated, the Generals took control of their respective countries, and war commenced, with only the strongest surviving. To the victors would go the spoils. But those spoils would be mere relics of a once-great planet. Left to the victors would be charred remains and an uninhabitable atmosphere for the few remaining species still alive. Soon, they would die off too."

Furrowing his brow, Carrick said, "I don't like where this is going."

"The war wasn't fought with foot soldiers, but rather space soldiers, in the form of satellites and ground laser fortresses. The laser garrisons on the ground attempted to wipe out the satellites, and the satellites attempted to wipe out the ground fortresses and every population center on Zenith."

"After that, the population centers were attacked by nuclear fission clusters, designed to pulverize infrastructure. The Generals only had one restriction; stay clear of The Triad. The goal was simple, win at any cost. What came after victory didn't matter."

On the screen was a digital recording made by one of the thousands of satellites orbiting overhead. The footage revealed nuclear holocaust. Thousands of laser beams, blue from the satellites and red from the surface, crisscrossed around the planet. The two sat and watched in horror. As the laser aggression began to subside, massive explosions could be seen on the surface. Rapid succession of atomic explosions pulverized the planet below, followed by hundreds of mushroom clouds. The media file continued to play until the screen was filled with white fuzz. It was an indication that the very satellite recording the devastation was itself destroyed.

Carrick weighed in. "If the Generals had all that power at their disposal, why didn't they just attack The Triad and take it over? "asked Carrick.

"The Generals were incentivized to protect The Triad. The promise they received was ownership of any land they conquered. If there was nothing left worth owning, they were promised luxury accommodations in The Triad. There, they would join their entire extended families who were already living there and seats on a subsequent shuttle Home. No General would risk the safety of their families, or the fate of the human race, by attempting a coup on the leaders of The Triad's Allied Assembly."

"Carrick, our world was on fire. Zenith literally went up in flames, and nearly every living thing went with it. Everything that drew breath from the atmosphere was eventually turned to ash, except for the few in The Triad."

"It was a violent end to an already dying planet, with an unplanned, unexpected, and unforeseen outcome. The massive trauma to Zenith's surface from the war, and the many decades of dehydration of the outer crust, began to reveal the lithosphere. The lithosphere would normally bond the mantle to the outer crust. However, once the outer crust thinned and the lithosphere started to erode, volcanic eruptions became more common and much more violent. And that accelerated the release of carbon and sulfur dioxides into the atmosphere."

"It was like a vicious cycle. More heat was released, and more chemically active fluids, like carbonites, escaped into Zenith's atmosphere. The carbonites, from volcanic ash and from the charred carbon remains of everything that had once lived, coated the outer crust and the planet's manmade ruins. Over the next several decades, the layers of carbonites mounted, and the world's surface became black. With no surface water or precipitation to cleanse it, it remained there."

"The now baked, black powdered crust began to absorb the Sun's heat at a furious rate. Within one hundred years, the surface temperatures had risen to more than 180°F. From there, it grew hotter and hotter with each passing century."

"My God!" said a horrified Carrick. "It was as if you just fast-forwarded through Earth's future. But why couldn't they have just built The Triad and simply not gone to war?"

"That's the question, isn't it?" Erik replied. "There is an answer, Carrick, but you're not going to like it."

In his heart, Carrick knew what was coming next. His face paled as Erik continued.

"The Triad could only house 360,000 people. Zenith's population was more than three billion. War had to happen to ensure The Triad would remain standing after it was populated. Otherwise, those who hadn't got in would have destroyed it as they sought its refuge."

Carrick took a deep breath and whispered, "Oh my God! Genocide!" He was filled with disgust. "I think I'm going to be sick!"

"It was necessary, Carrick," shrugged Erik. "Either the human species died, along with our planet, or 360,000 human beings lived, ensuring the survival of the human race.

"My God! What will become of Earth?"

"By your reaction, I'm guessing that planet Earth is heading down a similar path."

"Sadly, I do believe that to be the case," responded Carrick.

"Be on the lookout for the freshwater resources to start drying up. Once that happens, destruction and devastation will be upon your people, and, unfortunately, it will be irreversible. War will ravage what's left of the vulnerable atmosphere; there will then be a cascade of geological devastation coupled with mass extinction. This will result in the very extinction of humankind itself."

"When I get back," Carrick half-joked, "I'm going to start looking for a good architect."

"That's my boy!" Erik grinned. "Still got that sense of humor."

"Canfield Ripley? That was his name, right?" asked Carrick.

"Yep," Erik nodded.

"Maybe he's got some descendants on Earth I could reach out to," smirked Carrick.

Both somehow laughed off what they had just witnessed and headed back to Barrack 5. Dr. Carrick Michaels would spend a sleepless night reflecting on what he had learned; as a scientist, an astronaut, and as a fellow human being.

Chapter 22 – Operation Black Spear

Location: Planet Earth. Langley, VA. CIA Headquarters, The George Bush Center for Intelligence – September 5, 2022. 10:00 am, EST.

In a large meeting room, Director James Clapper addressed a group of CIA officers. The room was long and narrow, with a conference table taking up most of the square footage. The walls were adorned with framed pictures of the twenty-four former CIA Directors. A more prominent portrait hung at the head of the room, depicting President Harry S. Truman, who founded the Agency in 1947.

Attending the meeting were thirteen agents, the Assistant Director of the CIA, Cornelius Stanley, several assistants, and a stenographer.

"Ladies and gentlemen, thank you for being here today," said Clapper, standing in front of Truman's portrait and behind a small podium. "The reason we're here today is to discuss our plan for identifying the mystery man on Black Earth, who apparently goes by the name of Erik. So far, a total of four NASA astronauts have laid eyes on our subject. Of those four, one is currently still in his company."

"Dr. Carrick Michaels chose to stay behind on Black Earth. From what we know, he was not held against his will. That presumption is based on eyewitness testimony from the other three astronauts who encountered this unknown figure."

"So far, we know very little about our subject, Erik. By appearance, he's been described as an elderly man. He claims to live alone in a massive facility that he calls The Triad. He says he was born there and claimed to have lived alone on Black Earth for the past seventy years or so."

"There is one more thing, though," added Clapper. "We've been secretly monitoring surface transmissions from the moment our astronauts entered Black Earth's orbit, and we're hoping that Carrick can somehow reach out to us. Or, at the very least, that this Erik person might attempt to contact his country of origin."

"Our plan is to send a CIA interrogation specialist to Black Earth, in an effort to determine the following: Erik's true identity, his country of origin, how he came to be on Black Earth, how long he's been there and, finally, his reason for being there."

"At this time, I'd like to introduce you to the person who'll be heading up what we're calling Operation Black Spear. His name is Jordan Spear."

Clapper nodded across the room, and all eyes turned to Jordan Spear, who nodded back in acknowledgment.

"For those of you who've never met Officer Spear, please allow me to tell you a little bit about him. For the past twelve years, he's been working undercover throughout Europe, Ukraine, Russia, and Syria. His specialty is interrogation and counterintelligence. We pulled Officer Spear out of Moscow just two days ago, specifically for this operation, and he'll be flying out to Houston tomorrow morning."

"Officer Spear will begin astronaut training at NASA later this week. This type of training typically takes two years, but Jordan must be ready to go by December. We wish you luck Officer Spear. And with that, I give you the room."

Jordan Spear rose to his feet and walked to the podium. He stood an imposing 6 foot 4 inches tall, had an athletic build, and weighed a stout 230 pounds. His hair was dark brown and slicked back. Today he was dressed in an immaculate suit and tie, but one could get the impression that the thirty-five-year-old didn't have very many suits hanging in his closet.

Jordan Spear had been cultivated and groomed to be a CIA Officer from the age of six by his father, Jonathan, a legendary now-retired CIA Officer. By college-age, though, it seemed Jordan might take a different path. He'd attended the University of Virginia, where he'd graduated with honors, and had been a four-year starter for the Cavaliers, playing the position of Outside Linebacker. In his senior year, he'd achieved All-American honors. Then, in 2009, Spear was selected in the third round of the NFL draft by the Pittsburgh Steelers. A lucrative career in the NFL seemed to be beckoning. Instead, Spear went right to work for the CIA, following in his father's footsteps. The CIA was in his blood, and he was the only man the Agency considered for this mission. As an honor to Officer Spear, they included his name in the operation handle.

"Thank you, Director Clapper," said Spear, having taken Clapper's place at the head of the room. "It's an honor to head up this operation, but I'm not looking for accolades. I, or shall I say we, are here with one objective and one goal. To determine the identity of Black Earth Erik, and to find out who placed him there." Spear's voice was deep and intimidating, and everyone in the room gave him their full attention."

"While none of our foreign assets have reported hearing anything regarding our subject, our efforts will continue. My job will be to join the next manned mission to Black Earth and to interrogate our subject. Together with you, I plan on getting to the bottom of this highly-sensitive matter of national security."

"All of you have been briefed and understand your duties. We'll meet back in this room next Monday at 12:00 pm sharp. I will join you remotely from Houston, and we'll cover any and all updates you have. For now, I want you to get on the phones and ensure your foreign assets are all working synergistically in this effort."

With that, the meeting was adjourned, and the agents went their separate ways. As they filed out, Clapper remained behind to chat with Jordan for a moment in private.

"Jordan, the importance of this mission cannot be overstated," said Clapper. "The catalyst for a successful outcome to Operation Black Spear is for you to become space-worthy by December. If you are not, then Operation Black Spear will have to be scrubbed. Instead, we'll have to rely on some NASA astronaut with no interrogation skills to complete your job and get to the bottom of this mystery. As you can imagine, that would be an unacceptable outcome by Agency standards. Are you getting my point?"

Spear nodded in affirmation. "Yes, sir."

"On the other hand, if you complete the mission and achieve our objectives, we'll bring you home to work beside me here in Langley, not in Moscow, risking your life daily. I'm pretty sure that would make your father very proud."

Location: Houston, Texas. Christopher C. Kraft, Jr. Mission Control Center, Building 30 – September 5, 2022. 11:00am, CST.

"What?!" shouted Mars Johnston. "You've got to be kidding me, Jim!" He slammed a file folder of loose-leaf pages onto the table and threw his hands up in exasperation. "First of all, he'll never be ready by then. And second, if he's not ready, he'll be risking the lives of everyone else on board that ship. And third, whose God damned idea was this anyway?!" he yelled.

"Listen," Lorenstine said, trying to appease him, "this comes straight from the top. While Clapper likely lobbied heavily for this, it came from the White House, not the CIA. We've somehow got to get through to Michaels and see if he can shine some light on this guy Erik. If he can figure it out, then we might not have to take this Spear guy with us."

"Impossible!" said Johnston. "The CIA took over Operation Laser Focus, and I no longer have clearance! Plus, getting some garbled messages from Black Earth is a lot different than having a two-way conversation with Michaels."

"Well, just keep at it! And in the meantime, get your team ready to go; we've got to get this guy prepared for a seventy-five million-mile trip to hell!" Lorenstine then turned to walk out of the room and then swiveled back. "Oh, and Mars, one other thing. I'd like you to come up with the mission's name. Lift-off is officially December 12th of this year, which happens to be Dr. Michaels' birthday. We're bringing him home. Think up a good name," said Lorenstine, with passion in his voice.

"But I thought POTUS said the name was going to be New Beginning and that the launch would be on January 1st?"

"Close," said Lorenstine. "He said the spacecraft would be named New Beginning, which it is. The mission name, however, is our call. As far as the date, the POTUS speech was political. The goal has always been that we go when we're ready to go. Carrick needs to come home, and sooner rather than later. Come up with a good name for the mission."

"Well, in that case, I've got a great idea!" said Mars enthusiastically. "I figured they would move up the launch date to sometime in early December, but I didn't realize it was Carrick's birthday. I was flirting with the concept of Sagittarian Recovery, and now it makes perfect sense. Thoughts?"

"I love it!" responded Lorenstine. "Go ahead, leak it to the press! Give it to Johnson this time, though. Last time you gave it to Winston. I'm a Johnson fan," he smiled.

Mars was stunned. He couldn't stop his face from revealing what he was thinking: 'how'd you know it was me?'

Lorenstine chuckled and walked away without further comment.

Location: Washington D.C. NCN Studios, Studio of The Lead-Up with Jake Johnson– September 5, 2022. 4:45 pm EST.

"This just in!" Jake Johnson announced. "NASA has officially named its Black Earth rescue mission Sagittarian Recovery. The mission aim will be to bring home the international hero Dr. Carrick Michaels. You'll remember that Michaels is the astronaut who volunteered to stay behind on Black Earth, for reasons unknown, back in March of this year."

"The spaceship, named New Beginning, will be carrying the world's bravest scientists, aviators, and doctors, back to Black Earth. No word yet on the exact date, but December is circled on NASA's calendar. The prime objective is to bring Dr. Carrick Michaels home. But it will also provide scientists with more time to explore Black Earth's surface and conduct further tests and experiments. An interesting note for you; we've learned that Carrick Michaels will be celebrating his birthday on December 12th. Wouldn't it be a great birthday present if NASA launched on that day?" Johnson teased his audience.

Location: Houston, TX. Christopher C. Kraft, Jr. Mission Control Center, Building 30 – September 6, 2022. 10:00am, CST.

When Mars Johnston entered the office of the NASA Chief Administrator, he saw that James Lorenstine already had company. A man Mars had never seen before was sitting chatting with his boss.

"Come in, Mars! I want you to meet our newest recruit." Lorenstine hand gestured him to take a seat.

The man half-rose and extended his hand towards Johnston, offering to shake.

Mars declined the gesture. "From the size of you, along with the fancy introduction, I'm guessing you're CIA Officer Jordan Spear," muttered Mars, sulkily.

Spear's hand fell back to his side. "That would be me!" he nodded. "I'm honored to meet you, sir."

"Well, color me unimpressed!" said Johnston, staring Spear up and down. He knew Jordan was twenty years his junior and didn't feel he had to stand on ceremony. "I'm a retired marine, and I don't get why you CIA guys are always thought of as the heroes! Brought in to somehow save the day." Mars' tone dripped with sarcasm. "Let me guess, Matt Damon's your idol? I bet you have a Jason Bourne tattoo hiding up that sleeve, don't you?" He pointed at Spear's massive biceps.

"Actually, sir, my father is my hero. And with regards to your second question, hiding up my sleeve is a five-inch scar I earned while killing a man in Kiev after a double-agent blew my cover." Spear spoke firmly and looked at Mars squarely in the eye. "Listen, I can do this all day if you'd like, but I'd rather get to work if that'd be okay with you..., sir!"

Lorenstine put a stop to the growing tension. "Alright, alright, if this is going to be a pissing contest, the two of you are excused to go to the restroom. It's down the hall on the left!"

Mars came to his senses. "No, it's okay, Jim. Listen, it's nothing against you personally; it's just this whole messed up situation," said Mars. He extended his hand to Spear.

Spear reciprocated with a firm handshake. As his hand swallowed up Johnston's, he gave him a wink and a smile. Mars looked down at the clenched hands and smiled.

"Alrighty then," he said. From that moment, Spear had earned Mars Johnston's respect.

Later that day, Spear spotted Mars Johnston exiting his office. "Mr. Johnston, sir!" Spear flagged down Johnston, who was walking the other way.

"Ahh, Officer Spear, I was expecting you. Come with me for a minute; let's grab a coffee."

Moments later, in an empty employee lounge just across the hall, Mars was conciliatory. While pouring a cup of coffee, Mars said, "Listen, about earlier...,"

Jordan cut Mars off. "Don't worry about it," he said.

"No-no, let me say what I have to say. I want to explain. What you have to understand is that men and women wait their entire lives to go into space. They grow up dreaming about it; they study for years; they make crappy money. And they do it all for the slim chance that one day they'll be called upon to do something that was just laid in your lap. I don't like the fact that you were asked to fill one of the eight seats on that spaceship to Black Earth in December. In fact, I hate it!"

"Just because of some politician's decision, I have to tell one of my men or women that they're out and you're in. That doesn't sit well with me," he explained. "I'm not mad at you; I'm just mad at the whole thing. Now look, I took my frustrations out on you, and for that, I apologize. I'm sorry."

"No problem, sir."

"Call me Mars, please," said Johnston.

"Okay, Mars, it is then!" Spear responded. "Listen, I never liked flying, and I surely never dreamed of being an astronaut. However, I was called upon. I'm the only one that they considered. I was asked to go; they didn't tell me I had to. I might have thought twice about it if they had, but they asked, and I said yes. I have a duty. A duty to honor all of the hundred and thirty-three CIA officers who've died in the line of service. I will do whatever I am asked to do and not question it. I hope you can understand that" Spear finished.

"I do understand, but I also have to ensure the safety of my team. That's my entire job function. In the history of spaceflight, there've only been fourteen astronauts and four cosmonauts killed in the effort to advance space travel. Do you know why, Officer Spear?"

"Not sure, sir," fumbled Spear.

"I'll tell you why. It's because these were men and women who trained for years. Nearly six hundred people have traveled into space, and only eighteen have died. That's too many. Of course, it is. But the fact that the death toll is so low is because these heroes from around the globe spend years of their lives training and preparing. And it's also thanks to the hard work of scientists, engineers, mathematicians, and countless others on the ground." Johnston's voice was full of passion. "The vast majority of astronauts do come home. That's what training and preparation do: they bring you home."

"That means, when I send someone up there who isn't properly trained, the lives of all the others on board are also at risk. Their chances of coming home safely diminish greatly." Mars looked down at his hands, clasped on the table. "Do you understand, Jordan?" he asked quietly.

A conciliatory Spear nodded at his new mentor.

It was the beginning of a long conversation. The two men sat in the breakroom and talked about themselves, about life, about college football; Mars was a Tech fan. Eventually, Johnston changed the subject back to the task at hand.

"Jordan, have you ever flown at Mach 1 speed before?"

"I've never even flown first class before," replied Spear, looking a little embarrassed. "I been on a few hundred trips strapped to the back of a Hercules C-130, but those things move pretty slow compared to a jet. Or a rocket, for that matter."

Mars nodded. "A C-130 tops out at about 370 mph. Mach 1 is more than twice that speed at 767 mph. Meanwhile, a rocket launched from the Earth's surface needs to reach 4.9 miles per second or 294 miles per minute, or better yet, 17,640 mph, in an effort to achieve orbital velocity. That's roughly twenty-three times the speed of sound."

"Whoa!" Jordan nearly jumped from his seat.

"Listen, I'm not trying to scare you, but there's a reason it takes two years to train someone to be an astronaut. We must somehow prepare your body and mind for the extreme G-Forces that you're going to experience in a very short time. Have you ever heard of G-Force Centrifuge Training?" asked Mars.

"No, I haven't."

"Well, you're gonna be introduced to it tomorrow." Mars stood up and threw his coffee cup away, turned back to Jordan, and said. "You're about to do some extreme planet-hopping, Jordan. You'll travel on a spacecraft that will accelerate and decelerate violently, subjecting you to intense G-Forces your body simply isn't built for. There will be times when you're going to weigh fifteen times more than you do right now, and I'm guessing you're not especially light at the moment," Mars chuckled at his own joke before turning serious again.

"Let me tell you what happens if you're not prepared. Those bad-ass Gs can cause G-LOC. That's G-Induced Loss of Consciousness. It's when G-Forces prevent blood from getting to the brain, and if your brain isn't getting enough blood, you lose consciousness."
Jordan was now looking horrified.

"The good news is High-G training is routine for us. We use it to prepare fighter pilots and astronauts for those extreme Gs. Plus, you'll be outfitted in a G-Suit, which will squeeze the lower half of your body to try to force blood up to your brain. That should help a bit."

"This is serious stuff!" Jordan looked a little peaked.

Mars sighed. "If you lose consciousness at the wrong time, Jordan, you're not likely to be the only one that gets hurt. Dating back to the 1930s, hundreds of fatal accidents were caused by acceleration-induced loss of consciousness. It's my job to make sure that doesn't happen to you."

"Thanks for freaking me out!" said Jordan, who was looking a little pale.

"So, if you don't lose consciousness tomorrow, we'll be off to a good start!" Mars smiled as he clapped his hand on the shoulder of a pale-faced Spear.

Chapter 23 – Why on Earth

Location: Black Earth. Northwest Sector of The Triad, Sub-Level 7, The Culina – September 7, 2022.

"Mm-Mm, Brown Maize is pretty good!" said Carrick, admiring the metal cup in his raised left hand while wiping his lips with the right. Holding the empty cup to his nose, Carrick inhaled deeply. "That's weird, it tastes good, but there's almost no smell to it." He sniffed a second time as if to make sure.

"Who cares as long as it tastes good," Erik shrugged. He seemed moody this morning.

Nearly six months had passed since Carrick first arrived, and the two were becoming quite comfortable with each other.

"Gotta tell ya, I could really go for some steak and eggs right now," Carrick reminisced.

"What are steak and eggs?"
"God, you really need to get out more!"

"I don't get out at all!" Erik laughed without humor. "They really did brainwash you, didn't they?"

"Whatta you mean?"

"Every word you say is either God or Jesus related," snapped Erik.

"I guess so!" Carrick looked skyward as if to give Erik's words more credence.

As they washed their cups, Carrick explained that some people on Earth eat only plants, but most eat both animals and plants; and that human beings are near the top of the food chain. Erik seemed intrigued and listened for a while as Carrick fantasized about some of his favorite dishes.
After the two finished, they sat together in The Culina, and Carrick asked Erik an obvious question. "Erik, not once since I've been here have you asked me what life is like on Earth. Why is that?"

Because while I'm curious, it's better that I don't know," Erik replied dismissively.

"Why?"

"Because I don't want to know about a place that I'll never see. I would never subject myself to thoughts, images, or otherwise that might make me desire a home other than my own. Besides, I've seen plenty of aerial images of Earth, taken by migration shuttles over the centuries. They've painted a picture that satisfies all of my curiosities. I do not need to see or hear any more about Earth."

"Well, if you ever do come to Earth, I'll take you out to an awesome Mexican place. You'll love chips and queso!" said Carrick, his mouth-watering.

"I don't know what any of that is, and I'm never going to Earth, as I have told you," said Erik firmly. "I'll die right here like I was meant to. I'm just happy that the last shuttle to Earth was able to advance the human cause. Like I said before, the fact that you're here right now means that technology, medicine, and space travel, likely exploded after Earth's year 1947."

"You know, all I was trying to do was remember my favorite foods, and you had to get all grouchy on me. Either way, you're coming back with me to Earth, so you'll be going to that Mexican place with me eventually."

Erik shrugged off Carrick's words.

Until that moment, neither of them had discussed Erik going back to Earth. This left both wondering why the conversation had never come up before. Now that it had, they were both sure it would be the subject of many more discussions to come. That thought made Erik feel profoundly uncomfortable.

Of course, he'd always wondered what it was like on Earth. But what would be the point of going? By now, most, or perhaps all, of the Zenithians who'd migrated to Earth would be dead. He'd simply be going to satisfy his curiosity. And what if he didn't like it? Any journey to Earth was a one-way ticket, and he'd never again see his actual home. He was nearing the end of his life, and at least here, he was surrounded by memories of his family and of Lilly. Why would he want to leave that behind? He'd been asking himself the same question over and over since Carrick's arrival, "Why on Earth?"

Looking off into blank space and pondering the future, Erik was jolted back into reality by the young and energetic Carrick Michaels.

"Why? Why wouldn't you get on a ship with me and go back to Earth?"

Erik answered abruptly. "This is my home, and Earth was never supposed to be."

In disgust, Carrick threw his hands in the air and shouted, "That's bullshit! You said that from the time you were little, Zenithians were indoctrinated with the notion of going Home one day. You've told me that time and time again!"

Erik collected his thoughts before speaking again. "Carrick, listen, here's how it really played out for most of us. Many of my generation knew we'd be going Home on the very last shuttle because we were the brightest people remaining in the population. The problem was that shuttles didn't go Home very often. It could be as many as ten to thirty years between migrations. It became harder and harder to drop thirty-thousand people into an ever-growing population on Earth. So, we had to stagger the migrations of our remaining people in the final two hundred years. You must remember, the goal was to go unnoticed and assimilate discretely."

"The later shuttles made thousands of stops around your globe. We had to carefully drop small fractions of the shuttle's passengers near the biggest population centers so that the newcomers would be able to blend in without bringing attention to themselves. We also dropped tiny clusters of Zenithians in more rural locations."

"Back to my original point," continued Erik, "thousands were born, and thousands died between migrant journeys to Home. Most of us thought that we would never actually go. That's why there was such a big celebration when a shuttle manifest was announced. People wanted to go Home but weren't sure they ever would. I was one of those people, and I was right. I never did go Home." Tears of frustration began to pool in Erik's eyes.

Carrick put his hand on his friend's arm. "But now you can! Or at least I think so anyway." He suddenly wondered if he'd spoken too soon.

"What do you mean, you think so?" asked Erik, suddenly curious despite himself.

"Well, my logic is based on what I know to be true: That the people on Earth are all descendants of Zenith. I just realized, though, that we're the only two people that know this for a fact."

"As I said, I'm not going to Earth!" Erik's emotions were boiling over. "Just drop it!"

Carrick snapped his fingers. "No, wait! It's just a simple DNA test! When they come back, they're going to make pincushions out of both of us!"

"What's a pincushion?"

Carrick ignored the question. "They're going to do blood tests on both of us. They'll want to make sure you're human and not some alien wearing a human's skin. And they'll need to make sure I'm space travel-worthy. Then, when they get those blood samples back to Earth, they'll conduct DNA tests. Then they'll know conclusively that you're human. And if you are human, well then, they might want to bring you back anyway."

"If?" Erik questioned incredulously. Before Carrick could answer, Erik burst out in frustration, "For the last time, I'm not going to Earth with you or anyone else!"

Both men sat fuming, frustrated by the others' point of view.

After a few sulky minutes, Carrick asked. "Can I have another cup of this stuff? I know it's just one serving a day, but I'm still hungry."

"I don't care!" Erik sounded resigned now. "You'll be leaving soon enough, and I'll be dead not long after. I'm sure we have enough left. Just lay off the Red Fruit!"

"Brown Maize, it is then!" smiled Carrick. He served himself another cup and sat back down. His mouth half-full, he asked, "Are you gonna be like this all day today?"

"Like what?"

"Like a moody little boy!" laughed Carrick.

Erik didn't respond. He just sat there with a bemused look on his face. It was as if Carrick's voice was little more than white noise to the tired, old man.

Both were now feeling a little moody; they headed to The History Library for the 168th straight day. By now, Carrick had absorbed hundreds of hours of information, not just about Zenith's history but also about Earth's. For thousands of years, Zenith's shuttles had photographed, documented, and cataloged Earth's evolution through shuttle reconnaissance photographs.

Each time a shuttle visited Home, whether manned or unmanned, it brought back thousands of images. Carrick found this record of Earth's surface evolution fascinating. It had the potential to give scientists on Earth a better understanding of what Earth looked like through the decades, centuries, and millennia.

One question bothered Carrick, though, and now seemed like as good a time as any to raise it.

"Erik, I have to ask you a difficult question. It's been on my mind since we first came here to The History Library."

"Go ahead," responded Erik, less grumpy now that his body had fully absorbed the Red Fruit.

"Your suggestion that Zenithians populated Earth with human beings doesn't jibe with our scientific findings," Carrick put it gently. "Can you pull up Earth on the hologram again?" he asked.

Erik obliged him, and a translucent, slowly rotating Earth appeared. Carrick stopped it with his finger on a view of Earth that revealed parts of Africa, Europe, and Asia.

"Erik, I'm not a biologist like you. I am, however, from Earth, and I possess information that you do not. That information contradicts your timeline. It is true that modern human civilizations on Earth have only been around for roughly six-thousand years. And that fits with the Zenithian migration timeline. However, human-like species have been on Earth for roughly 1.8 million years."

"Some of these were archaic forms of human beings, for example, a species we call Homo-erectus. They were given the name Erectus because they actually walked upright. Our science indicates to us that they first appeared on Earth between 1.8 to 1.3 million years ago and eventually died off as recently as 70,000 years ago."

"By about 700,000 years ago, another human-like species had evolved, with a clear resemblance to modern-day humans. We call them Homo-heidelbergensis. They first appeared in Africa," he explained, pointing to the African continent on the holographic globe. "They then migrated from there to Asia and Europe, some 400,000 to 300,000 years ago."

As Carrick traced his finger in a triangular pattern on the translucent globe, he was reminded of the shape of The Triad. With a shiver, he also realized that these were the same three regions Erik had described as the settlement pattern for the three Zenithian racial classifications.

"Anthropologists believe Homo heidelbergensis migrated here," Carrick pointing to Europe on the globe, "eventually evolving into another species, the Neanderthals. While the group that migrated here to Asia evolved into Denisovans. And finally, the group in Africa eventually became Homo-sapiens, what we thought to be the ancestors of all humans," said Carrick.

"What are you asking me, son?" asked Erik, his arms folded in front of him.

"Stick with me; I'm getting there," said Carrick.

"Around 100,000 years ago, some Homo-sapiens left Africa and migrated to the Middle East. There, they encountered the Neanderthals, and they bred with them. That seems a remarkable fact on its own because most anthropologists view them as different species. But what we know for sure is that they interbred because most humans have bits of Neanderthal genetic material mixed in with their DNA. Are you following me so far?"

"I'm listening; please continue," encouraged an intrigued Erik.

"Okay. Well, somewhere around forty-thousand years ago, our fossil records indicate that Neanderthals went extinct. We're not sure what caused them to die off, but they certainly did."

"Now for the tough question." Carrick took a deep breath. "How can you possibly explain that nearly all human beings on Earth today inherited one to four percent of their genes from the Neanderthals." Carrick was speaking in a rush now as he tried to get the question out. "If human beings from Zenith didn't even arrive until as recently as six thousand years ago, how can that be?"

"Listen, I never told you that similar life forms didn't exist on Earth prior to the first arrival of Zenithian migration shuttles. I don't know who or what walked that planet before we got there. And while I certainly don't have all the answers, I can likely shed some light on your questions," replied Erik.

"Human beings, like you and me, are made up of matter that's ubiquitous throughout the Universe. Ninety-nine percent of the human body is made up of six common elements: calcium, carbon, hydrogen, nitrogen, oxygen, and phosphorus. Most of the other one percent is comprised of another five elements: chlorine, magnesium, potassium, sodium, and sulfur. All eleven of these elements are necessary for human life and those other life forms that may closely resemble humans."

Carrick sat attentively and absorbed Erik's words like a sponge.

"If a planet has H2O, light energy from a star, enough gravity to hold onto an atmosphere, and chemicals to make nutrients, then life can evolve and thrive. The surface temperature also has to be right. It's got to be somewhere between 59°F and 239°F for life, as we know it, to survive. It's likely that life might exist, in some form, on any planets that meet those conditions."

"If Earth is anything like pre-war Zenith, and it obviously is and was, then life would no doubt have evolved in many forms. I'd estimate that more than five billion different species have likely lived there over the millennia, as they once did on Zenith."

"So, wait a second! Are you saying that Zenith had other human-like species, which shared characteristics with humans?"

"Of course!" replied Erik. "Humans evolved from other creatures on Zenith. In fact, let me show you some examples."

Turning back at the hologram, Erik used the floating holographic slider to dial backward to a time before the climate crisis occurred on Zenith. He zoomed in on various parts of the planet. The images revealed a rich biosphere just like Earth's, with many species, including ape-like creatures, closely resembling those Carrick was familiar with, from Earth. Carrick's eyes lit up. It was starting to dawn on him that there were likely far more Earthlike planets out there in the Universe than he'd once thought.

Erik added, "But to be clear, Carrick, the chances of human beings, in the form of you and me as we stand here today, being found on different planets is all but impossible."

"Why, if our chemical make-up is so common?" asked Carrick.

"Because the processes that create all life are blind, our existence in this form is nothing more than a happy accident," said Erik. "We are the result of billions of species co-inhabiting a wet, rocky planet; mating and reproducing across millions of generations, their DNA copying imperfectly each time."

"Which ones live to breed again? Which ones die, removing their genes from the pool? The conditions on the planet itself control the answers to these questions. Sometimes conditions are conducive to life, and many survive. Sometimes conditions are harsh, and many die. And sometimes only the luckiest ones endure. The planet itself is the ultimate judge of that. We are quite simply the result of this process, one spanning billions of years of history," concluded Erik, sitting back reflectively.

Both men sat there for a moment and pondered life itself.

Erik then added, "Carrick, in lay terms, what I'm trying to say is that if along the way to first meeting your mother, your father took a left turn rather than a right, you and I would not be sitting here today."

Carrick shook his head and said, "Natural Selection."

Erik smiled. "While that term is familiar to me, I like to think of it as the lottery of life. That's precisely how humans came to be on Zenith."

"Back on Earth, we call it the Theory of Evolution."

Erik nodded and said, "On Zenith, we called it Darwinism."

Carrick stood in stunned silence and was looking a little pale.

Erik said, "You okay, son? You alright?"

Carrick whispered under his breath, "No." It took him a few moments to fully comprehend what he'd just heard. But by now, the revelations Erik kept delivering were becoming almost routine.

"It's nothing," he said. "Please continue."

Erik went on to say, "When we mapped out Earth, from many miles above the surface, we detected no life forms that matched those on Zenith. However, we were absolutely sure that they existed beneath all of those trees and in all of those oceans. How could they not?"

"To be clear though, human civilization, as humans on Earth know it to be, absolutely did not exist in the thousand years before the first manned shuttles from Zenith. There was no detectable infrastructure or traces of civilizations that we could find," added Erik.

"So, you're saying that if it were not for the mass Zenithian migration to Earth, human beings might not be there today?" asked Carrick.

"No, you're saying that I'm not," said Erik.

"However, it's unlikely that any species on Earth would look like you and I do today."

"How else can you explain the fact that in the millions of years before Zenithians reached Earth, essentially no human advancement occurred? And yet, in the mere six-thousand years since we arrived, your world, as you know it today, blossomed up out of the ground?"

"And how do you further explain this. Earth's modern technical advancements began only after we started sending our best and most up-and-coming people over the last one hundred and fifty years or so? Do you really think that's a coincidence?"

Carrick was speechless. He stood there and stared into empty space, seemingly trying to put it all together in his head.

To underscore his point, Erik showed Carrick images of Earth from seven-thousand down to six-thousand years ago. Carrick agreed; no life forms or infrastructure could be seen. Erik did clarify, though, that the images they were looking at were mere swatches from Earth's vast surface area. He stated that even though life, like human beings, had not been detected, it was surely there, living and thriving to some degree.

"Look, Carrick, all I can tell you is what I know for certain. Zenithians began their migration to Earth a little more than six thousand years ago. What was living there before that, in the dirt, in the trees, or the oceans, I couldn't say. I was never actually there, and I'm only one-hundred and fifteen-years-old. I can only rely on the documented evidence that I'm showing you now. Though you've studied far less of this evidence than I, the case is compelling, is it not?"

Shaking his head, Carrick muttered, "But the DNA makeup of nearly all human beings on Earth today includes genes from the Neanderthals. I just don't get it. There has to be some kind of connection." He stood before the globe in awe, shaking his head in disbelief. Finally, he turned to Erik and said, "I'm gonna need a cup of that Red Fruit!"

Erik, too, was perplexed. "There must be something we're not seeing," he thought to himself.

Location: Barrack 5 – Later that evening.

Long after Carrick had fallen asleep, Erik laid in his bunk, staring into the darkness. As he mulled over Carrick's question, he realized that he needed to know the answer as well. As quietly as he could, he pulled himself from his bed and returned to The History Library.

He was troubled by Carrick's question, and more importantly, why he was unable to answer it. "Carrick's riddle must be solved!" a determined Erik told himself.

Early the next morning, Carrick awoke to find Erik gone. He went to The Culina, and when he didn't find him there, he figured that he must be in The History Library.

Entering the library, Carrick found Erik at the back of the long, cavernous facility. Erik spotted him and said, "Come on back, son, I have something to share with you."

Carrick walked to where Erik was hunched over a small tablet. Beside him were two cups of Red Fruit; one half-empty, the other full.

"I've been expecting you," Erik grinned, sliding the full cup of his favorite flavor across the table to Carrick. "Take a look at this!" He handed Carrick the tablet.

"What exactly am I looking at here?" Carrick asked with sleep-filled eyes.

"Let me put it on the big screen for you." Erik activated the twenty-foot wide; liquid-glass monitor on the back wall of The History Library.

The images showed a more pedestrian time on Zenith. A time that resembled present-day Earth rather than the far more modern infrastructure of Zenith.

"I don't get it. What is this?"

"Carrick, this is Zenith 40,000 years ago, and these are five massive rockets getting ready to lift-off."

Erik hit the Play button on the sliding dial, and the images went from still frame to motion.

"Carrick, these rockets, destination unknown, never returned to Zenith. The records indicate that after this launch event, the manned space exploration program on Zenith was canceled. More suspiciously, all the data regarding the passengers on these rockets is gone from The History Library archives."

"What are you saying?" Carrick was now wide awake. "You're not suggesting that one or all of those rockets was headed to Earth, are you?"

"Son, I don't know. I'm not suggesting that this is a possible missing link or that it even remotely answers your question from last night. What I am saying, though, is that Zenith didn't continue its space exploration program for another 30,000 years after that mysterious launch. However, I can confidently say that the mass migration to Earth occurred as a result of our planet beginning to die off. It was due to the global climate crisis that we faced."

Both men were left to ponder the footage and what it meant. Did Earth and other inhabitable planets serve as a giant Petri dish for Zenithian scientists? Did those rockets land on Earth? Did the human contents of those rockets come into contact with the Neanderthals? Were Zenithians on Earth for far longer than the last six thousand years? What other species or plant life might have been on those rockets? What seeds of life from Zenith might have been planted on Earth thousands of years prior to the Zenithian Migration Program? And finally, would any of these questions ever be answered?

Chapter 24 – Centrifuge Training

Location: Houston, TX. Lyndon B. Johnson Space Center, Centrifuge Training Facility – September 7, 2022. 9:46 am, CST.

"I must admit, it's been a long time since I actually witnessed someone vomiting inside of the centrifuge simulator," joked Mars Johnston.

Two men assisted Jordan Spear out of the centrifuge flight training simulator. He looked wobbly and pale, and vomit dripped from his chin and his G-suit. Mars carefully patted Spear on the back to avoid getting vomit on his hands. "You know, somebody's gotta clean that up," he said, inspecting his palm to make sure it was vomit-free.

"In your defense, though, most astronauts, especially in the early days, were test pilots and were used to high rates of speed. Don't worry; you'll be fine, young man!"

Spear looked up at him. He felt utterly embarrassed but didn't want to show it. "I'm fine," he said with a false sense of bravado. "Let's do it again!"

"Nope, that's all the G-force training you can take for today. And besides, you passed your first test!

"How's that?" wondered aloud an unsteady Jordan.

"You did it, Jordan! You didn't pass out!" said an enthusiastic Johnston. "Now come on, let's get you cleaned up and into the classroom."

Jordan, still nauseous, didn't share in Mars' enthusiasm.

About an hour later, when Jordan had showered and changed, he arrived at Mars' office and stuck his head in.

"Knock-knock," he said, tapping on the open door.

"Jordan! Come in, son," said Mars, as he walked around his desk to greet his guest.

Jordan's eyes nearly popped as he entered. Littered around the room were dozens of statues and models of Saturn V rockets and Space Shuttles. The walls were adorned with photographs of Mars with presidents, space legends, athletes, and movie stars. As Jordan looked closer, he could see that some of them were autographed. "Geez!" whistled Jordan. "This place is amazing!"

"Yeah, that's what happens when you've been around as long as I have. People actually want to take their picture with you," said a humble Mars. Mars fooled no one, though, looking star-struck in most of the photos.

Taking a seat, Jordan felt terrible. "Mars, listen. I want to say I'm sorry. I hope I didn't embarrass you earlier this morning."

"Do you mean you hope you didn't embarrass yourself?" asked Mars grinning.

Half seated on the front edge of his desk, with arms folded and both feet on the floor, Mars reassured Jordan. "Son, listen, you're going to get sick again, you're going to get your hands dirty, you're going to fail. Failure is good... If you learn from it! Don't worry; no one here judges anyone. NASA is comprised of people that are at the top of their field. You don't ascend to the highest levels of anything without a thousand little failures along the way. The little failures of today help to prevent the big failures of tomorrow. The big failures are dying in a vacuum, a million miles from home, not some vomit on your chin just down the hall."

Jordan, looking contrite, rubbed his chin and didn't respond to Mars.

"Come on, let's go get breakfast... again," joked Mars.

The two men headed for the cafeteria for the second time that morning. Mars wanted Jordan to have a full belly before class started. Walking down the hall, Mars put his hand on Jordan's shoulder in a show of paternal affection.

After their second meal, Mars escorted Jordan to a room with about a dozen chairs set up in a classroom-style configuration. There, he introduced Jordan to an instructor named Dr. Conrad Schuyler.

At 6 foot 4 inches, the seventy-year-old Professor Schuyler was as tall as Jordan, if not as broad. His salt and pepper hair caught the light streaming in the windows as he welcomed his new student. "It's a pleasure to meet you, Mr. Spear," he roared in a heavy German accent.

Jordan extended his rather large hand to shake the even larger hand of Schuyler. "It's an honor to meet you, sir," Spear said respectfully.

"Call me, Professor Schuyler!" boomed the lanky teacher. "Mars has filled me in as to why you're here and what I need to do to get you ready in just a few short weeks. I hope that you're a good student and an attentive listener. That will make the process go much more smoothly."

"I graduated Magna Cum Laude from the University of Virginia!" said Jordan, proudly.

"Well, we won't hold that against you, now will we!" said the flamboyant Schuyler, practically elbowing Mars in the ribs while chuckling heartily. "I was actually hoping you'd tell me you were at the top of your class at Harvard, as those are the sorts of folks that walk these halls!"

At that moment, Jordan realized how difficult it was going to be to learn everything required of him in such a short amount of time. This was NASA, after all. This was life and death in deep space. It suddenly occurred to him that he was literally going to be surrounded by rocket scientists for the duration of his time at NASA.

Setting his jaw, he said, "I'm ready to do this!"

Mars turned for the door, looking at his watch. "Well, I'll let you two get to it then," he said. "Jordan, I'll see you in eight-hours! We'll do dinner!" Mars winked.

Wide-eyed, Jordan mouthed to him. "Eight-hours?"

Then Mars was gone, and Jordan was alone with Dr. Schuyler. "Okay, Mr. Spear," the professor pulled back a chair and invited him to sit. "Let's start with the basics."

Jordan pulled an unused legal pad from his bag in a show of enthusiasm. He immediately began jotting notes as Professor Schuyler began.

"Your training today will be geared toward the physical challenges thrown at you in space. Over the next six weeks, you'll also be briefed as to the conditions you'll face on Black Earth."

"During our time together, we'll be discussing not only lift-off and landing but the zero-gravity of outer space. It is equally important to note that the mind, as well as the human body, are put to the test when preparing for and experiencing space flight."

As Jordan listened dumbfounded, Schuyler explained several effects that launch, and landing have on astronauts. These included: elevated blood pressure, loss of consciousness, impaired vision, and lung respiration disruption.

Schuyler went on to describe the symptoms of motion sickness while living and working in changing gravity environments. He also went on to list what effects these symptoms can have on operational capabilities.

"Jordan, the vast majority of astronauts experience motion sickness at some point, particularly early on. Please understand, it won't be a sign of weakness should you become ill during training or while in space," expressed a sincere Schuyler.

Jordan was finding it increasingly hard to hide his sluggishness. The G-force training that he'd completed earlier that morning was wreaking havoc on both his physical and psychological state. His desk was in the front row, just three feet from Schuyler's. Luckily for him, Schuyler was busy drawing on an old-school chalkboard, with his back to the bored, tired, and hopelessly distracted Spear.

"The effects of motion sickness can last for days." Schuyler went on. "Even after returning from space, you're likely to feel ill for several weeks considering how long you'll be in zero-gravity."

The subject matter that Schuyler was covering was not helping Jordan stay focused, and just sixty minutes into the lesson, Schuyler felt compelled to ask Spear, "How are you doing so far? Am I going too fast for you?"

Jordan's head was spinning, and he was nauseous, but he summoned as much courage as he could and pronounced, "No, I'm good. I think I got it so far."

"That's very good, Jordan!" said a skeptical Schuyler as he continued with his instruction.

"Okay, let's move on to Cardiovascular events."

Jordan's eyes were heavy. He found himself expending every ounce of energy on keeping them open rather than focusing on the words of Schuyler.

For the next three-hours, Schuyler covered a multitude of subjects, from cardiovascular events to orthostatic intolerance. Jordan just sat there looking as if he was lost in space. Schuyler couldn't help but notice.

"Jordan, are you following me?"

"Yes, Professor," replied Jordan, slurring his words slightly.

"Okay, well then, let's now discuss the effects spaceflight can have on the human body," said Schuyler.

For the next hour, Schuyler discussed both the lethal environment of outer space and the environment within the craft, explaining that Jordan's body would have to be prepared for the dangers of both. Jordan would not only experience different gravities during the mission but would also experience two landings and two take-offs, as he was part of the surface exploration crew.

With his head hanging, Jordan decided that he'd had enough. He raised his hand and interrupted Schuyler. "Professor Schuyler, is all of this information really necessary if I'm just going along for the ride?" he asked.

Dr. Schuyler turned slowly from the chalkboard; hand still raised as if ready to write. He pointed the piece of chalk in his hand firmly at his student. "Young man, it's questions like that that will not only get you killed but could result in the unintended deaths of your crewmates. I strongly suggest you start taking notes instead of sitting there wondering if we should be occupying this empty room, wasting each other's precious time."

For the first time in a long time, Jordan Spear swallowed hard and bowed his head in compliance. He again realized that this was serious and that he was entirely out of his element. "Life and death in a vacuum?" he asked himself. He was beginning to believe that he was the wrong man for the job. He tore away the first page of his legal pad, and with it went the boredom doodles that he had sketched.

"Well then, may I take a fifteen-minute break?" the young Spear requested.

"I think that would be a good idea," responded Schuyler. "Make it thirty!"

It was during that break that the young Spear desperately tried to shake off the morning. After vomiting in the bathroom sink, he rinsed both his mouth and eyes. Staring at himself in the mirror, he made a silent commitment to himself and the others involved with the mission. He would do everything he could to make sure he was completely prepared for what was to come, no matter the challenge, no matter his level of fear.

As Jordan exited the bathroom, he unknowingly kicked a crumpled-up piece of paper that was balled up and lying on the tiled floor. As the door closed, the ball of boredom doodles came to a rest next to the wastebasket. From that moment on, CIA Officer Jordan Spear would be laser-focused on his efforts to become space-travel-worthy.

Twenty minutes later, now back in the classroom, Schuyler walked in and was impressed to see that Jordan was already back in his seat and appeared to be wide-eyed and ready to learn. The first page of his legal pad looked full of notes and diagrams from the earlier session.

A smiling Schuyler cleared his throat, picked up his chalk, and said, "Now, where were we?" staring down the now humble young man in front of him.

"Okay, continuing on...Jordan, you will be living and working in space for eight months and have to adapt to doing both while being completely weightless. That's not going to be very easy. The most seasoned veteran astronauts take days and sometimes even weeks to acclimatize to it. The human body must also adapt to isolation, confinement, and deadly radiation."

Jordan's pencil scratched heavily on his pad while his eyes no longer fought to stay open.

"Let's focus on isolation first," said Schuyler. "Though you are traveling to Black Earth with six other astronauts, you will likely go through periods when you feel isolated and confined. You may even experience claustrophobia and homesickness. The other issue astronauts face when traveling such great distances is the notion that they might not make it back. If you were to have a nervous breakdown up there, that could spell disaster to the other crew members and the health of the spacecraft itself."

Jordan interjected with several thoughtful questions that were well-received by a now more upbeat Professor Schuyler.

"Very good, Jordan! Let me try to answer your questions in a way that you can better wrap your head around. Until the mission to Black Earth late last year, astronauts had gone no further than the Moon. The Apollo astronauts traveled nearly 240,000 miles from home but were still able to look out their window and see the planet Earth floating in space. So, home was still within sight. It was still there the whole time. Are you understanding me, Jordan?"

"Not completely, Professor."

Schuyler's tone continued to soften. "Jordan, the fact that the astronauts could actually see their home planet helped them cope with being so far away from their homes and loved ones. Each time they looked out the window, it was kind of like getting a greeting card in the mail. But, when you travel to a planet that is seventy-five million miles away, separation anxiety can set in. The Earth will slowly disappear out of sight, and you won't see it again for many, many months. Now, do you understand what I'm trying to explain?"

"Yes, I think what you're trying to say, " said an astute Spear, "is that the human mind can tolerate great distances if it doesn't actually feel as if it's left home. But as home disappears, your mind can no longer be fooled and reacts upon its feeling of separation."

Schuyler looked on, somewhat surprised, and completely impressed. This was the first time Jordan had engaged him in the subject matter. He now felt as if his young student might actually have what it takes to become space travel-worthy.

Jordan continued. "My guess is that no one really knows how exactly they'll react until that moment arrives. Am I getting that right?" he asked.

"That's very good, Jordan! Conrad exhaled. "So, let's finish up the session with radiation effects, and then we'll call it a day."

"During long-duration space flight missions, astronauts can receive more than one thousand times the amount of radiation an average person here on Earth receives. Because of this, our training incorporates systems and processes for protecting our astronauts against radiation poisoning."

"Earth itself, like all active planets, has a protective dome around it called the magnetosphere; this deflects most solar particles coming from the Sun that contain high levels of radiation. All life forms are protected by this huge magnetic bubble. This magnetic field extends far out into space, nearly 36,000 miles. The Sun and all other geologically active planets have a magnetosphere, but Earth has one of the strongest in our solar system. Without this barrier, billions of species would die off very quickly."

Conrad was pleased to see that Jordan was franticly taking notes on his legal pad.

He continued. "In addition, Earth's atmosphere repels many of these particles and shields us here on the surface. Outside of this magnetic field, though, astronauts face harsh radiation. Our goal is to shield you from it as much as possible. To do that, we use insulated spacesuits, protective spacecraft, and there's even medication in development. The ISS as an example...,"

Jordan looked confused and raised his hand. "I'm sorry, Professor; what is the ISS?"

Schuyler smiled. "That would be the International Space Station."

"Of course!" said Jordan, lowering his eyes to his notepad to hide his embarrassment.

Schuyler understood that this was only day one of training and continued. "On the ISS, for example, we have instruments that measure the radiation environment both inside and outside of the station."

"These instruments can track both the short-term and long-term radiation doses astronauts receive. This information helps us to assess the risk of radiation-related diseases. We also mitigate health risks by providing special areas to serve as radiation shelters. These can be used during events like radiation storms."

Jordan looked up, about to ask another question.

"Radiation Storms," clarified Schuyler, "often occur after major eruptions on the Sun. They launch solar protons out into space at nearly six-thousand miles per second."

Jordan nodded and went back to his note-taking.

Schuyler spread his hands wide and gave a subdued smile. "Ultimately, we need to keep you as safe as we can, using medicine and technology, since radiation has one goal, and that is to kill you. The journey to Black Earth and back will keep you and the other astronauts away from Earth's protective bubble. You will be exposed to the deadly radiation levels in outer space. And, of course, you and the other surface explorers will get even less protection than those remaining on the craft when you descend to the planet. So remember, Jordan, keep your helmet on at all times when you exit the Lander!"

Jordan stopped writing. His pen hovered above his notepad mid-sentence. "Do I need to write that down?" he smiled.

Schuyler gave an eccentric laugh and shook his head. "I think you'll remember that one." He put down his chalk. "Okay young man, while I'm sure you found this information extremely interesting, much like radiation, I must give it to you in small doses. Class dismissed! I will see you back here tomorrow morning at 8:00 am sharp. Get a good dinner in you and get to bed early. Tomorrow, you'll learn about space food. Yum!"

Schuyler turned back to his chalkboard and began rubbing it clean, muttering quietly under his breath.

Jordan crept from the classroom. As soon as he was clear of the door, he leaned back heavily against the wall of the corridor. Like an exhausted football player, he curled over and put his hands on his knees, sighing deeply.

"Three months of this? You can do this, Jordan!" he thought.

Chapter 25 – Operation Sagittarian Recovery

Location: Houston, TX. Lyndon B. Johnson Space Center – September 15, 2022. 10:00am, CST.

In a large conference room on the third floor, adjacent to Mars Johnston's office, the new crew of the upcoming mission to Black Earth had assembled. There were less than three months to go before the scheduled launch date in December of 2022.

"Well, congratulations, team!" said Mars, with a hearty smile. "You have been selected to embark on the second-ever journey to Black Earth, formerly known as ILK-87b. While there are some familiar faces in the room, we also have some newcomers. I'd like to make special mention of them now."

"We felt it was essential to keep as many of the original crew members together as possible. Due to your ongoing experiments, continuity is a plus. Sadly, we did lose three members, but we think we've found some pretty good replacements to fill the big boots that have been vacated."

"While there are only seven of you in the room, keep in mind that the empty seat is for our boy, Dr. Carrick Michaels. Okay, now for some introductions."

"New to the team is Kyle Shaver." Mars pointed out a fit young man, his NASA branded cap set at a jaunty angle. Kyle nodded his head and raised his hand in acknowledgment as Mars continued. "He's considered NASA's best meteorologist. I refer to him as Rock & Roll because his Dad used to be in an '80s rock group called Silver Twilight. Kind of a fitting name for a band who had a member that would go on to have an astronaut in the family." Mars grinned. "Or maybe we should call him 'One Hit Wonder.'"

Shaver looked only slightly embarrassed as he'd heard Mars tell that joke several times before. The other crew members in the room could be seen rolling their eyes, each having become quite accustomed to Mars' dry sense of humor.

"Inside joke!" Mars laughed, looking pretty impressed with himself.

"Next, I'd like to introduce you to Kevin Yi," said Mars, indicating a man of slight stature who made eye contact with those around the room and smiled. "Born in South Korea, he now lives here in Houston, and we're lucky to have him on this team. Kevin was recently recognized as one of the top five geologists in his... cul-de-sac," joked Johnston. "Just kidding!" he said, slapping himself on the knee. "I meant one of the top five in the world!"

Some of the original crew members giggled and exchanged glances.

"All joking aside, I'd like to introduce you to our final newcomer. Last, but not least, Jordan Spear, who I like to call Rookie." Jordan smiled confidently; one eyebrow raised. He grinned at the other crewmembers around the table and made particular eye contact with Kinzi London, who seemed to return his glance with enthusiasm.

Mars went on to say, "As many of you know, Jordan has joined us from the CIA, by order of POTUS. This mission is not only aimed at continuing our vital scientific research, but also at bringing back our American hero, Carrick Michaels."

"When you reach your destination, Officer Spear, will have the delicate and sensitive duty of interrogating the Black Earth resident, Erik, as he seems to be known. We need to determine Erik's origins and reason for being there. Ultimately, everyone on this trip will be returning safely home," said Mars, not joking this time.

"The mission has been named Sagittarian Recovery for two reasons. One, because we will lift-off in December. And two, because Carrick Michaels will be celebrating his thirty-second birthday on the day we launch, December 12, 2022. Mark your calendars, people! It's official!"

"We expect to land on Black Earth on April 7, 2023, and we'll be on the surface for roughly forty-hours. This should get all of us back home by August 3, 2023."

Chatting amongst themselves, the new crew filed out of the conference room. As they left, Mars asked Jordan Spear to stay behind.

"Jordan, hang on a second. I wanted you to know that I've given Dr. Schuyler the rest of the week off." Mars smiled conspiratorially.

"You'll be stuck with me for the next eight hours, but then you'll have the following five-days off!"

Jordan first looked surprised and then excited at the prospect of a long weekend. "But what are we doing for the rest of the day?" he asked.

"Today, the two of us will be flying to Virginia. I've got a little field trip planned for you. Something to break up all of those hours in the classroom. I want to show you what's in store for you in the coming weeks."

"A field trip, huh?" asked Jordan, unsure of what Mars had planned for him.

"Yep! You'll be staying in Virginia when we're done today, so we'll need to stop by the hotel and grab your bag before we go. That way, you can go home after our little journey and get some rest before you end up back here on Monday. I'm sure you're a bit exhausted listening to our very own Doc Conrad for the last two weeks. Normally, he's got a whole class in there; I can only imagine what it's like being his only student."

"That's fantastic!" said Jordan. "A few days off will gear me up for another couple of weeks with Dr. Schuyler."

"You'll only be with Conrad for one more week, and then it's field training. We need to see how you perform in zero gravity; you're getting a little peek today in Arlington," responded Johnston. "And we're going to travel there in style."

Within hours, Jordan understood what Mars meant; they were catching a ride to Virginia on Air Force II. The V.P. of the United States had made a brief visit to NASA and was heading back to D.C. Fortunately, the flight time suited Mars' plan perfectly. Both Mars and Jordan were thrilled at being able to travel on such a famous plane. After a pleasant chit-chat with the Vice President, the two men settled into a small office in the back of the Boeing C-32.

Lounging in the tiny but plush room, Mars explained that, today, Jordan would be getting an advanced glimpse of the zero-gravity training he'd experience in the weeks ahead. Right now, Mars wanted to give him a bit of background on the topic.

As he talked, Mars put his feet up on the desk and, to Jordan's surprise, pulled out a cigar and planted it in the left corner of his mouth.

"Are you allowed to smoke that on this plane?" asked Jordan.

"Nah, I just like the taste of it."

"That stuff will kill you!" warned Jordan.

"Yeah, like I said, I don't smoke!" said Mars. "I just like the taste, that's all. Okay, where was I?" he asked Jordan rhetorically before launching in. "Back in the day, astronauts used to call the plane that they conducted zero-gravity training on the Vomit Comet. It all started in 1957 when astronaut trainees would fly on planes that would make roller-coaster maneuvers to simulate weightlessness. These maneuvers were sometimes so violent that they would make the trainees vomit during and after the experience. Hence the name Vomit Comet. It was pretty messy, as you can imagine. Well, I guess you don't actually have to imagine that at all, do you?" Mars chuckled, busting the chops of the already nervous Spear while gnawing on his cigar.

"Ha-Ha!', replied an unimpressed Jordan.

Mars went on as if giving a speech to an empty room. "These days, lots of people other than astronauts are encouraged to go through this training because it benefits the scientific community. Experiments in zero-gravity benefit mankind going forward since space travel is becoming more common. Plus, many countries and private companies are now growing their space programs, and Zero-G training has evolved a lot."

Mars had been talking for several minutes when he glanced over and saw that Jordan had nodded off.

"Kid! Wake up!" Mars shouted, tapping the younger man on the arm.
"Just resting my eyes, sir!" Spear responded groggily.

"As I was saying... Luckily, times have changed since the bad old days of the Vomit Comet. The planes that simulate weightlessness nowadays fly in a wave-like configuration, making it far less violent on its passengers." Mars made a waving motion with his hand and arm, reminding Jordan of a kid hanging their arm out of a car window, catching air under their palm. "As the plane climbs up the parabola, the passengers will experience up to five seconds of total weightlessness. The plane then dives back down toward the ground. When it pulls up again, the passengers will experience roughly twice the pull of Earth's gravity."

Jordan had been looking increasingly nervous throughout Mars' lecture. "It doesn't sound like my kind of fun," he confessed. "Is it dangerous? All of those ups and downs?" He waved his arm in a parody of Mars' demonstration.

"We've been doing it for a long time," Mars reassured him. "We normally log about three hundred flight hours per year. No one's ever been seriously hurt during this type of training. And civilians do it all the time. Do you remember the movie Apollo 13?"

"Yeah! I really liked that movie!" said Jordan a bit more enthusiastically. I'm a big fan of Ron Howard films.

"Well, some of the scenes were filmed in zero-gravity conditions, on an old KC-135A, the plane we retired back in 2004. It's wild! The set designers made the inside of the plane look like the inside of a spacecraft. Apparently, Ron Howard leased the plane for an entire six months to get what they needed for the film. So, all this is standard practice, even for Hollywood actors! Any questions?" smiled Mars.

"Just one," said an exhausted Jordan.

"Am I going to throw up again?"

"Based on your recent track record, I'd say that it's likely. But this training is nowhere near as hard on the body as the Centrifuge Simulator," smiled Mars.

Both men sat for a moment and looked out the window. With the short journey nearing its end, Mars needed to know something. It was something that had nagged him since he found out that a CIA interrogation specialist was being assigned to the mission.

"Jordan, let me ask you a question," said Mars. "What exactly will you be doing up there? I'm guessing you'll be doing more than asking questions," he suggested, not sure he was ready for the answer.

"Are you asking me what techniques I'll employ to gain the answers I need?"

"Yes. I'm afraid you won't be happy if you don't get the answers that satisfy your narrative or objectives. And if you don't, what then?"

"Torture," said Spear, with a straight face.

"What the fuck!" exclaimed Mars. "Intergalactic water-boarding?"

"Not quite," replied Jordan. "It's more psychological than physical. There's definitely some 'get in your face' stuff, but I don't plan on roughing the guy up if that's what you're worried about."

"Well, that's a relief!" Mars exhaled. "If any of my team witnessed something like that, it could upset the fragile psychological state of a human being that's seventy-five million miles from home. You get me?"

"Mars, listen. The first thing you need to know is that I will be filming the entire interrogation so that we can study it once back on Earth. In the end, I'm simply seeking the truth. I am not invested in what his answers will be," explained Jordan candidly. "I have a mission too! Yours is getting us there and back safely, but mine is to find the truth. I plan on doing that in a very effective but non-physical or lethal way," Jordan promised. "You said that we're on the surface for forty-hours. Is that right?" he asked.

Mars, still in a joking mood, said, "Yes, unless something silly happens, like that old man kicks your ass or pulls out a ray-gun and lasers you in half."

Spear chuckled. "Trust me, I'm not worried about my personal safety. I've tackled a bunch of 230 pound running backs coming downhill at me. I think I'll be okay, sitting with a little old man."

"I'm not worried about you specifically," retorted Mars. "I'm worried about all of you. My mission includes getting you back in one piece. The other thing that I have to assume is that this guy, Erik, is a pretty valuable asset. No matter where he's from or who put him there, he's holding onto a great deal of information that could benefit not just the U.S. but the whole of humankind. I just don't understand why the mission isn't to sedate him and get him back to Earth. It'd be a lot easier to interrogate him from Langley, wouldn't it?"

"Sedate him? For four months? That's crazy! You said it yourself, Mars. An unruly passenger on a spaceflight jeopardizes the entire crew and the spacecraft."

"Ugh!" Mars put his head in his hands. "There's got to be an easier way!"

"That's my point, Mars! We don't know how this whole thing is gonna go down up there. He might not make it even if we tried to bring him back! Anything could happen; anything could go wrong!" exclaimed Jordan. "You'll need to trust that I know what I'm doing."

Both men were a little uneasy as the plane landed at Reagan International Airport.

After deplaning, the two thanked the V.P. and hurried to catch a cab to the Virginia-based Zero Gravity Corp. The company had been taking civilians and NASA astronauts on parabolic training flights since 2005. In 2008, NASA selected the company as its sole provider of zero-gravity training.

The two men toured the facility and even boarded the modified Boeing 727 airplane, where Jordan's training would soon take place. While there, Mars was treated like a celebrity. Everyone there seemed to know his name. And he, theirs.

Jordan was impressed. "You're practically the mayor of this town, shaking hands and kissing babies," he said after Mars had had his photo taken with two star-struck interns. "Before you know it, you'll be running for political office."
Mars just grinned and shook hands with another senior executive.

In reality, the visit was making Jordan nervous, as well as excited, about the upcoming zero-gravity training. He was thrilled, though, that it wasn't happening in the next two weeks. In some ways, he was actually looking forward to getting back into a classroom that was planted firmly on the ground and had lots of gravity.

At the end of the day, Jordan took a cab to his parents' house in Northern Virginia, heading for a well-deserved rest. Meanwhile, a black SUV with government plates drove Mars to NASA Headquarters at Two Independence Square in Washington, D.C. There was no rest for Johnston.

Location: Titusville, FL. Cape Canaveral Air Force Station Space Launch Complex 41 – December 11, 2022.

"Jordan! Come on in, son," said Mars Johnston.

Jordan walked in and took a seat.

Mars looked like the father of a son who was going off to college. He was proud of his newest recruit and how far he'd come. "It's been ninety-six days since you're training started, and here we are, on the precipice of human history. What you are doing is far more than going on a trip to interrogate someone. What you're doing is making history. Your name will be forever mentioned with all of the other great space pioneers that came before you."

"Sir, when I joined the CIA, I didn't expect my name to ever be mentioned in any history books. That's not what I signed up for. I don't want to be remembered for this assignment."

"Jordan, It doesn't matter whether or not you want it. What matters is that you will. The only question is, what will those books say about you? How will history remember you? You get to write your own history, son. Write it well!"

The two men shook hands. This would be the last time they would see each other face to face until the Sagittarian Recovery mission was completed in August 2023.

Chapter 26 – Happy Birthday

Location: Titusville, FL. Cape Canaveral Air Force Station, Space Launch Complex 41 – December 12, 2022.

"We have lift-off!" exclaimed Mars Johnston.

The New Beginning spaceship successfully cleared the tower and seven-minutes later left Earth's atmosphere. The spacecraft and its crew were headed for Black Earth to recover the person who the world perceived as their global hero, Dr. Carrick Michaels. What the world didn't know was that a CIA interrogation specialist was on board and would be attempting to determine the true identity of a man called Erik.

"How're you feeling, Jordan?" asked Kinzi London as she checked his vitals several hours after the New Beginning spacecraft successfully escaped Earth's gravitational pull. "You look a little pale," she said as she checked his blood pressure, floating beside him, a little to his left. She noticed that his eyes were as wide open as a toddler's getting scolded for the first time by their father.

Struggling to find the right words, Jordan said, "Not two months or two years could have prepared me for that! For Christ's sake! What the fuck just happened? You never really see much of that in the movies. The pressure on the body is extreme!"

Kinzi giggled. "Don't worry, big boy; the hard part is over. Now we have four months up here before we make it to Black Earth." Stifling her laughter this time, Kinzi went on, "Hope you brought a good book to read; I hope it's a big one! You're gonna get bored up here."

The sound of ripping Velcro startled Jordan as Kinzi removed the blood pressure monitor strap from his left bicep.

Jordan flexed his fingers in an effort to inject circulation back into his hand. As he did so, he looked up and made eye contact with Kinzi.

"I heard you met him," he commented casually.

"Met who?"

"Black Earth, Erik!" replied Jordan. "What's he like?"

"That's what we're calling him now?" She stowed her blood pressure kit and shrugged. "He's just a little old man. He looks like he's a hundred-years-old. Not intimidating at all. In fact, he actually seemed quite nice... for an alien disguised as a human being," she joked half-heartedly. "How do you plan to go about questioning him?"

"Pardon me!" yelled Kyle Shaver as he whizzed by Kinzi and Jordan.

"Excuse us!" said Kinzi, grabbing a handle behind Jordan's head. She pulled herself clear of the speeding Shaver as he headed to one of the three lavatories onboard the New Beginning spacecraft.

"I'm just going to have a conversation with him. Just him, and me, and a camera," replied Spear.

"You know, he told me he's from Black Earth. He called the planet Zenith, and he said he'd lived there his entire life. He seemed believable too. But that, of course, would be impossible," she mused.

"As old as he looks, he must have been up there for decades. If he traveled there, it was many, many years ago. Who knows, maybe he's telling the truth!" She grinned at Jordan. "I mean, look at you. You're in perfect health; you're physically fit. And look at the toll space travel has taken on you already," she said. "He's way too old for space travel, and he has been for decades."

"There're only five space agencies in the world with the ability to go as far as ILK-87b." She counted them off on her fingers. "NASA, the European Space Agency, India, China, and Russia's Space Agency, Roscosmos. But decades ago?" She shook her head in answer to her own question.

"The U.S. is the only country to have taken human beings to another celestial body. In total, NASA's only sent twenty-four men beyond low Earth orbit, with just twelve landing on the Moon. And it hasn't been done since 1972. For any country, including the U.S., to travel as far as ILK-87b decades ago?" shaking her head again, "I don't think so. No other country has ever taken humans beyond low Earth orbit. None!" She arched an eyebrow at Jordan. "Perhaps there's something you're not telling us, Officer Spear?"

"He's not one of ours, that's for sure!" countered Jordan. "I'm planning on figuring it out, though!"

"He sure looked and sounded American. He had perfect English."
"What the hell does that mean, perfect English?"

"You know, no accent whatsoever. He just spoke in a normal way, with no dialect or regional flair. The way he enunciated his words. The manner of his verbal expressions. There was nothing to indicate where he might be from. It was weird, that's all. If he moved in across the street from you, you would just think he's a normal guy from nowhere... anywhere. He didn't seem like a secret agent, or a spy, or even an astronaut, for that matter. The other thing is that he was very respectful," she added.

"How so?" Jordan inquired.

"He saluted us and then offered to shake our hands. It was just all so strange."

"Saluted you? That's odd!" said Jordan. "Can you tell me anything else about him? Scars, nervous ticks, tendencies?"

"No scars that I could see, and I can't remember any ticks," she answered. But then she thought again. "There is one thing actually," she said. "He's clearly been to Washington, D.C."

"What makes you think that?"

"He knew a lot about the Pentagon. As if he'd been there. He suggested that the Pentagon was replicated from The Triad. He said it was some sort of monument to his people or his planet... Something like that."

"Hmmm, if he's been to the Pentagon, maybe he is one of ours," Jordan wondered aloud.

"I look forward to the blood tests, though!" said Kinzi enthusiastically. "The DNA will tell us what part of the world this guy's from. He won't be able to hide his origins then."

"That sort of data could be helpful with my interrogation. How long after you've drawn his blood can you provide me with that info?"

"Oh, no. I can't run DNA up there. That'll happen back on Earth after we return. I will only be able to tell if he's human or not."

"Or not?" said Jordan, a shocked look on his face. "How will you know?"

"Easy," Kinzi said straight-faced. "If his blood's red, he's one of us. If it's green, he's an alien." She winked at Jordan and floated away, calling out behind her, "We'll talk later, cowboy!"

Jordan Spear found himself blushing a little. He was left feeling as if Kinzi had the upper hand during their conversation. He looked forward to the next one.

Location: Black Earth. The Triad, Barrack 5, Sub-Level 7 – December 12, 2022. Early morning hours.

Sitting up in his bunk, Carrick had forgotten what day it was. He yawned and, glancing at the adjacent bed, saw that Erik was missing.

He was just thinking about going to search for his companion when the door burst open. It was Erik, holding a box. As soon as he saw Carrick, he started singing, "Happy birthday to you! Happy birthday to you!" Happy birthday dear Carrick, Happy birthday to you!" He walked towards Carrick. "Thirty-two today, huh?"

Carrick smiled. "You keep telling me that you're Zenithian, but then you start singing Happy Birthday, and I start believing you're from Earth again."

"They sing that song on Earth?!" asked Erik, surprised. "My people kept up the tradition, I see. That makes me really happy!" He handed Carrick the package. It was roughly big enough to hold an astronaut's helmet. "Here you go, kid!"

Carrick took it from him, rendered speechless for a moment. "What's all this about? I don't know what to say." He looked up at Erik. "What is it?"

"Just open it up! It isn't much, but it's the thought that counts."

Carrick carefully opened the box. Inside was something shiny and loosely wrapped in cloth. He unfolded the fabric and, at first, struggled to understand what he was looking at. The object resembled a glass ball with metal conductor prongs on the back. Shifting the contents, he suddenly realized what it was.

Erik grinned at him. "You keep talking about those damned wall-mounted light fixtures and how valuable they would be on Earth. Well, I removed one and boxed it up for you. I hope you like it, kid!"

Carrick held the light fixture up. It was big, about the size of a bowling ball. "Are you allowed to do that?" he asked.

Erik snorted in amusement. "In case you haven't noticed, I kind of run the place! I'm pretty sure I won't get in any trouble!"

Both men laughed out loud. They sat beside each other, looking at the birthday present of a lifetime. Carrick seemed delighted, and Erik knew that his gift had been appreciated.

Erik's gesture genuinely touched Carrick. He felt a deep connection with the old man. For two hundred and sixty-four straight days, he'd spent every waking hour with Erik, and the bond between them was undeniable, although neither man could really understand why.

Carrick abruptly came to his senses. "Do you have any idea how much this is worth?"

"Not much around here!" shrugged Erik.

"No, I mean on Earth?"

"Whatever it's worth, you've earned it! Hanging out with me for the last two hundred and sixty-four days," Erik replied.

"Ahh, I see you've been counting the days too, huh?"

"Yeah, well, I know that you'll be leaving soon, and I won't have anyone to talk to. My only friend is going to board a spaceship headed for Earth, never to be seen again! That's my life story." Erik sagged in resignation.

His words pricked Carrick with sadness. "I'm pretty sure there will be someone to talk to," he said gently. "Others will come."

"Yeah, but they won't be you." Erik looked away as if to conceal his emotions.

The comment hit Carrick hard. Although he desperately missed home, Carrick knew that when the time came, he'd have a hard time leaving his friend.

They both sat and pondered the inevitable fact that Carrick would soon leave. Carrick was still asking himself if and when the others would come back for him. After all, it had been almost nine months since his last contact with anyone who wasn't from Zenith. In the back of his mind, he sometimes wondered if they were coming back at all. Realistically he knew that they would, but perhaps he ought to try to reach out to them. Separation anxiety was real, and it was starting to get the better of him.

For the first time since he'd arrived, Carrick began to consider whether there might be a way to send a signal to Earth. With all the boundless technology in The Triad, could he get a message out? There must have been a mechanism for Controllers to stay in touch with the migration shuttles. If there was a way to send a simple sound wave or laser beam, anything, he had to find it. He owed it to his loved ones back on Earth, who were also waiting for, and wondering, about him.

Carrick started to say, "Erik, let me ask you something..." He turned, but Erik wasn't there. He'd gone. Carrick had been so deep in his reverie that he hadn't even noticed the old man slip away.

Carrick felt an unexpected and piercing sense of sorrow. Erik's absence seemed like a figurative, as well as a literal sign of things to come. He looked around, but the barracks, showers, laundry, locker room, and lavatories were all empty. There was no sign of Erik. After another twenty minutes, he actually started to worry. He couldn't hear water running in the showers, and Carrick didn't think Erik would have gone to The Culina without him. Not on his birthday!

Carrick jumped as the barrack door swung open violently, and Erik barged in a second time. This time he was carrying a smaller box and wearing a look of embarrassment because he'd pushed the door so hard.

Raising his voice, Carrick said, "You okay there, buddy?!"

"Sorry, didn't realize I kicked the door so hard," Erik blushed.

"Where were you? I looked everywhere!"

"Aww, you were worried about me! You missed me, didn't you, kid?" he poked fun at Carrick. "I wasn't even gone that long!"

"That's not the point! You left in the middle of a conversation without saying anything!"

"No, I didn't!" said Erik defensively. "You were sitting there staring off into space, so I left to go and get you something else."

"What do you have there?" asked Carrick.

"Well, I know you liked the broken light fixture, so I wanted to complement it with another small gift. Here, I got you this!" Erik pulled from the package a seemingly random piece of metal. It was about twelve inches by twelve inches, by one-eighth of an inch thick.

"What is it?"

"It's a piece of platinum! You seemed intrigued by it before, so I got you some to take home with you."

Carrick chuckled appreciatively. "First of all, thank you! Second of all, quit tearing apart The Triad; you're gonna get us kicked out of this place!"

Then something dawned on Carrick. "Listen, I can't take this stuff back to Earth! Every ounce on the spacecraft will be accounted for. Even the soil and rock samples. They won't let me take this stuff on the Lander."

"Now, you listen to me!" Erik said firmly, waving his index finger in Carrick's direction. "You're taking that back to Earth with you because I gave it to you as a gift!"

Carrick laughed at Erik's rigid tone. "Fine, fine! But what the hell am I going to do with this stuff anyway?" he asked.

"You said platinum and diamonds are precious commodities back on Earth, didn't you?"

"Yeah, but..."

"Yeah but, nothing! You're taking them back home with you. Period!"

"Okay, okay. But I would never sell them to make money. They're a gift from you!"

Erik reached for Carrick's hand and said earnestly. "Take a little piece of each and make a ring for Lola. Ask her to marry you. Don't make the same mistake I made with Lilly."

"I will!" said Carrick, with determination in his voice. "I will!"

Chapter 27 – Contact

Location: Black Earth. The Triad, Sub-Level 7, Barrack 5 – December 12, 2022. A few minutes later.

Both men shook off the conversation regarding what Carrick might do with his birthday gifts, and then the two men made their way to The Culina.

Along the way, Carrick said, "Erik, I need to ask you something."

"I can probably guess what it is!"

"Go ahead with your guess!" encouraged Carrick.

"You want to know if it's possible to contact Earth," replied Erik.

Carrick was astonished, wondering if Erik had suddenly become telepathic. "How'd you know what I was going to ask? Was it that obvious?"

"I read your mind," said Erik with a straight face. "Zenithians have that ability, you know."

Carrick's eyes widened. He didn't know what to say.

"Just kidding!" laughed Erik. "Of course, it was obvious. You're human, and it was just a matter of time."

Carrick just shook his head from side to side.

"You should've seen your face, son. You thought for a second I really could read your mind, didn't you?"

"Well, is it possible?"

"I knew that you would eventually ask me that question and was hoping to avoid it. I didn't want to get your hopes up. Carrick, I don't think it's possible," said a cautious Erik, trying very hard to manage Carrick's expectations.

At The Culina, the two men sat and savored a hefty portion of Red Fruit.

Putting down his cup, Carrick spoke. "When you were in the Command Center, controlling the migration shuttle to Earth, were you always in contact with those on board? Or did you just geo-track the shuttle through a pre-determined course?"

Erik nodded. "Not only was I in touch with it, but I could see the entire journey in real-time. It was like I was flying from the shuttle's cockpit," explained Erik. "But I had no communication with any of its passengers except for the highest-ranking officials onboard."

"Wait, it had a cockpit? I thought it was remotely piloted."

"It was. It had a virtual cockpit. When I remotely piloted it, I felt as if I was actually on board. It was heart-breaking when it arrived at Home." Erik looked dejected. "I felt like I was really there. But, of course, I wasn't."

Seeing the somber look on Erik's face, Carrick was reminded of how upset the old man had become back in April when the two discussed ditching the shuttle in the ocean on Earth. He didn't want to upset him again, so he quickly changed the subject back to contacting Earth.

"So, what was the means of communication? What technology was used?"

"Thermology radiation waves," Erik answered.

"What the hell are those?"

"*Thermology Neutrino Waves* or TNW are waves of radioactive energy that ride the Sun's radiation particles. Particle radiation is similar to a beam of light. The sub-atomic particles follow the Sun's rays. TNW also incorporates tachyonic particles, which propel the radiation particles 100x faster than the speed of light. In the middle of The Triad, beneath the shuttle pad, lies a Super Server Radiation Modem that communicates with a smaller server in the shuttle. That smaller server is roughly the size of ten shuttle transit rovers. The server beneath the shuttle pad is approximately half the size of the Northwest Sector. The Neutrino Waves bounce off the radiation particles and, as I stated earlier, move 100x faster than the speed of light."

"Tell me more!" said Carrick, hanging on Erik's every word.

"The radiation modem connects with the shuttle before launch and stays connected throughout its entire journey. Contact was never lost."

"Yeah, but... how did it account for the rotation of Zenith? As the modem and the shuttle lost sight of each other, didn't you lose contact?"

"No. The waves of radiation can move in any direction. They can travel through a planet, and they don't stop until they find their assigned target; in this case, the shuttle. As I said, contact was never lost!"

"Okay, so how would we go about contacting Earth?" Carrick implored him anxiously. "I've been gone for a long time. I'm worried about my family, and I'm quite sure they're worried about me. They don't even know if I'm alive or not."

"As I stated, Carrick, I'm almost certain that it can't be done. If it is possible, we would need to employ the Super Server Radiation Modem beneath the Shuttle Launchpad. The migration shuttle had a receiver that was designed to collect the Neutrino Waves. But..."

"But what? asked Carrick.

"Well, unless there's a similar receiver being used by the people you want to contact, I'm not sure how it would work."

Carrick cradled his chin and pursed his lips while Erik racked his brain.

"Wait a second!" Carrick snapped his fingers. "Earth has massive radio receivers pointing in every direction, and they're pretty damn sophisticated. They're designed to listen for alien transmissions. We also have hundreds of communication satellites in Earth's orbit and in deep space. I wouldn't be surprised if they had a comms satellite orbiting Zenith right now." A rush of adrenaline pulsed through Carrick's veins.

Erik perked up too. "Perhaps we can try to communicate with the last shuttle too! If we could somehow establish a connection, then maybe your satellites could pick up the signal."

"Alright, son!" exclaimed Erik. "There's just one issue. The Triad's Energy Conservation System will have to be manually over-ridden to channel electricity back to the Super Server. This could cause some portions of The Triad to lose power permanently. I won't know which sections until after we've done it. And once sections go dark, they stay dark. Also, it takes up so much power that The Triad could lose years off of its remaining electrical supply."

Carrick slumped; his enthusiasm gone. "We can't do it then. It could mean a death sentence for you. Doesn't the ECS control the oxygen supply systems too?"

"Yes, but the oxygen supply and water pumps will be the last things to go. I might be in the dark after you leave, but I'll have plenty to drink and breathe," joked Erik. "It doesn't matter anyway. We need to get a message out to your mother and to your Lola."

"Erik, I can't ask that of you! What if the lights go out in Barrack 6? You won't be able to visit or see the place where you and Lilly..."

Erik interrupted firmly. "Lilly's gone, but Lola and your mother aren't. We're going to try to get a message to them. Period!"

The two men went to the Northwest Sector's Command Center. There, Erik began entering data commands into a computer. The main wall of the Command Center had no fewer than fourteen screens. All of them had been dark for many decades, until now. When switched on, they almost looked like crystal gel until they warmed up.

Both men held their breath, neither knowing if the downed shuttle still had power. Then it happened. One after the other, the screens came into focus. The two men sat there stunned at what they were seeing. The monitors showed visuals of what appeared to be the bottom of an ocean: black, murky water. As the men watched in silence, ocean life appeared. Crustaceans and eels could be seen lurking near the camera.

"Erik, what are we looking at right now?" asked Carrick. Even as he spoke, the answer dawned on him.

Erik was melancholy. "You're looking at the final resting place of the last migration shuttle to ever leave Zenith," said Erik.

"Did you even know it was possible to make contact with the shuttle?"

"In my heart, yes, but in reality, no," he said. "I never even thought to try to contact it; that would have been torture. It would've only made my empty life seem emptier. I let it go decades ago."

"Erik, my father, went down in this general area," said Carrick nervously.

Erik quickly realized what Carrick was thinking. He swiftly tapped out several commands. Then he turned and looked straight into Carrick's eyes. "Do you want to search for the wreckage?"

Carrick took a deep breath and said nothing for a few seconds. Finally, he exhaled slowly. "Are you telling me right now that you can do that?"

"Well, the cameras are still working, which means there's enough power in the shuttle's Diamond Reactor to light up the ocean floor." Erik pointed to the screens as proof. "And there's one more thing. We transported migrants to the surface of Home on Carriages. The shuttle was far too big to land on the surface, and only a fraction of its human cargo would de-shuttle at each drop point."

"I don't understand." Carrick looked confused.

"There are cameras on each of the thirty carriages on board the shuttle; each was equipped with an elaborate camera system. The carriages were able to both fly and swim. They only had a range of ten-miles when submerged, though. After that, the signal is lost. But it can also search for structures or objects that don't match the surrounding landscape or terrain. We used the carriages to find and map infrastructure on Earth when our shuttles searched for previous migrant populations. They incorporated sonar, radar, and infrared laser technology, depending on the environment." Erik was clearly proud of the technology's capabilities.

Not sure what he was hearing, Carrick asked, "What are you telling me, exactly?"

"Let's go find your father!" Erik replied with a look of confidence on his face.

Carrick's head sunk, and he took a deep breath, not sure he was ready for the moment he'd always wondered about.

After several more minutes of data entry, the carriage separated from the shuttle. Within seconds it began to auto-search the area for anything that didn't match the ocean floor's landscape. Almost immediately, it detected a structure within two miles. Lights began flashing on the dashboard, and the men could hear beeping sounds. Carrick held his breath and then exhaled when he saw something that appeared to be the size of a naval vessel. As the carriage closed in, it revealed the unmistakable Japanese Rising Sun military logo. It adorned what looked like the flight deck of a massive ship. There was no mistaking what they were looking at. It was a sunken aircraft carrier from World War II.

After more than two-hours of scouring the ocean's floor, Erik and Carrick had not detected the remains of Mike Michaels' F8-Crusader aircraft. Disappointed, Carrick instructed Erik to "just shut it down."

He knew he was asking too much; to actually catch a glimpse of his father's final resting place. It had been a crazy notion. Erik reluctantly obliged Carrick and began shutting the system down. As the lights powered off, the console began to beep faintly. Carrick didn't give it any thought, but Erik said, "Carrick, it's picking up something far smaller than the numerous ships we found. Do you want me to fire it back up?"

"I guess," replied Carrick, not sounding particularly hopeful.
The video feed portion of the camera took its time coming back online, but the audio portion kept actively pinging a nearby object. The pinging got louder and faster as the video feed came back online. Carrick's eyes lit up, and his breathing seemed to stop for a moment. There it was. The unmistakable U.S. Navy aircraft roundel star. A white star in a blue circle, flanked by three stripes on each side; one red, between two white.

"Oh, my God! That's it!"

"How can you be sure?" asked Erik, trying to manage Carrick's expectations. "This part of the ocean is clearly an old battleground; we've seen so many aircraft and ships lying on the ocean's floor."

Carrick had tears in his eyes. "Do you see the star with the flanking stripes?" he asked. "That marking only graced U.S Navy planes between the years 1947 and 1999. That's not the remains of a World War II-era aircraft. And the plane we're looking at is a jet aircraft. During World War II, the U.S. Navy mainly used prop engine planes."

"I don't know what the words jet or prop engine means, but I understand the look on your face," conceded Erik. He gazed back at the screen in wonder. "That's your father's plane!"

Carrick sat and watched as the dark, murky waters and sea life swirled around his father's grave. There were no words. Just disbelief and fascination. How did all of this come to be? Everything in his life, every decision he'd ever made, had brought him to Zenith, brought him to this moment. It was all inconceivable and overwhelming.

Carrick was mesmerized, studying every inch of the view the camera could see. After what seemed like an hour, Carrick looked around for Erik. Once again, he had gone, probably back to the barracks, he'd reasoned. As he walked to Barrack 5, Carrick caught Erik exiting Barrack 6. He'd gone to visit Lilly's memory, likely afraid the power went out when they sent the signal to the shuttle, and with it would've gone the memories of his one and only love, Lilly.

What lay ahead for the two men would complete a life circle that neither could have imagined. Destiny was calling both of them. The only residents of Black Earth were about to be tied together by an unwoven thread that, when interlaced, would confound the world, and make the Universe a very small place.

Location: The Culina. December 13, 2022. The following morning.

"Carrick, about last night," said Erik. "After you retired and fell asleep, I returned to the Command Center and channeled the remaining power needed to activate the Thermology Neutrino Waves. They're now ready to transmit. After we're finished here, we should go back and try to send a message to Earth."

"Yes, let's do it!" said Carrick, with more conviction than he'd previously felt. "They might or might not receive the signal, but I'll be damned if I'm not gonna try!"

As the two made their way to the Command Center, Carrick asked Erik a curious question. "Erik, last night I wanted to ask you a question, but you left the Command Center before I could."

"What is it, son?"

"The carriages used to transport the migrants from the shuttle to their surface destinations...?"

"Yes?" asked Erik.

"Did you ever lose one?" wondered Carrick aloud.

Erik looked a little embarrassed before answering Carrick's question.

"Kind of..." answered Erik.

"What do you mean 'kind of'?" asked Carrick.

"In the entire history of the program, we never lost a carriage until..." he paused in embarrassment.

"Until what?" urged Carrick.

"Okay, the last carriage sent to your Earth's surface had Lilly on it," explained Erik. "After safely transporting the final few to Home, I was so distraught that I angrily drove the carriage into the ground instead of returning it back to the shuttle."

Erik, a little red-faced, asked Carrick, "Why do you ask?"

"They found it!" replied Carrick, shaking his head, and smiling at yet another revelation that confirmed everything that Erik had told Carrick.

The two continued on to the Command Center without further conversation.

Later, after their arrival, Erik pointed a microphone at Carrick and announced, "Go ahead, it's ready!"

Carrick nodded and began his message. "Hello! This is Dr. Carrick Michaels. I'm an astronaut from the United States of America. I am communicating with you from ILK-87b, also known as Black Earth. Its official name is Zenith. I'm reaching out to let you know that I am in good health and in good company. I have spent the past two hundred and sixty-five days with a man who is native to Zenith. His name is Erik." Carrick covered the mic and asked Erik something he'd never asked him before, "What's your last name?"

Erik responded with, "Erickson."

Carrick repeated into the microphone, "I am here with a man named Erik Erickson. He is the last living person on the planet Zenith. The story he has to tell is a great one. It is a story that will answer many questions. Questions that mankind has asked since it first came to be on the planet Earth."

"If you are getting this message, I need you to contact my soon-to-be fiancé, Lola Cook, and my mother, Maggie Michaels. Please get word to them that I'm okay and very much looking forward to returning safely to them both. If you want proof of my identity, I can offer you the following information: My birthday was yesterday, December 12th; I was born in 1990 in Suwanee, Georgia. I was born to a single mother, Maggie Michaels. She was widowed when my father, U.S. Navy Lieutenant Mike Michaels, died tragically on June 11, 1990, over the Southern Pacific Ocean. I graduated from Georgia Tech and went on to get my Ph.D. from Cornell University. Finally, on my NASA application exam, I scored a 100.
"I repeat. I am in good health and in good company. Over and out, for now!"

Just as he finished, the power supply that charged the Thermology Neutrino Waves was lost and would not return.

Location: Langley, Virginia. George Bush Center for Intelligence, CIA Headquarters – December 13, 2022. 4:18 pm, EST.

Two men were sitting around a speaker. The words, "Over and out, for now," were coming through loud and clear.

One CIA officer said to the other, "Did you capture all of that?"

"Yes, I got it all. I hope that was everything!" replied the other.

"Okay, get Director Clapper on the phone ASAP. I'll begin the voice authentication process, and I'll substantiate the bio facts that the subject shared. We have to make sure this isn't a hoax."

Location: Planet Earth. New York City's Upper Westside. 129 West 81st St. – December 14, 2022. Late morning.

In her New York City apartment, Lola Cook was packing to go home for Christmas when her cell phone rang. The screen reported that the caller was unknown.

Lola answered the phone. "Hello?"

"Lola! It's Mars Johnston. I have news about Carrick!"

Lola trembled and was unable to speak. Not since August 29th had she heard anything about Carrick's fate. She was about to get the greatest Christmas gift of all, with the words Mars would speak next.

"Lola, a message from Carrick was picked up by a communications satellite orbiting Black Earth, and his message was clear. He's alive and well, Lola! He wanted to get word to you and Maggie that he's doing fine and that he's looking forward to coming home."

Lola gasped and nearly dropped the phone. "How do you know it was really him?"

"He provided information that only Carrick would know. The CIA did voice authentication on the communication. It was definitely him." Mars went on. "Lola, I know what Carrick scored on his NASA application exam, do you?"

Still trembling, Lola smiled through her tears and said, "He got a perfect score! It was him, wasn't it?" she cried. "He's alive!"

"It was Carrick, Lola; he's alive!"

"When did this happen?!"

"Late yesterday afternoon. I just found out about it fifteen-minutes ago. I had to find a secure line before I could call you," explained Mars. "Listen, you can't tell anyone I called you. They have my phone tapped. They were aware that I called you back in August. They knew within five-minutes of me hanging up."

"I didn't tell anyone you called. I swear!"

"I know you didn't. But if anyone should call you to discuss this, you need to act very surprised, happy, and relieved! Do you understand?"

"Yes, of course, Mars! Thank you! Thank you!"

"Merry Christmas, Lola." Mars managed to keep his voice level low. He curbed his enthusiasm because he knew Lola was about to celebrate a second consecutive Christmas without the love of her life.

"Merry Christmas to you!" she replied.

Lola stood for a moment once the call had ended. She didn't know how she should feel. She was hovering between being relieved and broken-hearted at the same time. As she went to turn off the light in her bedroom, something caught her eye. She walked over to her nightstand. There, she picked up a picture of her and Carrick. It was the last time she'd seen him. Thanksgiving 2021, the day before he left for Black Earth. Since that day, almost thirteen months had passed. It seemed more like a million years, and she still had no idea when she would see him again, although her hopes were buoyed by Mars' call.

Lola's love and faith in Carrick had never diminished. She said out loud, "You're coming home to me, my love!" She kissed the picture and placed it back on the table. Then she grabbed her bag and left for LaGuardia Airport.

Chapter 28 – Mistletoe

Location: Outer Space. Onboard the New Beginning Spaceship – December 25, 2022.

The crew was celebrating Christmas in style; apple cider and the freeze-dried turkey were on the menu.

Kinzi approached Jordan Spear as he floated aimlessly in the galley, fumbling for some more vacuum-packed turkey and mashed potatoes.

"Do you know what I'm holding behind my back?" she said with a sassy smile.

"Well, I wouldn't be very good at my job if I didn't," he shrugged.

"What is it then?"

"Kinzi, you have Mistletoe behind your back!" replied Jordan, still rummaging through the ship's food supply.

"Do you know what that means?" she asked, leaning in while trying to regain eye-contact with him.

"As I said, I wouldn't be any good...," turning to look at Kinzi, Spear started to reply before she quickly cut him off.

"Well, I guess you're not that good at your job after all then!" Kinzi floated away. Moments later, she returned, held the mistletoe above Spear's head, and leaned in for a kiss.

Jordan obliged Kinzi's advances and said, "Well, my girlfriend's not gonna be happy about that!"

Kinzi had a visceral reaction. She shoved Spear and growled, "You son of a bitch! You have a girlfriend?"

"Nah! I just wanted to see if you'd be jealous or not. I guess I got my question answered." He eyed her with an insincere disdain. "Looks as if I'm pretty good at my job after all, huh?" he said, with a smile that wreaked of pay-back.

Kinzi said, "You suck!" and kissed him again.

Jordan continued to unsuccessfully rifle through cabinet after cabinet until Kinzi took pity on him. She pulled open a galley drawer to reveal the holiday stash of goodies, including Jordan's second helping of turkey.

"I'm going with you, you know!" she said as Jordan grappled with the foil packet.

"Going with me, where?"

"I'm going to be there when you interrogate Erik. You can't stop me. I know him; you've never met him; he'll respond to you better if I'm there too."

"Listen, Kinzi, you can't be there," said Jordan, as nicely as he could. "You're a medical doctor, not a trained interrogator."

"I have to be there to draw blood and to examine him medically. Doctors ask patients lots of questions during an exam to get to the bottom of what's ailing them. It's similar to an interrogation."

"Sort of," replied Jordan absentmindedly, trying to open his extra portion of lunch.

Kinzi grabbed the vacuum-packed meal from his hands and ripped it open, putting an end to his suffering.

"Thanks!" he grinned. "But just to be clear, you're not going to be in the room with me when I'm questioning the subject. It's simply not going to happen."

"Fine then! You won't be seeing any more mistletoe in your future!"

"Completely understood!" said Jordan, with a smirk.

Kinzi pushed herself away from Spear, did a 180° turn, and drifted off. She felt as if Jordan now had the upper-hand. And that bothered her.

Location: Planet Earth. Langley, VA., George Bush Center for Intelligence, CIA Headquarters – January 16, 2023. 8:55 am, EST.

In his spacious office, Director James Clapper was meeting with his special assistant, CIA Officer John Hall.

"Okay, that's great, John," said Clapper. "But have there been any more transmissions from Black Earth?"

"No, sir. Nothing since December 13th," replied Hall. "It's as if he had one chance to get a message out, and then all communications were lost."

"Have we tried to contact Dr. Michaels ourselves?" asked Clapper impatiently. "I mean, are we just sitting around waiting until he reaches out to us again?"

"Sir, we have nothing new to target. Other than the glass canopies on both the interior and the exterior of the Northwest Sector, there's nothing. We haven't detected a peep. I'm just as frustrated as you are. Since receiving his voice transmissions, we have been sending radio pings to that portion of the mega-plex in hopes someone will hear them."

"Well, keep me apprised if anything should change." Without making eye-contact, a frustrated Clapper excused his assistant with a dismissive wave.

Location: Houston, Texas. Christopher C. Kraft, Jr. Mission Control Center, Building 30 – April 7, 2023.

Left hand on hip, and right hand pushing his headset's earpiece closer to his head, Mars radioed, "Houston to New Beginning, do you read?"

"Copy that, Houston!" crackled back Mike Swimmer.

"Mike, everything looks normal from our end; are you getting standard readings?" Mars was standing in the middle of the Mission Control Center, which was bustling with no fewer than thirty NASA personnel.

"Roger that Houston. Everything is looking good on our end," said Swimmer. "Black Earth looks the same as when we left her. We've got T-minus twenty-minutes until commencement of our orbit insertion burn."

"Great!" came the answer from Earth. "Ease her in there and then get some rest. Tomorrow's a big day! Make sure everyone's in good spirits. We need to execute the separation of Black Horizon 2 flawlessly."

"Roger that!" said Swimmer. "We'll be ready!"

"Okay, I'll contact you at zero six hundred Houston time tomorrow morning. See you on the other side, Mike!" Mars signed off.

It was now early morning, the next day, and Mission Control was ready to assist the Sagittarian Recovery mission crew. The team had already been preparing to undock the Black Horizon 2 landing craft so that it could begin its powered descent to the surface of Black Earth.

"You ready to go?" Kinzi asked Jordan Spear.

"No, I think I'll stay up here. You go on ahead. Just be sure to get me Erik's autograph," joked Jordan, visibly apprehensive.

"You'll be fine; I'll be there holding your hand, so don't worry. Oh, and by the way, when we see Carrick, don't tell him about us. I think he has a crush on me," said Kinzi, trying to get a rise out of Jordan. "10-4! Will do!" Jordan saluted and half-smiled.

Kinzi helped Jordan get his spacesuit on.

"It's been four months; I forgot how to do this!" said Jordan, fumbling with the components of his protective suit.

"Well, let's see," she smirked while taking inventory of his EMU.

"We've got a set of big boy pants here. I'm guessing you put them on one leg at a time."

"Ha-ha, smart ass! Just give me a hand," said Jordan, looking hopelessly at the rack holding his EMU in place.

Within four-hours, Kinzi London, Jordan Spear, Kevin Yi, and Cosmo Popov were strapped into their couches and sealed inside the Black Horizon 2 Landing Module, ready to undock from New Beginning.

"3-2-1, mark undock," announced Mars Johnston.

"We have a clean separation Houston. Black Horizon 2 now has wings!" declared Swimmer excitedly.

One orbit later, Black Horizon 2 began its eight-minute descent to the surface. Jordan Spear grasped Kinzi's gloved hand, keeping his eyes firmly closed. Kinzi, having done this once before, was looking around, studying the faces of her shipmates. Yi's eyes were closed, but Cosmo Popov looked straight at her and shot her a wink.

Jordan appeared to be suffering badly during the 8G descent through the less than dense atmosphere of Black Earth. The abrupt, jarring maneuvers sent the Lander spinning and tumbling as the heat shield was jettisoned and the first of the drogue parachutes deployed. Jordan vomited into his helmet while Kinzi looked on. She toughed it out and actually took a little pleasure in Jordan's discomfort.

At 11:43 am CST, on April 8th, 2023, a thud signaled the Lander's descent engines cutting out abruptly, dropping the four of them the final two meters onto the surface.

Jordan finally opened his eyes. "Did we make it?" he asked. "Did we land? Are we okay?"

The other three crew members were busy high-fiving and laughing, happy to be alive. Jordan, however, looked exhausted and drained of color. After a moment, he realized that he was safe and broke into a smile, then exhaled in relief.

It had been one hour and twelve-minutes since they'd undocked in orbit. The riskiest part of their flight was behind them. Cheers from Houston, and New Beginning orbiting overhead, could be heard in the surface crew's headsets.

The successful landing meant that Black Horizon 2 would likely have no issues launching its upper stage Return Module back into orbit. It would reconnect with the New Beginning spaceship, which was orbiting some two hundred and fifty miles overhead in just under fifty-hours.

In place of the fifth crew member that the Lander could accommodate, the team carried with them two 200-pound battery packs. These would be used to charge the original Black Horizon Rovers 1 and 2. On the way back, the fifth seat would be used for the return of Carrick Michaels.

After roughly four-hours on the surface, Kinzi London would be the first to exit the landing module. As her foot touched the last rung of the outer ladder, she thought about what she would say as she stepped down onto the black surface. In a trembling voice, she began to announce, "I, Kaley London, with the next step taken..."

At that moment, the sound of Mars Johnston's voice filled her helmet. "Kinzi, we're not live back on Earth. The world will eventually see footage of you climbing down the ladder, but they won't have the audio. You're holding everybody up," he teased. "Get off that ladder and let the other three out of the module. In case you've forgotten, you already set foot on the surface last year. We have less than forty-hours left on the surface, so let's get a move on."

"Fine!" said Kinzi breezily. "Just dreaming out loud over here on Black Earth." With that, she put her boots on Black Earth's surface for the second time in thirteen months.

Over the next three hours, the other two scientists, along with CIA Officer Jordan Spear, exited the module and off-loaded the rover batteries, along with other equipment needed to continue their science experiments from the previous year. A mechanical arm was used to safely remove the two 200-pound battery packs. Kinzi and Jordan were responsible for removing the old battery supply from Black Horizon Rover 1. Though the conditions on Black Earth were hostile, there seemed to be little damage to the rover, which had been sitting in 800°F plus temperatures for the last fifty-four weeks.

Location: Planet Earth. Washington D.C., The Situation Center with Bear Winston – April 8, 2023. 11:59 am EST.

NCN – Breaking News.

"This just in!" said Bear Winston. "The mission to recover astronaut Dr. Carrick Michaels, who was left behind on Black Earth more than a year ago, hit a milestone just moments ago. NASA is reporting that the New Beginning's landing module has successfully touched down on the black planet. NASA, however, is not releasing live footage from mission Sagittarian Recovery but promises to issue still shots and some video very soon.

"With me now is NCN contributor and Assistant Editor for the Washington Post, Davin Schulten."

Winston swiveled briskly in his chair to face his guest. "Davin, what do you make of the cloak of secrecy around NASA's decision not to air live footage of the landing module's touchdown on Black Earth?"

"So, Bear, I think there are two ways of looking at this," Schulten replied. "One: not much to see here. This is the second landing and not the one that made history while being viewed by what was probably more than two billion people worldwide. Or two: NASA doesn't want us to see what they're doing because there might be some covert or nefarious 'goings-on' with the mission.

"What we need to keep in mind is that NASA doesn't know exactly what they'll find when it comes to the search and recovery of Dr. Michaels. They most likely feel that it would be prudent to keep a buffer between what they consider 'real-time,' or a live video feed, versus the 'right-time.' They also understand that they can share carefully edited video or photographic evidence of what transpired on Black Earth at a later date. Another thing to keep in mind, Bear, is that they bungled the last mission by leaving one of their astronauts behind."

Winston rebutted, "To be fair though Davin, Dr. Michaels chose to stay on Black Earth by all accounts. Isn't that right?"

"Bear, if you remember, it was days and even weeks before NASA came clean regarding the whereabouts and well-being of Dr. Michaels. They claimed that there were security concerns around what occurred, but my sources are conflicted about what really transpired up there to this day. My guess is that NASA is being prudent and doesn't want another public relations nightmare dropped into their lap," concluded Schulten.

Swiveling slowly back to the camera, Winston put on a big smile. "Alright folks, there you have it from our experts here at NCN. Stay tuned as we'll have much more on this developing story next hour."

Location: The Internet.

Conspiracy theories were swirling. Many people thought NASA had faked the Black Earth landing in March of 2022 and was now engaged in another hoax, claiming they'd landed there for a second time.

Photos were circulating that purportedly showed Carrick Michaels at a Publix supermarket in his hometown of Suwanee, Georgia, as recently as a month ago. Pictures also showed the individual exiting the grocery store and then entering a dry-cleaning establishment looking decidedly shifty. In the photos, the man was wearing a baseball cap pulled down low.

These reports were countered by one of the employees from the Majik Touch Cleaners. She claimed that the man pictured entering her location was not Dr. Michaels at all. The employee, Joshila Dahya, said that the person was actually a regular customer named Andrew Hill. Dahya did concede, however, that Hill might resemble Dr. Michaels from a distance. This, in turn, led some conspiracists to claim that Dahya was not an actual employee of the establishment but rather an undercover agent or even an actress. On various blogs and right-wing websites, some theorists actually alleged that the woman had played a bit-part in the 2008 movie Slumdog Millionaire.

Elsewhere, discussion forums claimed that no one named Carrick Michaels from Suwanee, Georgia actually existed. Some unnamed individuals professed to have graduated from North Gwinnett High School in 2007, without having any recollection of Michaels from that time. Making their argument implausible was an image published on the blogs that was taken from the Senior picture section of the school's yearbook. The photo revealed no one by name of Michaels appeared in the yearbook, as students were listed alphabetically. However, the image accidentally captured the page numbers at the bottom of the two pages represented in the photo. The page numbers clearly indicated that a page appeared to be missing. The left side of the image showed page one-thirty-seven, while the right side of the image was of page one-forty, suggesting that a page was removed from the yearbook prior to the picture being taken.

Location: Black Earth. Northwest Sector of The Triad, Surface-Level 5, Observatory Deck – April 8, 2023. 11:16 am, CST.

Erik and Carrick were sitting in the outer observatory, stargazing, and sharing a laugh about something that had happened days earlier.

Carrick was sitting in the large observatory chair while Erik occupied a smaller one off to the side. Each of them was enjoying a metal canister full of water.

"It's hot as hell up here," Carrick observed, "but the view of the stars makes the heat more tolerable."

Silence reigned for a while until Carrick spoke again. "They're beautiful," he said, taking in the splendor of the night sky and the stars overhead. "Without a moon, Zenith is so dark! You can almost see Earth from here."

"You can absolutely see it from here!" replied Erik. "It's right there!" "Where?" Carrick squinted at the sky.

Erik pointed to a position in the night sky, indicating the brightest point of light in their field of view. Carrick squinted and leaned forward in his chair. In that instant, the two witnessed a flash of light high up in the sky, followed by a fire trail.

"Whoa! Did you see that? That was awesome!" exclaimed Carrick. "Back on Earth, we call that a shooting star. What did... I'm sorry, what do Zenithians call them?" he asked, glancing at Erik.

"We call that a spacecraft entering our atmosphere," said Erik, impassively, standing up to get a better look.

"Stop joking around, Erik!" retorted Carrick, but he could clearly see by the look on Erik's face that the old man wasn't kidding.

Carrick stood beside Erik at the window. They followed the faint and sporadic fire bursts as they fell to Zenith's surface just a few miles away. Carrick recognized the location as the area where he'd landed the Black Horizon Lander thirteen months earlier.

"That's your ride home, son," said Erik in a somber tone.

"My God!" sighed Carrick, tears welling up in his eyes. "My message got through. They came back for me!"

A flood of emotions overcame Carrick. He realized that he would see Lola again. That his mother, Maggie, would have her only son back. After months of not being sure, he now knew that he would return from the dark abyss of Zenith and walk in the light of Earth again. He and Lola would hold one another. Carrick resolved that he would ask her to marry him the moment that he saw her face. He promised himself that.

As Carrick stood transfixed, it was an emotional moment for Erik too. His new best friend, his only friend, in fact, of the last seventy-six years, would soon leave him, just like Lilly had. He wasn't sure if he was sad or mad. He simply knew that, with the flash in the sky, his life was about to change for the worse. He would die alone on this dying planet. His heart was broken.

Carrick, meanwhile, was oblivious to his friend's grief. "We've got to hurry!" he exclaimed. "From the minute they touchdown, they'll only have about forty-hours of life support before they have to leave again."

He looked over at Erik, who wasn't showing any signs of urgency. "Let's go, Erik!" he said.

Erik remained static, just staring out into the darkness. "What's the hurry? You just said you have forty-hours."

Carrick nodded in agreement. He knew that after touchdown, it would take roughly four to five-hours to exit the module. He took that moment to step into Erik's shoes, and it slowly dawned on him how his companion must've been feeling. "Erik, I'll come back for you," he said.

To Carrick's surprise, Erik responded angrily. "I told you, I'm not going back to Earth!" I was meant to die here alone, and that's what I intend to do!" he snapped.

As he looked at Carrick with fire in his eyes, Carrick took a step back, surprised by his tone. He realized he felt torn about Erik staying on Zenith. But, in the same way that he had refused to go back to Earth the year prior, how could he force Erik to come? It also occurred to him that Erik was about to face some tough questions. There would be medical examinations and needles, as the mission medic would surely want to evaluate both of them.

"Erik, listen. The next forty-hours or so might be a little uncomfortable. They will be taking some blood from us. They may check that; they definitely will have lots of questions for the two of us," he warned.

"I'm up for it!" replied Erik. "I plan on savoring the last few hours I have with you. Just promise me you'll stay by my side no matter what happens."

"Until the last hour, my friend; I promise you that," said Carrick, with a somber tone to his voice. "So, what do we do next?"

"When you got here last year, I waited right here. We'll be alerted to an approaching vehicle or entity. Lights and sirens will sound. From here, we'll make our way down to the front entrance, the place where you and I first met."

"God, I remember that day. My whole life changed after that!"
"Mine did too," said Erik.

"That was more than a year ago!" Carrick couldn't believe how quickly time had passed.

"It was the best year I've had in the last seventy-five plus, my friend," said Erik.

"Erik, I can't tell you what it has meant to me. To know a man like you. You're not only a hero to every Zenithian that came before and after you, but you're my hero too," said Carrick, with tears of sincerity in his eyes.

A tear ran down Erik's cheek, too, as he listened to Carrick speak. At that moment, he felt he would never see his friend again.

Erik's only hope was that Carrick would go back to Earth and marry Lola. He even secretly wished to himself that if the two were to someday have a child and if by chance, that child was a boy, then maybe, just maybe, they would name that little man Erickson Michaels.

Chapter 29 – The Confession

Location: Black Earth. Northwest Sector of The Triad, Observatory Deck, Surface-Level 5 – April 8, 2023. 5:23 pm, CST.

Flashing lights and sirens.

With great anticipation, Carrick jumped up and said, "Here we go!"

Erik looked at him for a moment before saying, "Lead the way son," He gestured a ', please proceed' motion with his right hand.

The two men made their way down to The Grand Hall and took the elevator to Surface-Level 1; they barely spoke along the way.

Although he wasn't sure who'd be waiting for them at the front entrance, Carrick was contemplating seeing familiar faces.

For Erik, this was a day he knew would come, but for the last year had selfishly hoped it never would.

Without words, the two men chuckled as they walked by a hole in the wall where a diamond glass light fixture was once mounted. Minutes later, the two stood at the inner airlock door of the Northwest Sector's main entrance. Erik provided Carrick with the number code to open the exterior airlock door of the temperature regulation chamber.

"But there are no buttons to push," said Carrick peering at the panel, looking perplexed. "How do I enter the code?"

Erik rolled his eyes and shook his head from side to side. "This isn't Earth. You don't push any buttons. You just stare at the screen and, without blinking, think the number into the panel."

Carrick completed the mental command and heard the panel's computer say, "Code Accepted, Carrick." He smiled at Erik, eyebrows raised, and said, "Now that was awesome!"

A few minutes earlier, on the outside of the exterior door, two astronauts looked at each other and the massive structure that stood before them.

"So, this is it, huh? The Triad?" Jordan asked Kinzi. He was apprehensive and stood a half-step behind and to the right of his companion.

"This is it!" she replied. She, too, was nervous, although far more comfortable than she had been on her first visit to The Triad.

"Pretty big, huh?" she observed, looking skyward.

"Pretty scary!" replied Jordan.

"Listen, Kinzi, I'm supposed to be this big badass CIA interrogator, but frankly, I feel like I'm in over my head here," he finally confessed.

"No, shit!" said Kinzi. "You think I'm blind?"

"That obvious, huh?"

"Oh, yeah!" smiled Kinzi. "I bet your diaper's filling up right now."

Jordan, too nervous to acknowledge Kinzi's joke, said, "Listen, when we get in there, I need to be that big badass, or I'm going to get nothing out of this guy Erik. You need to go along with whatever I say or do; got it?" he added.

"Sir, yes, sir!" Kinzi replied, mocking him with a salute.

A few seconds later, the outer door began to open. Kinzi said, "You ready, Big Boy?"

Jordan gasped. "Nope!"

She then took his gloved hand, and they walked into the temperature regulation chamber.

On the other side of the door, Erik and Carrick stood waiting as the outer door opened. It would take several minutes to expel the heat from the chamber and from the materials that had been exposed to 800°F temperatures. This included the air surrounding the astronauts as well as their spacesuits and equipment. After the temperature regulation was complete, the inner door would open.

An impatient Carrick watched the liquid-glass monitor hanging overhead. On it, he and Erik witnessed two NASA astronauts entering the chamber. Carrick couldn't determine the identity of either of them but, based on the size differential, he surmised that one was a woman and the other a man. Carrick hoped that the woman was his old friend, Kinzi London.

After four-minutes of temperature regulation, the familiar sound of pressurized air being released replaced the sound of silence, and the inner door began to open. Jordan took a deep breath and then exhaled fully. Feeling like he did before running out onto a football field prior to a game. Kinzi, on the other hand, was anxious to see her friend, praying that he was still alive. After several seconds, the two astronauts stepped forward.

Before them stood Dr. Carrick Michaels and 'Black Earth Erik.' Carrick saluted the two astronauts and then extended his hand to shake. Kinzi dispensed with the formal handshake and immediately lunged to hug Carrick as Jordan rolled his eyes.

Though she still had her helmet on, Carrick could now see that it was his old friend Kinzi London. After an uncomfortably long hug with Carrick, Kinzi looked over at Erik, and Erik said, "What took you so long?" with a smile, repeating the words he said the first time he met her at the airlock door.

Carrick helped the two astronauts remove their helmets and realized he was staring at a man he didn't recognize. "Have we met before?" he asked the stranger.

Jordan's face looked stoic while standing as tall as he could, almost as if to measure himself up against the much shorter Carrick Michaels.

Carrick looked him up and down. "I know everyone in the program, but you aren't familiar to me."

Spear then looked Carrick up and down again and said, "No, we've never met before, but I've heard a lot about you. Kinzi seems to be a big fan," smirked Spear.

"My name is Jordan Spear," he said with a sardonic smile.

"O...kay?" said Carrick, with a look of skepticism.

Jordan Spear turned his eyes to Erik. "I haven't heard a lot about you, though," he said firmly.

Erik rolled his eyes in Carrick's direction. "Here we go." He sensed that things weren't going to go too well over the next thirty or so hours.

"Carrick, why don't you show our guests the way to The Culina. I'm sure they must be hungry," suggested Erik. "But first, let's get you out of those spacesuits."

Minutes later, in The Culina, the four sat down for some Red Fruit when Kinzi said, "God, this stuff is awful."

Erik offered a cup to Jordan Spear. Jordan waved him off and said, "Nothing for me, thank you." He then sat forward in his chair. "Listen, we're kind of short on time here, so, after you guys are finished with your little snack, I need to talk to Erik," he paused, "alone!" he said, with an intimidating and dismissive tone.

"Okay!" Carrick jumped up from his seat. "Who in the hell are you, and why are you here?" He stepped up to Spear, getting right in his face. As he did so, he swallowed hard and hoped that Spear didn't notice.

The size difference between the two men was clearly noticeable to all. A physical altercation was not what either man desired, as both knew it wouldn't end well for Carrick. Still, Carrick carried on, "You're neither a doctor, a scientist, nor an astronaut for that matter. So why are you here? What are you, CIA?"

Jordan smiled pompously. "It seems that you're as smart as you look. That's a compliment, by the way. I can see why Kinzi's so fond of you," he added, his voice turning sarcastic. "We all know why I'm here, as does Black Earth Erik!" said Spear, with an attitude.

Erik grinned. "Black Earth Erik, huh?! Is that what they're calling me back on Earth?"

Kinzi started getting the feeling that something was about to go down and said, "Okay, boys, let's all calm down a little bit."

"As I was saying," said Spear, "I'm going to need some time alone with our friend Erik," he repeated himself.

"I thought I was Black Earth Erik?!" said Erik with a smile and a chuckle. "I kinda like it....it has a certain ring to it!" he added while trying extremely hard not to sound insincere.

Jordan Spear immediately felt as if he were outnumbered and that the only way to regain control was to get Kinzi and Carrick out of the equation.

"As I said, I will need to speak to Erik alone," said Spear calmly. "That's an order," he added, looking directly at Carrick.

"Let me explain something to you, Detective Spear," said Carrick, with intended sarcasm. "You hold no rank over me here on Zenith, in the middle of outer space, or back on Earth. I can promise you this, pal; you won't be talking to my good friend Erik alone, not today, not tomorrow, not ever, for that matter."

Jordan countered with, "First of all, it's Officer Spear, and I'd like to remind you, Dr. Michaels, that you and I will be spending the next four months together on a very small spaceship." He paused before continuing. "I'd very much like that time to be filled with laughter and joy, as opposed to hostility and anger. I expect that you will allow me to do the job that I've been asked to do by the President of our United States."

Carrick was adamant. "As I said before, you will not find yourself alone in a room with my friend Erik!"

"Kinzi could see this discussion was going nowhere. Smiling, she interjected, "Well then, I'll be there too!"

With a look of capitulation, Jordan knew that he was no longer in control and would likely have to conduct his interrogation in front of a small audience.

Still smiling, Kinzi carried on. "Listen, I have a job to do too. So, why don't you two boys run along and let me get on with it before a game of tackle football breaks out." She seemed very impressed with her own joke. "I need to draw blood from the two of you later, and I also need to check each of your vitals. Let's get that done before you both start to experience tachycardia."

Jordan and Carrick looked at each other and then at Kinzi. "What?" they chorused together.

Erik shook his head, rolled his eyes, and said, "It means excessively rapid heartbeat."

"Nice job, Doctor!" said Kinzi, looking impressed. "I think we have something in common, an IQ slightly higher than these two gladiators."

The two looked absolutely dumbfounded and left out of the conversation. They excused themselves and left Kinzi and Erik alone in The Culina.

After the two men had walked out of earshot, Erik asked, "So, what's up with your rather large friend? Or is he a rather large foe?"

"He's a little of both, I guess. I'm still trying to figure him out. He is pretty, though!" Kinzi said with a smile.

"Can't argue with you there," Erik acknowledged, with a nod of his head.

Standing in The Grand Hall, Spear told Carrick that he was indeed a CIA officer and that he'd been sent here by the Office of the President of the United States.

"I'm not the enemy here, Carrick," said Spear. "but I can be if that's what you want, but I don't think you do. I can also have you taken into custody the moment we land back on Earth. In case you were unaware, impeding a federal investigation, with national security implications, has consequences."

"Listen, Spear," Carrick leaned in, "Erik is not what or whom you think he is. I strongly encourage you not to pre-determine the outcome of any conversation you have with him. Erik is neither a hostile foreign enemy nor is he a threat to our national or international security. He is a Zenithian. He was born here."

"Well, that's impossible!" exclaimed Spear. "So, you're suggesting he's an alien?!"

"There you go!" said a glowering Carrick. "You just did what I asked you not to do! You pre-determined something that you don't have the answer to. He's human, and he's not from Earth!"

Jordan was unblinking. "Don't be ridiculous! I know he's human, and I know he's from Earth; those facts are not in question. My job is to determine what country he's from and how and when he got here!"

After a few moments of silence and frustration, Spear spoke again. "He's definitely from Earth!"

"Okay, we're going around in circles here! How about this? I'll allow you to interview him alone under two conditions."

"I'm listening," said a conciliatory Spear.

"One, you don't lay a hand on him. I want to be clear, if you touch him, one of us won't be on that spaceship back to Earth!" Carrick said darkly.

Jordan smirked but nodded in agreement. "Fair enough, what's the second?"

"The interrogation has to happen in The History Library."

"What's that?" asked Jordan.

"It's the place where you're going to get all of your questions answered."

Meanwhile, back in The Culina, Kinzi had opened her bag and pulled out some items, including several foil-packed syringes and a pulse oximeter.

Feeling apprehensive, Erik pointed at the syringes. "What are those for?"

"I need to draw some blood. I've got to make sure you're human," smiled Kinzi.

"Boy, you're just full of jokes, aren't you?" Erik chuckled. "The last time I saw you, Carrick and I were picking you up off the floor. You ran out of here, screaming and crying."

"That was a long time ago, Mr. Erik."

"Seems like yesterday," said Erik, feeling a little melancholy.

"Feels like years for me!" she countered, pulling a blood pressure monitor from her bag. "I need to take your blood pressure. Is that okay with you?"

"Do I have a choice?" asked Erik.

"No! Now up with your sleeve," she instructed.

Kinzi wrapped the rubber cuff around Erik's left bicep. As she did so, he looked over the items laid out on the table and tried to get a glimpse of what else she might be hiding in her bag.

"So, how do I know you're not going to inject me with some kind of truth serum or something that will sedate me?" he asked.

"Got something to hide, Mr. Erik?" she asked with a smile.

"No, ma'am!" he replied.

"You see these syringes? They're empty! Nothing's going into your body, but something's definitely coming out," she said, with a look of determination. "Sure, hope it's red," she muttered under her breath.

"Have at it, Kinzi!" said Erik as he offered her his arm for the second time.

Back in The Grand Hall, the two men leaned over the top rail and looked down into a pit of darkness.

"What is this place, anyway?" asked Jordan. "It looks just like the Pentagon, inside and out."

"It's called The Triad, and it's been around for more than four thousand years."

Jordan looked skeptical. "Okay, I'll humor you; keep going."

"The Triad was the final safe-haven for the remaining human population of Zenith. Millions lived and died here, and the lucky ones got to go home to Earth. More than seven-hundred-thousand made the pilgrimage over a period of four thousand years."

Jordan sighed. "What is Zenith?"

"Erik will tell you more once you're in The History Library with him. But remember, keep an open mind," Carrick encouraged.

"Like any good interviewer, listen more than you talk. The answers are there. You just have to listen."

"That sounds like good advice to me. Perhaps we'll end up as friends someday," said Jordan.

"Perhaps," said Carrick, looking a bit skeptical.

"Unless, of course, you're lying to me, Dr. Michaels," said an unblinking Jordan Spear, who continued to wear a look of skepticism.

A frustrated Carrick shook his head and walked away, heading back to The Culina. Jordan was left alone in The Grand Hall. Before rejoining the others, he took a moment to look around at its dormant majesty. He couldn't believe how immense and frightening it was. Could Carrick actually be telling the truth? He struggled with all of it. But he was beginning to sense a ring of truth as he admired the circular atrium one more time before walking back to find the others.

Location: The Culina – Twenty-minutes later.

Carrick pulled Erik to the side and said, "I have to break my promise to you, my friend. I'm going to let Officer Spear talk to you without me in the room."

Erik was slack-jawed and questioned Carrick's decision. "You're really leaving me alone in a room with that rather large son of a gun?" using language he picked up from Carrick.

The two men both looked across the room at Jordan, who was conversing with Kinzi.

"You see the arms on that guy? asked Erik.

"Don't worry, I threatened to kill him if he lays a hand on you," said Carrick.

"Did you really? That's awesome!" said Erik, with a big smile, feeling proud of Carrick.

"Well, sort of," Carrick grinned. "Just tell him the truth. There's nothing he can do to change the truth, so just give the guy a history lesson."

Location: The History Library – Thirty-minutes later.

"Welcome to The History Library Officer Spear," said Erik.

"This place is pretty impressive; how long's it been around?"

"Longer than me, that's for sure," said Erik.

"No, really, how long?" insisted Spear, looking to validate what Carrick told him back in The Grand Hall.

"Four-thousand years, give or take," answered Erik.

"How long have you been here on Black Earth?" questioned Spear.

"Black Earth, huh? It's black, but it's not Earth. Earth is nowhere nearly as advanced as Zenith once was. It'll be another 6000 years before Earth reaches the pinnacle that once was the great planet of Zenith. From what Carrick tells me, humans don't have another 6000 years left; maybe a thousand, maybe less," taunted Erik.

"Again, how long have you been here?" asked Spear.

"I'm one-hundred-fifteen-years-old, Officer Spear."

"What is your last name, by the way?" asked Spear, also trying to validate the CIA's transcript of Carrick's message transmitted to Earth the previous December.

"Erickson. Doctor Erickson Michael Erickson," answered Erik. "Doctor, huh? I'm impressed," Jordan remarked while trying hard to look unimpressed. "Doctors are smart."

"Some are, some maybe not so much," thought Erik aloud.

"Well," Jordan continued, "if I were going to make up a phony name, I would've been smart and not used the same name twice."

"By phony, I surmise you mean spurious?"

Jordan, not knowing what spurious meant, gambled, and said, "Yes."

Erik just laughed and shook his head side to side, indicating that he'd had enough of Jordan Spear's line of questioning.

"What you just said sounds like a bunch of nonsense to me, son," he quipped. "You asked a question, and I answered it truthfully. You just questioned the truth, Officer Spear. How does it feel to have just lost the upper-hand?" he countered with a forged smile.

Jordan Spear was beginning to feel vulnerable and was desperate for control of the conversation.

He smiled and said, "You know what I call conversations like this one? Conversations that I have with people just like you? Conversations where I know all of the answers to every question that I'm about to ask?"

"Why don't you just tell me, son? Apparently, you have all the answers, and yet you find yourself stranded on an island looking for the truth. How does that feel?"

"First of all, I'm not your son!" Jordan paused for effect. "Second of all, please explain how it is that I've somehow found myself stranded on a proverbial island?"

Erik responded, "May I call you Jordan then?"

"No, you may not!" said an arrogant Jordan.

"Okay, Officer Spear, I'll answer your question. If it's true that you possess the answer to every question that you're about to ask me, then you certainly don't need me here. With that, I'll be leaving.

Erik stood in a spurious gesture and acted as if he were about to leave.

"Sit down, Mr. Erickson! You're not going anywhere!" said Spear, with a threatening tone.

Erik sat back down. "Now what?" He paused for a second and said, "Oh yeah, you were asking me a question a moment ago. Could you possibly repeat it?"

"I asked if you knew what I call conversations like this one?" Spear asked again, his face revealing utter disdain.

"Don't know. Why don't you just tell me? It seems like you're dying to do so," Erik replied with a grin.

"I call it the Confession," Jordan said ominously.

Erik, however, was not intimidated and knew that the young Spear was simply playing a role. An actor, and not a very good one, he thought to himself.

What Jordan Spear couldn't possibly know was that Dr. Erik Erickson had, for the last seventy-five years, been studying the greatest minds that ever lived on Zenith. From Julius Caesar to Johannes Kepler, Leonardo da Vinci to Louis Pasteur, Bernhard Riemann to Albert Einstein, Ferdinand Magellan, and hundreds of others. Erik knew that one truth was stronger than a million lies. Jordan Spear was about to learn something that he would take with him. Something that he would never forget.

"Officer Spear, can you tell me what's more powerful than the truth?" asked Erik, with a philosophical approach.

"Why don't you tell me, Mr. Erickson?" asked Spear.

Erik looked the young man up and down, shook his head from side to side, and delivered a measured smile. "Nothing. That's what," replied Erik. "Nothing is more powerful than the truth."

Erik's comments caught Jordan off guard and caused him to pause for a moment. At that moment, he felt like a novice chess player in a match against Garry Kasparov. This was no longer an interrogation where he could browbeat and intimidate his detainee. He was beginning to feel like he had prior to entering The Triad. In over his head. He knew he had to keep up the tough-guy façade, or else the interrogation would end abruptly.

"Why is that?" asked Spear, trying to buy a little time in an effort to change his strategy.

"The truth never lies," answered Erik. "The truth never changes. No matter how much time goes by, no matter how much the world, things, or people around us change, the truth never does. The truth unifies the righteous and fractures the corrupt," he professed as if he were the teacher and Jordan, the student.

"Please continue," said Jordan, as he needed more time to alter the course of where this conversation was going. The tables were turned, and Jordan knew it. It was an avalanche, a cascading reversal of control, and it couldn't be pushed back up the mountain.

"Let's try a little experiment, shall we, Officer Spear," suggested Erik.

"Call me Jordan," said Spear as his confidence began to wane.

"Jordan, it is then!" said Erik with a now warm smile. "Go ahead and share with me something that you think might alter the course of this conversation. I will then reveal to you how powerful the truth really is."

"Okay, I've got something to share with you," said Jordan. "No matter how smart you are, and you seem pretty smart, the truth cuts both ways. I happen to know for a fact that you are not from this planet. The only parts of your story that I'm stuck on is what country you hail from and why you're here," said Jordan, with a less than confident exterior.

Erik just smiled.

"Do I humor you?" asked Jordan, feeling as though he had just been exposed.

"Jordan, you had a look in your eyes as you were asking me that question. It's a look that I have seen many times before," explained Erik. "You see, Jordan, on the last shuttle to Earth, was a very smart man, a very good friend of mine. We used to play chess nearly every night in my barrack. He was very good at the game and could beat most with whom he played."

"The man's name was Kim Moiseyevich Weinstein, and he spoke with both conviction and with great confidence. He was so convincing that most of the people he was speaking to believed his every word and rarely ever questioned what he said. They were so taken with his confidence; they became convinced that what he was saying must be true. Many times, when at the end of a game of chess, he would pronounce checkmate, though he hadn't actually mated his opponent yet. He said it with such confidence that his opponent would almost always lay down their King in defeat and walk away. He would sometimes say it to me when we played, and many times my next move would checkmate him. The look on his face would be that of someone who was outsmarted and couldn't believe that I didn't concede."

"That look is on your face right now, Jordan. That's why I'm smiling. Not because I'm enjoying the charade that you're putting on, but rather because I'm putting an end to it," said Erik with quiet confidence.

"I'm confused!" confessed Jordan.

"I know you are, son," said Erik. "It's written all over your face. You've been wearing that look ever since you walked through the door. Now, back to our little experiment. A moment ago, you said that you knew, for a fact, that I was not from Zenith."

"That's correct. I know that you're from Earth," replied Jordan, with a false sense of confidence.

"That's checkmate, my friend!" exclaimed Erik, again smiling.

"How's that?" questioned Spear, with a 'prove it' look on his face.

"Jordan, the truth wins every time! I'm from Zenith, and your assertion that I'm not, tells me that you don't possess the answers to all of your questions, as you so confidently stated earlier. You're acting. You're simply playing the part of someone who is in control, someone who holds all of the answers, when in fact, you don't."

"What this tells me is that everything you're about to say or ask me is merely a guess, a lie, a tactic, or a ruse. Basically, your lie cost you your credibility. Any question that you plan on asking me going forward is now irrelevant."

"The two of us have been playing a game of cards. A game in which I have been holding a hand full of truths while you, on the other hand, have been holding a hand full of lies. Who wins that game every time, Mr. Spear?" asked Erik rhetorically.

It was at that moment that Jordan realized that he had neglected to record the interview. He decided that he would let Erik finish his thought as he desperately wanted to avoid Erik's recognition of his ineptness. The repercussions that he would face from his superiors at the CIA, back on Earth, regarding his massive blunder, would have to be dealt with later. For now, CIA Officer Jordan Spear just wanted to salvage some sense of credibility in Erik's eyes, but he feared that that moment had unfortunately passed. He hoped that the dread that befell his face was not obvious to Erik, but he somehow knew that it was.

"Okay, then. You win!" said Jordan. "Why don't you just tell me who you are. I then will assume you're telling me the truth until the point at which I catch you in a lie. Sound good?"

"That sounds like a great idea!" said Erik. "Here's my confession. My name is Dr. Erickson, Michael Erickson. I am from the once-great planet of Zenith. I am one-hundred and fifteen-years-old. I have lived in The Triad for my entire life, and I will surely die here. I have never been married, never had children, and have only ever loved one woman. Her name was Lilly. I have never harmed anyone. I have only served my people in the best interest of humankind and never my own. That is my truth Officer Spear; that is my confession," he said with a broken heart.

Chapter 30 – Torn

Location: Northwest Sector of The Triad, Observatory Deck, Surface-Level 5 – April 8, 2023. 4:18 pm, CST.

"You lost some weight, boy!" said Kinzi, beginning her exam of Carrick.

"Lil' bit," said Carrick, raising his eyebrows.

"They're going to start calling you Pebble instead of Rock when we get back," she laughed.

"Ahh, I missed that sense of humor, Kinzi."

"So, what have you been doing for the last thirteen months?" she asked as she began to draw blood from his arm.

"Learning as much as I can," replied Carrick. "So, did NASA fire me yet? How much trouble am I in?"

"Are you kidding me? You're their poster child! The world is your oyster when you get back. You're an international hero!"

"That's crazy!" Carrick was a little shocked by the news.

"You know, I almost had a nervous breakdown after I got back to Earth last year. I can't believe you stayed here on Black Earth! What the hell were you thinking? What on Black Earth compelled you to stay?"

"I see what you did there with the little Black Earth reference. That was cute," smiled Carrick.

Kinzi winked and smiled too, acknowledging her self-perceived comedic genius.

Carrick continued, "I don't know. Something just pulled me in. When I met Erik, it was as if I knew him. I felt safe in his presence. And, since getting to know him, he's become the most incredible person I've ever met. He's changed my life."

"I don't get it," said Kinzi.

"I don't expect you to. But if you were alone on this planet for one day with Erik, you'd know exactly what I was talking about. Profound is the best word that I could use to describe the man."

"Hang on!" Kinzi butted in a stunned look on her face. "You seriously believe that he's actually from here, don't you?!"

"Kinzi, listen to me! Erik is from here, and he's as human as you and me. The DNA test will prove it. We have to get him back to Earth. He's got a story to tell, and the entire world needs to hear it. Is the landing module still equipped with the back-up EMU?"

"Are you crazy! He's not coming back with us!"

"You don't understand!" Carrick shook his head.

"Carrick, the module can only carry five of us. Even if it were possible, we couldn't take him back with us."

"Oh God!" said Carrick, sounding panicked. "Are you telling me four of you came down in the Lander? We can't leave him here! I can't tell the world his story; only he can! Fuck! Dammit! What are we going to do?" he yelled.

"Carrick, listen to me; it would take a U.N. Security Council Resolution to gain approval to bring him back. Until we can confirm that he's not a threat to mankind, no one will ever authorize it. The world would riot, and the stock markets would crash if they knew he was coming back! You don't understand! The religious right thinks he's the devil, and the anti-government conspiracy nuts have guns; who knows what they'll do? He wouldn't be safe," stressed Kinzi.

"You're right! I hate it, but you're right! Dammit!" yelled Carrick.

Calming himself, he suddenly realized he needed to know Erik was ok. "Let's get back down to The History Library before G.I. Joe eats Erik for dinner," he said grimly.

As the two friends walked down a long dark hall, Kinzi studied the building's features. "What the hell is this place really all about? It's creepy!"

"I'll fill you in during the four-month trip back to Earth," offered Carrick. "If I can manage to pull you away from Captain America, that is," he joked. "So, what's up with you two, anyway? It seems like there's some chemistry there." He paused before continuing, "And I should know, I'm a chemist," he said, laughing at his own joke.

Kinzi pushed him playfully and laughed along with him. "I knew you were going to say that. You're so predictable! God, I missed you, man!" she added, with a more serious look on her face. "Don't pull a stunt like that ever again!" She grabbed Carrick's arm. "Life wasn't good for me after I got back to Earth. I felt responsible that you stayed. I should never have left without you."

"Trust me," said Carrick, "staying here was the best decision I ever made."

After a moment of silence and reflection, Kinzi conceded that she did, in fact, have a crush on Jordan as she untangled her arm from Carrick's.

"You think he likes you too?" asked Carrick.

"I wish!" Kinzi wore her frustration like a crown. "I'm still trying to figure him out. He's basically unreadable."

The two wrapped up their conversation and opened the doors to The History Library. To Carrick's shock, they found the place empty. He started to panic and began yelling.

"Erik!!! Erik!!!" he shouted, turning to look in every direction. "Calm down! Jordan would never hurt him!" Kinzi reassured him, although, in her heart, she couldn't be sure.

Carrick ran from the library and started down the long corridor leading to The Grand Hall. From there, he raced on to the barracks below. Kinzi had to sprint to keep up with him, not wanting to get lost in the massive, dark structure.

Carrick flew through the doors of Barrack 5, but it was empty. He searched some of the other barracks but found nothing.

At that point, Kinzi yelled, "The Culina!"

Without a word, Carrick ran as fast as he could, screaming that he would kill Spear if anything happened to Erik.

As the two approached the doors to The Culina, they heard two men laughing.

Carrick burst through the door and yelled, "Where the hell did you guys go? What's going on here?!"

"Calm down," said Erik, "I was just sharing a cup of Red Fruit with my new friend Jordan!" He smiled as he reached over to squeeze Jordan's massive shoulder.

Carrick was utterly astonished. He couldn't wrap his head around the situation.

At that moment, Jordan confessed, "It's crazy! This old man read me like a book!"

Kinzi just rolled her eyes and shook her head. Under her breath, she muttered, "Oh, brother!"

Spear directed his next surprising comment at Kinzi. "We've got to get Erik back to Earth!"

Carrick nodded in agreement, and the two men pleaded their case while Kinzi valiantly argued back. "Guys, it's not possible! There's only room for five on the Lander!"

Carrick and Jordan quickly came back to reality and were sobered by the notion that Erik wouldn't be going back to Earth with them.

Erik listened to the three-way discussion from a distance, then quietly excused himself and exited The Culina. Though he'd always thought he would die in The Triad, he now pondered the thought of dying on Earth. After all, he could be close to Lilly again. He could die on the same planet where his mother, brother, and Lilly had all died.

He was torn. Zenith, or Home? Now that he was getting to know people from Earth, he was actually entertaining the notion of going there. He knew it wasn't possible, though. The old man felt hopeless. He drifted off into the darkness that was The Triad. The very darkness that consumed his heart would undeniably consume what few days he had remaining.

"Wait, where's Erik?" asked Carrick, experiencing the same anxiety he'd felt moments earlier.

He ran to the hall and saw Erik walking into the black void. Carrick ran to catch up with his friend.

"Erik! Wait, where are you going?" he asked, short of breath.
"I'm tired, Carrick! I'm heading back to the barracks. I need to rest."

Erik knew that when they left, there would be no third mission to Zenith in his lifetime. He knew that he'd likely be dead within a year and never have human contact again.

Carrick let Erik continue on to the barracks and rejoined the other two in The Culina. There, Jordan was explaining to Kinzi the truth about Erik. That he really was from Zenith and that he had a story that needed to be told on Earth.

Carrick overheard their conversation and said, "Kinzi, that's what I've been trying to tell you the whole time!"

It didn't matter, though; Erik would have to stay on Zenith.
At the end of the night, the three went to Barrack 5 to retire until morning. When they arrived, Erik was nowhere to be found.

"Shit!" said Jordan, "Where could he be?"

Carrick replied, "I know where he is. He's fine. We'll catch up with him in the morning."

In Barrack 6, lying in Lilly's old bunk, Erik cried. He just wanted to see Lilly's face again. He wanted to see if her wrinkles matched his. But in his heart, he knew that she was gone. He knew that she must have died years ago.

In going to Earth, he knew he could never be as close to her as he was on Zenith. In body, perhaps. But in spirit, no. The Triad was as close as he could ever be to her memory. This was the place where the two had consummated their love for each other. She might have lived and died on Earth, but their love for each other had lived right here, and in his heart, that love had never died.

Erik knew, at that moment, that he would never leave Zenith. He came to peace with the fact that he would never leave her memory here, to die alone in The Triad. This was his home, after all, and it had once been Lilly's home too. This is where Erik Erickson would die.

Location, Barrack 5 – The next morning.

Carrick awoke to find Jordan and Kinzi gone. He could only imagine where they might be and what they might be doing. With all of the bunks they had to choose from, they might have finally sealed the deal.

Carrick made his way to The Culina. No one was there either. He began to worry. He cradled his chin for a moment and surmised that they must be in The History Library. When he arrived there, he heard a commotion in the back of the room. He walked back and soon saw that the hologram was up. As he got closer, he observed Kinzi standing on the circular hologram platform, dodging traffic on a futuristic street. It was almost as if she were in the middle of a virtual reality game. She laughed hysterically, as were Jordan and Erik, as they watched her jump around like a kid playing dodge ball in middle school. Standing at a distance, he too began laughing.

As Jordan helped Kinzi step down from the hologram platform, Erik motioned for Carrick to join him in the hallway, just outside the door.

Once they were away from the others, Carrick asked, "Is everything okay?"

"Let's walk, son," said Erik. He put his arm around the young man's shoulders. "Carrick, it's time, my friend."

Confused. Carrick asked, "Time for what?"

"It's time for you to go Home. You need to go Home, son." Erik had tears in his eyes. "Please don't come back for me because I'll be gone."

"What are you saying? The people of Earth need to hear from you. They need to hear your story. They need to know their story." Carrick pleaded. "The story of how we got there! You're the only one who can tell them!"

"You have been a wonderful student, and you will go Home, and there you will share the wonderful story of Zenith and how Zenithians saved human civilization, how we preserved our species while wiping out billions of others. Go, Carrick! Go tell them!" urged Erik.

With tears flowing down his face, Carrick said, "I will. I will find Lilly! I will put a flower on her grave. I will find her! I will tell her that you loved her. She will somehow hear my words, Erik! I promise you!"

The two men hugged, tears flowing. Then Erik turned and disappeared into the darkness. He would not be seen again by the others before they left for Earth.

Location: Black Earth. Northwest Sector of The Triad, Observatory Deck, Surface-Level 5 – April 9, 2023. 11:43 am, CST. Earth time.

Erik watched the flames of the ascent stage light up the sky. He cried for the loss of his friend but took heart in the promise Carrick had made him. Lilly would somehow know that he loved her. That he always had and always would.

Erik was also thankful. He knew that even if he never saw Carrick again, he'd spent three hundred and eighty-three days with someone who felt like the son he'd never had.

Location: Black Earth Orbit. The New Beginning Spaceship. Two hundred fifty miles above the surface of Zenith – April 9, 2023. 12:47 pm, CST. Earth time.

In the background, Carrick heard aviator Mike Swimmer tell Mars Johnston, "Black Horizon II has docked, and Michaels and the others are safely on board." Then everything went quiet in Carrick's mind. He gazed out of the ship's window and took one last look at the fading planet. Though his heart was broken, he would keep the promise he made to Erik. He would find Lilly. He would tell her that she had indeed been loved.

Chapter 31 – Paternal Consanguinity

Location: Houston, TX. George Bush Intercontinental Airport – August 5, 2023.

NCN was reporting that a massive reception was occurring at the George Bush International Airport in Houston, Texas, to celebrate the return of the Sagittarian Recovery mission crew from Kazakhstan.

The crew members were greeted on the tarmac by NASA officials and a limited number of family members, who were eager to see their loved ones after the eight-month mission to Black Earth. The airport itself was flooded with thousands of curiosity seekers who wanted to get a glimpse of their new hero, Carrick Michaels.

Some protesters were also in attendance, waving signs that read: CONSPIRACY but were vastly outnumbered by the supporters of the returning astronauts. The crowds would have to wait to get a glimpse of the returning astronauts, though, as they would have to enter into a quarantine protocol for the following two weeks.

In a private moment between Carrick and Lola, he whispered in her ear and asked, "Will you marry me?"

Lola emphatically said, "Yes!" and the two parted ways again until Carrick was released by NASA physicians several days later.

Carrick also spent a few moments with his mother, Maggie, who was overcome with tears of joy as she thought she might never see her son again.

Maggie said to Carrick, through tears, "You're not going back up there! You're not leaving Lola and me again!" she cried.

For security purposes, the crew was whisked away to a private NASA facility. From there, they would be debriefed and have a battery of medical tests completed on them.

After seventy-two-hours of routine observations, the astronauts were medically cleared and released to a secure housing facility for several more days of mission debriefing meetings.

In a side office at the NASA housing facility, Mars sat at a desk and waited for Carrick to join him. On the desk was a box, roughly the size of a small suitcase. An hour earlier, Mars had summoned Carrick so that the two could have a one-on-one conversation prior to a meeting with the rest of the Sagittarian Recovery crew.

Carrick arrived, and Mars invited him to take a seat. Carrick, looking exhausted, sipped on a bottle of water, and waited for Mars to finish a call.

Mars hung up the phone and said, "Hi Carrick! How are you feeling?"

"Exhausted and hungry!" Carrick replied.

"Yeah. Looks like they're bringing in pizza and wings for you guys."

"That's great!" said Carrick, too tired for chit-chat. He chugged the remaining water in his bottle and sat back in his chair, interlocked his fingers behind his head, and stretched out his legs.

"Listen, Carrick, what's with these items you brought back from Black Earth?" Mars flipped open the box and removed its contents, laying them on the desk. "I mean, what in the hell is this, a diamond?" he said, rotating the light fixture in his hand. "And what's with this piece of metal? Is this platinum?" he asked, tapping the metal with an ink pen. "You know, NASA officials will never let you out of here with this stuff. They'll have to be taken to a lab for further examination and testing."

Carrick pulled his hands from behind his head, leaned forward, and spoke firmly. "Let me be clear about something Mars. I don't say a word to anyone about the events of the last thirteen months on Black Earth if I don't get to take those items home with me. Not a word!"

Mars held his ground. "What are they?"

"They are gifts from my good friend, Dr. Erik Erickson, from planet Zenith, and trust me, they're going home with me!" he stressed for the second time.

"Doctor?! He's a doctor?! And what in the hell is Zenith?!" exclaimed Mars, looking perplexed.

Carrick sat back in his chair while Mars shook his head and muttered, "Zenith? That's what we're calling it now? The damned name keeps changing! I like Black Earth better! It has a nice ring to it!"

Mars went on to explain that the items would need to be tested for radioactivity first. Additionally, they would be labeled as material evidence from Black Earth, and many government officials would want to take a look. However, he promised he would do his best to get the items back to Carrick in the near term.

Location: Langley, VA. CIA Headquarters, The George Bush Center for Intelligence – August 18, 2023. 8:59 am, EST.

In a substantial and lavish corner office on the third floor of the secure facility, CIA Director James Clapper sat working. Hearing a knock on the door, Clapper invited his guest into the room.

"Ahh! Jordan, thank you for being here. Welcome back, son! Please come in," said Clapper. "Have a seat." He motioned to the chair in front of his desk.

"I want you to know that I've read the report regarding your time on Black Earth, as you've detailed it in this dossier." He held up a half-inch thick file folder and paused for a moment. "I must say though, Jordan, I'm deeply concerned," he revealed, now dispensing with the niceties.

Jordan looked exhausted but perked up with the revelation of Clapper's concern and changing tone.

"It's very important you know that just yesterday we deposed Dr. Carrick Michaels for eight-hours. I just want to make sure you're comfortable with your story."

"Story, sir?" Clapper now had Jordan's full attention. He sat erect in his chair just across the desk from Clapper. "I'm a little confused. What are you asking me here, sir?" questioned Jordan, with a high level of disdain in his voice.

"Son, listen, we spent thousands of hours and nearly a million dollars preparing you for your mission, and you come back with a story that quite frankly doesn't wash. So, for the second time, I'm asking if you're sure you want to stick with this story?" Clapper's voice was filled with skepticism as he continued. "Additionally, are you telling me that not recording the most important interrogation of your life was simply an accident or a mere oversight?"

Jordan rose from his chair, stood as tall as he could, and addressed his boss. "Director Clapper, as I stated in my deposition, I did not record the interview due to the circumstances that were presented to me at the time, sir!"

Clapper exhaled and sank back into his chair. He needed a moment to formulate his next question.

Before he could speak, Jordan continued. "With all due respect, sir, the words that I carefully dictated in the report you're holding in your hand do not tell a story. But rather, they constitute the facts as I see them, sir!"

"As YOU see them?" asked Clapper leaning forward in his chair.

"Yes! As I see them. As I was there, and you were not...., sir!" Spear exclaimed soundly in his famously threatening tone of voice.

Clapper stood up from his chair and leaned forward with his fists supporting his weight on the desktop. He had a pained look on his face. "Son, I strongly encourage you to exercise caution when addressing me. Do I make myself clear?"

Jordan replied, "Abundantly clear, sir!"

Both men sat back down in their chairs. Jordan was red-faced and fuming. Clapper, though, quickly regained his composure.

"Jordan listen, I've known you since you were a small child. I worked with your father for nearly three decades. So, I'll be as forthright as I can. I need to ask you a question. Exactly how much time did you spend in Russia over the last eight years?"

"I'm sorry, sir, I'm having trouble with this line of questioning," said Spear, confused and incensed at the same time. "What does one have to do with the other?"

Clapper was starting to look a bit uncomfortable too. "Officer Spear," he said, frankly. "I need to know if you've been compromised."

"Sir, with all due respect, again, I need to know what the hell is going on here," said Spear, no longer trying to hide his anger.

Clapper hit a single button on the phone positioned to his right and said, "Send him in."

Clapper waited for a moment until a man entered the room and then said, "Officer Spear, I'll need you to go with Officer Solstice to the *Blue Room* for further discussion."

"This must be some kind of a joke!" exclaimed Spear angrily. "I trained Matt in the art of interrogation, and now you're going to have him interrogate me? This is absurd!"

Clapper excused the two men, but Spear stopped at the door. He turned to Clapper and, with Solstice looking on, said, "Director Clapper, I have a question for you."

"Go ahead with your question, Officer Spear. What is it?" asked Clapper.

"Director Clapper, can you tell me what is more powerful than the truth?"

"What would that be, Jordan?" asked a now stoic Clapper.

"Nothing!" said Spear, a look of total calm on his face. The truth was on his side, and nothing that the Director of the CIA, James Clapper, otherwise believed would change that. "Nothing is more powerful than the truth! The truth never lies. The truth never changes. No matter how much time goes by, no matter how much the world, things, or people around us change, the truth never does. The truth unifies the righteous and fractures the corrupt," professed Jordan Spear, in the words of his friend, Dr. Erik Erickson.

Clapper half-smiled and said, "Hmmm. Thank you for your insight, Officer Spear. You're excused." Clapper turned to Solstice.

"Matt, stick with me for a few minutes. Officer Spear is free to go home for the time being."

"Thank you, sir," said Jordan. He walked away as Solstice moved back into Clapper's office.

Shaking his head, Solstice approached Director Clapper and respectfully asked, "What just happened, sir?"

Clapper told Solstice to have a seat and said, "Matt, I didn't actually invite you in here to interrogate your mentor. That was just a ruse. I simply wanted to see how Jordan would react to the situation. Spear's story matches the account given by Dr. Michaels', word for word. They both have the same exact impression of this fellow Erik Erickson. Neither of the men believes that he's either foreign, or foe, and both agree that he's not an immediate threat to the United States or the world for that matter."

"Yes, but they did have four months to get their stories aligned on the return trip home," offered Solstice.

Clapper stood and looked out his window, hands in pockets. "That may be true, Matt, but Michaels and Spear had no connection before their meeting on Black Earth. And while it's possible that the Russians compromised spear, Michaels almost certainly was not. At any rate, we know a lot more about this person today than we did six months ago, but we need to be vigilant and find out more." He paused before announcing, "We're bringing him home, Matt!"

"Sorry, sir?" Solstice looked confused.

"We're bringing Black Earth Erik home," repeated Clapper, turning to face Solstice.

"Holy Shit!" responded Solstice.

"Matt, what I just told you is classified. The only reason I'm telling you at all is because you'll be assigned to interview this Erik person when we get him back here on Earth. Do you understand?"
"I'm honored, sir. And yes, I understand!" replied Solstice, beaming with pride.

Location: Houston, TX. NASA Science & Research Laboratories – August 22, 2023. 9:57 am, CST.

"Dr. London, I'm Dr. Aubrey Carin, NASA's senior administrator in their genetics lab; thank you for taking my call. Listen, we're having an issue with the blood samples you brought back from Black Earth."

Kinzi gasped. "Oh, my God! Do you have the DNA results yet?"

"Yes, I do, but there's an issue," said Carin.

"Oh?" questioned Kinzi.

"Yes, the sample you sent for Subject A matches someone in our database. I cannot share the name of that person with you over the phone, but I'll be able to do so once you come down here to the lab."

"Of course. I can be there within the hour," said Kinzi.

Two-hours later, Kinzi finally arrived at NASA's Science and Research Laboratories and walked into Carin's office. "So sorry I'm late, Dr. Carin," she apologized.

"Not a problem, Dr. London," said Carin. "Please sit down." She motioned to a chair across from her desk.

As Kinzi sat down, Carin picked up the phone. She pushed a button and spoke into the handset. "Please send in our guest from Washington."

Within seconds, a stout man dressed in a black suit walked into the office and sat down in an empty chair next to Kinzi. It was someone she had never seen before, and she immediately felt like something was wrong.

"Okay, what's going on here?" she demanded. "Why did you ask me to come down here?"

"Kinzi, this is CIA Officer Cole Slater, Dr. Carin explained. "He's been assigned to this case. I am obligated to have him here to witness your testimony and your reaction to my questions. I'm sorry it seems so formal, but this is a matter of national security."

"No, I completely understand," Kinzi acknowledged, still feeling apprehensive.

Carin handed Kinzi a file folder with some loose-leaf pages in it and asked her to take a moment and look them over.

"Okay, so what exactly am I looking at here?" asked Kinzi.

"The blood sample you provided for Subject A, Erik, is a perfect DNA match for Dr. Carrick Michaels, your Subject B."

Kinzi was relieved. "Oh, for God's sake! I must have mislabeled the two samples," she said, feeling very embarrassed.

"Yes. You did, in fact, mix them up. Of course, that, in and of itself, isn't that big of a deal as we are only talking about two samples and two subjects...," said Dr. Carin, before being interrupted by London. "So, what are the results of Erik's blood work?"

"I wasn't finished speaking, Dr. London," said Carin.

"I'm so sorry; please continue, Dr. Carin."

"As I was saying, the samples were mixed up, and the actual results of Subject A are shocking. That is why Officer Slater is with us right now."

"Okay, what is it? Are you going to tell me?" Kinzi demanded, her heart pounding. "Please don't tell me he's not human! I'll have a heart attack!"

"Dr. London, have you ever heard the term consanguinity before?" asked Carin.

"No, I haven't."

"Well then, you likely won't understand the term paternal consanguinity either," said Carin. "It means blood relationship."

Kinzi's eyes widened as she put two and two together. Before she could say another word, she fainted back into her chair.

After a few moments, Kinzi regained consciousness and began incoherently asking if Carrick and Erik were related. "Are they related?!" she repeated, with much trepidation.

"Yes, they are related, Kinzi. Carrick is a direct descendant of Erik on his family's paternal side, with the genetic markers suggesting that Erik is Carrick's grandfather. Our conclusions are based in part on a blood sample of Carrick's father."

Kinzi couldn't hold back tears as she sat still in shock.

Carin continued. "The United States Navy has kept DNA records of all its officers, dating back to 1988. When comparing the paternal side of the family, the markers are an exact match for Carrick, his father, Navy Lieutenant Mike Michaels, and our Subject A, Erik Erickson."

"Dr. London," said Officer Slater, "prior to being told the actual results of the DNA match by Dr. Carin, you seemed to make the connection between Dr. Michaels and our subject from Black Earth. Can you please explain to me why that is?"

Wiping her tears, Kinzi said, "I don't know." She took a moment to collect her thoughts. "It just makes sense!" she reflected. "They seemed connected. They had a lot of the same mannerisms. The same sense of humor. Similar physiques, eye color, you name it. I didn't think it then, but now that I know what I know, it just makes sense." She shook her head and said to herself, "But how?! It all makes sense, but then it doesn't."

"Dr. London, we're going to have to ask you to stay here at the laboratory for another hour or so," said Slater. "We've asked Dr. Michaels to come down here and join us. And I'm going to need your phone, as we can't have you speaking to anyone about this until Dr. Michaels has been briefed as well."

Kinzi looked at him sideways, and before she could say, "Go to hell!" he reminded her that it was a matter of national security. "I'm sure you understand," he said politely.

Two-hours later, In a conference room down the hall from Carin's office, Kinzi was joined by Carrick Michaels, Officer Slater, Dr. Carin, and three other NASA and CIA officials.

Dr. Carin began with Carrick the same way she had with Kinzi. "Dr. Michaels, my name is Dr. Aubrey Carin, with NASA, and I have some news to share with you. Only a few people in the world know what I'm about to share with you. The people in the room, CIA Director James Clapper, who is en route as we speak, and the President of the United States. We do apologize that you were not the first to know, but we simply couldn't get you here in time," explained Carin.

Carrick looked puzzled but remained silent.

Carin carried on. "Your DNA results came back, and there's something important to share."

Carrick felt sick to his stomach, wondering if he'd been exposed to dangerous levels of radiation on Black Earth. "Radiation poisoning?" he asked nervously.

"No, you're in perfectly good health," Dr. Carin smiled. "Whatever you were fed on Black Earth has agreed with you. But there's something else, Dr. Michaels."

An imposing African-American man in the room stepped forward and interjected. "Before we share the results of the test, Dr. Michaels, I have a couple of questions for you," said the unknown man.
"I'm sorry, who are you?" challenged Carrick.

"I am the Assistant Director of the CIA, Cornelius Stanley." The man stood an imposing six foot eight inches tall. The salt and pepper-haired sixty-year-old was every bit the 300-pound menace he'd been during his professional football career back in the 1980s. "I report directly to Director Clapper," he explained. "May I proceed with my questions, Carrick?"

"Please do," replied Carrick.

"Dr. Michaels, I understand that your father, U.S. Navy Lieutenant Mike Michaels, died before you were born. Is that correct?" asked Stanley.

"Yes, my mother was just three months pregnant with me when he died."

"I also understand that your grandmother, Dr. Lillian Michaels, the mother of your father, died shortly after your father. Is that correct?"

"Yes! But what's going on here?" Carrick was as exhausted as he was confused. "Why are you asking me all of these questions?"

"Dr. Michaels, what I'm about to tell you is going to be difficult for you to understand and, quite frankly, hard for me to explain," said Stanley.

"Get on with it!" insisted Carrick.

Kinzi stood by, tears welling up in her eyes. Carrick looked around the room, making eye contact with everyone before Stanley spoke again.

"Dr. Michaels, your father, was the son of Erik Erickson," explained the Assistant Director. "Erik is your grandfather on the paternal side of your family."

At that instant, Carrick burst into tears and fell to his knees, sobbing uncontrollably. Kinzi stood weeping, her hand covering her mouth. After regaining his composure and climbing back to his feet, Carrick yelled, "Get me back up there! Get me back to Black Earth!" He turned to Kinzi. "I knew it! I knew it! Lilly is my grandmother!" Striding over to the Assistant Director, he grabbed his arm. "We have to get back up there! He's not going to last much longer; he's going to die soon!"

Kinzi walked towards Carrick, hysterical, and embraced her friend. The two had experienced something life-changing on Black Earth. None of the people watching their display of emotion could possibly share in their combined heartbreak.

After Carrick had calmed down, he was taken to a private office in Building 30 at the Christopher C. Kraft, Jr. Mission Control Center. In the large room, Carrick sat with Kinzi and Mars Johnston. Kinzi held Carrick's hand, trying to console him. Within fifteen minutes or so, the door opened, and CIA Director James Clapper walked in. With him was CIA Officer and fellow astronaut Jordan Spear. He made eye contact with both Kinzi and Carrick and gave them a subdued smile and a nod.

Clapper thanked them all for coming and for their service, not only to their country but to the entire world.

"Folks, I have an announcement to make as well as a request," said Clapper. "Should any of you decline this request, your wishes will be honored. All of you have already given more to your country and the world than anyone should be expected to. That comes straight from POTUS," he added. "Not even Mars knows what I'm about to ask." Clapper took a deep breath. "So here goes. We're going back to Black Earth, and we'd like to request that the three of you be on that spaceship. Our hope is that you're up to the task. We're bringing back Dr. Erik Erickson, Carrick's grandfather! We lift-off in just six weeks!"

"It's Zenith," Carrick stated without hesitation.

"I'm sorry?" asked Clapper.

"It's Zenith! We're going back to Zenith!" clarified Carrick. He looked over at Kinzi and Jordan. "And you two are coming with me! Mars, we'll need Swimmer and Taylor again. We can't mess this one up."

Mars nodded in agreement.

Jordan Spear exclaimed, "I'm in!"

Kinzi emphatically agreed, and the three of them hugged and patted each other on the back. Mars looked on like a proud parent.

Clapper informed the group that they would need to stay healthy in the six short weeks before lift-off and get some rest. After several more details were discussed, Clapper excused the room's occupants.

"Carrick," Clapper paused. "Stick with me for a moment; would you, son?"

Carrick nodded, and the two waited for the room to clear.

Once they were alone, Clapper said, "I don't pretend to know what exactly to make of all of this, and I most certainly don't know how your grandfather came to be on Black Earth. I have lots of questions, no doubt, but I want you to bring your grandfather home. We'll sort out the details once he's back here on Earth."

"Let me tell you something, Director Clapper," said Carrick, "my grandfather has a story to tell, and the story he'll bring home with him will be a wake-up call for all of humanity. Now, if you'll excuse me, I have to go visit my grandmother's grave."

Carrick turned to leave the room, and Clapper called out to him. "Carrick, wait, there's one more thing." Pulling a sizeable box from beneath a table, he handed it to Carrick, "I have some items here that belong to you."

Carrick opened the lid. Inside were the diamond-light fixture and piece of platinum that his grandfather had given him. Carrick began to cry again as he was holding objects that were once held by Erik. Carrick had a momentary flashback to the morning of his birthday when Erik barged through the door with the gifts. He stood there and laughed to himself as Clapper looked on. If only for that moment, these items closed the planetary gap between Carrick and his only living paternal relative and best friend, Erik Erickson.

"You know that's a diamond, don't you, son?" asked Clapper. "It's been valued at more than a billion dollars. No one, not even me, can say that you haven't earned it. I would find a rather large safety deposit box to keep it in."

"It's worth far more than that to me, sir!" said Carrick.

Clapper placed his hand on Carrick's shoulder. "Listen, I have a few agents downstairs who can assist you in getting that rather pricy light fixture to a safe place," offered Clapper.

Carrick smiled. "Can we stop by a jeweler along the way?"

"You bet, Carrick!" Clapper nodded. "Whatever you need, son!"

The two men shook hands and parted ways.

Over the next six weeks, Carrick and Lola planned their wedding and did some much-needed catching up. NASA granted each of the five astronauts a two-week vacation. Carrick and Lola used theirs to visit his grandmother's grave in Suwanee, Georgia. From there, they made the pilgrimage to Artesia, New Mexico, where they visited the house that Lilly had lived in after migrating to Earth from Zenith, back in 1947.

His grandmother had willed the house in Artesia to his mother, Maggie. Carrick's mom had signed over the deed to Carrick when he turned twenty-one. Carrick had only ever been there twice, once as a small child and once again after college. On that last visit, he'd worked out the contract details with a real estate management company that would manage and maintain the property.

For the last five years, the house had been occupied by a young family, who were originally from Texas. The Spencer family had taken good care of the property, even though the house was in a state of disrepair. Carrick never really felt a connection to the property, but he had never sold it for some reason. Now he understood why.

He and Lola met the Spencers at the house and offered to buy them a brand-new home in a new subdivision being built in North Roswell, on the condition that they'd be willing to break their lease and vacate the house immediately. The family was stunned by the gesture and gladly accepted the generous offer.

As Carrick and Lola were saying goodbye to the Spencers, they heard a little girl begin to cry in the next room. She'd overheard the conversation about the family moving. The little girl pleaded with her father, begging him to stay. She didn't want to move to another home. But all Carrick heard was Home.

As the screen door closed behind Carrick and Lola, they heard the father say to his daughter, "Don't worry, Lilly. It'll be okay. You'll make new friends when we get to our new home." This time Carrick only heard the name Lilly. It took his breath away. He stopped in his tracks and told Lola that he'd meet her in the car.

Meanwhile, Carrick knocked on the screen door and asked to come back in. The family welcomed him back into the house and seemed a little fearful that perhaps he'd changed his mind.

"Hey..." Carrick paused for a moment before speaking. "Listen, I know I said that I'd buy you a new house in North Roswell, but I don't want to be responsible for taking little Lilly away from the people she cares about."

The family held their breath for a moment before Carrick continued. "How about this? You see that empty lot across the street with the For-Sale sign?" he asked.

"Yes, that's been vacant for several years now. It's a real eyesore," said little Lilly's mom.

"Well, what if I built you a custom home right there?" Carrick offered.

"That way, Lilly wouldn't have to migrate... I mean, move to a new home?"

Once again, the family was stunned and happily agreed. As Carrick was walking out the front door, he felt a tug on his shirttail.

"Hey, mister!" said little Lilly. "Can I give you a hug?"

Carrick looked at her parents for approval, and they nodded, smiling. He knelt down, and little Lilly whispered in his ear, "Thank you for not making me and my family move away from our real home. I love it here, and I never want to leave!" she said, clinging to Carrick's neck for an extra couple of seconds.

"I'm so happy to finally meet you, Lilly! I'm sorry it's taken me so long to get here!" said Carrick, with a smile and a tear, as if he were actually talking to his grandmother.

Outside, Carrick got back into the car. Lola asked, "What's wrong, babe?" when she noticed tears in his eyes.

Carrick replied, "Nothing. I'm good now."

He asked Lola if, while he was gone on the mission, she would ensure that the Spencer family got the house of their dreams. A house that they could call Home, and one that they'd never have to leave.

As they drove off, Carrick thought about how, if Erik could somehow make it back to Earth, he could live out the rest of his days in Lilly's home. There, he would be able to look out his window every morning and see little Lilly growing up right before his own eyes.

En route to the airport, Carrick noticed that a part of the interstate they were traveling on was dubbed Extraterrestrial Highway. Along the way, the two passed an old, tattered sign that read, UFO Crash Site Tours – 623-8104. He and Lola looked at the sign and then at each other and laughed.

A few moments later, and after the laughter had died down, Lola gazed over at the man for whom she'd waited so long for. Carrick was looking ahead, studying both the road and the now more certain future. Lola, instead, studied the lines on the face of the man whom she had always loved. Gently running her fingers through his blonde hair and down onto the nape of his neck, she read those lines. The lines, which had only appeared since his journey to Black Earth, told the story of a man she realized she'd never really known before. She saw that his once hopelessly unfinished puzzle was nearly complete. And only now did she feel part of that puzzle. She turned toward the road that lay ahead and, for the first time, felt that her and Carrick's once-separate destinies were now one.

Chapter 32 – Lilly

Location: Zenithian Migration Shuttle. Somewhere between Zenith and Home – Early 1947. Six weeks into the expected eight-week journey.

In the private quarters she shared with her mother, Lilly awoke, feeling unwell again. After more than six weeks in space, it appeared space food didn't agree with her. Whether it was the food or the artificial gravity in the shuttle, her head was spinning. She always seemed to be nauseous. This had gone on for days now.

Lilly's mother, Laila, approached her and asked how she was feeling. Lilly replied that she'd be fine.

Laila sat down on Lilly's bed and said, "I didn't realize you and Erik were that serious."

"What are you talking about?" asked Lilly.

"Lilly, you're pregnant! You're a doctor; you should know that!"

"Mom, I can't be!"

"Are you suggesting that you and Erik didn't consummate before you left? I've been by your side this entire journey, so I know it didn't happen on board this shuttle."

"Mom, we only did it once, the night before we left. It was my first time... I can't be pregnant!"

"Did you know that I became pregnant with you the first time I consummated with your father?" asked Laila.

Lilly fell into her mother's arms and began to cry. "How could I have left him? He was the love of my life. The only man that I ever felt close to. He was my friend, my equal, my love."

"How could he have been so selfish as to let you leave?" her mother retorted. "He should be on this shuttle with you right now!"

"Selfish?! Mom, you just don't get it, do you?" Lilly exclaimed, turning away from her mother. "He stayed behind so that the two of us, and the thousands of others on board this ship, could carry on our lives in a better place. To live a life outside of that prison, The Triad; a life away from that wretched and dying planet. Zenith was never a real home!" she cried. "He'll die alone; he'll never know that I loved him and that he gave me a child."

"Do you think he loved you in return?" asked her mother.

"I do. He never said it, though."

"But what was his response when you told him that you loved him?"

"I never told him!" Lilly cried a little louder.

"You never told him! Why?"

"I don't know! We just never talked about it. We always seemed to sidestep the question. We were always too busy."

"Don't worry, Lilly," reassured her mother. "When we get Home, we'll meet with the Liaison. He'll provide us with a story that will support a young, unwed pregnant woman."

Location: Home. Artesia, New Mexico. A remote farmhouse near a heavily wooded area – June 1947.

Lilly, her mother, and a group of others from the shuttle disembarked the back of an old pick-up truck. From there, they were instructed by the truck's driver to walk over and meet a small group of people standing outside of an old, dilapidated house. The building was nestled between a large field and a densely wooded area. It was very dark, with only the Moon providing light for the migrants to see the trail that led them away from the dirt road. The group followed a well-beaten path to the dark, abandoned-looking farmhouse.

As they nervously approached the strangers, Laila turned and looked for her daughter. Lilly was still standing near the road. Her mother went back to retrieve her, just as the truck's red taillights evaporated into the darkness.

Lilly was staring up at the Moon, seemingly in amazement. "Come on, Lilly!" said Laila. "We must hurry!"

Unmoved by the tug on her arm, Lilly said, "Mom, wait. Look at it! It's so beautiful! It must be Zenith," she wished aloud.

"Don't be ridiculous! Zenith is black and millions of miles away. That's nothing more than a moon."

While Lilly knew that must be true, she had never seen a moon before. For the rest of her time on her new planet, she would look up at the Moon and imagine that it was Zenith. She would think of it as Erik's home. She would do whatever she could to feel close to her lost love, Erik Erickson.

"Welcome Home. You must be Laila and Lilly," said a conservatively dressed, middle-aged woman. "My name is Ollidean Mitchell, and this is my son Edgar. Please call me Ollie."

The young man, wearing a flannel shirt and a pair of jeans, appeared to be in his late teens. He tipped his newsboy-style hat out of respect and simply said, "Ma'am."

"You look cold, Lilly. Here, take my sweater," Ollie offered. "I am your Sponsor here on Earth. The two of you will stay with my family until you get acclimated. Lilly, you'll be first. The Liaison is inside. He'll assist you and provide you with your Book. Please go in; he's waiting for you." Ollie motioned to the door.

Lilly looked at her mother with fear and apprehension. Her mother pointed to the door and encouraged her to go inside. "Go ahead, Lilly. It'll be alright."

Lilly hesitated for another moment and then walked in.

Once inside, she found herself standing in front of a tall, slender, dark-haired man who looked to be about twice her age. The strange man was seated behind a tattered table.

The room was dimly lit, and to Lilly, looked like an old and very small Culina. Next to the table was an open box that was overflowing with books.

The man slid a candle on the table to the side and looked Lilly up and down before speaking. Using his foot, he pushed a chair from beneath the table, and with a raised brow, offered Lilly a seat. She declined.

"Lilly, do you know what it is that I do?" asked the Liaison.

"Of course I know what you do!" she exclaimed, tightly clenching the top of her sweater. "You help Zenithians assimilate into society on Home."

"It's not Home anymore," said the Liaison. "Now that you're here, people call this planet Earth. Neither Home nor Earth is a destination any longer. Now it's where you're from. You must focus on your story now, what you do, and who you are. I am about to give you a story that will define you to everyone you encounter going forward. Do you understand?"

"Yes, I do," replied Lilly.

"You'll have to memorize your story, Lilly. You must!" stressed the Liaison.

The man-made her feel very uncomfortable. Lilly found it hard to look at him directly. Instead, her eyes danced with the candle's flicker, focusing on nothing except the parts of the room that the tiny candle would reveal.

The place was dark and humid, and nothing like Lilly had envisioned Home would be. Everything Lilly had ever known on Zenith was modern, advanced, clean, well-lit, and climate-controlled. She found herself regretting leaving the prison she and Erik once lived in, The Triad, her real home.

"I'm actually going to give you two different story choices, and then you must decide on one of them," said the Liaison. "The first choice is that you are a twenty-eight-year-old physician from Voorhees, New Jersey. You relocated to Artesia after your husband, a World War II veteran, died tragically in a car accident last month."

"But I'm forty-years-old!" said a confused Lilly.

"People live longer on Zenith, so the age of twenty-eight will suit you better here on Earth. Additionally, as a twenty-eight-year-old woman, you will be afforded more opportunities in your profession."

"That's fine, but what's a Voorhees, and what's a physician?" asked Lilly.

"Voorhees is not a what; it's a where, and a physician is a medical doctor," the Liaison explained.

"What's the other choice?" asked Lilly.

"The other choice is that you are my young bride," said the Liaison, with a predatory smile, "and you just moved here from where we were both born, southern New Jersey."

Lilly, looking ill, said, "Okay, I think I'm going to be sick!"

"Is it the pregnancy?" asked the Liaison.

"No, it's you!" she responded with disgust. "I am officially a widow from New Jersey. And I won't be getting remarried, I'm afraid. Just give me the Book, and I'll be on my way."

He handed her the book. "Memorize it, Lilly," he urged.

Before exiting the farmhouse, Lilly turned to the man and said, "I need to get a message back to Zenith. Can you do that for me?"

"No," said the man, shaking his head. "I'm afraid that won't be possible."

Lilly's head slumped, and she walked out the door in tears.

The Book was a journal that all Zenithians received when they first arrived on Earth. Zenithians were brought up being educated that the Book would detail who they are and who they were. It would tell the migrating Zenithian their life story up until this point in their life on Earth; after that, they would write their own story. Their past, however, must stay true to the Book, or else they risked compromising their new identity.

The Book included instructions on how and where to acquire history books about the world and their new home country. It also included an atlas of the world. The study of history and geography would be critical during the migrant's amalgamation process with the existing population.

Zenithians were taught to leave behind their former life on Zenith. However, Lilly would never forget her past, nor would she forget the only man that she had ever loved. She desperately hoped that the child inside of her was a boy. She hoped that the baby had his father's blue eyes and brilliant mind. She would love that child, which would help fill the black void in her broken heart.

Five months later, Lilly delivered a baby boy at the local hospital where she worked. The midwife was also Lilly's new best friend and Sponsor on Earth, Ollidean Mitchell.

As the new baby squirmed in Lilly's arms, Ollie asked, "Have you picked out a name for the little man yet?"

"Yes, his name is Michael Erickson Michaels." Lilly smiled and cried at the same time.

"What a lovely name!" said Ollie. "He'll be a man someday, just like my Edgar. He's going to make you very proud, Lilly!"

Ollie was soon called away, and Lilly was left alone with little Michael Erickson. She gazed into his crystal-clear blue eyes as if looking for her lost love, Erik. Through her tears, she laughed out loud for a moment, remembering when she teased Erik, calling him by his middle name, Michael. He hated it, but Lilly liked the name, so she gave it to her son. And, as a tribute to his father, she gave him the same first and last name, with his middle name being Erickson. She wanted his middle name to stand out. His new name would be similar to a palindrome.

Lilly wanted the name Erickson to be the center of her newborn son's entire universe. She wanted him to see Erik jump off the page whenever he saw it, said it, read it, or wrote it. His name would be a tribute to her love and his father, Dr. Erickson Michael Erickson. The man who countless Zenithians knew simply as Erik.

Little Erik clung to his mother, and Lilly held him tight. She knew that, although the world would know him as Mike Michaels, she would always look at him and see little Erik Erickson, named in his father's memory. Erik would forever be a Zenithian and a hero to his kind. She promised that her newborn son would become something special; the world would know his name. She knew that his children would grow up and make a difference, not only to her new world but to the shared universe of Earth and Zenith.

Additionally, she vowed never to remarry and promised herself to always tell the ones she loved that they were indeed loved. She would never hold back those three words again. Never!

Lilly would never forget where she came from or the only man that she ever loved. The man who sacrificed everything so that she could go on and thrive in her new beginning, her new world, her new Home.

Lilly never did remarry. And after her mother died in 1954, she and her son relocated to Suwanee, Georgia, a northern suburb of Atlanta. She had accepted a prestigious professorial job working for Emory University, where she would teach advanced medicine in the field of cancer research. Lilly went on to become dean of the school in 1969 and retired in 1984. Her son, Mike Michaels, graduated from North Gwinnett High School in 1965 and then went onto study at the United States Naval Academy in Annapolis, Maryland. There, he graduated at the top of his class. Mike 'The Hammer' Michaels, like his mother, was career-minded. Getting married was not a priority. At the age of forty, though, he did eventually marry a woman named Maggie Walters. Walters was just thirty at the time.

Lilly, and her adult son, would spend little time in the same cities as the military kept Mike Michaels on the move. He was always in her thoughts, though. The two would get together once a year at the house she still owned back in Artesia, New Mexico. Mike visited his mother in Georgia whenever he had an extended layover there. He always knew she'd sacrificed a great deal for him and always hoped that he'd made his mother proud.

After finding out that he and his wife Maggie were expecting a child, he couldn't wait to tell his mom but wanted to do it in person. That announcement would never come. On June 11, 1990, Lieutenant Mike Michaels died when his F-8 Crusader crashed into the ocean, just southwest of Guam.

Lillian Michaels passed away just six weeks after her only child had died. She never knew that her daughter-in-law, Maggie Michaels, was pregnant. Maggie never told Lillian that she was expecting. At the funeral, the two were both too bereaved to have a coherent conversation.

In her will, Lillian Michaels requested to be buried next to her son's empty grave in Suwanee, Georgia. She also willed her estate in Suwanee and the tiny home back in Artesia, New Mexico, to her daughter-in-law, Maggie Michaels.

On the first anniversary of Mike Michaels death, Maggie Michaels, and her infant son Carrick, flew to Guam, compliments of the U.S. Navy. There, she boarded a U.S. Navy Cruiser, traveled to the approximate location where her husband's plane had gone down, and tossed a wreath into the ocean. Along with the wreath, Maggie fulfilled one of her mother-in-law's wishes by dropping in a necklace that Lilly had always worn. It was made of diamonds and platinum. The centerpiece of the necklace had three letters encrusted on it, E.M.E., the initials of the only man she'd ever loved.

Lilly could never have known that the shuttle Erik guided Home, with her and the other 27,912 Zenithians onboard, lay not far from her beloved son's final resting place. The necklace was a gift from Erik, which she found in her bag only after she arrived on Earth. It would come to rest somewhere between the final migrant shuttle and her son's watery grave.

Maggie Michaels, holding her seven-month-old son in her arms, waved goodbye to her husband and vowed never to remarry. It seemed that Michael Erickson Michaels had married a woman who was a great deal like his mother.

No one knew how Lilly had died. It was speculated that she died of a broken heart. One could surmise though that, had she known her beloved son and his wife were expecting a child, she surely would've lived long enough to see him born.

When Lilly died, she was seventy-one Earth years-old, although she was actually eighty-three in Zenithian years. The same age as her beloved Erik back on Zenith. At the time of her death, she would have been completely broken-hearted, knowing that her only child was gone and not knowing whether the man she foolishly left behind on Zenith was alive or dead.

Lillian Michaels died without ever knowing that she connected the dots between the present and past, between Zenith and Earth, between her and Erik. The message she would eventually send to Erik would be one of family, of hope, and of love. The message she sent was her grandson, Dr. Carrick Michaels, and it showed that his sacrifice had not been in vain. That his sacrifice had allowed their son and grandson to live in a world where they could breathe in air and dream of dreams. A world that would allow them to touch the sky and, ultimately, the stars. The love between Lilly and Erik would transcend time and space, life and death, and Earth and Zenith.

Chapter 33 – What took you so long?

Location: Black Earth. Northwest Sector of The Triad, Sub-Level 7, Barrack 5 – January 26, 2024. Early morning hours.

Erik awoke alone for the two hundred and ninety-third day. Looking in the mirror, he again realized that he had no future, only a past.

He splashed some water on his face, there'd be no need for a shower today, and then wiped it away with a cloth that was in desperate need of being laundered. He looked more resigned today than he had on others. After getting dressed, he began his daily routine. Exiting the barracks and walking through the dark halls, he headed to The Culina for his breakfast, lunch, and dinner of Red Fruit, thanks to his not so old friend, Dr. Carrick Michaels.

Today, unlike all the others, Erik would forego his trip to The History Library. Erik was tired. He had lived for a long, long time. He was one-hundred and sixteen-years-old, and he was ready to retire. Retire from his daily routine, retire from being alone, and retire from being the final chapter of a story called Zenith.

After savoring his daily protein intake, Erik prepared himself a second portion and made his way to The Triad's infirmary. There, he rummaged through cabinets and drawers until, finally, he found what he was looking for. Erik collected a handful of foil pill packs and headed for the outer observatory deck, on Surface-Level 5, the top level of The Triad. This was the hottest place in The Triad, a balmy 98°F, due to the massive diamond-glass, triple-paned, heat-shielded façade.

Though it was warm, it was the only place in The Triad that gave Erik true peace. It was here that he had spent some of his best days talking, laughing, and sharing stories with his friend Carrick. Erik walked over to the master console that had recently gone permanently dark due to The Triad's Energy Conservation System. There, he laid out the foil packets and began striking them with his fist, not in anger but with determination. He pounded them until he was sure that their contents were crushed. Erik smashed pack after pack until his hand was swollen and sore.

He emptied the powdered contents into his metal cup of Red Fruit and then prepared himself to enjoy his second meal of the day, and the final one of his life.

Before ingesting his final meal, Erik sat in the over-sized command chair, propped up his feet, and took in the splendor of the night sky. The sky was so clear, and the stars so bright, Erik could easily pick out Earth. He sat and wondered what might've become of Carrick. For many years after Lilly had gone, he would do the same. Just sit and wonder. Finding the star in the sky that was Home, he would think of her.

He stared at Home and thought to himself, it must be brighter with Carrick on it, just as he had thought when Lilly made it Home. He missed his friend, and he missed his Lilly.

Erik hoped that his new friends, Carrick, Kinzi, and Jordan, had all made it safely back to Earth. He wondered if Carrick had proposed to Lola and if he'd given his mother a big hug. As he stared into the cup in his swollen hand, he also wondered if Carrick had kept his promise of finding Lilly.

Erik exhaled and then took a generous drink of the elixir he'd created. He pondered again what life must be like on planet Earth. What might it have been like for Lilly? Did she ever marry? Did she ever have children? Though he often wondered about these things, he never regretted his decision to stay. He never regretted his sacrifice.

Erik knew that his sacrifice had allowed his mother, brother, Lilly, and thousands of Zenith's greatest minds, to live in a place with no walls, boundaries, or limits. Whether they contributed a little or a lot, they'd added to Earth's history and made a difference, either big or small.

As Erik raised his cup to take another drink, his eyes went skyward. At that moment, he witnessed a flash of light high up in the night sky, followed by a fire trail. He put down his cup and recalled the conversation he'd had with Carrick, when the young man had shouted, "Wow! Did you see that? That was awesome! Back on Earth, we call that a shooting star."

Erik vividly remembered what he'd told his friend back then. "We call that a spacecraft entering our atmosphere!" He looked at the cup in his hand and thought that perhaps his life was passing before his eyes. Feeling a little woozy, he looked up at the sky again and could clearly see thrusters slowing the descent of a landing craft.

Erik was confused; he told himself he would wait two-hours and no more. If flashing lights and sirens didn't go off to indicate a landing party's approach, he would finish the remaining contents of his cup, and that would be that.

Two-hours passed, and still no lights or sirens. Then Erik remembered that the ECS had shut down power to many of The Triad's systems. Could that be the reason no sirens were sounding? After another thirty minutes had passed, Erik wondered if he'd simply imagined the whole thing. Perhaps it was the lethal cocktail in his cup, taking ahold of his psychological state.

Erik decided he would go down to the main entrance and wait by the inner airlock door. If no one came within thirty-minutes of his arrival, then he would finish his drink. If it all ended there, he would be okay with that because, after all, that was the place where he'd first met his good friend Carrick Michaels.

Erik finally made it to the main entrance but needed to sit down as he was feeling groggy. He tried to stand minutes later, and in doing so, spilled the cup of liquid onto the floor.

Location: Black Horizon 3. Two-hours and thirty-minutes earlier

"Houston, we have touchdown," said Carrick Michaels. "All circuits are functioning fine, and we're awaiting your word for module exit."

In the lander were Carrick Michaels, Kinzi London, and Jordan Spear. Overhead were aviators Mike Swimmer and Ollie Taylor, orbiting in the Erickson Recovery spaceship.

"Roger that!" said Mars Johnston, back in Houston. "T-minus two-hours, and you should be ready to go. Complete egress checklist and report back."

For the three astronauts on board, it would be the longest two-hours of their lives. For the last one hundred and nineteen days, they had thought about what they might find when they made it back to Zenith. Would Erik still be alive? Would he come willingly? Would they all return safely to Earth? Nearly all of their questions, hopes, and fears would be answered in just a matter of hours.

Two-hours later, Mars' voice filled the comms. "Black Horizon 3; our readings indicate that you're good to go!" he announced. "Disembark carefully and report back to us with updates on Erik's whereabouts."

Carrick responded, "Roger that!"

As Carrick was about to exit the module first, he looked over at Jordan, who had no expectations of the order in which they would exit the lander. He said, "Hey, Spear! Why don't you go first!"

Jordan looked at him, wide-eyed, and exclaimed, "Roger that!"

As Spear stood on the last rung of the ladder, just before stepping down onto the ground, he wondered what he would say when both feet sank down into the charcoal surface.

As he pondered his next words, Mars Johnston, back in Houston, covered his mic and said, "Here we go again!" He uncovered his mic and, half-serious and half-joking, said, "Houston to Crewman Spear! If you're reading me, please get the hell off that ladder and let the others exit. We have a pretty important job to do, and the clock's ticking!"

Jordan, feeling slightly embarrassed, acknowledged the command. "Roger that, sir!"

As he stepped down, Jordan's boot got caught up on the last step of the ladder, twisting his ankle slightly. Gripping the ladder and steadying himself, he yelled, "God-damned motherfucker!"

Mars, the crew orbiting above, and the astronauts in the module all laughed, thinking that those were some unceremonious first words. Chuckling, Mars said, "Those words will, unfortunately, go down in history!"

Once the crew had successfully disembarked, Kinzi examined the Black Horizon Rover 1. It appeared to still have plenty of battery life left. The plan was for Jordan to stay behind and collect rock samples while Kinzi and Carrick traveled the two miles or so to The Triad. There, they would attempt to gain access through the Northwest Sector's main entrance.

While Kinzi was completing diagnostics, Carrick loaded a large tantalum carbide trunk onto the rover. He then positioned himself in one of the two passenger seats.

When Kinzi finished her objectives, she walked over to Jordan. "You keep the engine running, big boy. Don't even think about leaving without me!"

"I'm not going anywhere without you, London," replied Jordan.

The two touched helmet shields in what they called a Space Kiss. Crackling in their ear, Carrick's voice interrupted the moment.

"Ah-hem! Can we please get a move on for the love of God?!"

Twenty minutes later, Kinzi and Carrick stood at the front entrance of The Triad's Northwest Sector. The rover tracks from the two previous missions were still there and appeared to be pristine. This made getting back to The Triad far less time-consuming.

The two offloaded the trunk, and Carrick said, "Are you ready, Kinzi?"

Kinzi looked a little sheepish and said, "This one's on you, cowboy! I'll stay right here should you need me."

Carrick looked at her. "Are you sure?"

"I'm sure! This is about you and your grandfather," she added, tearing up a little.

Carrick nodded as if to say thank you.

As Carrick turned towards the door, Kinzi grabbed his arm, pulled him close, and gave him a space kiss on the side of his helmet. "Good luck, friend!" she said, almost whispering.

"Thanks, Kinzi. Stay close, would you?"

"Friends always do," she replied with a wink and a warm smile.

With comms open back in Houston, the lander, and in the Sagittarian Recovery 2 orbiting overhead, everyone listening appreciated the touching moment between two friends and didn't dare add commentary. In Houston, Mars made sure that no one at Mission Control could see his tears of pride.

With that, Carrick walked up to the door and awaited its opening. Two-minutes later, nothing had happened. Carrick began to panic a little and looked back.

Kinzi shouted, "Is there another way in?"

Carrick studied the frame of the massive door, looking for a keypad. As he brushed away the fine, powdered carbonite, he exposed a keypad that was void of buttons. He wracked his brain for a moment and said, "Come on. Come on!"

Finally, he remembered the code to the door, 12121965. "I've got it!" he declared. Keeping his eyes wide open, he began to recite the number in his head. After repeating the number several times to himself and staring into the screen, the exterior door began to open.

As soon as the exterior airlock door opened fully, Carrick dragged the carbide trunk into the temperature regulation chamber.

Carrick looked back at Kinzi and said, "If I'm not out in two-hours, head back to the module and return for me in four-hours from that point. Six-hours from right now. Got it?"

"Roger that. Six-hours from now!" said Kinzi, in the affirmative.

"Go get 'em, Carrick!" crackled in his ear. It was Mike Swimmer orbiting overhead.

Mars chimed in from Earth. "Carrick, you get back to us the minute you have him. You copy that? No overnight stays this time, son."

"Copy that, Mars!" Carrick smiled.

Three-minutes after the exterior door had closed, the interior door began to open. Erik was sitting on the floor awaiting his guest, one leg extended, and one leg bent at the knee.

Erik wondered if this was a hallucination or a dream. It was the moment he'd hoped for but never actually thought would come. A day that when it came, could change everything, or might change nothing at all. On this day, however, change everything, it would.

The inner door opened and in walked Carrick. He saw Erik sitting on the floor, leaning against the wall to his immediate right. At Erik's feet was the spilled concoction, a reddish batter with threads of white foam running through it.

Carrick fell to one knee at Erik's side. "Erik, are you okay?"

Erik replied with a subdued smile and uttered the words, "What took you so long?" His hand finding Carrick's glove.

Carrick smiled and knew that Erik was okay. "What are you doing on the floor?" he asked.

Erik replied, "I'm just a little tired; that's all."

"Here, let me help you up!"

"Would you mind just sitting with me for a moment?" asked Erik, who was feeling groggy.

Carrick obliged his friend. He removed his helmet and gloves then joined him on the floor, sitting awkwardly to Erik's left, his PLSS back-pack flush against the wall.

Erik asked Carrick, "What are you doing here? And what's in that trunk?"

Carrick smiled. "It's a gift for you, old man!"

Erik's face turned serious. "Well, did you find her? Did you find my Lilly?"

"Well, Erik, that's just it. Lilly kind of found me."

"What does that mean?"

"Listen, I've come to take you home!"

Erik replied, "This is my home, son."

"No, it's not!" said Carrick, with tears in his eyes.

"Why are you crying, son?"

Carrick stood and dragged the tantalum carbide trunk in from the temperature regulation chamber. "I have something I want to show you," he said as he began to unlock it. Erik remained seated. "Erik, do you still remember the exact location that Lilly was taken to when she went Home?"

"Of course! Why? What's going on?"

"What are those coordinates again?" Carrick was looking for further confirmation of what he already knew.

Erik wasn't sure why Carrick was asking but recited the coordinates anyway. "Latitude N33.373442°, Longitude, -104.529393°."

Carrick entered the coordinates into his Honeywell armband computer and awaited verification. "That's what I thought!" he said. He nodded his head in silent confirmation.

"Carrick, what's going on here?" Erik demanded drowsily.

Carrick replied, "You asked me if I found Lilly. As it turns out, she was never really lost."

"I don't understand!" said Erik, feeling more lucid now.

Carrick released the buckles on the trunk, breaking the seal, and the quiet sound of releasing air replaced the silence. He lifted the handles and opened it up. Carrick pulled out a vintage photo album. He sat back down next to Erik and opened it up. There, on the first page of the album, was a picture of Lilly on a horse. She sat tall in the saddle. She had a smile just like daybreak and sunlight-colored hair.

Fully back to his senses now, Erik exclaimed, "My Lilly!" He looked over at Carrick and started to cry and then began flipping through the pages.

"Where did you get these photographs?" he sobbed.

Carrick motioned him to turn the page.

On the pages, Erik saw pictures of Lilly at the beach, driving in a convertible car, and receiving awards from the medical profession. There were images of her wearing a white lab coat, newspaper articles touting her successes in the medical field, and even one of her standing at the top of a mountain, planting a flag. Erik sat speechless, tears covering his unshaven face.

With the turn of the next page, everything would change for Erik. The notion that The Triad was home would soon disappear.

"Turn the page," Carrick quietly encouraged.

Erik looked at him and then down at the album. He tentatively turned the page, almost afraid of what was awaiting him. The next sheet revealed a picture of Lilly in a hospital gown; only this time, she was the patient. In her arms was a beautiful baby boy. Erik's breath was taken away for a moment, and then he cried, "She had a child? She married?"

"No, Erik, Lilly never married," said Carrick.

"Then whose child is she holding?" he sobbed.

"That baby is your son, and my father, Michael Erickson Michaels," said Carrick gently through his own tears. "Lilly was my grandmother! I'm your grandson, and we're going Home, grandpa."

Erik closed the album and clutched Carrick's arm. He put his head on Carrick's shoulder and cried inconsolably.

"I tried to tell you when you first told me about Lilly," said Carrick.

"Tell me what?" The spacesuit muffled Erik's voice.

"That my grandmother's name was Lillian," replied Carrick. "I never knew her, but my mother talked about her all the time, and I always loved the name. I was going to tell you, but you just carried on with your story," said Carrick. Fighting through his tears, he added, "Let's look at the rest of the pictures."

The two wiped their tears and flipped through the remaining pages. They saw Lilly grow older and Erik's son grow up. There were pictures of Mike Michaels playing football as a small child and photographs of him dressed as a fighter pilot for Halloween. Then, pictures of him as a young man, graduating high school and holding an acceptance letter to the United States Naval Academy, and another photograph of him as an actual fighter pilot.

As Erik turned the pages, he absorbed the images and tried to wrap his head around the fact that he'd had a son. It didn't escape Erik, though, that the pictures had also revealed Lilly was getting older. At that moment, he looked at Carrick and realized that these weren't just pictures of Lilly and his son but also images of Carrick's father and grandmother.

Erik sobbed, "She loved me! Lilly loved me! She sent you here to bring me Home."

"We're going home, grandpa!" cried Carrick.

All at once, Erik now knew why the bond between him and Carrick was so strong. Erik never knew his son; Carrick never knew his father, but their relationship bridged that gap. No matter how much longer Erik lived, they would have what each of them had always been missing, a family.

Erik then shocked Carrick by saying, "I don't know if I can go. I don't know if I can leave this place. This is where Lilly and I loved each other; it's the only home we ever shared. This is my home, Carrick! This is my home!"

Carrick responded with words that would touch Erik's inner core. "Grandpa, home isn't where you're from," he paused, "it's where your family is." And with that, they were going Home.

Carrick reached back into the metal trunk and pulled out a helmet. At the top of the helmet, etched across the front, just above the visor, were the embossed words, Dr. Erik Erickson.

Erik proudly held it in his hands and said, "Thank you, Carrick."

Erik knew he was leaving The Triad and Zenith behind. He knew he wouldn't last long in Earth's deteriorating atmosphere, having never breathed air outside of The Triad's artificial environment. He was scared, but most of all, he was thankful.

The two men cried in each other's arms for a while, and then Erik said, "Carrick, how long do we have before we have to go?"

"About five hours."

"Good, because there's something I need to do!"

Carrick offered to help Erik to his feet. Erik obliged him by reaching out with his good hand. Seeing Erik's other hand, Carrick asked, "What the hell happened to your hand?"

Erik brushed the question off. "I bumped it on a drawer when I was reaching for some pain killers."

As the two men walked away, Carrick looked back at the spilled concoction and again at Erik's hand. He pondered for a moment and then refused to consider what might have been.

The two men walked for a while and then entered an elevator in The Grand Hall. They traveled to Surface-Level 5, the top of The Triad's Northwest Sector. Carrick had a pretty good idea of where they were headed. They exited the elevator and took a right. Within minutes the two were at the Northwest Sector's Command Center. Once inside, Erik began entering data commands into the main computer. Within minutes the cameras on the last migrant shuttle came to life. They illuminated the bottom of Earth's deepest ocean.

Carrick asked his grandfather, "What are you doing?"

Erik simply said, "I want to see your father before we go. I want to see my son!"

Before long, they saw the wreckage, and then the familiar U.S. Navy's roundel symbol icon star and bar came into focus.

As Erik zoomed-in, Carrick asked, "How close do you want to get?"

Erik replied, "I want to see my son!"

Carrick held his breath as the camera zeroed in on the cockpit, with the canopy still in place. As the camera scanned the cockpit, all the two men could see was a helmet. On the top, at the front of the helmet, they could see the words, Lieutenant Mike Michaels. That was it. That was all they needed to see.

After another moment, Erik exhaled and shut down the system, saying, "I'm ready now."

Carrick put his hand on Erik's shoulder, and the two walked into the darkness.

Several hours later, the outer airlock door opened, and two silhouettes stood in the airlock chamber. The frozen image of the two men standing there was both symbolic and heavy. The Triad behind them and an uncertain future ahead. Studded out in their two hundred and fifty million-dollar spacesuits, each holding a handle of the metal trunk that Carrick brought with him from Earth. The two men with a shared DNA and future would begin their journey Home.

As they walked out of The Triad, Erik realized that he had never exited the exterior side before. He'd only walked out of the interior into the central launchpad area.

"Nice view out here!" cheered Erik as he looked back at The Triad. "It looks bigger from this side, don't you think?"

"Yeah, it kind of does, now that you mention it," Carrick replied. He looked around for Kinzi and the rover but didn't see either. He and Erik began to walk back along the rover's tire tracks.

"How old are these spacesuits, by the way? They're pretty nice!"

"These suits are likely the most advanced space gear in the entire Universe," Carrick grinned with pride.

"Hah, I see what you did there... Just answer the damn question; how old are they?"

Carrick chuckled. "Mine's brand new, but yours is eighty-five-years-old," he joked.

"Nice try!" Erik countered. "You Earth humans weren't even in space eighty-five years ago! I bet you still wouldn't be in space if we hadn't sent a child prodigy to Earth."

"Yeah, who's that?" Carrick decided to humor him.

"Wernher von Braun. Heard of 'em?"

Carrick shook his head in shock, and stuttered, "Wait, what...? He was from Zenith too?"

Carrick's astonishment confirmed what Erik had always believed about the young lad who had left Zenith.

"Oh yeah!" Erik smiled with pride.

He thought to himself that if von Braun had never migrated to Earth, then Carrick wouldn't be on Zenith right now. He would never have known that Lilly had a son who, in turn, had a son. The idea frightened him, and his smile dissolved. Carrick didn't notice through his helmet visor.

"Watch your step!" said Carrick, tugging on Erik's heavily uniformed arm. The two had to make their way around a random ditch that looked like a small crater.

Carrick offered, "After one of our great wars, World War II, von Braun migrated to our country from the losing side, Germany. He became a pioneer of space exploration and rocket science."

"He didn't become anything; he already was, long before he went Home," bragged Erik. "He was already advanced in propulsion systems by the time he was ten-years-old. He left for Home a year later. From what I read, when he wasn't studying propulsion, he was analyzing Earth from the Astronomical Research Observatory. Apparently, like Einstein, he desperately wanted to go Home, swearing he would transform the place."

Carrick was speechless. If his helmet could have shaken back and forth, it would have.

"I actually knew him," Erik continued breezily. "He was a little younger than me, but we actually had a couple of educational classes together. That kid was a genius! He blew past all of us."

A few minutes went by without any words.

"So, Germany, you say?" asked Erik.

"What's that?" Carrick was caught off guard. He was distracted by the absence of Kinzi.

"You said von Braun was from Germany; is that right?"

"Yeah," said Carrick. "Why?"

"Well, there was a section in The Triad called Germany. It was a small section of The Triad that the residents named after their ancestor's home region of Austriaca. I recall that we sent a radical youth named Adolphus, something or other, from that section. He was on the same shuttle as Einstein. From what I understand, he was a real trouble-maker with controversial views. He actually led the vocal opposition to the de-segregation of The Triad, as sector populations dwindled and had to merge."

Carrick's face went white inside of his helmet, and his hands went cold. He could hardly catch his breath.

"Listen, we sent both the best and the worst that Zenith had to offer. I hope he didn't end up causing too much trouble on Earth," added Erik, apologetically.

Inside Carrick's helmet, his head shook from side to side. After a moment of stunned silence, and with eyes wide open, he mouthed the words, "Wow. A radical young man named Adolphus from Germany?" To Erik, he responded, "Man, they're not going to believe your story back on Earth."

"It's not a story. It's a matter of fact. A matter of our combined human history, of both the good and of the bad."

Carrick shook his head again, and the two kept trudging forward in the rover's tire tracks.

After an hour of walking, the two men needed to rest. They put down the trunk and sat on it, wondering where Kinzi was. Just then, they saw the headlights from the rover coming towards them.

Kinzi pulled up and said, "You fellas need a lift?"

Carrick exclaimed, "Where the hell have you been?! We've been walking for an hour!"

Kinzi seemed flustered. "Ahhh, I was helping Jordan collect samples back near the module," she said nervously.

"Helping, huh?" Carrick paused. "You know, your suit's on backward!" he said with a straight face.

Kinzi seemed panicked and tried to look down to inspect her suit. The two men just laughed.

"Ha-ha! Go to hell!" said Kinzi, laughing along with them.

"So, you and Officer Spear, huh?" said Erik. "I saw that coming from seventy-five million miles away!"

Kinzi blushed and stayed quiet, not saying a word.

Four-hours later, Carrick's words rang out, "Houston, we have lift off from Zenith's surface and are heading skyward."

"We read you loud and clear!" replied Mars Johnston.

Chapter 34 – Home

Location: Planet Earth. USA, Suwanee, GA. Level Creek Cemetery –
June 24, 2024. Five months later.

Carrick and Erik made their way to Erik's beloved Lilly's grave, their
feet matting the overgrown grass and weeds along the way to a
pristine grave and headstone. While many had neglected or
forgotten about their loved ones buried there, Carrick had not. He'd
made sure both his grandmother's and father's grave were well
maintained and remembered.

Without speaking, the two stared at the graves. Carrick had tears in
his eyes, while Erik was more stoic. He wondered if perhaps he
didn't know how to feel. Perhaps he couldn't fully comprehend that
the only woman he had ever loved was buried beneath his feet. On
Zenith, people were cremated after death.

Carrick broke in on his thoughts, "I'll leave the two of you alone for a
moment." He turned and walked away, leaving Erik standing before
the grave.

The tombstone read:

Lillian "Lilly" Michaels

Born: June 11, 1907

Died: July 25, 1990

Here lies a woman who only loved two men in her life: Michael
'Erickson' Michaels

While the world would read Lilly's tombstone and see one name, Erik looked deeper and saw two. He saw the name of his son, Michael Michaels, embracing the father he had never known. Erik read the words etched there and, for the first time, knew that he had been loved by Lilly and his son. He never knew his son but intended on getting to know his grandson as completely as a grandfather could. Before walking away from the grave, Erik stared at Lilly's engraved name on the tombstone and mouthed the words, "I love you."

Later, as the two were driving to the airport, headed for New Mexico, Erik said, "You know, Lilly's last name wasn't Michaels. It was Koss, Lillian Koss."

"She took your middle name, grandpa, and made it her last!" said Carrick.

Erik smiled and then laughed. "She used to call me Michael all the time. She always said I should go by my middle name; she said it was her favorite name."

"Looks like she got her wish, naming her child Michael Erickson Michaels while the love of her life was named Erickson Michael Erickson. It's kind of like a palindrome!" said Carrick. "Do you know what that is?"

Carrick answered his own question. "It's a name or a phrase spelled the same forward or backward."

"Thank you, Carrick! I know what it means. The word originates from Zenith. It also refers to the two antiparallel nucleotide strands in DNA. You know, a double helix? Please tell me that you're familiar with the subject, Doctor Michaels.

"Thank you for that biological definition, doctor!" smiled Carrick, rolling his eyes and shaking his head.

Location: Artesia, New Mexico. The next day.

Carrick and Erik stood in front of a tiny, old house that had been recently remodeled and decorated with contemporary furniture and fixtures. Before his last journey to Black Earth, Carrick had asked Lola to ensure the house was equipped with the latest technology. This included an elaborate air-filtration system that would ensure Erik only breathed in air that was free of micro-dust. Additionally, Carrick had had platinum-plated walls installed in the longest hallway of the house. The hall also had wall-mounted, custom-made light fixtures that resembled those in The Triad. Along the base of the walls were track lights that ran the length of the hall. Carrick wanted his grandfather and best friend to feel at home.

Like a proud father handing over the keys to a new car, Carrick presented Erik with a remote-control device that unlocked the front door.

"This is your new home, grandpa!" he announced.

Erik smiled and said, "It's beautiful, Carrick! Thank you."

Erik's smile disappeared and, after a moment of silence, he requested, "Can you take me to where Lilly used to live?"

Carrick smiled and said, "Grandpa, this was Lilly's first home after she migrated from Zenith. She lived here from 1947 to 1954, and then she moved to Suwanee, where she's buried. Lilly never gave up the house and would vacation here every summer with my dad. When she died, she left it to my mom, and then my mom gave it to me. I've never lived here. I just let other families rent it," he explained. "I never sold it and never knew why until I found out that you were my grandfather and that your Lilly was my grandmother Lillian. All of this was meant to be, grandpa!"

Erik couldn't hold back his tears. "I get to lay down my head at night in the same place that Lilly laid hers. I will live out the rest of my years here. Carrick, thank you!"

"Well, I sure hope so. You see that house being built right there?" Carrick pointed to the lot right next door to Erik's house.
Erik looked and said, "Yes?"

"That's where Lola and I will be living once it's complete. It should be done by the time we get back from our honeymoon!" said Carrick, with a big smile. "And" he turned around to point, "in that new house across the street lives the Spencer family. They're really nice people. They used to live here before I built them a new home."

"You removed them from this house for me?" asked Erik.

"Of course!" shrugged Carrick.

The two men hugged on the driveway and started walking toward the house. As they did so, a school bus stopped in the middle of the street. When the bus pulled away, a little girl was revealed standing on the curb. She waved at the two men and yelled, "Hi, Uncle Carrick!"

Carrick waved back and motioned for the little girl to come across the street. She looked at her mom, standing on the front porch of her home as if to ask for permission. Her mother nodded, yes. Then, looking both ways before crossing the street, the little girl ran over to Carrick and jumped into his arms.

Carrick lifted her up, and she said, "Thank you for the new house Uncle Carrick. We love it!"

Carrick put the girl back down and said, "Erik, I'd like you to meet someone."

Erik knelt and shook hands with the little girl and asked, "What is your name?"

The little blonde-haired, blue-eyed girl looked at him and said, "My name is Lilly! What's your name?"

Erik responded, "Lilly, huh?" He looked up at Carrick and smiled, then back at the little girl and said, "My name is Erik, and I hope that we can be friends!"

At that moment, Erik flashed back to a time when he and Lilly were just toddlers, and he'd asked her if she would be his friend. Then and now, little Lilly replied the same way. "I would like that very much, sir!" Erik just smiled, closed his eyes, took a deep breath, and then exhaled.

As Lilly turned to go home, the two men looked at each other and smiled. Words were not needed at that moment.

A few minutes later, inside the house, the two men shared some Red Fruit, recently smuggled back from Zenith in the carbide trunk.

Carrick gave Erik a tour of the tiny, ranch-style house. Exiting the living room, the two men walked down a long hall that led to two bedrooms and one bathroom in the back of the house.
"Are these what I think they are?" asked Erik examining the wall-mounted light fixtures.

Carrick smiled. "Those are made of crystal. They're not quite diamonds, but they do sparkle in the darkness."

Erik shot him a smile. "Well done, Carrick."

"Follow me to the sleeping quarters." Carrick walked ahead of Erik. In the back left spare bedroom, Carrick said, "Well, whatta ya think?"

"Not bad," said Erik, with a look of approval.

Carrick tried to explain why there were two twin-sized beds in the room. "The reason I had two beds installed is because...,"

Erik quickly cut Carrick off and put his hand on his grandson's shoulder, and gave it a squeeze. "I know why, son." No other words were needed.

Carrick walked Erik to his actual bedroom. "So, this is your bedroom. I hope you like it."

Erik nodded in approval.

On the bed was a package wrapped in solid black wrapping paper. "This is for you, grandpa," said Carrick, handing the gift to his grandfather.

Erik was genuinely surprised. "What's this?"

Carrick reminded him that on Zenith, Erik had told him that he'd never actually seen a book. He'd only seen images of them. Erik had asked Carrick to let him know if he had any recommendations. Erik opened the package and found a book inside. It was the first time he had ever held a book in his hand. The title was Where Once We Stood.

"This was illustrated by a good friend of mine, a visual poet named Martin Impey," said Carrick. "The book is about the twelve American astronauts who shot for the stars and landed on Earth's moon. The first of the six manned missions landed on a part of the Moon called The Sea of Tranquility," he explained. "Erik, I give you this book as a memorial to 'where once we stood' on planet Zenith. Your Triad was my Sea of Tranquility. I thank you for those lucky thirteen months. The time spent with you on Zenith changed who I am, who I will become, and revealed to me who I always was, the son of your son."

Erik smiled and teared up a little. As the two left the room, Erik took a right-turn into the spare bedroom instead of heading back down the hall to the living room. Carrick watched him go, puzzled. Back in the tiny room, Erik placed the book on one of the two twin beds.

A curious Carrick asked, "What are you doing, Grandpa?"

Erik looked at him and said, "I'll take this bunk. You can have the other." Carrick laughed out loud. He immediately realized that Erik would be more comfortable in the room with an empty bunk across from his. The two men laughed until they cried.

Location: A once-vast Universe. Three years later.

Lola and Carrick welcomed into the world a set of twins, a boy, and a girl. They named them Erickson Michael Michaels and Lillian Koss Michaels. Little Erik and Little Lilly were named after their late great-great-grandfather and great-great-grandmother.

The previous summer, Dr. Erik Michael Erickson was laid to rest in Suwanee, Georgia, right next to his eternal bride, Lilly, and his only son's empty grave.

His tombstone read:

Erickson Michael Erickson

Born on the planet Zenith

June 12, 1907

Died on the planet Earth

July 25, 2026

Here lies a man who traveled seventy-five million miles to be with the only woman he ever loved, Lillian Michaels, forever known to him simply as 'Lilly.'

Epilogue: The Secret

In his two-plus years on Earth, my grandfather and I spoke to the masses around the world. Dr. Erik Erickson gave an impassioned speech to the United Nations. He even accepted an invitation from Pope Francis to speak in St. Peter's Square.

Subsequently, the two of us traveled throughout thirteen countries together, speaking about the fate of Zenith. Erik chronicled the climate crisis on Zenith that resulted in an apocalyptic world war. A war that finished off an already dying planet. Dr. Erik Erickson also spoke of the decades-long search for a planet that could support human life.

Zenith's was a cautionary tale. Erik reminded all of us that, to save the human species, a billion others had to die.

Erik spoke about the origins of segregation and racism. How barriers, borders, and walls fed the isolated, the ignorant, and the angry. But mostly, Erik spoke of sacrifice, although not of his own. Rather, he spoke of the sacrifice that humanity would have to make if they were to save their dying planet if they were to save humankind.

Dr. Erik Erickson, my grandfather, and the greatest man I ever knew, was a hero in both life and in death. He always thought he would leave the Universe with one question unanswered: did Lilly, my grandmother, ever really love him? That question was answered. At the time of his death, however, Erik still had two burning questions. One, would mankind finally have the ability to learn from its past mistakes? And two, would the human race be able to save itself... again?

After my grandfather's death, thousands of cities around the world posthumously erected statues and monuments to Erickson Michael Erickson. Earth's universal hero would live on in memory for all time. How much time is left, though, I wonder?

You see, before Erik Erickson died, he whispered a secret to me about Zenith's quest to find an inhabitable planet. He revealed that Zenithians determined Earth to be the only planet within thirty-two light-years of our solar system that could sustain human life. Erik knew what humankind did not; that Earth was indeed the last refuge and our only hope to avoid the extinction of the human race.

The End

Michael Cook

Follow Me On Twitter

@BlackEarthHWGH

@AuthorMichaelC

@MichaelwCook

and on Goodreads

and on Medium

@AuthorMichaelCook

Black Earth – How We Got Here

Also available on:

www.BlackEarthNovel.com

In Loving Memory of:

Tracy Lynn Ray buck

1970-1978

Never Forgotten!

Made in the USA
Monee, IL
21 March 2021